SETH MORGAN'S

HOMEBOY

"The strength of the novel is Morgan's obvious intimacy with the world he writes about, his selection of just the right details...the powerful, resonant images....This is good writing."

—*San Francisco Chronicle*

"Funny and fast moving." —*Time*

"Sometimes shocking, sometimes funny, but always enthralling... *Homeboy* is an intriguing, festive book, populated by a grand assortment of characters, with action on the dark and comical side, and language that is so striking you wonder if it can sustain itself. But it does."

—*New Orleans Times-Picayune*

"A graphic, funny novel that reads like Armistead Maupin meets Mickey Spillane and *Fritz the Cat*, with an affectingly gruesome look at prison life." —*Vanity Fair*

"A tough, raucous book about San Francisco's lowlifes and prisons...[an] exciting debut." —*Cosmopolitan*

"*Homeboy* is big and blustery, using a huge, colorful cast of characters and its author's obvious love of language to tell the story of Joe the Barker, Baby Jewels Moses, and other shadowy denizens of San Francisco's Tenderloin district....The percolating rhythms make [the] prose seem to bubble and jump off the page."

—*Los Angeles Reader*

HOMEBOY

SETH MORGAN

VINTAGE CONTEMPORARIES
VINTAGE BOOKS
A DIVISION OF RANDOM HOUSE, INC.
NEW YORK

for my father

FIRST VINTAGE CONTEMPORARIES EDITION, MAY 1991

Copyright © 1990 by Seth Morgan

Grateful acknowledgement is made to the following for permission to reprint previously published material:

Leiber and Stoller: Excerpt from "Jailhouse Rock" by Jerry Leiber and Mike Stoller. Copyright © 1957 by Jerry Leiber Music and Mike Stoller Music. Reprinted by permission.

Milene Music, Inc. and Warner/Chappell Music, Inc.: Excerpt from "I'll Never Get Out of This World Alive" by Fred Rose and Hank Williams. Copyright © 1952, renewed 1980 by Milene Music, Inc., 65 Music Square West, Nashville, Tennessee 37203 and Aberbach Enterprises Ltd. All rights on behalf of Aberbach Enterprises, Ltd. administered by Rightsong Music Inc. All rights reserved. International copyright secured. Used by permission of Milene Music, Inc., and Warner/Chappell Music, Inc.

University of Illinois Press and Frederick Morgan: Excerpt from "Meditations for Autumn" from *Poems: New and Selected* by Frederick Morgan. Copyright © 1987 by Frederick Morgan. Published by University of Illinois Press. Reprinted by permission of University of Illinois Press and Frederick Morgan.

Library of Congress Cataloging-in-Publication Data
Morgan, Seth.
Homeboy / Seth Morgan. — 1st Vintage contemporaries ed.
p.   cm. — (Vintage contemporaries)
ISBN 0-679-73395-7 (pbk.)
I. Title.
PS3563.0871485H66   1991
813'.54—dc20   90-55669
CIP

Manufactured in the United States of America
10   9   8   7   6   5   4   3   2   1

From the being born to the dying
life is a butchery.
The primitives got it right
with their ritual compensations

For those more enlightened, however,
the unacceptable lurks
just beyond the visible circle—
knife at the ready.

—FREDERICK MORGAN, "MEDITATIONS FOR AUTUMN"

CONTENTS

||||

HOMEBOY

RINGS'N'THINGS

||||

That afternoon was the first time in her bustout life Rings'n'Things had met a man who wanted to know her real name before banging her silly. Daddy didn't count—naming her after Rosemary Clooney was his big inspiration in the first place. So it wasn't exactly like intros were needed that night in the garage when she was twelve and he was drunk and bent her over the Pontiac's front fender and went to town.

Rings'n'Things had been her handle ever since a biker called Sugarfoot broke her out of the Encino splitlevel where she'd been held POW fifteen years. Sugarfoot was prez of the Ventura chapter of the Satan's Slaves and the business end of a dozen felony warrants—which pedigree spelled G-O-D to an echohead Valleyette. She took on faith his solemn word that chasing a fistful of Seconals with a quart of Thunderbird was the righteous way to celebrate her liberation. Three days later, when she came to, Sugarfoot was croaked from lead poisoning, like forty SWAT-issue rounds worth; and Rosemary Hooten, lollisucker of the shopping mall, was trans-mogrified into Rings'n'Things, shedevil bike bimbo and certified Satan's Slut.

Dozens of cheap golden hoops dangled from her ears, nostrils, nipples, and—"*Gag me with a blowdryer!*" she Valleyshrieked, shivering cracks in the gas station mirror and setting the towel dispenser to vomiting its endless soiled tongue while dogs in the next county howled at moons unrisen—good ole MAJOR LABES!

Yet even the horror of the hoops paled beside her next discovery. The rings at least could be removed. Not so the fresh tattoos beneath a crusty canopy of scabbing stretching from her neck to ankles. Some designs she could make out through hot helpless tears: serpents slithering along her limbs, horned toads and hobgoblins, winged insects amidst deadly orchids; and emblazoned on her schoolgirl tummy a hybrid spawned in a Methedrine delirium, a sort of freeway centaur, half mad biker, half flamethrowing shovelhead Harley-Davidson.

Now that she was good for nothing else, she figured why not fulfill Sugarfoot's highest ambition for her and sling pussy on Sunset Strip. If for no better reason than to consecrate his memory performing the most spiritual exercise to which her knees were adapted; and she'd been at it ever since, up and down the coast from Tacoma to Tarzana; in massage parlors, for escort services, in no-tell motels, on street corners.

"Sometimes I feel rode too hard and put up wet," she confided to other working girls. Yet told the social workers and probation officers who wondered how she kept it up year upon flatbacking year: "It's just a piece of gut, you cant wear it out. Like, you ever seen one in a junk yard? Huh? HUH?"

God, squares gave Rings'n'Things a pain in the bahakas. Especially the way their eyes shone and they wet their lips pumping her with questions about the Life. Though she couldn't have spelled hypocrisy on a bet, she had a hooker's nose for its faintest fume.

Not that this kept her from deciding that afternoon she'd fallen in like atomic love with the buttondown square of the millennium. Everything else in her silly sad twentyfive years had been upside down and wrong way around. "I was *born* backasswards," she liked to explain, referring to her breech birth. "Why switch up now?"

It was rush hour on the 3 Kearny and this cacahuate was standing like right over her seat taking a megachomp a weenie extra world when the bus lurched and the chilified tube steak shot right out of its bun and slithered down the front of her Frederick's of Hollywood Kasual Kitten kreation with builtin padded bra and hip inserts. She shrieked, jumping up; down it sluiced between her knockers and torpedoed out between her legs like a greasy tampoon. Nothing kasj about *those* brown and yellow stains. What was Rings'n'Things to do but like sob her eyes out of their Maybellined sockets.

Stammering apologies, El Dorko whisked her off the bus into a cab and straight to I. Magnin, where he insisted she pick up something pricey from the New Choices collection in the Career Girl department. Rings fur shur knew she had a career, as in like the Original Gig, though how much choice was less clear.

The Bus Bozo wouldn't let up until she told him her real name and it just so happened his fourthgrade biology teach was another Rosemary, which seemed to clinch the thing. He begged her to call him Marty and have dinner at a ritzy frog joint on Geary, where, over garlicky snails and teeny lamb chops with frilly booties, he asked her to come meet his mama at the rest home the very next day. It was as if he couldn't see the rings and tattoos and all. Though if he did, Rings had the old chestnut all heated up about when she was a kid and ran away with the circus. During dessert the beeper she carried in her purse went off and she explained she was a lab technician on twentyfourhour call and scooted back to the ladiesroom to phone her escort service and say she couldn't book any tricks that night, she'd just started her period and was it a whopper.

In the cab hailed by the tophatted doorman, Marty asked where she wanted to be dropped, and Rings had to do some fast thinking. Girls with any kind of choice, forget new ones, didn't live in the Tenderloin. Right off she remembered her friend Gloria Monday and gave her Nob Hill address. Glorioski had a mysterious new sugardaddy and was living on cocaine and caviar with a view of the bay, a Maserati Mistral, and expense accounts like everywhere.

She told Marty she had errands in the morning, please meet her at the Sir Francis Drake bar, noonish. Kissing goodnight, she let him swizzle his tongue in there just a little for something to dream on. She stood on the curb watching the cab's taillights wink out like coals dropping down the Taylor Street hill, imagining how she'd like to hop Marty up in a highchair and spoonfeed him forever. Suddenly her wistful smile went woeful. The happy everafter reverie featuring Marty in Pampers had juiced the crotch of her new Career Girl getup, as in *damp* . . . D-A-M-P.

Luckily she was already at Glori's crib and Rings was sure her friend would loan her one of her thousand and one designer dresses for the next day. She couldn't wear one of her own peekaboob whoredrobe numbers, not if she wanted to spare Marty's mom a coronary. While she was there, she thought, she might as well phone back her service and announce her period had backed off its attitude and she was like a big Ten Four for the rest of the evening.

The elevator was paneled in old walnut and carried a faint familiar scent Rings remembered from some highrolling trick. The carpeted hallway was dimly lit and quiet, like old money. Tiptoeing down it, Rings caught herself holding her silly breath. At a palmed alcove opposite Glori's door she paused to appraise its occupant, a plaster toddler making weewee in a giant seashell. Frowning, Rings flicked at the multiple hoops compassing her left earlobe, adding their twinkly chime to the fat brat's tireless tinkling. She shrugged then, deciding the only Art she needed to appreciate was the usedcar salesman from Half Moon Bay who paid full freight once a week just to play dolls.

Gloria Monday was scripted on the brass nameplate over the bell. Some handle for a Polack from the wrong side of Milwaukee. Rings was about to push the bell when she noticed the door was ajar. Gingerly, as though it might be boobytrapped, she pushed it inward. She snatched a breath and let it go in a long whoosh blending horror and amazement: "Combat decoratin, *fur shur* . . . "

New furniture all overturned, upholstery slashed; expensive art prints hurled to the floor and everywhere broken glass. Upsidedown drawers lay around, their hoards of lace and satin strewn across the floor. A mattress had been dragged from the spare bedroom and disemboweled. Clothing, makeup, magazines, kitchen spices, and smashed potted plants contributed to the domestic demo derby. In the corner, by the toppled bust of Prince, glittered the delicate shards of what was once a blownglass crack pipe in the shape of a dolphin, stained citrine with use. At the clawed feet of a Victorian loveseat spurting tufted guts sprawled Glori.

Her wrists were bound with electrical cord, both her eyes were moused. Her nude body crawled with bruises like bloodsuckers; her throat was collared with a glowy welt, as if someone had tried ringing her skull by hammering her adamsapple up her throat like a carnival strongman contraption. Rings thought fur shur she was dead, then she saw the pale ribs shudder. She rushed over, fell to her knees and freed Glori's hands; then, cradling her friend's head in her lap, kneaded her swollen larynx and lightly slapped her face until Glori girl coughed up bloody foam and started sucking air, great ragged sobs. She tried to speak, but all that came out was *"ach . . . ach . . . "* like a rusty rachet wheel turning in her throat.

"Glori girl! What came down here? I'm callin the cops."

Glori's puffed lids trembled. She clutched Rings's sleeve, shaking her head in terror. She made a shaky drinking motion. Rings fetched a glass of water and held Glori's head until she choked it down and croaked, "Gimme phone."

Rings thrashed through the detritus searching unsuccessfully for the instrument, then she found its cord and reeled it in like a fish. Taking drunken aim, Glori stabbed seven buttons. "Mr. Moses, come quick. He fucked me up."

Picking up and recradling the receiver dropped from Glori's hand, Rings scarcely wondered that she was calling her pimp, Baby Jewels Moses, instead of real help. Most working girls were like that, their noses open wider than their cunts. Rings'n'Things counted first among her virtues that she flatbacked for no man . . . well, maybe Sugarfoot's ghost. A girl needs some inspiration.

Ignoring the catarrhal ruckus Glori raised in warning, Rings made a beeline for the bedroom to forage through the closet. Like, another thing a girl needs is to look out for herself. Trouble was, Glori had so much stuff Rings couldn't make up her mind which outfit might best impress Marty's mama.

"Make . . . history," she heard Glori creak from the livingroom.

"Girl, I dont need a bullet between the eyes to take a hint," settling on the cutest little peachcolored outfit still in its drycleaning bag.

She turned with it over her arm and was starting back into the livingroom when she heard another sound added to Glori's rattling, a flaccid wheezing like a blowup sex doll leaking from a seam. She knew it was the Fat Man before she whiffed his trademark lavender lozenges. She flung the dress on Glori's canopied babydoll bed and scooted beneath it. No way Rings wanted to run up on the Pimp Blimp. He made a practice of sending to hell in small pieces freelance flatbackers dipping his girls' business. But how'd he gotten there so fast? . . . *Fur shur* . . . The cellular phone in his limo! That was Glori girl's intended warning. For the hundredth time that week Rings rued that thinking wasn't part of her M.O. Through the litter beneath the bed of spent rubbers that squished like slugs, she wriggled, suppressing gag after gag until she was positioned so she could part the bedspread's ruffled taffeta trim just like Grandma's kitchen curtains and peek terrified into the livingroom.

Smirkily the Fat Man surveyed the wreckage. He wagged his neckless glabrous head, shivering jowls talced like sugared aspic, and clucked his tongue, his standard expression of avuncular reproof for his girls' each peccadillo. But for the tiny black eyes sunk deep in fat like cloves in ham, he would have been albino. Something obscenely prenatal about him incarnated all the blind importunate guilt of original sin.

"Gracious, Glorioski," he said. Such an eerie incongruity, that squeaky glottal lilt so like a pullstring doll's voice. "Your greed got the best of you, hmm?" Beneath the bed Rings rolled her eyes—*Like, when was it even a contest?* "What did you get on him? Polaroids? Maybe a video of you pissing in his mouth? . . . Wasnt all this enough?" His multitude of rings twinkled with the truncated gesture meant to encompass the penthouse, the clothes, all the accoutrements of a kept life. Behind her ruffled curtain Rings lifted a tired brow which said anything was too much, and all the world too little, for the likes of Glori M.

"No, I suppose not," the Pimp Blimp chortled, unwittingly endorsing his unseen watcher's estimate. "The shvarze's a shlemiel, he should have known better."

A second man prowled the room, lifting debris with shiny, pointed shoetip, peeking behind the one print remaining on the wall. If the pancaked nose and cauliflowered ears weren't enough, the simultaneous neck roll and shoulder hitch gave him away. They were the vestigial reflexes of an expug staying loose between rounds of fights he no longer remembered. This was Bobby "Quick" Cicero, factotum to the Fat Man.

"No prints," snapped Baby Jewels. From his hip pocket Quick produced a pair of kid gloves, flexed them over his knuckles, and resumed his casual, yet narrow sweep.

Baby Jewels turned back to Glori. The slow smile was swallowed in fat before reaching his eyes.

"Quick suspects the shvarze didnt find what he was looking for. Panicked and sprouted wings, I'd guess. But there's no reason for us to panic, hm?"

Rings felt like telling Fatso to speak for himself.

"Mister Moses, I swear . . . " Her voice was nearly recovered now, a hoarse whisper. Gathering the blanket around her, she lifted herself on the loveseat. "I wasnt tryin to shake him down or nothin. Just keep his respect so he dont take me for granite. But he nutted up. I was *tryin* to tell him where the necklace was . . . "

Fool bitch! Clutching the coverlet's ruffles in angry frustration, Rings nearly yanked it off the bed. Talk makes two things your mouth does without thinking, whore.

"Necklace?" the Pimp Blimp coyly simped.

Why stop now? Rings telepathed rhetorically on the channel to which she knew Glori's brain was permanently tuned.

"Some bigass piece of blue ice belongs to his fancy white wife. I was tryin to tell him where I stashed it but he thought I was callin him a name I sometimes do and started sockin me up. He was crazy, like big time. See, he was blowin that rock cocaine . . . "

"Tch." Baby Jewels shook his howitzershell head, sucking a fresh lozenge whose aroma recalled to Rings a shoe deodorizer favored by footsie freaks. Quick, to her relief, had ceased his perambulations and stood, head cocked, absently punching gloved fist into gloved palm, attending to this exchange. Then the Fat Man's ancient infant voice, wheedling as it might for a bon bon: "What name did you call Justice Bell?"

Something behind Glori's eyes crumbled and, were her face not blued already, she might have blushed. "Douchebag. Only it wasnt a name, it was where I hid it."

At a glance from his boss, Quick passed through the bedroom to the bathroom. One shoetip sharp as the stiletto that Rings imagined rode in the garter above it passed inches from her face, stalling her heart. Momentarily he returned, heels splashing sparks through the Herculon cutpile, carrying back into the livingroom a rubber douchebag of the variety that hangs from showerheads. Inquiringly, he lifted it by its plastic hanger; Baby Jewels nodded. The expug squatted and shook the upended sack over the floor. Crystal blue light shuddered the room, sequining even the shadows where Rings lay.

Baby Jewels gasped liquidly and shook a handkerchief from his breast pocket to sop his brow. "Oy vey," he wheezed with reverence.

Quick scooped up the vaguely Egyptianlooking neckband, shaped like an open caliper with teardrop blue diamond glittering at its V. He handed it to his boss, who lifted it to the light. Prismlike, the gem refracted an arctic aurora around the walls.

As in a trance the Fat Man wheezed, "The Blue Jager Moon. The legendary Devilstone. His wife's family heirloom."

Her drawn face drenched in the diamond's cold blue light, Glori's words tumbled over themselves: "He took it out of the vault to get it appraised the next day. See, he was borrowin money against it to take care of me. His wife didnt know. The insurance company made her wear a *fake*. Anyway, it was the only way I'd go to the opera if he let me wear it. I hate them people struttin around, wavin swords and screamin their heads off. Then we spent the night here. Next mornin he went to a bar meeting, as in lawyers, and I went to my own, as in bocoo bourbon and beer backs. Then I come home first n hid the ice. Then he come to take it to the appraiser but first he bazooka'd a couple of crack rocks big as the diamond itself, I swear by the time he got around to askin me for it you could hear his brain sizzlin through his ears, and like a fool I told him ixnay, if you aint gonna make me an honest woman you can damn sure make me a rich one, and he went bananas. I shoulda known better, I shoulda stayed in school . . ."

"Shut up," the Fat Man lisped drearily. He turned the necklace; the room shivered with scintillant cold colors washing the lights from his rings the way dawn enfeebles streetlamps. Shaking his huge head as if to shake a spell, he quickly tucked the stone beneath his jacket. At once the room shrank back to flat and finite hues.

"Mr. Moses, I think something's broke inside. You gotta call me an ambulance."

Fur shur, Rings mocked silently. Like charter you a Learjet straight to the Mayo Clinic. Turn on your front porch lights, whore. If you know a prayer, say it.

"All I gotta call you is a dumb shiksa."

"Huh?" Mystification wrung Glori's face.

"Tch, child. Not only couldnt you shake down a couple of bucks with the Devilstone, you nearly got snuffed by the shvartze for trying. Now what if he believed he *did* kill you? What do you think the diamond would be worth then? What do you think *I* could shake him down for?"

"Beats the shit out of me." Glori's titter reminded Rings of a gerbil's death chatter. She yanked shut her ruffled curtain, darkening her world to the horror.

"His soul," she heard the Fat Man hiss. "Only not with you alive. Then it's just another diamond . . . Quick, will you do the honors?"

Rings couldn't help it, the same way she couldn't help peeking at the frogs her brother used for batting practice. She parted the bedspread to see Quick drop a pair of pantyhose over Glori's head, snapping the legs tight, noosing her neck with a static shriek of nylon. He lifted her, toppling the loveseat.

Again Rings shut her curtain, to keep from getting sick. In a moment she heard the door close with a casket's muffled click. She counted to ten, then squirmed out from beneath the bed and stood shakily. Picking a rubber from her hair and another from her leg, she stepped on tingling legs into the livingroom.

Above the overturned loveseat, Glori's feet twitched like a girl's about to come. Gnawing her lip, Rings circled slowly, then froze.

"Gag me with a DC-9!"

Glori girl lay on her back, blood like sherry syrup pumping from both nostrils. One rolledup eye bulged big as a pingpong ball. The other was sprung from its socket, hanging by optic fibers the way a button hangs from threads where once a doll's eye smiled.

Forgetting completely the outfit planned to wow Marty's momma, Rings rushed from the apartment, though she did remember to use her sleeve closing the door so as not to leave her prints. No way was Rings going to mix herself up in this scene. She knew what happened to girls who fucked with the Fat Man. Die for the birdie, that's what.

Down the hall she ran and jabbed the elevator button. It took like a week to groan upstairs. Before it swallowed her in its expensive scents leavened now with lavender, through an open hallway window breathed the first chill breath of night bright with a cable car's brass syncopated carillon, a streetsweet elegy that dingalinged for whom Rings just didn't want to know:

Lights Out for Glorioski.

CHINESE RITHMETIC

||||

Other lights were just then coming up only a few blocks down the hill, along the Strip once known as the Barbary Coast. In countless flophouse rooms countless girls painted on faces as lurid as the sinking sun slung hugely in the Golden Gate's cats cradle. The Strip itself was awakening; dressing itself in lights, cloaking the stink of backbar rot and curbside garbage with a fresh admixture of popcorn, beer, stray bottled scents. Spitting banks of neon began their nightcrawling, hissing and humming the names: The Casbah, Blue Note, Gaslight Follies, Pepper Patch; Kyoto's Oriental Massage, Fleur de Lis Nude Encounter Clinic, the Tender Trap, Lucky Louie's Sexporium, the One-Stop-Smut-Shop. Everywhere red, yellow, blue, and green bulbs flashed promises as old as they were empty.

The purveyors of these promises were arriving with the rise of a gibbous moon. Dropped from cars and cabs, on foot; strippers lugging gym bags, hookers out for early luck, sleevegartered bartenders masked with professional boredom, barkers wearing loud clothes and practiced leers.

One of these last, a pale joker in his late twenties with slickedback hair, squashed nose, and a nervous smirk, was already at his station in the laserblue neon haze fogging the entrance of the Blue Note Lounge. On the back of his black velveteen jacket was embroidered a dragon amid constellated Chinese characters. A toothpick traversed his mouth in sync with the restless eye gunning the street, identifying in less time than it took to name the hookers, hustlers, thieves, and thugs; pennyweight ponces and flyweight flimflammers; diddyboppers, deadbeats, and dopefiends. Cops he could feel with every sentient fiber; highrollers scent as a shark does blood.

One pallid cheek bulged big as a baseball pitcher's, though it was hardly a chaw of Beechnut wadded there, but a dozen tightly rolled party balloons the size of jawbreakers packed each with a gram of brown Mexican heroin guaranteed to hitch any hype a ride on that tragic magic carpet.

"Murder one," is how Joe Speaker pitched his merchandise to the evening's first customer, a bloatchested dwarf in top hat and tails who barked at the Pepper Patch; adding "Knock yer dick inna dirt," as if Rigoletto's had far to go. A special munchkin was Rigoletto, twice a freak by virtue of a monstrous member which qualified him to moonlight for Climax Produxions, the porno movie mill owned by Baby Jewels Moses.

"Whip me a deuce, homeboy," piped the dwarf.

This familiarity bunched Joe's nostrils. A homeboy was someone you trusted more than money, and Joe trusted Rigoletto less than himself. Not that he hesitated spitting twice in his fist and shaking the dwarf's nubby hand, palming in exchange for his folded twenties the balloons Rigoletto stashed in his mouth by covering it to cough. They stood side by side surveying the populating Strip like livestock bidders sizing up cattle chuting into auction pens.

"Dentist convention in town," the dwarf noted. "Fat City tonight."

"Every night's the same to me," said Joe. By which he meant that Maurice, the Blue Note's manager, no matter how often or eloquently he promised a bonus percentage of gross receipts over a certain figure, always kicked the same lousy fifty dead presidents across the bar at closing. Not that Joe cared. He would have stood each night in the Blue Note's door for free, talking more shit than a Chinese radio—because in between felonies he supported his own oilburning habit slinging the same dope he shot. Barking at the Blue Note was a license to stand in one public spot for eight straight hours without attracting police attention, a pusher's wetdream.

And there was a further bonus. Kitty Litter, his squeeze, stripped at the Blue Note, and Joe pimped her to its customers to make up the nut when he shot more dope than he could sell. For this heroin absolved him of guilt, becoming its own morality. Its fleet sweet spell reprieved Joe of the conscience he couldn't otherwise abide.

"Our girls really clean up when dentists or doctors are in town," Rigoletto was chirping. "The only bigger marks are lawyers. The ABA convention is some kinda bustout Christmas."

Nodding at a passing whore in lemonyellow Capris, Joe shrugged. The Pepper Patch girls always made money because they freelanced handjobs under the tables and blowjobs in the backbooths. That's why it was called the Snatch Patch: it was a scumbucket. Yet every strip needed one to lay off their scum action.

Not that the Blue Note rated even a single star in the Michelin Tour Guide. Their girls weren't exactly on the Vegas circuit. But they didn't jerk just *anyone's* joint under the table for the price of a drink. Un-unh. To shlep a girl back to a hotel cost two hundred up front. One yard for Maurice, one for the girl. The Manager had *some* sense of propriety. But if they were savvy enough to confer with the bentnosed Barker, well . . .

As if on cue the Manager's dinged and dusty Coupe de Ville careened to the curb, and Rigoletto made dwarf dust down the street. Once he'd worked the Blue Note door and Maurice caught him hustling French ticklers and dropkicked the do-wrong dwarf into the middle of the Strip. Ever since, Rigoletto gave the Manager his share of air.

Out popped the Manager, swirling over his shoulders a motheaten furtrimmed cape that made him a ringer for a thirdrate magician shooting for a comeback on the cartoon napkin circuit. Clung to his arm was a dragqueen named Oblivia DeHavilland. Like most shemales on the Strip, Oblivia's forte was B-drinking. She wore mirrored contact lenses and a sequined sheath splashing kaleidoscopic neon. Her ratted platinum hair burned an electric blue nimbus.

Maurice smirked seeing Joe, "Cops were looking for you last night. Had warrants for you and your sidekick, Rooski."

"I know. Kitty put me wise, she pulled my coat already. Must be a mistake."

"Right. A mistake," sniffed the Manager. His lip was chewed, his eyes brittle and birdbright with cocaine. "Maybe you should catch a southbound freight."

"Barker's too slick for that," husked Oblivia, her chrome eyes lubing Joe with Crisco'd surmise, flashing back his twin miniature reflections. "He knows the best place to hide's in plain sight. He's been doin it all his life."

"You dont get it," Joe blithely insisted. "Aint been misbehavin."

"They'll carry you to jail until you prove it," said Maurice.

"They'd be doing me a favor. I need some fucking rest."

"Ha! You'll get plenty of both in there."

Inside swept Maurice with Oblivia slinking at his heels, raking metallic eyes across Joe like barbed wire.

The joints were juking open throttle now, up and down the Strip bass notes spilling out the doors like ladles of hot grease. Joe added his own voice to the barkers' caterwaul: "Walkin n talkin n crawlin on their bellies like reptiles . . . You, sir. Dont be no meanie to yer weenie. Dont pass by, give us a try"—though barking with a mouthful of junk balloons was as hard as hogcalling while gargling ball bearings, Joe netted the night's first rube; by his highwater Sears Roebuck slacks and hickified overbite, a Future Farmer of America.

"Got money fer yer honey," a voice at Joe's shoulder huskily echoed his spiel. "Got cash fer yer trash."

"No time fer yer line," Joe answered looking down into tombstone eyes leaned between temples scooped deep as shooter spoons. "You still owe for last night, Fay."

Fay DuWeye tugged his velveteen sleeve, pleading, "I just need one to take off the sick."

Joe sighed. Once upon a long ago the Strip's own neon heart skipped a blink when the emcee growled her intro: "Love is real not Fay Du-Weye." Now her G-string was traded in for a jar of K-Y jelly and a hand towel; and when the parlors were finished with her, she was into the streets until none would buy even a nickle blowjob behind a backalley dumpster from a drooling scabrous junkette; then—and Joe knew she hoped, *prayed* she wouldn't survive that long—she'd hijack a shopping cart and join the Tenderloin's mad hag legions, hank and hair like her of what had once some dim yesternight been dream flesh. And when at last they zipped her in a welfare bag and dumped her in some forgotten hole on the backside of Colma, the coroner might note heroin addiction on his report, though that powder was just the bitter seasoning of her direful days. Fay was strung out on hotel and dressing rooms and sex metered to the hour; hard times and easy money and fast thrills that could only be spoken in the language of the street. She was jonesin' on that carnal metaphor for her soul: the Life—in a minor key, played on a G-string tourniquet.

"If you dont tighten me up I'll be too sick to work, Joe. Then you'll never see your money. Look at it like protectin your investment. Please . . . "

Joe ducked his head, ruefully wagged it and whitelied: "Fay, you still got what it takes to make me go out robbing 7-Elevens, busting hot checks, throwing good junk after bad . . . " He slipped her a single sack with a kiss, thinking *some pusher.*

Turning, Joe rebounded two feet off the fortyfour triple-D bionic bumpers attached to Bermuda Schwartze, the Blue Note's headliner—"head-shiner," the Manager would crack, obliging Joe to demonstrate her lesbian preference by jamming together forked fingers and grinding the conjoined

V's. "That bimbo dont buff penis helmets, Manager. Pussy's her game."

"What's the forecast?" Joe asked now, reaching to honk a Schwartzian hooter.

Bermuda's barometric bazooms were a standing joke on the Strip to all but her. She'd gotten her boobjob back in the days before implants. A Van Nuys surgeon had simply injected a couple of gallons of silicone into her chest with a syringe the size of a cake decorator. And all he asked in payment was to be strung up by an engine hoist in his garage and sodomized with a caulking gun. "But you get what you pay for," Bermuda philosophized: the first cold snap, the miracle mammaries lumped up like two sacks of golf balls. Only when both the thermometer rose and barometer dropped would the silicone decongeal and jiggle as it ought. Put simply, Bermuda's tits looked approximately real only when it rained cats, dogs, and fleas, and the Strip was deserted of the rubes to relish them.

Not that this whiffle ball in heels cared. Ironies were things girls used to curl their hair. She even *liked* playing the bustout meteorologist. "Just quit callin em leche bags," she'd beg the Manager. "Be a mensch. Show some respeck. They'w bwests."

This neon dawn she slapped Joe's hand away and squeezed one herself, rolling up her eyes and sweeping a speculative tongue like a windshield wiper across her polished upper lip.

"Fair to partly cloudy," she decided. "Business should be aw-reety."

Then she got down to her immediate concern: the whereabouts of Dwan Wand, her neo-Nazi roommate. The perfect homo companion for a junkie diesel dyke who relaxed listening to CD's of the Ontario 500 while selfirrigating with homemade herbal colonics. Together they performed the Blue Note's "Love Act." Dwan would fluttertoe down the runway, handcuffs and thumbscrews twinkling from his studded leather G-string, swishing a whip fashioned from strips of cherry licorice. "BEAT ME, EAT ME," Bermuda would shriek where she lay lashed to a ratty stage chaise. The geeks were the ones to eat it up. How could they know the mere sight of a male member tossed Bermuda's cookies? "Like old turkey necks," is how they looked to this bulldagger fitted with boobs bigger than her head.

Joe said he'd seen neither fifi'd hide nor moussed hair of Dwan. "What's he done *this* time?"

"Silly little fruitloop woke me up this mawnin all excited. Said he had a mission. Asked me would I call n see if the peace corpse would take him . . ."

"*Whose* corpse?"

"Peace corpse. Yuh know, the folks teach niggers in Africa how to use rubbers. That's his mission, come to him in a dream. Though I speck he's what cum in the dream."

"Corps. Peace *Corps.* Like in apple."

"Yeah?" She snapped her gum. "So how come there's an *S?*"

"It's silent. French."

This made sense: the only French Bermuda knew cramped conversation. "Awreet. So I call n ask, could they use Dwan? They sez, what can he do? I sez, dance, exotic like. They sez they meant vocation n I sez, gee he couldnt carry a tune in a bucket n they sez they meant trade. I asks, how bout shepherd? I know them sand niggers got all kinda sheep and camels runnin loose. And you know what they did? They *hung up* on me. Can you imagine? Upset Dwanny so bad he run off to one of his bondage bars . . . Phew! It aint a pretty picture when those Folsom Street fistfuckers get done with him, I'm tellin ya . . . Say, you holdin that dandy candy?"

"Is a pig's pussy pork?"

This stumped Bermuda for a moment while she reviewed her knowledge of porcine anatomy. She stood hipshot fixing Joe with a slantendicular dogeye. Wiseass barker dopeslingers, particularly ones with girlfriends she'd trade her entire David Bowie record collection to bump bellies with, bulleted straight to the top of Bermuda's Bummer Parade, right after turkey necks.

Maurice poked his permed head around the doorway curtain, breaking up the romance by reminding Joe he wasn't being paid to bump gums with the weather girl. Joe and Bermuda consummated their business pronto.

"*SsshOAH* time!" Joe howled into the hurlyburling night. The human-scale pinball machine was ringing fulltilt now: gridlocked traffic, squalling barkers, roaring drunks; from everywhere fevered rockenroll and somewhere a saxophone's bestial arabesque. "Let's go, let's go, let's rodeo. *No* cover, *no* minimum, *take* a free look. She's doin what her mama tol her not to, bendin over n shakin a tail feather. And gents," orbiting his eyes, growling, "it's jist gotta be jelly cuz jam dont *shake* lak that—"

Joe sliced off his spiel in midbreath; a turf challenge was slanting across the Strip, a precision patrol of crackoids swivelhipping between stalled bumpers straight for the Blue Note. They wore full gangbang gear: designer jogging suits, unlaced Reebok hightops, baseball caps fixed askew over clear plastic shower caps, and sunglasses blacker than their skin. They advanced with the dip and slide stride rehearsed on project sidewalks for performance on prison yards.

It was going to be a facedown. Joe took a half step back into the doorway. He sidled his legs apart, hooked his thumbs in his belt, and ducked his chin. The troop leader hopped the curb. Rap music hectored from the boombox on his shoulder. He reached over his head to turn it down, then snapped his fingers, and the rest of the troop dressed out in a rank facing Joe. Now the leader lifted his atomicblast shades up his brow, holding them there with a peculiar female daintiness, pinky out, staring with blinkless boreholes Joe was careful to look into but not see.

How alike we are, Joe thought to keep himself distracted—yet how alien. Both addicts, but I to escape the life I was given and he to gain the one withheld. It's no coincidence that cocaine and heroin are called boy and girl on the street. This youngblood staring at me exalts the ego that I shun, surcharges the reality I dim, uses the violence that sickens me to get his dick hard.

"Yo!" woofed the leader finally. "You got group rates?"

Slowly Joe shook his head, keeping a bead on the eyes that seemed to boing now, as if attached to his skull with springs.

"Yo *mama* did."

What! How did he *know?* Tears of mirth irrigated Joe's parched eyes. The effort to constrain his laughter spazzed the corners of his mouth, making him tremble. With rage, Joe hoped the leader would believe, not fear.

But the subtleties of body language were lost on the crackedup leader. Men whose mothers were called whores should attack, reckless of odds. He turned to his cohorts, lifting his palms as much as to ask, What I gotta do to get a rise out of this whiteboy? The troop laughed and highfived, declaring victory by default. The leader dropped his shades, shuttering the toxic stare. He cranked up his San Quentin briefcase, reawaking its raging rhymes. As one the blood pack swung out, dipping and sliding down the sidewalk, backslamming phantom Cadillac doors, swiveling their heads like gun turrets. They measured their warrior cakewalk to a boombox beat as deadly and mechanical as automatic fire.

Keep on cracklin, Joe wished them with affection. *Hell's just half full.* Junkies appreciated the crack epidemic for the heat it drew off their traffic. They wished the crackerjacks continued success in filling headlines and prison cells.

Across the street, Holy Hubert, as common a Strip pestilence as the clap, mounted his orangecrate pulpit and crackled through his bullhorn the customary call to curbside services: "Sinners, repent! The Reckoning draws nigh. When all who ever walked to and fro and up and down the Earth, and the dead given up by the sea and delivered up from Hell . . . the Lord's bullpen, yuh see . . . "

"Shitfire, boy . . . " Kitty Litter's wild glossy mane was poked around the curtain, flickering like black fire in the breeze. "You tendin mass or barkin? The girls asked me could you crank it up. They need the pictures."

"Tell em to chill out, the night's still young."

She laughed. "Well, that's more than I can say for us bimbos inside."

A frown then flickered between her screwball eyes. "No sign of the Man? . . . "

Joe glowered. "I thought we decided *if* and *when* . . . "

"You decided," she reminded him; then smiling too brightly, "Got a kiss in your pocket?"

They swapped quick spit, Joe murmuring, "Kitty gal . . . "

She cut him off, "Gotta run, boy. I'm on next," and was gone. Leaving him with the wax candy flavor of lipgloss before he had a chance to say he loved her, hearing the backbeat of her opening number *Ecstasy* BA BOMP BA-BOMP *When you whip that stuff to me* BA-BOMP BOMP-BOMP when she'd strut down that runway switching fire off those Texas hips.

Holy Hubert was exhorting the small crowd gathered at his crate: "Dipsos, deviates, harlots, and hooligans! Who'll plead your brief? Satan, that's who. Ole Nebucanezzar will cop you a plea straight to Hell . . . "

"And who'll be your mouthpiece, you pious putrefaction?" bawled a voice through truly ecclesiastical whiskers, stained though they were with cheap port and puke. "Judas Iscariot?"

Pete the Packrat extracted a shortdog of wine from the shopping cart filled with trash harnessed to his Dalmatian bitch, Daisy; drilled it with a drunk's perfect panache and bowed from the waist, acknowledging the crowd's applause.

Oh whoa whoa ecstasy BA-BOMP

"Hurry, hurry," Joe urged two bozos caparisoned in burntorange leisure suits that might have been cut from Motel Six drapery remnants, accessorized with white vinyl loafers and matching belts: the Full Cleveland. "She's wet if yer ready. Watch Miss Kitty Litter perform *ee*rotical acts unknown outside the seraglios of Istanbul *not* Constantinople. See her go slow like turtle . . . " Joe demonstrated sending his thin hips around the world "then quick like bunny . . . " He pumped them rapidly and slipped in a sotto voce personal imprimatur. "Getcha harder 'n Chinese rithmetic."

It was only the nametag that saved Cleveland One from being taken for a bowling trophy salesman: Claude Sweeny, DDS. He put it to Joe slyly, "Any chance of some side action with the girls?"

Joe winked and leered, careful to hide his junkrotted teeth. "What the girls do on their own time is their own business."

"That's all we needed to know!" Cleveland One cried squaring his cowboystitched shoulders. "Once more unto the breech, eh Larry?"

"Tallyho!" caroled his Dacron clone, shining a shoe on the back of his pantleg before charging inside with his chum.

When you whip that stuff on me BA-BOMP BOMP

And Joe's mind saw Kitty all creamy fold of breast and buttock opalescent above the candycolored lights and wondered why he bothered always saying he loved her. Sure he loved her coarse mestiza hair, her dimpled coccyx and obloid nipples. He loved her screwball wandering eye that looked like the five ball off the eight, the hard way; loved the consumptive blush rising to her cheeks when she needed a fix; and especially the way when they were walking and she got excited over something and would spring ahead to skip backward before him, corralling his full attention. But it was only love's delusion, its desperate carnal charade, he sadly acknowledged. By blocking his heart from hurt he'd stopped it from love, and until he'd earned the courage for the one he was denied the other's grace. Dopefiends dont take lovers; their hearts seize hostages on the long retreat.

That same morning Kitty had cut straight to the quick. Still astride him after sex in their sixdollar room at the Jupiter Hotel overlooking the Strip, she laughed: "Big ass and chichis is all you love."

The laugh became a growl as she stretched, arching backward, tossing up her hair with the backs of her hands to fall in a whispery black mist. She froze then, staring up at the strands of crumbly plaster hanging like stalactites from the flophouse ceiling.

"What?" he'd asked, reaching lazily to toggle one raspberry nipple.

She seized his wrist, stared down hard at him. "I was asleep when you come in last night. Then you got me so hot wakin up this mornin I forgot . . . "

"Forgot what?"

The cops was what. Come swooping in four units from both directions on the Blue Note door and it was only luck that it was Joe's night off. Because these weren't your regular cops, your SFPD cracking wise and goofing with the girls, but state police units, Kitty saw the shields on the doors, clean young silent plainclothes troopers with faces blank as paper, whose leader wore a cheap black suit and smoked a cheap cigar. When the Manager asked what warrants they held, the Cigar said none of his fuckin business in a way that gave Kitty the geewillies; then, later one of the girls said she was in the dressingroom directly over the mensroom and heard one of the troopers at the urinal grumbling to another about enforcing the law for people the color of his piss bent on rotting democracy with cheap TV's and subcompacts.

Joe screwed his mouth sideways, tonguing a broken tooth. "The gook pharmacy Rooski and I boosted last week."

"What came down?"

It was the first Joe'd told her. How Rooski swore he cased the place, guaranfucken*teed* the chink pharmacist went home at six; and how Rooski went through the backdoor locks and alarm box like a hot knife through butter and then Joe handed him the flashlight while he jimmied the narcotics box and all of a sudden up popped the Chink in his nightcap like a Mandarin fright puppet and Rooski panicked and whacked the flashlight over his head. Joe heard something break, whether aluminum casing or skull he couldn't be sure.

"You can be sure now. Shitfire! Leave it to Rooski to panic and probably croak the gook. That's murder during the commission of a burglary, fella. Under the felony murder rule, you guilty as Rooski. *And* it's a special circumstance . . ." she paused a beat. "Capital."

"Even if Rooski killed him they aint got a case, they're shootin dice in the dark. The light was in the Chink's eyes, he couldnt make a deathbed mug ID. No one saw us go in or leave, we wore print mittens."

"Why take the *chance*, fella?" She gripped the iron bed railing above his head, lifting herself, plopping out his wrung cock; then resettled atop him, urgently clinching his hips with her big Texas thighs. "Shitfire!" again she exclaimed, jerking a thumb over her shoulder. "They could bust in that tragic door any second." Everything from nukes to broken nails was *tragic* to Kitty. Leading the list was heroin, that tragic magic. "Why not cut n *run*, fella?"

"Because like another Joe once said, you cant hide. Not from the law. Runnin's just another charge and circumstantial evidence of guilt. Jump state and the feds get sicked on you and those boys dont *know* quit. Had a father I never told you about once played rabbit from the Federales. They ran him to ground in the hospital an hour before I was born . . . No, this one we gotta play on Front Street."

"Listen to the tragic desperado."

"They aint got squat diddly do, girl."

"But the caper fits yall's M.O. like a rubber. How you figure they swore out warrants so fast? And when they get Rooski he'll turn over in a heartbeat. Rooski cant go back to the pen. With his snitch jacket, he wouldnt last a week. You told me yourself, boy. And if he ratted inside, he'll rat twice as fast on the street."

"Even if he turns state's witness, an accomplice's testimony has to be corroborated by independent evidence."

"Shitfire and piss bullets, Joe. You've been watching too much TV"—

an odd accusation since their's had been in hock these last two weeks—
"this is the real world." As if to show him how real, Kitty scissored her
long legs out of bed and crossed the room to squat on the sink sagging in
the corner and piss like a cow. Finished, she hopped off and honked the
rusted pipes running the water. The drain sucked down the water and
urine with a sob drowning her own.

"Dont cry baby . . . "

"I'm not!" She leaned against the collapsing dresser with its top drawer
stuck halfway open like a moribund tongue stuck in the act of vomiting
up its bellyful of cheap underthings, feather boas and tangled G-strings.
Making a face, she concentrated on fluffing her pubes with a broken-
toothed comb. She held the comb to the dirty orange light strained
through the oilcloth window shade, flicking out tufts of hair to float
spiderlike through the murky silence. Then her hand froze. She cocked her
head and slanted Joe a savvy slantendicular. "You layin for Rooski."

"Give the little lady a kewpie doll."

"Cuz they aint got nothin till they got him n he turns over to keep from
goin home again."

"Throw in a threedollar ring."

"Where *is* that tragic wingnut?"

"Dont know. He ran one way down the alley, I ran the other. Aint seen
him since. He must've known he did something stupid to put the Man
on us and was too scared to tell me. The only good news we got is that
the cops aint got him. Not yet." Joe watched a slice of golden light
projected onto the ceiling through a nick in the shade.

"Shitfire, he's the cause of all the trouble . . . "

"It could've been me," Joe said abstractly. A wind nudged the shade;
the slice contracted like a junkie's pupil. "Rooski's holed up somewheres.
I gotta find him before the cops do . . . "

"And? . . . "

He lowered his gaze. "I dont know. Christ, I just dont know," and fear
seeped from his eyes.

Kitty stared at him. Comprehension congealed, drawing her face into
a mask of sorrow. Shaking her head, she shoved off the dresser and stood
naked at the room's center, arms akimbo and hands backward on her hips,
bunching together her heavy breasts with their nipples still lipsticked from
the night before. One mimicked her screwy eye, staring at the wall. Usually
he'd laugh, and wanted to now, but Joe could only blink and softly smile.

"What*evah* comes down, boy, it's you n me . . . "

"Till the wheels fall off, baby," he'd mumbled, "right to the hub."

"Shitfire." She raised her fists like sixshooters, cocking their thumbs,
pointing them at his chest. "I'm talkin love, boy. Big as Dallas . . . "

"Uncle!" Joe had shouted, reaching for the flophouse ceiling, toward which another appendage arose with only slightly less alacrity. And she'd run that morning, laughing to his arms, grabbing for that dang ole Dallas . . .

I'll start huntin Rooski tonight, Joe resolved within the Blue Note's thumping neon cloud. *Soon as the club closes I'll beat the night bricks.*

Voices suddenly rang on his ears like clashing pots and pans. He was surrounded by a giggling gaggle of gooks. From the inverted quartermoon eyes, expensive dark suits, and ubiquitous cameras, Joe made them for Japs. *Dozos,* in Stripspeak. Prime fleshpot fodder; spent dollars like dimes on proscribed pleasures.

"*Dozo! Ichiban! Hairu suguni! Skippy show! Iza!*" His Japanese exhausted, Joe resorted to the international vocabulary of smut, jobbing a forefinger into his fist.

Giggles riffled through the group, the sound of wind through temple chimes. Americans were both fearsome and funny, despots in diapers. Several unslung their Nikons to immortalize with insectoid *whirclicks* this antic young man with a wolf's grin and dragon jacket. According to their custom when visiting foreign lands, they had a spokesman prechosen for his command of English and knowledge of Western wiles.

"How much?" this toothy delegate inquired with a jerky bow.

In pidgin English that drew a fresh crop of giggles, Joe explained there was no charge to enter, but to stay for the show cost the price of a drink. "Dlink," he caught himself saying absurdly, nearly spewing heroin balloons in their faces.

"*Ahh . . .*" the delegate nodded knowingly and, turning to his constituents, repeated the richly nuanced syllable. "*Ahh . . .*" The whole gang now chorused "*Ahhh . . . ,*" turning each to the next and nodding amazedly as though Joe had revealed the secret to some ancient conundrum. He wondered if Jap doctors bothered stocking tongue depressors.

The ensuing discussion amounted to an audio root canal. Joe divined a dispute was in progress whether to test the waters at the Blue Note or first canvass the rest of the Strip. The pros shrilled; the cons barked and grunted. With their waving arms and contorted faces, they resembled wrathful oriental dancing gods.

Joe stepped back and snatched aside the curtain to hiss "*Dozos . . .*" The girls all knew this cry for assistance with Orientals. Luckily it was Candy on point, the girl perched on a barstool just inside the curtain whose charge it was to gaga, goose, or garrote incoming rubes into buying a drink before their eyes could even adjust to the dark. Hard was the only sell these girls knew.

Out poked Candy's spunsugar wighat, baby blues agog. At once the dozo caucus fell silent. Suckers for Amazonian blondes, those zipperheads. Doubtlessly from being weaned on thirtyfoot B-movie bombshells. Candy squeaked dropping the curtain exposing a beachball boob dusted with sparkles. "They call her Candy," Joe explained, "because she's hot n sticky n *sweet*." The dozos signified a unanimous quorum with a concerted fullthroated *AHHH!* and nearly bowled Joe over banzaiing into the Blue Note.

Across the street, Hubert was getting down with some Big Tent revelating. Conjuring for his motley flock the reek of brimstone, the scorch of the hellfire coursing through veins and igniting eyeballs; summoning the fiends of Hell vomiting molten rock. He was just wrapping up the travelogue along rivers of burning flesh, past the smoldering tar pits to the very shores of the Great Lake of Fire; and in conclusion was wheeling his eyes apocalyptically, cupping a hand to his ear, saying: "Hearken! I hear the roar of cleansing fire . . ."

Yet the roar he heard was his assembly's laughter. Looking down, he spied Pete, laceless brogans spread for support, pissing on his orange crate. His bladder drained, the tramp staggered backward, fencing his wizened member at Hubert.

If Joe hadn't been standing at the curb, he would've needed Velcro sneakers to keep from being blown into the middle of Strip traffic by the blast of Bermuda's chainmail lungs: "AND STAY OUT!"

Out onto the sidewalk reeled the dental Clevelands followed by Bermuda in nothing save stiletto heels, G-string, and dishonest sweat. No shame in her bustout game when it came to affairs of *honor.* Squalled she, "Whaddaya think this is, a *whorehouse?* This is a *night* club, dicklicks. We sell drinks, not pussy."

Horns blared as cars slowed pretending to glare down the Clevelands like choirboys caught with dirty pictures in their hymnals, but really only memorizing those silicone monuments for dreams as yet unwetted.

"But we gave you a hunnerd dollars."

"You didnt give me nothing but a hard way to go . . ." Bermuda could snap that gum like a smallcaliber automatic. "What kinda girl you think I am anyhoo?"

Wisely the Clevelands declined informing her. Instead they turned to Joe. "*You* said . . ."

"I said nothing," he corrected them curtly; then, just to show there were no hard feelings, pleasantly shared perhaps his only conviction unattached to a penal code number: "You want something for nothing, jerk off."

Cleveland One turned to Cleveland Two. Between the two a fresh resolve was forged. Goddammit, they weren't just fifty percentilers but

U.S. citizens as well, with godgiven rights! "You cant just rob us . . . "
"We're getting the police!" "Fuckin A."

"No you aint, *I* am," Bermuda volunteered. She jammed two fingers in
her mouth and split the night with a whistle that belonged on a steamboat.

"You callin the cops?" the Clevelands harmonized in horror.

Bermuda read them the law west of Oakland: "You've been soliciting
for prostitution, which carries six months and five thousand dollars, butt-
breaths."

Across the street, Patrolman Daniels was cajoling Hubert into moving
his ministry off the Strip, suggesting other neighborhoods equally hungry
for the Word; while Hubert likened him to Pharaoh and called down all
manner of loathesome plagues on his head. At Bermuda's summons, Daniels abruptly wheeled and nearly fell off the curb. Yet he wasn't so drunk
he couldn't read the situation in front of the Blue Note. The Manager gave
him all the free bourbon he could guzzle and, if he could still get it up,
some Oblivious backbooth skull just to discourage the likes of these two
Clevelands from filing complaints.

This time his help wouldn't be needed. The Clevelands knew when the
deck was stacked against them. Off they grumbled with Bermuda's vilifi-
cations raining on their bowed Dacron backs: "Twistos, weenie wavers,
panty sniffers . . . Show up again n I'll break yer faces!"

Passing back into the club, she palmed Joe a twenty, his cut of the
Murphy, as any bunko prostitution game was called. The variety Joe and
Kitty played was the simplest and most common. When she was too sick
to turn a trick, she'd just pick one up, take him to a motel, drop the keys
out the bathroom window for Joe. Waiting an appropriate interval for the
mark to get naked, he'd bust in and impersonate an undercover Vice
officer willing to take all the john's cash and valuables to forget the matter.

At that moment a stakebed truck cruised by the Blue Note. People
crowded to the curb, waving their arms, clutching at whatever a gang of
blackrobed women were tossing from its rear. A banner strung between
the stakes read SISTERS OF PERPETUAL INDULGENCE, LATEX FOR SAFE SEX,
MAKE LOVE NOT DEATH. But wait, these weren't women, but men, bearded
mostly, in whorey makeup and nuns' habits with obscene décolletages
flashing flabby hairy titties squeezed in pushup bras. And the foilwrapped
objects they tossed were hardly devotional aids but Ramses brand prophylactics. The Egyptian trademark seemed a fulfillment of Holy Hubert's
biblical maledictions; and, indeed, a handful showered on Officer Daniels's
besotted head. What more fitting plague when frogs were scarce, Joe
sniggered, than cheap rubbers.

On Joe barked beneath the neon stars and honkytonk moon, promising humiliations to match any guilt. The music throbbed, the neon fried, the lights cartwheeled across waxed hoods and spun in chrome hubcaps. He downed a few more balloons, hustled another dozen rubes into the Blue Note. Intermittently he dreamed that instead of standing at the center of a blue neon cloud, he was alone in the subaqueous gloom of Steinhart Aquarium, within its soothing liquefactive geometrics, where often he went secretly to rake the ashes of his junked soul.

But now his nose was flowing and skin squirming. The writhing lights needled his eyeballs; his bowels ground like broken glass, making him fart abjectly. He touched his cheek, clammy and unalive. His reprieve from feeling was running out; the Big Hurt was coming home to be fixed once more.

How long Poppa Whoppa had been standing in the shadows beyond the border of blue neon Joe didn't know. He motioned him closer. The Whoppa wore a purloined Shriner's fez and a dashiki that had seen better days at sixties sitins. Formerly he'd been a yegg, safecracker, the best on the Coast. "Shittin in tall cotton," was the style to which the Whoppa in those days was accustomed. Then arthritis gnarled those virtuoso digits that could pickpocket little girls' hearts as easily as tickle tumblers behind six inches of steel. Now he was reduced to hustling streetcorner threecard monte. And only the stuff, Poppa Whoppa's holy *hairwine,* could thaw the frozen fingers sufficiently to make those cards whisk and whir, snap and blur so that the one eyed pimp faced up where the rube purely swore he couldn't.

"I'm short n sick, Homes," moaned the Whoppa. The old yegg's withdrawal was a palpable effluvium, a contagion bathing Joe with microwaves of misery. With his own sick coming on Joe was too weak to withhold the junk from another sufferer, he lacked that essential pusher's obduracy. He took Poppa Whoppa's short money, telling himself he'd have to hustle up some action for Kitty. And he could hear her now, "Shitfire, fella, why you gotta give up your stuff so I gotta give up mine? Sometimes I feel like my big ass and chichis is supportin the habits of half the dopefiends in San Francisco," and him rejoining, "It's that or go sick," wondering *Why dont she leave me, why wont she?* until she returned flushed and flustered maybe but never hurt half so bad as he would hurt until that tiny prick plunged away all feeling, swept aside the shards of shattered self like broken mirror that cuts to look into.

"The Man be after you n Rooski," Poppa Whoppa said once his balloons were safely stashed behind a cheek ashblack and cracked as his ancestral riverbanks.

"They know where to find *me,*" Joe cracked brave. *Why did I ever hook up with Rooski in the first place?* he raged. Why caper with an informer unless to foster your own betrayal? In his sleep he'd heard the whisper in the telephone, the murmur at the bluesleeved elbow, the sob before the squadroom desk. Yet he meant only to deliver himself from the streets, not life; he didn't count on murder. But Christ! Why not? What else remained but more of this? And since he hadn't the iron to extinct himself by bullet or Big Shot, it was just as well he set up another of the damned to do the dirty work. Yes, this was best. Far less terrifying than his fate was the prospect of regaining a hand in it. Fervently Joe petitioned the Bearded Madman presiding over the nightcourt of his soul that the cops might find Rooski first and relieve him of what he'd inherited with breath, this requirement to survive.

"I reckon they do at that," solemnly agreed the Whoppa.

"What?" Joe felt his voice stretching like catgut, twanging.

"Know where to find yo ass," shuffling off humming a dirgelike ditty soon swallowed by the thumping jukes and traffic.

NEVER BAD ENOUGH

||||

Two blocks down the Strip, in the basement offices of the Tender Trap Massage Parlor, Baby Jewels was in conference with his lawyer. Sidney Dreaks had mournful eyes, a long patrician nose, and looked more like a seedy headwaiter than San Francisco's premier defense counsel. "Civic morality undergoes these convulsions every four years," he was explaining. "They're called elections. Mayor Mancuso and D.A. Faria are in real danger of losing their reelection bid to the Clinton Marks ticket. Marks has portrayed them as being 'soft' on crime. Actually, real, violent crime's declined during their administration. But that doesnt matter. All that matters is public perception, illusion. So the mayor and the D.A. have to brandish hardons for socalled victimless crime. Statutory, service crime. You, Jules . . . The City Council appropriated the funds for Faria's Victimless Crime Task Force with just you in mind . . . "

Across the ivoryinlaid desk Baby Jewels wheezed indifferently. He was absorbed in the gems strewn on blue velvet trays before him. One after another he picked up to examine through a jeweler's glass screwed in his fatty eyefolds. The way his neckless head coned to a point recalled Cold War cartoonists' renderings of human H-bombs.

"The first statute they're going to use on you is the Red Light Abatement Act," Sidney continued. "It was passed before the turn of the century to contain prostitution on the old Barbary Coast. Under its provisions they can conduct warrantless searches and padlock any establishment suspected of operating for immoral purposes. I'm sure Faria had no idea it existed until one of his paralegals exhumed it. It's fucking medieval, forget unconstitutional. But then so are statutes prohibiting watering your horse at public fountains and kite flying west of Van Ness Avenue. But you can go to jail for either. These relics stay on the books because there's no political mileage to be gained removing them."

On the padded wall behind the Fat Man babyspots were trained on a gallery of framed and autographed photographs: Baby Jewels gladhanding politicos, grabassing showgirls, squeezed into nightclub booths with minor celebrities, lolling in his box at Candlestick Park. In one, the Fat Man in a Hawaiian shirt the size of Maui actually dwarfed a giant marlin strung up from a dockside hoist.

Sidney lowered his voice in the habitual manner of a man who is, by virtue of his profession, an accomplice after the fact to innumerable felonies. "They're raiding you tomorrow night. Luckily our man in Muni Court informed me. But such tipoffs are going to get scarcer than hen's teeth if we dont regain some initiative."

Baby Jewels set down the jeweler's glass and popped a lozenge in his cupidsbow mouth. That cloying lavender bloom always reminded Sidney of a mortuary. "*Tch,*" went the disembodied baby voice. "Those shleppers in Faria's office might just as well hire skywriters, Sidney. I knew they were coming. I have sources you dont know about."

His client's nonchalance began to nettle Sidney. He said, "Cant you see this is just the beginning, the kickoff? They've already impaneled a grand jury, which will surely hand down indictments." When Baby Jewels cavalierly screwed the glass back in his eye, picking up a stray emerald, Sidney took off the gloves: "Faria's not just going to padlock you. He's sure to bring multiple pimping and pandering charges which I dont see how we can beat. They wont deal, of that I'm certain. Not in the public spotlight . . . " Sidney scooped air up his long nose. "Jules, I cant guarantee I can keep you out of jail."

"Sidney, tomorrow night every girl upstairs will be a licensed physical therapist. And every shmuck will be getting a real massage . . . As for your guarantees, maybe I dont need them. They might convict in Superior Court, but I got a stopper higher up . . . Or will, shortly."

"Very good, Jules. I'm glad you're so sanguine. What I cant understand is why you're even making a fight over it. Why dont you follow my advice and close up? Johnny Formosa and the tongs have slammed all the mahjongg parlors and doll shops, Connie Truck, his lowball rooms. They've got enough salted away to wait this thing out. Certainly you do." Sidney swept his hand over the desk. "You've enough right here to live like fuckin Farouk until after the election. Then, with the administration back in office, reopen your whole operation. All you're doing fighting them is playing into Marks's hands. And with him in office you may as well open a string of dry cleaners . . . Jules, if you close yourself, you beat them at their own game. Why not?"

"Because I'm right."

"*Right?*" Sidney thumped the heel of his hand to his tall forehead. "What's *that* got to do with anything? This is business." He leaned forward in his chair to coax his client the way he might a witness in the box. "You know better than anyone, Jules. As soon as the last editorial is printed, the last speech made, and the last pulpit pounded, all the Dudley Dogooders will be the first back down here for a little fun. It's been that way since time immemorial. You've nothing to prove fighting them."

"Wrong. I have two things to prove. First, that Jules Moses backs down from nothing. Second, that I offer services as legitimate as any priest or doctor . . . not to mention lawyer. See, without me those johns would be out catching AIDS and getting rolled. Without me those girls would be in the streets getting maimed by pimps and murdered by sex maniacs. There's a saying in the Life, Sidney—'You can always treat a woman too good, but never bad enough.' It's the girls themselves who promote that kind of mentality, so you could say I protect them from their own worst enemies—themselves."

Sidney Dreaks shrugged helplessly. Baby Jewels wasn't the first crook he'd represented who was convinced he was a misunderstood philanthropist.

Baby Jewels lifted a cabuchon blue sapphire to the cyclopean magnification of his eye. Between appreciative kissy sounds, he absently simped, "Look what happened to that girl Gloria Monday."

"What girl Gloria Monday?"

"*Tch.* I thought she made the evening edition."

"Why should she?"

Removing the glass Baby Jewels smiled his patent smile lost in fat before lighting the chips of anthracite pressed deep beneath his hairless brows. From above thumped the night's moronic pulse.

"You'll read about her over your morning coffee, Sidney. I hate giving away a good story."

THE FIX

||||

Midnight a stepvan doubleparked in front of the Blue Note. Out hopped a boy in orange coveralls humping a bundle of newspapers. A quarter flipped from the polished digits of a longlipped horse degenerate in a snapbrim hat. Joe smiled in the Blue Note doorway—*Just the jerk to spell me while I fix.*

The carrier snatched the neon twinkle in midair and handed Club Charley the top racing form before locking the rest in the curbside vending machine. Club set immediately to work, licking his pencil, picking ponies, and Joe had to call out twice for his attention. Club sniffed and hitched up his pants crossing the sidewalk. What? he asked, dogeyeing the Barker. Would Club mind watching the Blue Note door while Joe rounded up a girl from another club to replace one the Manager sent home for getting too drunk? Well, okay—but don't expect Club to talk dirty, he had a wife and kids at home. Naw, all Club had to do was stand there looking sharp as a jockey's prick in his pearlgray threepiece.

Lucky Louie, proprietor of the One-Stop-Smut-Shop, perched on a stool behind a tall glass display case. Within were ranked triple-X videos, rainbowhued and roostercrested French ticklers, an arsenal of vibrating missilery, brass benwah balls, silver cock rings, batteryoperated Autosuckers trimmed with Gen-U-Pube nylon hair like Astoturf, Pocket-Pal Buttholes and heroic dildos of every color and configuration, including one candystriped doubledonger affair that promised a trip to the emergency room for the uninitiated.

Louie looked more like a longhaul freight dispatcher than the weapons broker for the aging shock troops of the sexual revolution. Bloodless lips sucked one of those gnarly dago cheroots that put one in mind of a smoking cat turd. Cold greasy sweat waxed his brow; fingers smudged with Treasury ink blindly changed Joe's two dollars into quarters. Goatlike eyes followed the embroidered dragon vanishing through the footfreak and rubber racks.

The mingled reeks of crusted sperm and Pine Sol flipped Joe's stomach like a gaffed fish. The clicking hum of projectors was interspersed with slurps and muffled grunts. Joe refused to meet the wet importunate eyes floating through the haze of a single red bulb dangling in the aisles between the booths—until a breathy whisper at his elbow: "Oh Jo*whee* . . . "

"Dwan! What are you doing here? . . . No, dont tell me."

"I was going to ask you the same thing." Dwan Wand's swastika earring twinkled like a rhinestone spider.

"You get to work or the Manager'll fire you."

Pouting fiercely, Dwan stamped a Cuban heel. "I quit! I'm joining the peace corpse, teach those Negroes what time of month to fuck. Goodness knows they got every other kind of rhythm," adding selfeffacingly, "A shitty job, but someone's gotta do it."

"Sure'll be shitty the way you'll go about it."

Joe ducked into the closest booth and locked the door against Dwan's urgent little knocks. He had to threaten to tell Bermuda on Dwan to make him go away, sobbing.

In the rank dark Joe extracted the paraphernalia stash from his boot, arranging on the narrow ledge beneath the coin meter the water vial, syringes, cotton balls, and cooking spoon. He deposited a quarter, the loop began its run, something with two men taking a woman orally and anally. Deftly Joe bit open and shook two balloons into the cooker, snapping them to empty each last grain of Mexican brown heroin. He drew up 50 cc's of water into the syringe and sluiced it into the cooker. The booth went black; he fed the meter another quarter.

Next he lit an entire book of matches, quickly folding it back and setting it on the ledge to stand freely. The sputtering sulphur pinched his olfactories, making him sneeze. By passing the cooker lightly over the flame and stirring the sediment with a plastic needle sheath, in seconds he had an injectable solution. Once more, darkness; another quarter. Into the cooker he dropped a tiny cotton ball, delicately setting the needle into this crude filter. He drew up the amber solution into the syringe's slender barrel. He was ready to fire.

Darkness again while Joe unbuckled and slithered off his belt. He clamped the buckle beneath his boot, cinched the worn leather tightly around his bicep, and clamped its tongue between his rotten teeth. He levered his arm then, raising ravaged veins, and dropped another quarter. The winnowing light was just sufficient to reveal the nasty cicatrices littering the crook of his arm. Gingerly his finger prodded for a vein tender and defined enough to drink the shot. *Oooh,* there we are; hush now, slowly, breath held, *slooow.* Set the minute, steely gleam against the tender ridge. Tap the plunger, penetrating, flesh opening, swallowing steel . . . Christ! Out went the light. Joe left the syringe impaled in his flesh while he fumbled another quarter into the hungry slit. Looking back down he saw in the amber lumen a filament of blood, the merest undulant tendril. Sucking air through his teeth, whimpering softly, he adjusted the needle's depth. Bingo! A mushroom cloud of blood exploded into the barrel, billowing, blooming a crimson orchid. Weeping gently, Joe raised his boot, releasing the belt's tension, and slammed the syringe like a detonator, plunging the flower of forgetfulness into his bloodstream.

Orbits of panic and astonishment collided across Lucky Louie's brow watching the Barker weave out of the arcade, almost capsizing the watersports and bondage racks. The bentnosed geek seemed *too* relaxed. Like a deboned chicken or an underinflated Stan the Man, Yes-He-Can blowup party stud. His leadlidded eyes kaleidoscoped around pupils reduced to pinpricks.

"Yous awrite?" Louie asked solicitiously. The Health Department made him keep a first aid kit on the premises, he just hoped he wouldn't have to remember where. The Barker stood before the counter scratching his goddam nuts and swaying like a man in a typhoon, though Louie's labored breathing was the biggest wind around.

At times like these Joe truly did stand within a wind that whirled around just him; transfixed at the center of a religious instant in which Louie's display case, for instance, became a shrine of sexual sacraments, an altar of latex amulets, anal idols, priapic periapts, fertility fetishes. Tonight he noted two new additions to the fluorescent reliquary: a Day-Glo neoprene gag and a brutal lowtech buttplug (this one with wire bristles like a bottle cleaner), each ritually situated within the others' ranks on the glass shelves according to a divine order beyond his knowing, augmenting an iconographic sense of concealed message, an intent to enlighten, like the voices within his whirlwind, tremblings of revelation Joe felt yet couldn't hear.

"Hey!" Louie shouted, "I asked you if you wuz okay."

Joe smiled secretly and slurred, "I'm fine, Louie," ungluing his gaze from the numinous case, "if I felt any better I'd be unconscious."

The pinwheeling eyes were making Louie dizzy, like one of those gismos that hypnotists use. He was glad when the Barker, taking two steps sideward to each one to the fore, headed for the door. Louie stared after him, marveling that it must be true, fags could outsuck any broad, because that geek looked like he'd just gotten the Cosmic Bigdaddy of Blowjobs.

They grabbed Joe just outside the One-Stop-Smut-Shop. Slapped him on a squadrol's hood (reflexively he swallowed his remaining balloons), frisked, cuffed, Mirandized him—"I know the drill." *"Shut up, punk."* Head squashed sideways against cool metal, Joe saw the Manager down the sidewalk waving his arms screaming Why couldn't he get good help these days and would they pul*leeeze* hustle Joe out of there, cops all over worked no wonders for biz; and Kitty in her stupid hotpink peignoir crybabying in the doorway with that heliumheaded gashgrinder Bermuda Schwartze patting her back going *it's all right now baby* with her mouth while her eye meeting Joe's wished him a oneway ticket to the House of Many Slammers; and there, Club Charley, he had to be the one to tell them Joe'd gone to Louie's, hiding behind his tip sheet.

Then he was derricked up from behind and wrenched around by his cuffs to face a narrow dark man in a narrow dark suit with a narrow black Hav-A-Tampa Jewel aimed through Joe's heart like a stake.

"Lieutenant Tarzon," twitched the seegar. "Homicide."

"Huh?" The Strip spun slowly, an outsize neon roulette wheel.

"You're under arrest on suspicion of felony murder."

"Oh," Joe mumbled as if someone had told him his fly was unzipped.

BLACK MAN'S BURDEN

||||

Ducklike the bluntnosed ferry breasted the choppy bay confettied with the sails of Sunday mariners. High in a blue sky scrubbed sparkling clean overnight by north Pacific winds hung a single highprowed cloud, serene and magisterial as God's own hairpiece.

The ferry's main contingent, a battalion of krauts, scrambled around the deck, exclaiming and snapping one another's photos against a backdrop equally spectacular in its entire ambit. Children shouted and scampered underfoot, interlocked lovers leaned over the rail, watching the foaming wake; elderly couples in lounge chairs against the sundrenched deckhouse held hands, eyes closed, transported by the brisk salt air and throbbing diesels.

But one blot marred this maritime idyll, a giant bald blot suited in black with wraparound blackglasses screening eyes to which sunlight was anathema. For Baby Jewels hated the outdoors more than the national anthem, fresh air worse than renegade whores, and bay excursions with the same venom apportioned waiters who introduced themselves by their first names. His time was afterhours, his action peddling hot celluloid and cold women, his passion pawnbrokering dreams, his spiritual home the neon strip of the soul. Baby Jewels would sooner coach Little League than ride the Sausalito ferry. It was Gloria's sugardaddy who insisted on meeting with the repository of his darkest, most lonely secret in the lightest, most populous of places—on a Sunday, when no local commuters would be aboard to recognize him.

But after today, Baby Jewels consoled himself, I call the shots; keeping an eye on a large seagull hovering menacingly off the stern as if about to make a bomb run, telling himself again: *After today we'll meet at home-plate at Candlestick Park if I want. Or in any public toilet stall.*

A small boy stood transfixed by the black lenses squeezed onto the conical fatty pod. "Mister, could I have my ball back?" Baby Jewels's tiny tasseled loafer kicked loose the red ball lodged beneath the bench. The boy scooped it up and scurried across the deck to peek back around his mother's hip at the monster at the sternrail. His was the odorless musk of evil best sensed by animals and children.

Beneath the tawny hills and crazy cantilevered homes of Sausalito the diesels roared in reverse and the ferry skidded on the tide, crashed, gulped broken water, slid, settled slowly into its slip. The common wharf stink of oil and tar and dead fish was scented with oranges. The gate lifted, the krauts jostled down the plank like apples fed down a chute into a press. An equally ruddy Australian delegation swarmed aboard, wearing khaki shorts and talking T-shirts.

But where was the shvartze? Baby Jewels removed the wraparounds. Two eyes that could have been shaken from a box of tacks scanned the parking area. Briefly he experienced the terror of every blackmailer who knows if his bet is called there can be no winners, only twice the losers.

Watching the ferry approach from his car, Gloria's sugardaddy had seen his life pass before his eyes once already and was, like a film loop, returned to the beginning, his first recollections in that tin and tarpaper shack halfsunk in the Alameda mudflats, where his mother and he studied the Bible; hearing again her cadences worldweary and melodious metering the Oriental rhythms of Deuteronomy, Job, and Judges to the strident cries of marsh fowl . . . *inhaling the cocaine coal, bonfiring my brain* . . . the same birds that in a boy's dreams clamored over the fishing boats of Galilee . . . *memory's all wavery, like things seen in flame* . . . His mother, the slight and slighted granddaughter of slaves, first taught him that faith's sinew was selfsacrifice . . . *papers said strangled, I cant remember—the whitehot howling!—think maybe I clotheslined her when she called me that name, maybe to a doctor it could look the same* . . . and he wondered at how far he'd come and how much faith worked until his flesh betrayed.

The ferry was docking now. He spotted the fourhundredpound venereal wart spread across the sternrail and imagined it was mad Noah returning on a diesel ark to invoke once more the curse of Canaan. With a prayer that the brassy taste on his lips was not the final cup's, he opened the car door.

Tch. There the shvartze was—slinking between parked cars, sliding across the dock, scuttling up the plank; wearing a widebrimmed Stetson and long leather coat, sunglasses the size of frisbees and a preposterous stageprop beard. California Supreme Court Justice Lucius Carver Bell looking for all the world like an Eddy Street pimp on his way to sparrow-hawk runaways at the bus station. Baby Jewels picked a lozenge from its scrolled tin and pushed it into an effeminate puckery smirk.

The ferry tooted derisively as if it too was in on the joke; then roared, plowing a bluegreen bow wave back to San Francisco, gleaming like a Pacific Jerusalem across the waters. The day was lengthening, purpling the deep downtown defiles. The lowering slants of sun flamed the high windows and shone off the smaller houses spread across the city hill's like carelessly strewn sugarcubes.

The way Bell skulked around casing the ferry reminded Baby Jewels of an actor in a lowbudget thriller. His mirthful baby gurgle was lost on the wind. Didn't the shvartze know the only suspicious person on board was himself in that cockamamy outfit?

When the ferry passed within the huge cold crenellated shadow of Alcatraz—shrine to another pigeyed pimp, Al Capone—Judge Bell finally approached the stern in the wary, circuitous manner of a bird closing on food held by a hand that might snatch it. He perched at length on the stern bench, close enough to be heard over the wind and engines.

"You better have a good reason for insisting on this meeting." The judge's implied threat was about as convincing as the shrubbery glued to his lips.

"As good as yours for agreeing to it." Seeing the judge stiffen, Baby Jewels pursed his lips amusedly. "A fivefootfour reason with a butter meringue keister and marzipan naynays."

"Cant you speak respectfully of the dead?" Bell weakly admonished.

Twin folds of fat reared above the wraparounds. "I dont think she'd want respect any more dead than alive."

"The papers said they found partial prints."

"Yes. And skin beneath her nails." Baby Jewels sighed. "Black."

The judge smacked a fist in his palm. "There's an *animal* out there. I only pray they bring it to bay . . . "

"Havent you learned to take care what you pray for?"

"If they dont catch the killer it wont be the media's fault." Bell barked two ironic notes. "I wouldnt have thought a harlot's murder would excite front page attention."

"A *white* harlot, your Honor . . . a *black* slayer. You of all people should be familiar with the emotions ignited by black on white." He was alluding to Bell's publicly scorned marriage to Daphne Riordan, a white heiress to a sugar fortune who was drummed out of the Junior League for posing nude in a national stroke rag. Her dowry included the Blue Jager Moon. It was less a marriage than uxorial hoax; she to taunt her race, he to tout his. Gloria Monday's murder may have been page one; their miscegenetic nuptials fifteen years earlier made headlines.

"Isnt it amusing," chuckled Baby Jewels, "that marriage could be considered a greater outrage than murder."

Bell ignored the remark. "The apartment was ransacked. The police suspect narcotics. Paraphernalia was found."

"Yes. The crack pipe from which the partials were lifted. You would have been wise to remove that. But I suppose the crack blitzed your better judgment. Toxic psychosis, I believe it's called. It might be a defense. But then you'd be the better judge of that."

The judge whirled on the bench. "I see your game, Moses. But if you try dragging me into this I'll simply deny everything. I left nothing traceable. She paid for the apartment, the car, the clothing . . . she paid for everything with cash I gave her. In public I wore this disguise. We made restaurant reservations under assumed names, attended the theater inconspicuously in the gallery. I was . . . discreet."

"Not the night you shlepped her to the opera. Not the night before she was scrambled. Trying to be discreet with the Blue Moon's like playing darts with cruise missiles. I still cant imagine a man of your intelligence slinging that rock around Gloria Monday's neck. The ditz would have attracted less attention naked."

"Wha—?" Bell snatched off the outsized shades, half ungluing the ersatz whiskers to reveal the deep claw marks beneath.

The Fat Man's dewlaps shivered with hilarity. He produced a golden toothpick and plucked his pearly little teeth. It was a prearranged signal. From the rail circling the deckhouse roof, Quick flashed the diamond necklace, an electric blue burst like an exploding camera bulb instantly extinguished when Quick stepped back from view.

Baby Jewels sucked a pink glob of lobster from the toothpick and waved the implement like a tiny baton, silencing the judge's expostulant gulpings. "One of our girls found her and called us. From the apartment's condition we deduced her killer had searched it for something without success. After we found the Blue Moon I had the police called anonymously."

"But I looked everywhere! I thought she removed it from the apartment, gave it to an accomplice."

"You have to understand that splendid oxymoron, a whore's mentality, to know where one hides things."

Bell gestured between his legs. "Here?"

"No. But you should have checked there first. It was in her douche-bag . . . "

Bell's face collapsed like a struck tent repeating it, hearing her shriek it perhaps, *"Douchebag?* She was calling me that . . . "

"No, the poor girl was trying to tell you where she hid it when you strangled her."

Justice Bell measured his words gingerly as gunpowder. "I beat her, yes. She was trying to shake me down. But I didnt kill her, not purposefully."

"As I said, a good lawyer might make a case for diminished capacity."

The judge collected himself with a deep breath. "How much must I pay for the diamond's return? It's worthless to you . . . "

"Au contraire." Sidney Greenstreet had nothing on Baby Jewels. "It's worth far more than it would fetch on any diamond exchange."

"What are you driving at?" The sudden teeth in Bell's voice were cut razorsharp from amputating courtroom dilations.

"Just this, your Honor. If the police found it, they would have linked it to you, matched the partials and skin samples, and you'd be under arrest for murder. The same can happen any time in the future that the Blue Moon surfaces in connection with Gloria Monday. Any time I choose."

The judge slumped. He stared at the vicinity of his navel as though it were an opened plug and he were watching his life leak slowly out. Then he asked softly, "What is it you want from me?"

It took the remainder of the ferry ride for Baby Jewels to explain. His plump beringed hand dismissed Bell's halfhearted objections that he couldn't interfere with grand jury proceedings. For starters Bell could use his influence to deliver the city's black vote in exchange for Faria dropping the charges—"No deals, I'm talking dismissal." Failing that, Bell could engineer the overturning of all Moses's convictions in the Appellate Division. The court of last resort, of course, was Bell's own.

"I cant control which cases they hear," Bell pleaded, "much less how they rule. No justice has that kind of influence."

"You better win yourself some. Start handing out markers to call in."

"The State Supreme Court isnt a political arm of government." The mediagenic baritone was shredded to a parrot's squawk.

"Quid pro quo. I like the noble spin you lawyers put on things."

A light suddenly flared in Bell's eyes. "The opera? . . . How did you know?"

As quickly as they dented, the fatty brows smoothed themselves. "I have friends who attend the opera," he said with deadpan irony. "How apt that it was *The Rake's Progress* that evening. But my friends found the production so dismal they amused themselves surveying the audience. And *mira-*

bile dictu, they reported seeing you two. It's only at my . . . encouragement that they havent reported the same to the boys on Bryant Street. The police would love toppling you. They know cutting your legs out would cripple every other black politico in the state. So you see, you have to cooperate. If not to save your own skin, then for the sake of every other who shares its color. You owe it to your . . . people."

The light guttered and died in the judge's eyes. Bitterly he considered the unjust burden of the black man: that his glory was always the fleet exception to his race, but his shame forever its rule.

"By the by," smirked Baby Jewels, "did you know the Africans who originally mined the diamond called it the Devilstone? They believed it cursed anyone who carried it across water."

The roar of the ferry's engines shuddered the pier buildings. Baby Jewels heaved his bulk upright, hugely crossed the deck; took the waiting arm of Quick Cicero at the head of the plank and descended to the Mercedes awaiting dockside.

"What's with the dumb disguise?" Quick wondered holding open the limo's door. "They all look the same."

One last time Baby Jewels wetly chuckled at the forlorn spectacle of Bell slumped at the sternrail, clutching the phony beard which one last impish gust of wind had ripped entirely away, miserably conspiring against laws he was sworn to guard.

THE SALLY

||||

Rooski crouched shivering inside a soggy refrigerator carton beneath the Bay Bridge. He listened to the mutter of traffic high above, waiting for rushhour when the police changed shifts and it was safest to move. When the cables hummed with a thousand idling engines and the girders screamed with horns, he scuttled from his hiding place down the garbage sloped high around the great abutment, tripping and falling, stumbling out of the roaring crisscrossed shadows onto the Embarcadero. Through the stalled traffic he bounded, all elbows, knees, and kangaroo ears, startling motorists as he jetéed past their windshields through the ultraviolet streetlamp vapors like a hobgoblin from a modernist ballet.

He reached the Salvation Army on Harrison Street in ten minutes. The Sally was Rooski's second home away from the home he never had, the first being jail. He took his place in the line stretching to the next block; attached his chinless profile to the sooty frieze of faces as stricken and bleak as the Tenderloin twilight. Beggars, bummies, and bindlestiffs of every bent; the hardtiming homeless street haunters whose hearts busted out just behind their luck. Men crouched against cold lightless buildings passing shortdogs of synthetic wine; women, many cradling a child on one arm and holding another by the hand, shifted uneasily on tired feet. Now and again someone bravely laughed when a joke was found not on himself.

Once the Sally soldiers admitted them they thronged the transient lounge. Quickly the air grew close with sickly sweat and sour breath and sharp blue tobacco smoke; murky with nameless guilt, burdened with furtive regret. A hundred Sally feet scuffed fresh marks atop linoleum already tortured by a thousand others toiling beneath unseen crosses toward anonymous Calvaries.

Rooski stood at a corner table beneath a stuttering fluorescent tube. He was trying to tailor a cigaret using a rolling machine whose greasy apron needed replacing several hundred smokes ago. Being legally blind without his glasses made it all the harder. For the third time his trembling fingers fumbled the tin roll bar, exploding Sally tobacco in his face.

"Lemme hep," offered an oldtimer with a face like ten miles of bad road. Deftly he tailored and handed Rooski a cigaret and said sympathetically: "Usta be a firebreathin alkie my own damn self. First got into my daddy's shine out back of the barn and it got worser n worser till I got them DDT's. I shuck jist like you."

Rooski sobbed a lungful of smoke with a force that set his ears to flapping and hacked, "It aint *buh-buh-*booze givin me the whips n jingles. See, the shrink said I was socialist or sumptin and . . . "

Suddenly vigilant, the oldtimer backpedaled a piece. "I dont truck with no cumniss," he whistled through broken orange teeth. He spun clumsily on his heel to join the line forming at the messhall doors.

Rooski shrugged, pointy shoulders nudging pink translucent ears. He didn't mean to scare the old fart; probably should've just let him go on thinking he was a rummy. He couldn't tell the truth, that he was fixing to shatter spontaneously from heroin withdrawal, like blown glass at a rock concert. The Barker drilled that into his head: never cop to your jones. Rooski was trying to blame his shakes on his multiple overdoses of electroshock. Only he could never remember the illness for which it was so frequently prescribed; that name he first heard when he was fourteen, sitting across the Youth Authority psychiatrist's desk, asking: "What's that fivecenter you called me?"

Switching off the recorder, the Y.A. shrink crimped the corners of his mouth and said, "A sociopath? Oh just something somewhere between psychopath and K-mart Republican."

A picture on the Sally wall caught Rooski's attention. To make it out he had to lean over an old fogy passed out on a metal chair, head tipped back, fat fuzzy tongue unhinging his jaw. It was a CERVEZA TECATE calendar featuring a sexpot Aztec warrior queen with little armored pasties tipping big copper jugs. One sandaled foot was planted on a fallen conquistador's breastplate, braced to yank out the spear sunk deep in his chest. Behind her feathered headdress a volcano reared against a scowling sky, erupting suggestively. Kitty Litter could've posed for it, he concluded. The Barker's TexMex squeeze was some kind of goddess in Rooski's slim book.

That Y.A. evaluation wasn't his first, nor would it be Rooski's last brush with stateissue psychology. From some of the later encounters he even emerged something of a Pyrrhic victor. Case in point: during a short layover at the State Hospital at Atascadero, Rooski's doctors as usual decided electroshock therapy was indicated. It was Brer Rabbit into the brier patch all over again: by now Rooski loved Edison medicine better than LSD. There he'd lie strapped to the stainless steel table, wired up like Frankenstein's amphappy stepmonster, screaming "More! Crank it up! I'm runnin a juice jones!" He really was, he'd built up a tolerance, a *habit*. And with an addict's typical ingenuity figured out how to surreptitiously ground himself to the radiator with a wire smuggled off the ward. Finally on his sixteenth treatment he snatched the saline sponge from the horrified technician, doused his testicles, and looped the wire around his penis. Like a lightning rod it sprang erect, buzzing blue and white, shooting sparks like sperm. "Bringin the rush *home!*" shrieked Rooski just before the hospital's central circuits blew. To his awestruck fellow loons back on the ward he offered this modest yet manly explanation: "Just to show em I could take it."

But excepting such occasions when correctional prescriptions jibed so cleanly with Rooski's sense of fun, his life had been a pitiful, abusive progression of foster homes, youth detention facilities, county jails, and lastly state prison. His brief forays into society met invariably with disaster. There was no job so menial that he wouldn't botch it and get fired, no social obligation so trivial it didn't render him impotent with anxiety, no woman so chaste she didn't carry a disease just for him to contract, no pastime so innocent he couldn't convert it into instant criminality, no crime so petty he wouldn't be immediately caught. He was alcoholic before he ever tasted beer and addicted before he swallowed his first aspirin.

It got so the inmates of the various institutions that periodically loosed him on an unsuspecting public started betting pools. Not as to the number of years, months, or even weeks Rooski might remain at large, but days. The lowballers always won.

This last stretch of freedom had set a record: nine months, one week, six days so far. Rooski marked free time the way most recorded sojourns in stir.

"It's the Barker keeps me on the good foot," he was quick to share the credit. "He knows how to stay in pocket and out of trouble. He's got more learnin than just the paperbooks ridin his hip alla time. That Barker's got *street* smarts."

What Rooski shared with no one was his most compelling reason for staying on the bricks this time. There it hung hidden behind all the stateissue jackets, the one with the target on its back he'd have to wear through those penitentiary gates next time: SNITCH.

Rooski joined the mess line. From speakers hidden overhead rockabilly guitar trailed notes sad as tinsel at an unattended party.

It was a dry snitch that came down at San Quentin. A number of the cons housed with Rooski in a North Block honor unit kept pet cats. For some time the guards winked at this technical rule infraction. Yet for some reason when Rooski acquired a kitten, it was confiscated. He lost his head and demanded why he was being singled out for persecution. The guards were forced to prove he wasn't by staging a general feline roundup and using the critters for moving targets at the range. The North Block cats were more than pets, they were the only living things in a lifer's stone-shrunk world from which he could expect the unconditional reciprocation of his affection. No matter that Rooski didn't *mean* to front off the other cons. One can dry hump the local roundheels without fear of infection, dry fire a pistol and spend not one day in jail. But dry snitching in prison carries the same mortal penalty as the real thing. Rooski survived that jolt in Protective Custody. He'd be sprouting shanks like a human porcupine before he was processed through Receiving and Release the next time he was sent home.

A caged red bulb above the messhall doors flashed to the accompaniment of a raucous alarm. The doors whumped open. A chunky Sally matron with sooty fuzz on her lip, a bulldog scowl, and a nametag introducing SGT. ETHEL RAMIREZ took up station collecting meal tickets. Smartass Rooski saluted; she growled, "Shove it along, Stretch."

On the steam line was standard Sally fare: rubberized cream chicken, mashed potatoes, sludgy boiled greens, lime Jell-O. Though his guts roiled like a tub of scalded rattlers, Rooski begged extra helpings out of instinct born from foster home famine.

He stood with his loaded tray squinting around for an empty place at the crowded tables. He saw the beckoning wave of a vaguely familiar fatdimpled arm sheathed in bright bracelets, but couldn't remember to whom it was attached until he heard that tenor honed by cigarets and oiled with bourbon: Penny Bliss. Tray held high, he executed the difficult field maneuver through the sea of bobbing heads.

"You still skinny as an honest alibi," crowed the Bliss miss. "Still tryin to keep up with the joneses . . . Take a load off your sex appeal." Her plastic bracelets clacked, gesturing to the table's last empty stool. Rooski sat and asked Miss Bliss how she was doing. "Better than a hand job," was how.

Beside her sat her twelveyearold daughter, Clarissa, who gunned Rooski a slow onceover, the corners of her mouth turned down in habitual faint revulsion. Her casehardened stare reminded him of Y.A. juveniles convicted of crimes they were not yet old enough to commit, yet purely dedicated to pulling once they were.

"Where your specs, Rooski?" asked Penny, watching him bent two inches over his tray, trolling for vagrant shreds of fowl in the suety paste already setting like concrete.

"Lost em," he said. Remembering when and where galloped his heart.

"Not that you need them hangin out all day down in Cosimo's gallery," she said, adding quickly to quell his sudden alarm, "Dont getcher fuzzy red nuts in an uproar. The Bliss miss has ears like everyone else on the street."

Pete the Packrat also sat at their table. The growlings through his polychromatic whiskers lamented the repair a bottle of *vin fin* could work on this excretal offering. Never mind that he hadn't tasted corked wine since V-J Day. He kept up a running denunciation of the Sally kitchens for undercooking what he was certain was seagull. Suddenly dramatizing the point, he used his fork to flick a morsel over the heads at nearby tables with the exhortation: "Fly, gull! You aint hurt so bad."

"They catch you throwin food, they'll throw you out," Rooski warned. Pete ignored him according to the chauvinistic code by which winos and junkies held each other in mutual contempt. Not that the Dean of the Dumpsters needed someone to look down on. His was the special gift of lying in the gutter staring down the whole world through a sewer grate. Just now he was staring at a cockroach embedded in his lime Jell-O like an emerald scarab.

"Listen, you tall drink of strawberry soda water," said Miss Bliss, her clownish face turned serious. "In case you dont know it, you runnin a high temperature. The Man's dragging the streets for your ass. Your mug's on the top of every squadrol's clipboard. And you know what's waiting for you in the pen. If luck were money in the bank, you're way overdrawn. It's time to get out of Dodge."

"The Barker'll fix it . . . "

"The *Barker?* You crazy? You cant trust the Barker. A pick n pressure bar's all you are to Joe Speaker. Operators like him throw people away like used rubbers . . . " Her eyes untracked. "Like someone threw away that girl on the news."

"I *knew* that girl," said Rooski, grateful for the chance to switch topics. "Usta work for Baby Jewels. Gloria Monday was her handle."

"I knew her too. A *nice* girl, but she trusted everyone. Including her killer. No sign of forced entry, the papers said. Trust'll earn you the same, Rooski—your own morgue drawer."

A secretive smile bespoke Pete's glee at stumbling across a piece of drift knowledge somehow left high and dry by the alcoholic ebb tide wiping his mind blank as wet sand. With a hand the color of wood layered with generations of varnish over dirt he crossed the air, intoning: *"Sic transit Gloria Monday."*

"Shet up yer monkey gibberin," commanded the Bliss miss, who of all things Latin liked only tortilla chips. She turned back to Rooski, tears milky with makeup tracking down her cheeks. "She's just a number now. One hunnerd and twentyeight. I dont want you to be one hunnerd and twentynine . . . "

"Number's already taken," the fourth diner at the table broke his silence. "Last night they pulled the plug on a gook druggist who'd been brain dead since he was whacked during a burglary last week."

Rooski yelped.

"What's wrong?" cried Penny Bliss. "You shakin worse than a whore in church!"

"With a tendollar trick waitin outside," sneered the baby pokerface fronting Clarissa.

"It's this jones crushin my bones," sobbed Rooski. *I killed him, I never killed no one, but I busted his head like a rotten apple. Oh Barker, help me.*

He leaped up tipping his tray to the floor and ran to the transient dorm where he lay staring blindly at the ceiling. *I was jist skeered, dint mean to squash out his life like a bug.*

Later in the stale dark, wrapped in the smells and sounds of a hundred transient dreams, his trembling subsided. Rooski *knew* the Barker would save him. Miss Bliss was wrong about Joe, she didn't understand. With others he might be the way she said, but not with Rooski, his truliest homey. The Barker was magic almost. He could make down seem up and low look high; and bad so good you scoffed at anything better. If there was any swingin' dick who could save Rooski this time, it was the Barker.

ROOSKI BUSINESS

||||

"**Y**ou dont have to talk to me," jerked the Hav-A-Tampa Jewel like an artillery piece on a halftrack. "Twenty years ago an Arizona rapist named Miranda fixed that."

How could Joe tell the homicide cop that he was too scared not to talk with him? They didn't have Rooski, calling him out of the tank proved that. But what did they have? Imagining the worst was more terrifying by far than knowing it.

"Beats playin dominoes in the tank, Lieutenant Tarzan."

"Tar-*zone*. Lieutenant Tarzon."

Joe knew the correct pronunciation; he only hoped by low wit to negate the other's advantage. "As in erogenous?"

"As in combat."

"I'll settle for twilight," Joe said.

Watching Joe across the desk, Tarzon rolled the ash off his cheroot on the lip of a Firestone promotional ashtray, a miniature facsimile of a steelbelted radial. A gooseneck lamp, a wooden In-tray, and a heavy black telephone were the desk's only other accessories. On the shadowed wall over the lieutenant's shoulder hung a photograph in a stainless steel frame. The dark little girl behind the glass wore a frilly white dress like a Mexican tablecloth; a first communion portrait, Joe guessed.

Joe was about to crack that he'd visited mensrooms with more character when Tarzon's frayed white cuff spun an eightbyten glossy across the desk with the casual contempt of a blackjack dealer busting out a desperate gambler. "Look familiar?"

Joe hunched forward, twisting sideways for a better look. It was a morgue shot of the Chinese druggist. PIOUS WING read the placard. Blazing white bandages swathed his high head, sweeping gracefully up in the shape of a bishop's miter. The sheet drawn to his chin clung to him as if wet, lending his peacefully clasped hands the look of polished marble. The eyes in his long ascetic face were halfopen, glazed with secret knowledge, possessing something as well of the luminous blank perfection of a cathedral carving.

"I asked you a question."

"No," Joe answered truthfully. The flashlighted yellow face that night was a blur. He disguised a shiver as a shrug and leaned back from the desk.

"Wing was the druggist you whacked."

"You got the wrong dude," Joe said watching a fly crawl onto the Smith & Wesson handcuff securing him to the chair. He wondered if the steel was as cold to those threadlike legs as it was to his sweating wrist. *Dont get cold feet lil feller.* "I'd no sooner hurt a fly."

"If the fly was carrying less than a sawski . . . " Tarzon banged a fist to the desk, jumping the tire, jiggling the light. "Look at me!"

Joe lifted his head, cocking it slightly and lidding his eyes to screen their fright.

"I know your game, Speaker. Narcotics, bunko, burglary, *pimping,*" spat Tarzon. "But this is a redhot One Eightyseven. Doesnt matter which of you bashed his brains out the back of his skull, you're both guilty under the felony murder rule." He leaned back beyond the lamp's small circle of light and puffed the cheroot, flashing dentalwork from the shadows. His voice dropped, coiling confidentially. "They just might drop the pill on you."

Joe knew he meant the gas chamber but played it dumb. "Pill? I dont fuck with pills." He was adept at whisking up courage with the wind of his own voice; courage as false as his words, yet courage just the same. "Maybe to taper off the stuff, that's it."

Tarzon lunged forward with a shriek of chair casters. His blueshadowed grimace aimed the Hav-A-Tampa between Joe's eyes. "You know goddam well I'm talkin about the big *plop plop fizz fizz.*" Joe did his best to look as if he knew nothing of the sort. Slowly Tarzon leaned back out of the yellow puddle of light. "Word on the street's you're runnin a jones longer than your record," all casual cop again, sveltely intimate, "a nuclear habit. You must be hurtin pretty bad by now."

Of course, Joe realized. That's why he waited two days to call me out of the tank. He counted on me being sick, in the throes of withdrawal, screaming to give Rooski up. How could he know that when I was arrested I swallowed six bags, then used a plastic fork in the tank to pick them out of my shit? I've held off the bonecrushers two days, rationing that stuff up my nose—horned the last just an hour ago.

"I threw in that junkie's hand, Loot. Cleaned up my act . . . " He wished his legs weren't chained so he could cross them to better join in Tarzon's spirit of false intimacy. "Just got to where I had to run as fast as I could to stay in one place. To get anywhere, I had to run twice as fast. I think the Red Queen said that . . . No, no," he added, seeing Tarzon reach for a pencil, "that's a character from a kids' book, not the streets."

Tarzon tossed down the pencil and reached for the top file in the In-tray. Joe knew already it was his jacket, he'd seen his name stenciled on the tab. Once more from the top, he inwardly bemoaned. He'd suffered through these flapdoodle attempts at intimidation by official omniscience before. But nothing from his past could hurt him any longer, and his confidence swelled like a bully's chest.

"I have your NCIC jacket here. There's just one or two points I'd like to go over . . . " Tarzon invested his voice with the same putrid strain of spurious concern the others used. "Born 1958 to Beatrice Holly and 'unknown' father . . . " The lieutenant's brows seesawed, surmising what sexual misdemeanor conceived Joe. "How'd you get the name Speaker?"

"Just the alias used by the stumblebum married my mom. Feds picked him up on a John Doe fugitive warrant just before my birth. Extradited him someplace on a murder charge. Hell, I hope."

"Your mother never bothered to find out who he was?"

"Why? He was just a vicious drunk who socked her up every night for the paper she made slinging hash on Highway 12. Far as she was concerned, the feds who gaffled him up were angels of mercy. Same as she never bothered divorcing a man who never existed, she didnt bother switching up my birth certificate. Just switched back to slinging pussy."

"What about you?"

"Me, I never knew him. Far as I was concerned, he was just another of her supply of deadbeat daddyos. By the time I was five I had more 'uncles' than any little monkey."

"Yeah, but later. When you were old enough to understand. To care . . . Werent you even *curious?*" Tarzon blued the cone of light with an indignant cloud of smoke. It pricked Joe's olfactories like burning brush, and he sneezed twice rapidly, a sure harbinger of encroaching withdrawal.

That and the cold sweat tracing rivulets down his back like the tips of icicles. The interview was spurring his adrenal gland, galloping his metabolism, wringing the heroin from his system.

"Later I already had enough people to hate."

"With yourself at the top of the list."

Joe just shook his head at the fatheadedness engendered by psychology extension courses.

Tarzon lowered his eyes again to the NCIC jacket. "So you lived with your mother and . . . 'uncles' until you were nine, when she copped one B case too many and the state took you away . . ."

"She might have been a whore, but that last bust was humbug. Sheriff had a thing for her and she had nothing for him. He got miffed and one day caught her in a bar and whipped a case on her when all she was soliciting was another beer."

"Soon after, the sauce killed her. Well, not exactly. She passed out with a lit cigaret and incinerated herself in her trailer. Not even thirty. A tragic waste of a young life."

Oh gimme a fivecent break, Joe wailed silently. "Why dont you light her a candle next time you're in church?"

Tarzon vaulted to his feet, rocketsledding his chair against the wall. He sprang halfway around the desk, then gripped it with white knuckles, checking himself. "One more crack about your's or anyone else's mother and I'm taking you upstairs to a quiet cell and kicking your balls up between your ears."

Joe slitted his eyes staring up at him, seething, *Fuck your spic mammy plexes.* This mother, bad as she was, was Joe's to cop attitudes over, not Tarzon's. He chewed his lip furiously, flipping through his mind like a Rolodex for any memory of her that might justify taking a beating. Yet the only sad pride of Beatrice Holly's life had been that once she was a racehorse, a pricey L.A. pro. But the years took a heavier toll on her than others, then the booze. By the time she was twentysix, she was scalylegging the taco trade; rented a trailer next to the wetback camp; day in, day out goldtoothed pachooks scratching on its screen door hissing how they do for cooz. "Get em in, get em up, get em off, get em out," the work song of the working girl became her requiem. So he ducked his head and said it both for her, and for himself for having taken root within her: "I'm sorry."

Slowly Tarzon backed around and regained his chair. He relit the Hav-A-Tampa Jewel. *Why doesnt he ask where Rooski's at?* Joe fretted. That or charge me with a crime? He'd been booked on suspicion of murder only.

The cops had fortyeight hours to bring formal charges or release a prisoner. If not for the murder, Tarzon could book Joe for the paraphernalia found in his boot, simple burglary of the pharmacy, or any number of stray cases fitting his M.O. that needed cleaning off the blotter. Why play *This Is Your Life?* Unless out of boredom and loneliness, a cop's chief occupational hazards after alcohol. Joe checked the wall clock. Eleven thirtyeight. Twentytwo minutes until the witching hour when he must be either charged or cut loose.

Tarzon's eyes had followed Joe's to the clock and met them back at his own with a wintry smile. He skimmed over some jacket entries going *dum dee dum* as if Joe's pathological loathing for people who popped tuneless ditties was recorded there.

"Whoa!" Tarzon stabbed a finger at an entry as though squashing a bug. "Here in seventyone you won the Eleanor Lasker Rider Cup . . . Where'd you learn your way around horses?"

"That's an eighthgrade composition prize. Miss Rider was a patron of the Monserrat School."

"What school?"

"A Jesuit boarding school in Napa County. Three years after my mother died, an aunt I never knew I had kicked the bucket. She left money for me to attend Monserrat. It was the only break I ever got, though I didnt appreciate it then." Joe paused, remembering nighttimes peeling the scabs from his knees so they'd bleed afresh on the chapel stone next dawn, dramatizing his devotion. "I got a crash classical education from the fathers," hearing the Latin declensions ringing against stone walls rough as excavations. "When the money ran out, Father Aloysius picked up the tab for another year. Then cancer wormed his brain and the blackrobes turned me back to the state." His memory tripped a reckless whim and Joe slanted Tarzon a twinkler. "Father Aloysius loved puns, the cheaper the better. He would have called this conference rooski business."

Tarzon betrayed no sign that he knew a pun from poontang. He chomped on the cheroot with a renewed ardor that had Joe wondering if he wouldn't rather eat than smoke it. Then he launched into the meat of Joseph Holly Speaker's computer portraiture; the recitation of California Penal Code numbers, Health and Safety violations; the panoply of arrests in various California counties and one in Washoe County, Nevada, where the authorities took a dim view of Bay Area junkies coming to dump hot traveler's checks at their tables; the numerous probations, the stints at the work farm.

Joe listened absently as though learning of the doubleganger reflection staring curiously back at him through the office window. Beyond, thick night fog rolled in through the Gate, chasing ghost ships with running lights like misty halos. The Alcatraz horn bloomed wetly; another answered, deeper; a freighter bellowed back like an enraged bull sea lion. Orange lights bedewed the Bay Bridge. Across black water a refinery belched fire. The doubleganger looked away.

"Huh?" He'd waited so long for the question it came as a surprise.

"Where's Peter Chakov?" Tarzon had set aside Joe's jacket and reclined backward so only the lower half of his narrow face was lit. "Rooski to you."

Joe knit his brow. "Rooski . . . Rooski . . ." With the junk wearing off, he couldn't keep up the bluff much longer. He snapped his free hand's fingers. "Oh yeah. I've heard of the dude. Heavy snitch jacket, they say." He frowned hurtfully. "You dont think I run with informants, Loot?"

With that cheroot perfectly centered, it was impossible to tell Tarzon's grimace from a grin. "He's your known crime partner. You've fallen together on several raps. Tell me where he's hiding and I can still talk to the D.A. about a manslaughter or second degree."

Artful consternation drawn on his face, Joe chinked his chains shrugging. A pair of smashed blackframed glasses spun into the light.

"Recovered at the scene of the crime," the Hav-A-Tampa Jewel fired short bursts. "State issue. From the pen. Etched on the frame, Peter Chakov's prison ID number . . . I was trying to give you a break asking his whereabouts. But now I've changed my mind. I'm tired of your bullshit. The only true thing you've said since you walked in here was that your crimey's an informant. Snitch. He'd be dead his first night back in the joint. Rooski knows it. That's why he'll be turning his guts inside out like a rubber glove right at this desk soon as we find him. And we'll find him, Speaker. Make book on that. And he'll turn over on you like a bitch in heat. Punch you a oneway ticket to the little green room with the funny windows across the bay."

Joe's stomach churned feeling cold perforated steel on the seat of his pants, a hand tapping his shoulder saying, "Take a deep breath, son. You wont feel a thing"; the dreadful sound of the thin chain pull and the cyanide pellets hissing into the bucket of acid like angry snakes.

Tarzon set the Hav-A-Tampa in the Firestone ashtray and sighed. A small shiny key suddenly skipped across the puddle of light. "It fits your legirons too. Unlock yourself and get out of here. I've got reading to do."

Fumbling with his locks, Joe watched Tarzon reach for the next file in the In-tray. It bulged with computer roll and graph paper. Autopsy reports, Joe guessed. The name on the flag was Gloria Something Polish that looked like spilled alphabet soup. Oh yeah, he'd heard some scuttlebutt in the tank about Gloria Monday buying it. Whores might live by the bed, but they rarely died in one.

Tarzon's voice stopped him at the door. He turned, facing eyes bright as meat hooks. "Like they say in the movies, Speaker. This aint goodbye, just *au revoir* . . . motherfucker."

FRONT STREET

||||

"**S**hitfire, it was good this morning."

"What?" Joe's naked body glowed orange through the oilcloth window shade. Lifting back its edge, he squinted in the crack of gray light.

"What else? Fucking. It was Texastype good, which is plenty fine. You kept a slow hand and when you come it rung my ovaries."

"No sale, I hope." Joe ducked for a better angle through the rusted fire escape slats. A squadrol whispered along the rainslick street; the traffic light at the corner blinked its feverish yellow eye. Last night's dreams lay smashed with the bottles in gutter puddles reflecting dirty clouds raked by a broken skyline.

"Tarzon wouldnt have cut me loose except to follow me. He needs me to find Rooski. Cops dont have a dopefiend's special antennae. Set a junkie to catch a junkie."

Kitty sighed. "Guess it's just as well you took your time. How long's it supposed to hold me?"

Joe looked at her, dropping the shade. "They'll be playing me like frog pussy, watertight. I wont be coming around until I . . . take care of Rooski."

"How you going to take care of that idiot?"

"I keep tellin you I dont fuckin know. I only know they left me no choice but to find him first. Then I'll worry about what to do with him . . . " Joe flung back his head and cursed the ceiling. "They could send me to the chamber. Talk about limiting a dude's options!"

"I wouldnt want Rooski hurt, fella."

He dropped his jaw, staring at her in outraged disbelief. "You think maybe I would? You think I've been waitin all my life to whip a world of hurt on Rooski's freckled ass? Fuck!" He balled his fists, reeling clumsily, searching for an object to strike. He loosed an agonized groan, slammed the heels of his hands into his temples and sat defeated on the bed, bouncing. "Christ."

Kitty was reaching to stroke his bent head when it shot up.

"There's one chance," he muttered fiercely. "One caper I've had on the drawing board only I didnt have the stones. I dont now either, I'm just plain desperate enough. We might score enough to get Rooski out of the country, not just fuckin Dodge. We *might . . .* " biting the word like a bullet.

"What caper?"

His mouth sprang open, then slowly shut. "You dont want to know, Kitty."

"I reckon not. I reckon all I want to know is my baby is gonna get off Front Street in one piece. I dont care how." She sat beside him, resting her hand on his shoulder, and made a glowering survey of the desolate room. "Sometimes you gotta do what you gotta do."

"Yeah, and it's got me blue to the bone."

"Cmon, fella." She punched his arm. "Keep an eye on the sunnyside. Turn this last trick and we're free. We can get out of this Life before it kills us." She seized the arm and shook it. "We got what it takes to square up, Joe. Between us we got the grit and savvy to put all this behind us."

"You always loved long shots."

For a long moment she gazed at him with that veiled look with which women distill thought from feeling. A siren dopplered past; from the hallway a cry followed by thudding like falling down stairs. Lightly slapping her knees then, she rose and scudded on bare callused feet to the dresser. She shook a Winston from its pack, lit it, and turned jetting smoke through her nostrils.

"You ever wonder why I stick with you, Joe?"

He snorted without raising his head.

"You have to. You got to wonder why I put up with all this shit. So I'm gonna tell you. A lot of men have loved me. I'm talkin *bo*coo. And there were a few I thought I loved back. But that's all it was, a thought. An idea. I wanted to love so bad I could talk every part of my body into it but my heart . . . "

"You dont need—"

"I do so. Then I met a fella who wanted to love but couldnt. He believed in love, he'd just never known it. And watching him I realized I was watching myself, and I seen that wanting to love, struggling for it, is more real than just loving. It's deeper, stronger, more honest. The other's too easy and cheap. For cheap, easy people. The sort who fall in love like falling off a horse. Our kind has to suffer." She took his hand and pulled him to his feet, leveling their eyes. "So we're in this together, fella. You aint a long shot, you're my only shot."

Joe ran both hands back through his matted hair, swallowing hard. With her nail Kitty underscored the tattoo over his heart, BORN TO LOSE, chuckling, "It's only got one letter wrong . . ."

Joe grinned reaching for his Levi's. He turned to the window, buttoning them. "I cant spot them, but they're there."

"Phew!" She fanned her hand beneath her nose. "What's that smell like fish oh *ba*by! . . . Cmon," she stepped to the sink and wrenched a tap. The pipes brayed their rusty jeremiad while she wet a towel. "You got cum plasterin your pubes. Lemme clean you."

"No, I gotta book . . ."

"Sure. The cops wont have to keep up with you, they'll just follow the cats."

"No time," Joe said shrugging into the dragon jacket. "Tarzon's out trackin Rooski. I cant afford him gettin too big a jump on me."

"Be careful. If they catch Rooski he'll give up all the drawings."

Through the wall a radio wondered how hard times came so easy.

"Bye, Kitty . . ."

"Shitfire! Aint you got a kiss in your pocket?"

He didn't know she was crying until he tasted salt on her lips. He reached with his thumb to dab at a tear shivering from the corner of her eye. She loosed a tiny snarl; her hand flew up slapping his aside. Staring at her, Joe groped behind his back for the pair of visegrips that served as a door knob. With a screech of rusty hinges he was gone.

Kitty listened to the tumble of his bootheels down the stairs, then flung herself on the bed and stared at the fuckedup flophouse ceiling. Funny, now that he was gone, so were the tears. Wait a minute! He forgot his keys. Snatching them off the Pacific Gas & Electric spooltop which served as their nightstand, she jumped to the window. She snatched the shade aside and wrenched it open. The sooty cold wind snatched away her breath. She ignored the derelict flaked out in the doorway across the street, lifting his shortdog inside its paper sack, toasting her nudity. She leaned out . . . . shit. The dragon was almost a block away, stretched skinny across his back by Joe jamming his hands in the pockets the way he did in a hurry. Tragic.

Wrestling the window closed, she saw the derelict wasn't taking a drink—he was talking fast into a radio hidden in the sack.

Double tragic.

||||

Rigo La Barba slumped on the nod in the crushedvelvet front seat of his '62 Impala lowrider at the corner of Sixth and Mission. He was called La Barba, the Beard, after his carefully groomed goatee.

Next to the highgrade chiva he dealt, La Barba was proudest of his lowrider. It had jeweled vanity mirrors attached to the sun visors, a miniature crystal chandelier in place of the dome light, a goldplated chain steering wheel, and, next to the ivory Virgin atop the minklined dash, a keyboard on which he could play "Besame Mucho," "Don't Cry for Me, Argentina," or, more to the point, "Chinga Tu Madre," according to his cholofied caprice. Over twentyeight handrubbed coats of topazflake lacquer, sequined rococo script announced La Barba's philosophy on one rear fender: *Low 'n' Slow*; and on the other he christened his chrome galleon *Crystal Blue Persuasion*.

This whole automotive confection rode just inches above the pavement on electric shocks powered by a dozen Sears Diehards in the trunk. At the push of a button, La Barba could catapult the entire car three feet in the air. Or, should he scope a particularly oomphy muchacha rumbaing down Dolores Street, dump the front end, beneath which was welded a steel bar, and plume a roostertail wake of sparks down the street. *Que macho,* heaved each *rucca*'s brown barrio bosom. Every day was Cinco de Mayo in *Crystal Blue Persuasion*.

The voice from the hungry face framed in the Impala's window was like a bad long distance connection. La Barba turned down the oldies throbbing from satin door panels.

"Que dice?" The cholo shaded his eyes squinting into the Mission forenoon.

"Front me ten sacks, Barba. I'm out of pocket."

"I heard you were in la pinta, Joe."

"They rolled me out last night . . . "

"No fronts. Too risky. You no pay me from la pinta. I give you just one so you no beg." In a single swift motion La Barba reached behind a visor and palmed Joe a balloon.

"You seen Rooski?"

The cholo hissed like fat in a fire. "Fock no. Undercover down here onny dis morning asking me same ting." He dug a crucifix from the nest of hair glistening where his chest spread the unbuttoned top of his Van Heusen. He touched it to his forehead, breast and shoulders, then kissed it. "In Mehico we say such as Rooski are *tocado* . . . " He tapped a forefinger to his brow. "Touched by God . . . He protex them and ponishes any who fock with them . . . "

Suddenly La Barba sprang rigid; his arm shot up, pointing across the dash. The motion was so violent Joe thought at first he'd been electrocuted by his highvoltage beanmobile. He stared horrified at the trembling fingertip, waiting for the first wisps of smoke.

"*Mira!*" La Barba croaked.

Joe tracked the finger's direction and his stomach opened like a trapdoor. A white fourdoor Plymouth was parked in a loading zone on the next block. Two heads were silhouetted in the front seat.

"They watching now. Watching you for Rooski. I no know you no more . . ." La Barba's quick wrist flicks started the rolling chivaria's engine and cranked up the Delco Powermatrix booster. *Crystal Blue Persuasion* glided from the curb low and slow, leaving behind a trembling echo of colored girls' voices wondering *will you still love me tomorrow* . . .

Joe scowled at the unmarked. The heads were motionless, locked on him. How were they dogging him so close? He was sure he'd shook them. All that folderol at the Hyatt Regency; up and down the service and guest elevators, through the kitchens and basement storerooms; and finally, trademark jacket over his arm and sunglasses lifted from the gift shop on his bent nose, out the front entrance with a herd of Midwesterners boarding a tour bus. Angrily he snapped his fingers. They must've picked him up again when he checked at the methadone clinic where Rooski often begged state juice.

Joe stumbled jumping the curb and bolted down an alley.

The last section of track where the Hyde Street cable car reaches Market at Powell is embedded in a giant turntable. The conductor rolls his car onto this circular slab of concrete, locks his brakes, and alights to push the car completely around facing uphill for its return trip to Fisherman's Wharf. For this spectacle, the corner of Market and Powell is a tourist hub—and prime hustling locale.

Hymie the Hat, wearing his trademark homburg, stood near the turntable hawking racing forms stacked in his toy red wagon. Hymie used to print and sell his own tip sheet titled *Gift Horses* at Bay Meadows until cataracts sealed the dapper little horse savant within a white waxen world and he was reduced to flogging forms. Gamblers old enough to remember his halcyon days traveled from miles around for the auspicial bonus attached to getting the last line from the Hat.

"Golden Gate Fields, Hollywood Park, New Awleens *Fayyyr*-grounds . . ." The fabled track names floating off his tongue, hanging in the racketing downtown forenoon like golden sonic globes. "Hiya*leey*ah,

Churchill Downs, Pimlico, Belmont, aannduh *Ahhhh*queduct . . . " Hymie the Hat could have been the conductor on some horse degenerate's fantasy rail junket.

Hearing his name, Hymie turned smiling as though truly recognizing who hailed him. He wouldn't admit his blindness, though he saw only shadows, as through gauze.

"It's the Barker." Sometimes Joe flogged Hymie's leftover forms from the Blue Note door.

"Joe." Still the short con smile, smooth and cute as a baby's ass. Hymie held his palms reversed before him to ward off clumsy shadows. "You need a pony?"

Joe told him he only needed to find Rooski this morning, who often cadged Demerols from Hymie's migraine script.

"Have I *seen* him? Yesterday afternoon the idiotski came tearing down Powell like a bat outta hell. Tripped over my wagon and spilled my forms all over the street. I asked what the hell was going on. He said he was in plenty trouble and could he borrow a few bucks to get off the streets. I told him no way, I work too hard for my money to put it on losers and lunatics. Next he hit me up for pills. What? You think they're jellybeans, I said. Get outta here. Go to the Salvation Army with the rest of the bums. You see him, Joe, you tell him to stay outta my face."

"He's in a little over his head," Joe said. Behind him the cable car bell rang *All aboard.*

"Funny. That's what the other guy said."

"Other guy?"

"Yeah. Come around bout an hour ago askin for Rooski. I could smell stogie tobacco, but no smoke . . . Say, what kind of trouble *are* you two in?" Turning, searching for a shadow in the tall columns of Market Street sunlight. "Joe?"

Fuckin Tarzon's all over me like a cheap suit, cursed Joe swinging off the cable car and running a block to catch the 15 Columbus bus to Fisherman's Wharf. Noontimes Rooski often hustled bunk hash there and Joe planned to do the same in hopes both of catching him and collecting some dead presidents himself. Killing two birds with the one stone. But how'd Tarzon make the Hat?

It gave Joe some kind of creeps whose crawling he tried to still by planning where to steal the hashish mix: All Seasons sage, butter, vodka. He needed a store with a restroom to mix them and a sandwich microwave to bake the flat cakes of ersatz blond Lebanese. He decided on a Kwik Fixx two blocks from the Wharf. He regretted the store was already a mecca for every grifter and garden variety shoplifter between Chinatown and the Bay. Like mercy, Joe preferred to dispense his larceny evenly around.

The decision made, Joe relaxed. He smiled feeling the throbbing bus diesel knead away the backache he incurred combatfucking Kitty the night before until his hip gristles creaked like oarlocks. He tipped back his shaggy head against the window and dreamed himself within the blue underwater world of his private refuge, the aquarium.

The moment he stepped off the bus, Joe spotted Pete's Dalmatian, Daisy, hitched by old belts to her shopping cart beside the glass doors. The Kwik Fixx was her master's first stop of the day. And Joe knew just what the irascible wino was up to in there. Back in the cosmetic section guzzling Rub-a-dub or Green Lizard, his affectionate cognomens for rubbing alcohol and Aqua Velva Lime. For "Squeeze," Sterno to the rest of the world, he'd stop in Ace Hardware down the block. Pete liked kicking off his alcoholic days with the *outre* stuff; later he'd switch over to more conventional potables, usually Fleishman's Tokay or, in his more villainous moods, Mad Dog—as Mogen David 20/20 was known to the doorway wine set.

Although the convenience store was lax enough to be worked by several thieves at once, Joe preferred waiting until Pete had drunk his fill. He occupied himself meanwhile inspecting a Dungeness crab languishing in a pail of water atop the rest of the garbage heaped in Pete's cart.

"Stop molesting my menagerie!" came a blast of lime aftershave. At least one drunk in San Francisco had sweet breath today. "You and your Slavik sidekick are always meddling in my affairs."

"Rooski?" Joe yelped. He hadn't expected help from this quarter. "You seen Rooski? Where?"

"Tellin me how to eat my vittles down at the Sally," bawled Pete. "If I never see that varmint agin it's too soon."

"He didnt say where else he'd been?" One could stay at the Sally just one night a week.

"What are you? The Mind Police? 1984's over and gone, me bucko." Pete's slack growl and dangerous list to port signaled his total inebriation. Without a liver, the alcohol went as straight and surely into his blood as if he'd injected it. "But come to think of it . . ." Pete staggered, grabbing the cart's handle for support. "The bawd alluded to him frequenting a cosmic galaxy."

The shooting gallery in Cosimo's basement! The Troll's dope lair. Of course that's where Rooski would go to ground, there to run errands for the Troll and beg cottons from the other dopefiends. Joe frowned watching

Pete mush Daisy toward Burger King for a spot of lunch from its bountiful dumpsters. Why hadn't he thought of it sooner?

Wrong question, he upbraided himself, running into the middle of Columbus to snatch a cab. What if Tarzon already had?

THE TROLL'S

||||

Out of the rumbling ruby gloaming a stringy squincheyed bird with Dumbo ears and red hair fine as duckling down came winging around the corner of Post Street and ricocheted smack off a streetlamp into a mailbox.

The gallon jug of Clorox bleach beneath one arm, intended to disinfect needles, rolled willynilly down Post Street—at the corner of Larkin it jumped off the curb and exploded against a Yellow Cab. The sack of lactose beneath his other arm, purchased to cut heroin, burst at his feet, caking his face like a mime's. When the blood loosed from his brow by the thoughtlessly situated streetlamp mixed with the sweet white powder and trickled into his mouth, his tummy shouted: *If this is what blood pudding tastes like, me for seconds!*

Flapping his arms like flightless wings, he vroomed straight through the beveled leadglass doors of Cosimo's Billiard Parlor.

Three old wops sat hunched over tiny cups, crinkling the bronze light with cigaret smoke, listening to *Una Furtiva Lagrima* grieving from an antique Wurlitzer. If they thought anything of this Central Casting dream of a rabid mooneyed vampire with a chalked face and bloody mouth contorted in a soundless yowl, they revealed nothing. Past the billiard tables he bounded, fluttering aged Italian travel posters and *giornales* draped on wooden spindles; through the empty storerooms he zoomed, raising dust devils in his slipstream. He came to a skidding halt at the locked basement door. For a moment he stood moaning lowly, wringing long freckled hands; then remembered and pressed the digital combination on the Simplex lock. The sixteengauge CECO door popped open, and he passed down the rickety wooden staircase to the Troll's subterranean shooting gallery.

Addicts called the legless man on a wooden platform the Troll after his practice of levying tribute from the dopefiends who used his premises and paraphernalia. A tenspot was his toll, more than twice the going rate, but the Troll's was hardly the regular chippy joint that got raided every week—he was protected. What's more, he kept on hand an endless supply of PlastiPak disposable syringes and plenty of bleach for flushing them, which alone in this age of AIDS excused the extortionate tariff.

None knew how long the Troll had held court on his rolling dais behind the line of votive candles in the corner of Cosimo's basement. His gray hair was long and matted and tied around his waist to keep from fouling in the platform casters. His breath rotted the basement air, his nails were grown into hard hooked claws; and his eyes, like those of any creature of the deep, were enfeebled by desuetude, vestigial, glistening in the dark like poisonous berries.

Once tribute was paid, his phantom patrons repaired to Bunsen burners to perform the central ritual of their blighted existences, afterward withdrawing into the writhing darkness along the walls, ranking side by side, enfolded in their junk spells like bats within their wings. *Ssshh, no swoon so sweet this mean side of paradise.*

Until some whirlybird came crashing down the stairs and, missing the last three steps entirely, stumbled halfway across the basement before regaining his balance wildly windmilling his arms. Violently shaken from their nods, the shadows tensed. Could it be a crackling crackoid penetrating their sanctum? Then, seeing it was but the pest who was known to them all too well, they loosed a weary broadside of obscenities. One voice with a twang like a jew's harp put it most succinctly: "Rooski, you could fuck up a wetdream." "Sorry . . . sorry . . . " The spellbuster tiptoed in a circle peering into the shadows going *hush, hush* with a finger to his bloodied lip as though the others, not he, were the cause of their own distraction. Soon they relapsed into their trances and the basement again was silent save the faint jabbering of the Troll's portable TV.

"Where the stuff I sent you after?" the Troll demanded.

Rooski stammered, fumbling for an excuse, remembered the bleached cab. "Goddam cab knocked me on my ass, busted all the stuff. You want I should go out again?"

"No," the Troll said. "Maybe later. Now you stay right here."

No argument from Rooski, who was too sick for any more gofering just now anyway. The three codeines he'd copped with the Troll's change and coldcooked and shot in the bathroom of Johnny Drum's Body Electric Tattoo Parlor hadn't touched his jones. Holding off the bonecrushers with codeine was like trying to rob Fort Knox with water pistols. Rooski shook like a pup passing a peach pit, the treacly brown smell of cookedoff heroin turned his legs to wet noodles; any minute now he knew he was going to shit in his pants.

Then, from the tenebrous region beneath the stairs, he heard a familiar feminine hissing: "Please God lemme have this hit."

Rooski could recognize Belinda Batista's voice anywhere. He'd heard it a hundred times screaming from the TV about how she'd like to eat this bimbo's face off or grind that one's ass up for taco filler or squeeze that bitch's tit in a wringer. Her ring name was Belly Blast and she'd been captain of the Tinsel Tarts in Distress, a female tag team, until retired by her jones.

Rooski knew she was having trouble injecting herself and sprang to her side. "I'll do you, Belly. I'll do you good if you lemme pound your cotton." By which he meant add more water in her cooker and strain the residue from her cotton, something like percolating coffee grounds a second time.

With black lambent eyes Belly Blast scrutinized the deranged scarecrow. Blood webbed her arms and hands where she had repeatedly plumbed for extinct veins. She held the syringe close to a burner's flame. The barrel was black with blood. Even if Rooski could find a vein, how could he detect a register?

"No es una problema, chiquita," he said confidently, flashing a little chili chatter he'd picked up in the tomato fields of the Youth Authority. "I'll fix yer neck."

Her hand flew to her muscular throat, eyes sprung wide.

"You got it. Expressway to your skull."

The dark eyes hooded suspiciously, then dulled with resignation as she considered the alternative, drinking the bloody shot, and she sighed, handing him the rig. "Help me, Crazy Red."

She followed his whispered instructions: lie back, face the wall, blow on your thumb. Her cheek ballooned like a trumpeter's; her jugular swelled like a highpressure hose. In a twinkling Rooski tapped a register. *"Cut!"* he whispered. Out popped her thumb; her breath escaped with a *whooosh;* the great artery slurped the barrel dry.

"Sweets for my sweet," Rooski softly crooned withdrawing the spent rig. He bent and quickly kissed the teardrop of blood at her throat.

She lapsed into her native tongue, moaning from very far away: "Que bueno."

Rooski set right to work preparing his own injection. He was undeterred by the traces of blood in her cotton—in fact, he was pleased. A little hot spic sangre might liven up his own shot, shoot smoke from his ears. Ears that were just now flexing as he worked, rotating like radar dishes to scan a news flash interrupting one of the Troll's gameshows.

> "... *masked gunmen burst into Chinatown's Golden Boar Restaurant during the lunch rush and executed two reputed members of the Wah Ching gang in a blazing fusillade, killing one busboy and wounding three other diners. Police say members of the rival Joe Sing gang are suspected* ... "

Joe Sing and the Barker were old homeys, he remembered with pride as he drew up his hit. He fixed himself without even tying off. He was one of those wiry guys with veins forever; he could even fire at will into the rollers around his wrists and ankles. Before he'd withdrawn the point, his eyes were blurred and his features smeared like a melting wax mask.

It was then a voice from the nearby shadows first spoke: "Hey, Scarecrow. You wanna sell a coupla them ropes?"

The Barker! Rooski scooted around on his knees squinting into the dark. "Joe? Joe! You're here!"

"The more veins I lose, the more you got. You stealin mine?"

Rooski still couldn't see him. "They're fixin to lay me low, Barker. What do I do?"

"Dont worry. I got you." The voice paused, then: "Why didnt you pull my coat? How come I had to get it from the Man?

"I dont get you, Barker ... "

A weary something tainted the voice like a parent scolding a child for forgetting his galoshes at school. "Your glasses."

Rooski's rabbiteyes twitched, his cheeks fluttered. "I'm sorry, Barker. I feel so low I'd need stilts to walk under a snake ... just too scared to tell you."

Joe emerged from the shadows and squatted in the undulant orange light of the burner. His slitted eyes stared at his crimey; then he spit in the basement dirt and shook his head, laughing softly.

"You aint gonna sock me up?" twittered Rooski.

"What for? It's too late ... "

"Or yell even? ... " Hope dawned on his goofy face.

"*Hush,*" Joe said suddenly, holding up his finger. The ceiling shook with pounding feet; then fists thudded on the basement door. A muffled voice shouted: "The door's double steel with nonrising hinge pins. Tell Lieutenant Tarzon we're gonna have to bust it out of its jamb . . ."

The shadows along the walls went rigid; several leaped upright.

"Cool yer jets!" bruited the Troll, a Browning ninemillimeter suddenly in his hand. He waved it at Joe and Rooski. "They only want them."

"That's why he didnt send you out again," Joe hissed. "It's part of his protection plan giving up dudes."

The Troll swung the automatic on Joe, leering livid confirmation in the murmurous blue video wash.

Suddenly out of the darkness flew a boot kicking the Troll's head, shooting his platform sideways with a screech of metal wheels, toppling the cripple in the dirt. The Browning clattered from his claw. Belly Blast leaped out of the shadows through which she had circled the basement undetected. She snatched up the gun. The Troll screamed horribly, flailing on his back, rocking his legless torso like an overturned tortoise. Belly squatted and with both hands thrust the automatic in his face.

"Dont zip him," Joe shouted, springing across the basement. "The Troll aint worth a bullet."

His voice was swallowed by a shuddering boom. Again—Boom. The basement door was being rammed. The jamb creaked and splintered, about to cave in. Police voices swelled and Joe heard Tarzon bark an order.

Belly sprang to her feet. "We gotta book—fast. Get Rooski. We use the Troll's own escape route."

Rooski was in a daze, and Joe had to grab him, push him across the dirt floor, kicking aside the Troll's picket line of votive candles. Past his gibbering thrashing form they scrambled into the dumbwaiter whose door Belly held up, hissing for them to hurry.

Above, a great shout arose as the whole door frame crashed inward, and the halfton slab of steel slid booming down the stairs, followed by thundering feet.

Then they were in the dumbwaiter, its door shut, Joe and Belly hauling on its pulleys for all they were worth.

"I never seen a dumbwaiter so big," Joe huffed.

"Joint usta be a mortuary," gasped Belly. "They got embalmed in the basement and hauled up in this thing."

"They still get embalmed in the basement," Joe quipped, then: "Why're you helping us?"

"That was Rick Tarzon bustin down the door," she said, adding between breaths in a tone which forbade further inquiry: "We got a personal problem."

"Plus it's good luck to help out nuts," chirped Rooski.

Between their climbing arms Joe saw a smile flash beneath her straight bangs and button nose. Then the dumbwaiter thumped against a ceiling and Belly hitched its pulleys around the cleats affixed to its interior. She threw open the gate and out they stumbled into a deserted topfloor room four stories above the billiard parlor. Out a window and up a fire escape they clambered, then off across the steep night roofs.

The Red Light Abatement raid was staged promptly at eight. Baby Jewels and Sidney Dreaks met the crush of police and press at the Tender Trap's door. In the glare of a dozen kliegs, District Attorney Faria preached City Hall's commitment to eradicating fleshpots like the Tender Trap; while Moses, ignoring Sidney tugging on his sleeve counseling restraint, denounced the Mayor, the D.A., and the media for scapegoating him to disguise their failure to apprehend real criminals like the psycho who murdered Gloria Monday.

The cops herded all the girls out and into the paddy wagons. Warrant checks were run on all the customers before releasing them. All receipt books and files were carted out. The doors were closed and posted with dire proclamations. For the final padlocking ceremony, Faria struck a heroic pose as though preparing to lock the very gates of Hell. But in all the hubbub and hoopla some nitwit cop had misplaced the goddam five-pound nickleplated padlock specially requisitioned for this civic charade. After much vociferation and confusion, a rookie patrolman's lowly handcuffs were substituted.

Later, long after the clubs and porno shops and peepshow arcades had closed and the Strip had gone dark like an unplugged pinball machine, along came swishing a slight figure in a leather greatcoat and stormtrooper boots. It was Untergruppenfräulein von Wanditz—and was little Dwan ever in a snit. Just that afternoon he'd answered a promising want ad, dressed just for the occasion. Only to find out they had something else in mind in advertising for someone "bondable."

The fascist fruitcake gasped when he saw the handcuffs securing the Tender Trap's door handles. So *shiny* . . . and regulation tempered steel too! His nipples hardened. Not like those rinkydink toys sold in S&M shops. Just what that lumberjack back at Bermuda's needed to teach little Dwanny the lesson of his life. Ooh, his sphincter squirmed. *Pull yourself together, Mary!* he scolded himself. He just couldn't help it, he felt so deliciously, well . . . *Third Reich* this evening.

Naturally, Dwan Wand was an expert with constraint devices. He set to work with his swastika roach clip, and in a twinkling opened the cuffs. Off he traipsed down the blackedout Strip whistling "I'm in the Mood for Love."

STREET COURT

||||

The state of war with the Wah Ching mandated that the Sing brothers stay constantly on the move. To find them, Joe loitered in Chinatown Park, searching out one of their minions for instructions. There, dozing behind his pulleddown porkpie hat beneath the checker pavilion's snapping pennants, the wizened pigtailed dopepeddler known only as Firecracker.

"Barkersan!" Firecracker cackled once Joe roused him from his stupor. Bright beady eyes laughed from a face like a desiccated apricot. "Doggone no see, long time."

Hastily Joe asked where Joe and Archie Sing were to be found. Firecracker knew the Barker was trusted by the brothers and issued a convoluted set of directions. Thanking him, Joe halfturned to leave, then stopped, flinging back his head and puffing his cheeks disconsolately. Releasing his breath with a curse, he turned back.

"Front me a dime of your gunpowder, Firecracker."

Surprise further wrinkled Firecracker's face. He'd never known Barkersan to use coke. But his next knowing cackle guessed Joe had a good reason for wanting it now. With a motion subtle and fluid as the T'ai Chi performed by nearby youths in martial pajamas, Firecracker swept off his porkpie hat, plucked a plastic pane of white powder from its band, and palmed Joe a quarter gram.

||||

The vast import warehouse near the piers at the foot of Telegraph Hill was owned by one of the brothers' innumerable relatives. A loft that could be reached only through labyrinthine secret passages was on their rotation of hideouts.

"Heard you booked Rooski out of the Troll's just before the cops nailed him," said Joe Sing, the elder of the two almost identical Chinese brothers seated on futons facing Joe in the tan speckled light of bamboo blinds. Their tight facial skin was a luminous saffron not unlike the multitude of ceramic Buddhas sold below.

Joe sat crosslegged, facing them. "News travels."

"Where you got him?" Archie asked.

"Stashed at a chick's crib in the Tenderloin. She's out running credit cards, he's on a nod."

"You figured what to do with him?" Joe Sing asked.

"Book his skinny red ass as far out of Dodge as I can." Joe tipped his head. "You know the Fat Man's porno movie palace on Jones?"

"Yeah, only I thought it shut down with the rest. You know, home videos, new blue laws."

"The Kama Sutra's about the last. The Fat Man only keeps it open for the betting bank he runs out of its basement. I'm gonna rip it."

The elder Sing's obsidian stare narrowed; the Barker wasn't known for daring capers. "You taking down the Fat Man?"

Joe nodded. "Had the idea for months."

"Dangerous dude to fuck with," Archie observed.

"Not as dangerous as the cops if they get their hands on Rooski. I'm dogmeat then."

It was Joe Sing's turn to nod. "What are your drawings?"

The brothers listened with implacable half smiles as Joe outlined his plan. From below arose the sound of the engines and crashing gears of delivery trucks picking up orders. A large ceiling fan stirred the smells of sandalwood and cane, sawdust and varnish, and from somewhere frying fish.

"Right on Front Street," Joe summed up. "Blast in big as Dallas, have Rooski cover the patrons while I throw down on whatever motherfuckers are in the basement."

Joe Sing's brow arched lazily, like a cat stretching. "You're using Rooski?"

"Got to. Cant do it solo. And I need more firepower. I cant use this . . . " Joe withdrew the Browning from the back of his pants. "Rooski's been dropping things lately and I cant risk the cops tracing this through the Troll to us."

Joe Sing's eyes vanished when he laughed. "We thought you might bring along the Troll's piece to barter . . . You must have heard about . . . lunch at the Golden Boar yesterday."

Joe grinned crookedly. He'd counted on the Sing brothers giving him the ordnance used in the restaurant massacre. It was a switch they'd pulled a year earlier. The Sings had knocked off a Republican campaign office fat with cash contributions. The next day Joe and another addict used the same guns and disguises to jack an abortion clinic overstocked with painkillers. Both were alibied for the hour of the others' crime, flummoxing the cops.

Joe dry fired and shot the sliding bolt with a clang, then handed the automatic across. Archie Sing took it behind a screen and emerged with a slideaction, pistolgripped Mossberg Bullpup and a Smith & Wesson Bodyguard, a .38 favored by criminals for its trigger shroud, which prevented snagging on belts and clothing at critical moments.

"Just ditch em close to the scene." Joe Sing's eyes disappeared again.

Archie also handed Joe a paper sack. Peering in, Joe chuckled. He pulled out two rubber masks, the kind that pull down to cover the entire head. One was Ronald Reagan, complete with textured pompadour; the other Donald Duck, blue tasseled cap and all. At the sack's bottom were other essentials: plastic wrist restraints, surgical gloves and tape, extra shotgun shells, wire cutters.

"I owe you guys one," Joe said.

"No," Joe Sing said. "We owe you."

Joe gathered his booty and rose. "You guys figure you can find a party or something to go to around six or seven tonight?"

The Sing brothers nodded in unison.

"Playing against the Fat Man's a dangerous game," Joe Sing warned one last time, "and teaming with Rooski only lengthens the odds."

"Aint no long shot, it's my only shot," Joe said with a peculiar laugh. He halted halfway through the beaded curtain, smiling slyly. He reached in the paper sack and lifted out the Reagan mask like a Medusa head.

"But I'm bettin I can win just this one for the Gipper."

If Nadine Ackley had her druthers, she would have used surgical gloves to collect their money and issue tickets to the Kama Sutra's patrons. No telling where the hands slipping the bills through the cutout glass halfmoon had been. Better yet, Nadine would have preferred the ticket kiosk was fitted like a NASA lunar unit for collecting moon rocks, with robotic arms. That way she wouldn't have to worry about their icky breath either. Breath from strangely breathless mouths which also seemed always, well . . . *wet.* Her ticket booth was a shark cage, and her leaking innocence, the blood drawing the solicitors, slobberers, outright flashers, and—though it hadn't happened yet, she was certain any night—rapists.

This nippy evening a copy of *People* magazine lay open on her lap. With her customary seamless blend of outrage and astonishment, she read between ticket sales the perky paeans to people who feasted at the same groaning boards of life where she starved. From time to time she inadvertently touched the photographs as though feeling for the substance behind the designer sportswear, capped teeth, and flashbulb eyes.

She was feeling up Sylvester Stallone and scowling at the tart towering at his side and thinking as long as Rocky was going to wear elevator shoes, he should at least make sure they made him taller than his bimbos, when there came two taps on her glass. It was growing dark, and her vision was impaired by her own reflection in the glass, and at first she thought someone was furiously squeezing a tube of Finesse Creme Rinse at her, like the kind she used at home. That's what the chubby pink tube and stuff splatting the glass looked like. Only when the tube accordioned back into itself like a giant clam's head did she shriek and grab for the Mace. By then the "perp," as she'd heard TV police call them, was long gone around the corner of Jones to Turk. She replaced the Mace with a jug of 409 and roll of paper towels she kept for just such emergencies. Only she couldn't reach the drippy smear through the small halfmoon aperture. And it was so wet, so . . . *alive.*

"*Tu*-two, please." A pale freckled hand slipped through a ten.

"Help me clean up *that* n you can go in for free," Nadine pleaded, pushing back the ten along with the 409 and a wad of paper towels.

"Help her," said the second man. He stood with his back to the street wearing one of those dimestore rain ponchos. He clutched a big paper sack beneath his arm. Probably obscene ointment and such, Nadine didn't *care*. All depravity paled next to the secretion crusting her window like a squished jellyfish.

"You're so kind, sir," wheedled Nadine, "but you're only spreading it."

"Oh. Sorry." The hand fleeced with pale red hair redid the job somewhat better, although with some difficulty since its owner kept his other hand hiding his face. Nadine didn't wonder why, only why he bothered with her window smeared with that opaque . . . *shudder.*

"Thank you," she said primly and let Joe and Rooski into the Kama Sutra for services rendered.

IIII

"Ha . . . Ha . . . Ha," Fabulous Frank honked sarcastically when he saw Ronald Reagan clomping down the concrete steps to the basement office; he hummed a few bars of "Hail to the Chief": "Dum dum dee dum dum . . ."

The bookie was playing gin with Quick Cicero on the metal desk. Quick didn't seem to get the joke. His snaky pale eyes slitted; his lip shivered and curled.

"What's the matter? It's just Lou playin one of his practical jokes." Lou was the bartender down at the Silk'n'Spurs on Geary, Frank's favorite watering hole. "For a guy named Quick, sometimes you aint . . . Hey, Ronnie! What's in the paper sack? Rubber turds? Ha!"

El Fabuloso was still laughing, discarding the deuce of hearts, when the muzzle rose from beneath the poncho.

"Both of you pootbutts. On the floor." Rather than muffle Joe's voice, the latex mask acted like a diaphragm to amplify and resonate it. When the expug made a move for the open drop safe, the Gipper's likeness loudly vibrated: "NOW! Out here, side by side. Face down! And nothing sexy, I'll dust ya, I swear you'll die . . ."

Fabulous Frank had too often heard the selfhypnotic cadences of men desperate enough to kill to lose any time hugging the concrete. Yet Quick lay down slowly and carefully beside him as if worried about his goddam drycleaning bill. Trying to stall. *Now where's the percentage in that?* The gambler in Frank was real curious. He felt something plastic looping and cinching his wrists. Those nifty new disposable cuffs the cops had started using. Seemed every new wrinkle the cops came up with, the crooks turned around and used on registered Republicans like Francis Stutz.

Joe sprang to the open safe. He set the Bullpup on the desk and scooped out several buff envelopes stuffed with cash and betting slips. He didn't have to open them, he could feel they contained only a few hundred. That's why the safe was open, the runners hadn't come in yet.

Oh shit, Rooski, howled Joe's heart as his hand searched the safe's bottom—hardly enough cash to get you to Oakland . . . Hold the phone, what's this?

Joe withdrew a velvet pouch. He used his teeth to untie its drawstrings and shook out what resembled a big compass with a blue stone hinge. Joe held it up close to the mask's eye slit, regretting that the Gipper had always to grin, narrowing them. Christ! The hinge stone was a blue diamond bigger than Joe's left nut! Could it save Rooski? . . . No, too hot to hock, raced Joe's mind. Too big to fence. It would have to be hidden for a long time. But there wasn't any time, not with Tarzon breathing down their necks. Time for Joe to defend himself from Rooski was running out where Front Street deadended in a basement on Jones.

"Take the Moon n you're dead n stinkin, punk," Quick Cicero spit.

Ronald Reagan leaped across tromboning a round in the gun and jammed the muzzle in Quick's ear. Fabulous Frank waited for the roar, squeezed his eyes tight so flying skull shard wouldn't poke one out.

Suddenly, commotion above; Ronnie looked at the ceiling, cursed. With wrist flourishes worthy of a rodeo roper Ronnie whipped surgical tape three times around their heads and across their mouths. Then he stuffed the cash envelopes in the paper sack, replaced the diamond necklace in its velvet pouch, stuffing this inside his clothing, and snatched the Bullpup off the desk again.

The next thing heard by Fabulous Frank, Dean of the Daily Double, was the gallop of boots up the concrete steps. The lights went out, the upstairs bolt was shot, and he and Quick Cicero were left in the dark trussed up like Christmas turkeys.

The scene upstairs did what the White House never could, aged Ronald Reagan eight years. He *told* Donald Duck to just wait for him at the top of the basement stairs situated right inside the entrance. Station himself in the back by the projection booth and make sure none of the audience got wise—and *wait.* Nothing too out of place about a jackoff in a Donald Duck suit in *this* theater. When Joe finished robbing the basement bank, they could slip out unnoticed.

But *nooo,* not *this* Donald Duck. The lights were up, the movie still running—looked like the Statue of Liberty blowing a freight train. And beneath the screen it looked as if Donald had organized a summary round pound. Waving the Bodyguard, he had all eleven moviegoers ranked buck-naked before the first row of seats, clothing piled at their feet like guys at an Army physical. Except half these guys had hardons in various stages of tumescence. Nervously they shifted from foot to foot, one eye on the guntoting duck, the other fastened to the Bearded Clam That Ate San Pedro, which was being squeezed down by dirty fingernails the size of steamshovels onto a fleshtoned Washington Monument.

Ronald Reagan ran down the aisle crying, "What is this, a circle jerk?"

Some porno buff *al buffo* was just destined to ask: "Who *are* these masked men?"

"Shut the fuck up!" screamed Ronald. The comic saluted. "Yo, boss."

"Dont get mad," begged Donald. "The projectionist opened the door and asked what I was doin in this . . . " Rooski touched his duckbill.

"Pack that meat in, you cumsuckin bitch!" kibitzed the comic. It was hard not admiring her enthusiasm as, vigorously posting up and down on the monument, she began blowing a shiny black submarine, glans to gonads. The comic was flogging up a big one. Ronald had to slap the Miracle Fibre feathers on the back of Donald's head to retrieve his attention.

"Thu—that's it. Before I could get out the gun, he slammed the projection booth door and locked it. I knew we was made so I did this . . . " Donald swung the twoinch barrel at his prisoners.

"Dont point that thing at me!" one yelled.

"Sorry," Donald mumbled, dropping his bead obligingly.

"*Squish . . . SLURP . . . squish,*" went the onscreen orifices.

"Phone! Is there a goddam phone in the booth?" cried Ronald.

"I forgot to check. I was just waitin on you to help me clean out these guys."

Ronald snatched the .38 from Donald and slapped the shotgun in his hands. He shouted at him to cover these perverts and ran back up the aisle. Behind him the Clam That Ate San Pedro was going whole hog, wedging the black sub up its companion valve. The screen filled with two pistons chugging in tandem into twin cylinders someone had the practical sense of humor to disguise as human genitalia.

Joe banged on the projection booth door with the Smithy butt and hollered, "Open up or I'll blow the lock off."

"*I'm comin, OH GOD I'M COMIN!*" the soundtrack answered.

Christ, and that emetic soft rock endemic to department stores and airport lounges. That shlock street characters called shoplifting music. Bad enough alone, but accompanied by the stagey grunting, arty *ooomphing,* and all the other phony phonetics these method players had read some smutty where and were faithfully reproducing for the silver screen—Joe was grateful that the mask was so faithful to the Gipper's physiogomy as to reproduce his partial deafness by stopping the ears with latex.

He decided to skip shooting the doorknob. Probably only worked on TV. Just his luck, it'd ricochet and blow off his foot. He checked for telephone wires. None. Probably just an intercom to the basement.

BOOM! The shotgun blast from below stopped Joe's heart two beats. He stared aghast at the silver screen, where the two Titan missiles had withdrawn their warheads from the Great Divide and were supposed to be geysering like twin Old Faithfuls to the strains of the *Star Spangled Banner* according to Herb Albert and the Tijuana Brass—there instead gaped an enormous ragged hole ringed with smoke.

Rooski had gotten too far into the spirit of the thing and discharged at the same climactic moment.

His neglected fold bolted up the opposite aisle.

Up the ruptured screen rose the pathetic wail: "Jo-*WHOA!*"

No time to stop the runaway audience. And the zip damn fool just used his real name. Luckily it matched that of the mask's last user. In this instant Joe acknowledged to himself what perhaps he'd known all along he had to do. Had to do before Rooski did the same to him. *It'll hurt me more than you,* ran the old nursery con through his head.

He rushed down the aisle, grabbed Rooski, and hustled him out the fire exit giving onto an alley. There, in an abandoned Pontiac, he ditched the masks, the robbery gear, the Smithy. He wasn't breaking faith with the Sings by keeping the Bullpup. It was enough that it was seen.

In any event, it would be found with Rooski at the end.

While outside, Nadine Ackley was telling herself she always knew it would come to this. A screaming horde of bucknaked smutcrazed rapists banging on her glass ticket kiosk. She crossed herself, and with a single prayer commended her soul to the Lord's Everafter and consigned her flesh to the Devil's own Here and Now.

It was a firegutted Victorian on Treat Street, pooled with black water, where wind through the gashed roof dirged and the homeless and hunted found hospice. In the front parlor Joe shook out the paper sack into the trough of a soggy mattress. Rooski tore open the envelopes, making a paltry pile of betting slips and cash. And nary a dead president could so much as smile; they shared the same look of bemused reproof as the characters staring down at them.

"We would have done better breaking into video games," Joe announced sourly.

"No, it's enough," Rooski wanted him to believe; and began raking the bills together. They rustled like dead leaves.

"Enough for what? Coupla weeks of jailhouse canteen?"

"Cmon, Barker, dontcha *look* so blue." Quickly he counted the money. "Over five hundred. Six, if we down the trombone. Enough to blow town."

"Christ, Rooski. If it werent for bad luck we'd have none at all."

"We gotta make a little good luck of our own," Rooski remonstrated, "cantcha see?"

"Sure," Joe tried shoring up his voice with conviction. Truth was they were trapped like the rats scrabbling behind the charcoaled walls.

"Keep the faith. You always say that, Barker."

Right. Faith. You got to have a little, he always said. But faith in the sidepocket bank shot and that talk walks and money talks; faith in the sucker around each corner and the perennial next score. Not the Faith illumining mean days with grace; not the Faith brimming empty hearts with hope—that faith like a shell game had mocked Joe all his life. Though never so cruelly as now Rooski's fate was subordinated to his biological imperative to defend his own worthless breath.

Nearby mission bells tolled vespers. It was time. Ice twisted along Joe's sinews and lumped under his heart. Now he had to act. He said, "I got one of La Barba's sacks we can split."

"I'll second the fuck outta that emotion!"

Joe always went first. Fumbling and cursing over his ruined blood mains, daggering himself repeatedly. Rooski knew better than to offer help or even talk. Joe liked doing his penance right along with the sin. Taking off his Levi's, he at last struck strong blood high in his groin. With an exhalation mixing weariment and wonder, he handed the works to Rooski the way an officer might hand a blooded sword to his batman after a hard day on the killing field.

"I got it all figgered, Barker," Rooski was saying preparing his shot. "Hook a bus, hook a freight, anything making southward smoke. Sunup day after tomorrow we'll be waking up on the beach at Mazatlan. They got little boys there, Barker, for pesos . . . mere *pennies* . . . they'll catch you a fish and cook it for you right on the beach . . . What you puttin in my cooker?"

"Lil Andes candy . . . "

"I hate coke," Rooski whimpered. "I get the wrong kick." But the glitter was already melted in his heroin solution.

"I need you to fire a bombida, Rooski," Joe said softly.

"Why? With the Edison medicine, shootin speedballs makes me double crazy . . . " But he already had the point poised over a vein.

"I need you a little extra crazy."

"Why?"

"I'm goin out to steal a car to run for the border. A *nice* car, Rooski. We got that comin . . . But while I'm gone I cant have you noddin out n the police come creepin on you. If they do, you gotta hold court in the streets."

Rooski plunged the bombida into his bloodsteam. His angled frame snapped rigid, his brow sprang a halo of sweat; his eyes shot fire like sparklers. Joe asked if he'd heard what he said; Rooski nodded tightly, eyes spinning now like slot machine lemons.

"Down at city prison I seen one of the cons whose cat you got killed,"

Joe lied. "He said soon as you fell he'd get you. Said whether its firecamp high in the Sierras or the deepest hole at Folsom, he was going to find you, cut out your heart . . . and *eat* it, Rooski."

"Hold court in the streets," Rooski repeated the dire oath with squinch-eyed resolve.

"Got to, my homey. You cant let em take you."

"You know," Rooski said, "even if they caught me I wouldnt give you up. I'd die first. We all gotta go sometime. Why you cryin, Barker? It's gonna be all right."

"Aint cryin, Rooski." With the hem of the dragon jacket he wiped away tears not even heroin could staunch. "It's somethin in the air here. They must have used chemicals to put out the fire . . . "

"That's good, cuz I dont want you worryin, aint nothin gonna happen. No one knows we're holed here. What in hell you doin?"

Joe was trembling so violently he jammed the Bullpup trying to jack a fresh shell in its breech. Rooski took the weapon, spit in the breech, and tromboned the shell home with a clash, saying "And I thought I was the one who could fuck up a wetdream."

"Guess I'll be goin," Joe mumbled.

"Guess I'll just pray no police come while you out."

"That's a good idea, Rooski boy . . . So long and good luck."

"You're all the luck I ever needed, Barker," said that ghost about to be born.

In the blackened hallway, Joe stopped and pulled the bigass diamond from beneath his shirt. It burned a depthless blue. He had to hide it, but where? Its light licked the walls with tongues of flame, blue wavey shadows reminding Joe . . . Then he knew where to stash it. Not just in plain sight. On exhibit.

But first the call.

On the corner across the street, a booth stood empty. Its light seemed both to beckon and rebuke—*Come, none will overhear your treachery on my dark corner.* He ran to it, stepped in, and covered his mouth with his jacket sleeve. If 666 was the number of the Beast, then the number he dialed was the Judas code—911. "Gimme Homicide . . . Homicide? Take this address, 183 Treat . . . Chakov's holed there . . . He's hopped up and heavily armed and swears he wont be taken alive . . . "

Oh, that black sump pump in his breast only a doctor would call a heart. Fast, so he needn't further ponder the enormity of the betrayal—steal a car to drive to Golden Gate Park. He couldn't chance a cab. Joe wanted

no one to know the watery repository he'd chosen for the diamond Quick
Cicero called the Moon.

The valet parking lot attendants at Rossi's Famous Seafood Restaurant
hustled hard for tips. Otherwise they wouldn't make it on the minimum
wage Mr. Rossi paid. When patrons were preparing to leave, the head
waiter called them at their shack at the front of the lot. That way they
had the cars waiting at the curb, one hand holding the door open, the other
palm up for the dollars Mr. Rossi liked to call gratuities.

Often both were absent from the shack delivering cars at the same time.
That night neither saw the Porsche Carrera drive off the rear of the lot
or noticed its keys missing from the shack until it was called for in the
midst of dinner rush two hours later.

Joe was the day's last paid admittance to Steinhart Aquarium. The usher
at the turnstile tore his blue ticket, returning him the half bearing the
imprint of a leaping dolphin, and warned him the building would be
closing in fifteen minutes. Joe smiled—"Long enough."

He knew the aquarium's corridors as well as the hallways of half the
city's flophouses. Times like this when few visitors were around he liked
best. When the teeming colors were brightest, the symmetries more fantastic, the liquescent shadows most hallucinative.

Here he was. The plaque introduced the MAKO and TIGER sharks, with
a profile of each and world maps showing their ocean ranges. A brief
description noted neither was dangerous to man—unless provoked. Joe
looked up smiling into the flat black eye of one gray form gliding past, its
flexing speckled gills recalling the bamboo blinds in the Sings' loft. Certainly whatever hand brought forth that shape was possessed of the maca-
bre. No more perfect articulation of sudden, silent death was imaginable.

He turned his attention to the tank display. A shipwreck motif. From
the Jolly Roger tangled in the helm canted in the sand, a sunken pirate
craft. Beside the helm a cutlass, cannonballs, a binnacle, and belaying
pin—all arranged around the centerpiece: Davey Jones's locker, an overturned treasure chest spilling its hoard of jeweled dirks and diadems, gold
doubloons, and crucifixes; rubies, sapphires, pearls, and diamonds; yes,
diamonds, within which galaxy the birth of one more star, a blue one even,
would go unnoticed until Joe returned for it.

"We're closing, sir," a guard reminded him politely.

"Yes, I'm coming." He leaned across the railing and peered upward, spotting several gaffs hanging from hooks along the catwalk that crossed over the tank. He'd use one of them to retrieve the Moon when the time was right. He slanted both ways to make sure he wasn't being observed, then used the stolen credit card he kept in his boot to slip the lock on the door marked: NO ADMITTANCE, EMPLOYEES ONLY.

Out went the lights; the aquarium corridors became tunnels of wavery marine light. The colors of the shark tank were cobalt and coral. In a moment, a gasblue scintillance attached to a golden V fell, swinging slowly like a jeweled leaf to land near the treasure chest. The Tiger shark flinched at the puff of sand; then sculled its scythelike tail, gliding on.

"COURT'S IN SESSION!" was Rooski's last scream. The concussion of the first blast blew out the parlor's last remaining window. The second round of Double 0 exploded a door in a maelstrom of cinders. The third rocketed straight through the ceiling from where he lay in puddled black water, the .357 Magnum verdict burrowed deep in his chest.

All Joe had to do now was ditch the Porsche, then get Kitty and maybe they could get shut of this old Life. Go to Galveston, lay low until it was safe to return for the diamond; escape the cooker, crooks, and cops, who had nothing on Joe now if court was adjourned.

But he had to make sure, see for himself. He turned up Divisadero toward Twin Peaks. *You're almost home, you're almost home,* the tires whispered on the fogdamp asphalt . . . *Oh no, Rooski boy. Was it me laid you low? Me?* raved his heart. With an effort he steeled himself. It was selfdefense, pure and simple. More: it was euthanasia. Better to die a man in the streets than an animal behind walls.

He turned onto a side street and parked in its culdesac over the streetcar tunnel. He walked to the railing overlooking the tracks and leaned against a streetlamp that looked, in the swirling mist, like a giant dandelion atop a wrought iron stem. The N Judah car burst out between his legs, rattle-trapping down the cutbacks through the steep backyards, jiggling in its yellow windows like corn in a popper newspapers, crossed legs, a woman applying lipstick. Scanning the gray density of buildings, Joe spotted the house on Treat Street by the police lights. They pulsed in the fog like red amoebas.

He was just in time to see the morgue attendants lug out the stretcher. Coming down the front steps, they lifted it perpendicularly, raising the corpse, and Joe thought he saw Rooski's face splattered once, twice, three times with spinning red . . .

Then, with a suddenness snatching a cry from Joe's throat, the circular chill of steel at his neck, the familiar cold, clipped voice:

"I knew I'd find you close. A rat's never far from its hole. You found him first, saved your ass by setting his up for me to blast. You made him hold court in the streets. You better pray you wont have to pick a jury on a prison yard. Because you're going down for the car. You're penitentiary bound . . . motherfucker."

RINGS TAKES
A TUMBLE

||||

The colored whores sang a cappella in the rear of the tank, where the echo was best:

> *Shebop my baby shebop shebop*
> *Hello stranger*

Darcie and Rings'n'Things slowdanced, boxgrinding around the dayroom, husking sweet nothings in each other's ear like the longlost lovers of the song

> *Ooooh it seems like a mighty long time*
> *Shebop shebop my baby oooohhh*

which in a sense they were. Coupla years ago they both worked the Femme Fatale escort service, since defunct, and Darcie and Rings did the specialty shows where the conventioneers paid pretty pictures to watch a coupla bimbos sixtynine on their banquet table—only then it was makebelieve; "stimulated," Rings remembered it called. But there was no faking here in the women's section of county jail. Rings couldn't get enough of Darcie's ass like an upsidedown valentine and boobies firm as boxing speedbags.

"When the lights go out I'm gonna toot your twat till it tweets," Darcie whispered, raising gooseflesh on Rings's neck.

"Kasj!" gushed Rings. "Fur shur! Just like last night?"

"Better, girlfriend. With us it gonna just get better."

Rings was like, Wow, I never thought to find love in the clink! She'd just come in last night and right off got into it with a cholita who called her a comicbook whore. Rings was getting the best of it, had the puta down chopping her face with her fists, when the bitch pulled a razor from her ratted hair and sliced Rings's cheek. The matrons stormed the pen then and rebooked the tacotwat for a concealed weapon and transferred Rings to the women's felony section.

It was fur shur a relief seeing Darcie in the tank—such a relief Rings let her make it with her in the shower, washing off the blood. Darcie knew all the secret places and the sweet slow way of reaching them, until Rings had to snatch a washrag and stuff it in her mouth to keep from screaming.

Shebop my baby oooohhhh

Now Darcie danced Rings up against the bars, gripping them above her head, pelvising her clit through her jeans until the Illustrated Hooker was fixing to melt in a cum puddle, when she felt a tap on her shoulder.

"Can I cut in?" It was Big Lurleen the Sex Machine, grinning her grungy teeth.

Big Lurleen was just that, humongous. She waddled around with her thick arms stuck out sideways like a cop, only she didn't have a big belt with a radio and handcannon and six pairs of handcuffs for an excuse. She always put her foot on a bunkframe or stool when she talked to you and carried her cigarets rolled up in her T-shirt sleeve. She smoked filters, which she bit off before lighting up, demonstrating how she'd chomp off any bitch's clit who doubted Big Lurleen was boss of female county.

"I *like* dirty dancing," the grungy teeth announced.

"Oh gag me with the phone book!" Rings screeched. "My dance card's full, dildohead."

Big Lurleen turned on Darcie. "Not if I break her legs."

Up leaped Rings and grabbed Big Lurleen's pigtails. Before the giant bulldagger could get her balance, Rings tied them through the bars. Big Lurleen bellowed like a she elephant yanking her knotted hair, trying to free herself. Other girls took advantage of the situation to get in a few licks of their own.

"Cmon." Rings took Darcie's arm. "That dieseler wont fuck with us no more."

They went and sat on Rings's bunk, and Darcie said she was sure glad she was raising up any day because she was sick and tired of the shit that came down behind bars. "But the way you handled that, baby. Ooohh— got my jalobies harder n jawbreakers."

Rings looked. Sure enough, Darcie's nipples looked like rocks in her jumpsuit pockets.

"What you mean glad you raisin up?" Rings asked.

"Didnt you know? I just finished a stretch at the women's prison at Frontera. They're just holdin me here in county until they find a halfway house, one of my parole stips . . . Why you cryin, girlfriend?"

"Because I thought we were goin to Frontera together," sobbed Rings.

"You mean you're goin to the pen? Since when's slingin pussy a felony?"

"Since I copped too many cases in too short a time," Rings said dismally. She turned teary eyes on her new lover. "You wanna hear my Tale?"

"That's what these jailhouses are for, tellin them Tales. And that's what lovers are for, lissenin."

Rings sighed. "Love's a many splendored thing."

"I knew you got poetry, I seen it in your eyes. Now tell me your Tale, baby." Darcie squeezed her knee.

Rings told her of Marty, how she was so totally sure it was like megalove that she even found room amid the tattoos adorning her ass to add Marty's name inside a heart. And what did it get her? State time. Well, maybe that wasn't fair. Marty didn't exactly sentence her or anything. But it was his fault just the same.

What happened was, Marty was kasj in the beginning, everything was peaches and cream. They went to the movies and toney boites where Rings learned not to drink from fingerbowls. One afternoon they went to the yacht club where Marty had a sailboat. Only Rings got so seasick, like totally *scuzzed* the first wave even, that they were back in the lounge in twenty minutes where they hung out tossing back Singapore Slings until the sun set over the Marin Headlands.

Thing was, Marty never got down to doing it. You know, *it*. Boinking. She tried accidentally on purpose dropping her towel coming out of the shower and playing with his weenie while he was driving—but nothing doing. Marty kept saying he had to have maximum respect for her first. Rings wasn't sure what that meant, she only wished he'd get around to it in a hurry. If you don't use it, you lose it. And Rings hadn't used her's in so long she was afraid it was going to heal shut like a pierced ear you dont wear a post in.

Finally Rings woke up one morning feeling like, Hey, enough's enough, it's all about Boink City. She scarfed a bowl of Cap'n Crunch and beat cheeks straight down to Frederick's of Hollywood, where she ran Marty's Visa up to like its total limit. When he got home from work, she was sprawled on the sofa in sixinch spikes, rubber garter belt, crotchless panties, and a pushup bra with nipple ports—the whole beatme, boneme tostada.

The sight of his gaslight Galatea greened Marty's gills. "I'm g-goin out for p-pizza," he stammered.

"Oh gag on yer pizza! Willya do me a favor and fuck my fillings out?"

Marty started bawling then, and Rings had to beg him just tell her what turned him on. Having her make weewee was what tripped his trigger— put on her Jordache jeans, lean over the dresser and wet them. If that's what it took to get his respect, she sighed. Rings prided herself on her tolerance, her flexibility. She watched him in the dresser mirror getting hard, offering up silent thanks that at least he didn't want it in the mouth like most weewee worshipers.

Lickitysplit she ran into the bathroom, peeled off the icky jeans, jumped in and out of the shower, and dashed back in the bedroom to climb aboard . . . But Marty was crying again and his little pecker was all shrunk and it was back to square one, where Rings just couldn't bear to be.

Nothing to do but cry her eyes out and call her service right in front of Marty. She had to make sure *someone* out there needed her for more than just a ditz to teach the difference between a booger and an escargot.

Her first trick asked so many questions, at first she feared he was another like Marty who wanted to pick her brains instead of fucking them out. When they finally got down the gitdown, she was afraid she'd have to use Rustoleum it had been so long, but good ole K-Y was grease enough. Still, he had such a fat one and pumped so hard, Rings got some kind of gas. With like an *at* titude. Started farting like a tuba. When he got off he asked if the jet assist was extra and Rings said, no, organic power boosts were on the house, so to speak. Next thing she knew she was staring through her tears at a gold shield. So *that's* why all the questions.

But her troubles had only started. The lady judge bumped her up to the felony docket on account of all her priors, and whipped deuces wild on her, consecutive two year sentences. Rings's public defender argued till he was blue in the face, and the judge relented just a little, running the deuces bowlegged instead, as in concurrent. Still, it was state time just for renting a piece of gut.

"The old bitch in her black rayon muumuu!" sobbed Rings. "And now Marty wont even accept my collect calls. So much for love."

"I love you, girlfriend," Darcie said.

"Fur shur?" Rings turned to Darcie dabbing donewrong drops from her cheeks. "But what good's that? We're going opposite ways through the gate." An intimation of like atomic love was mushrooming in her heart. "Will you wait for me?"

"I'll stitch my pussy shut meanwhile." Darcie crossed her heart.

TANK COURT

||||

No seasons in a jailhouse, only time. No sun to rise and set, just Lights On, Lights Off. At five ayem the central circuit was thrown with a WHUMP that hummed the bars and flooded Felony Tank F with electric pissyellow from fortywatters recessed behind steel mesh.

"Christ!" Joe jerked the blanket reeking of creosote over his face. Dismally he registered the sounds: prisoners growling up from sleep; cursing, farting, rasping bare feet across concrete, and loudly pissing; roaring toilets, the rumble and bang of distant steel, sleepthick voices. He moaned, "Why'm I always wakin up in jail?"

"Maybe cuz you got a habit of fallin to sleep in em," suggested a drifter of indeterminate years brushing his dentures at the steel sink beneath Joe's upper bunk. Unbidden, he introduced himself: "Smoothbore's the name," flashing smooth pink gums, "crime's my game. I'm a rambler, a gambler, my gun's by request. From Sparks to Key West, I'm known as the best . . ."

"Best gum beater, peter eater," sneered a white voice from beneath his wooly shroud stenciled CITY AND COUNTY OF SAN FRANCISCO.

If only Joe could still laugh, the way he could when cops and robbers was still a game and jail just like old home week. But now Rooski lay ten floors below in the basement morgue, racked on a cold steel slab with a sinkhole between his feet dripping gore into a bucket; his bloody clothes stuffed in a paper sack between his knobby knees, his guts coiled atop his sawn chest, an ID tag wired to his big toe.

"COUNT TIME!" boomed from the front bars. "Drop yer cocks n pull up yer socks!"

Joe tumbled off his bunk and stood with the others gripping the bars where the paint was worn to naked steel by generations of wringing hands. The deputy ticked the wristbands off with a mechanical hand counter, *click click click.* He stopped where a barechested black with a shaved head shiny as an eightball stood.

The deputy drawled, "We put a boy in last night needs some of your religion, Reverend Bones."

"Which one?" Bones had tonsils like bronze bell clappers.

"You'll see," winked the deputy.

Ardor glowed the green eyes sunk beneath Bones's beetled brow; anticipation shivered his thick plates of chest muscles. Retiring from the bars at the completion of count, there was no mistaking the menace in his rolling simian carriage.

Safely out of earshot, a peachfuzzed punk named Clovis wondered who this Reverend could be that the other prisoners tolerated his parlaying with the deputies. Smoothbore hitched a foot on a bunkframe, struck a match off the tightened pantleg to a cigaret, and reported as surely as if he'd booked the badass himself:

"Reverend Ismael Bones is his name, n rapin up pretty young black boys is his game. Run himself a Tenderloin storefront church, *loored* them boys in there with free coffee and instant salvation."

"But I thought rapists got no respect in jail," piped Clovis, a nice enough kid—though a few years behind bars would fix that. "Especially *homo* rapists."

"*Shh*, boy . . . " Smoothbore lifted a stained finger to his lips. "Yuh dont want the Rev hearin sech talk . . . Forgit everythin you ever heard bout these jailhouses n lemme put you wise. It took the whole SWAT team to bring Bones in—n the Rev werent even armed! When you that bad, you gonna get respeck. I dont care if you raped yo mama. You gonna get shit on yer dick or blood on yer blade . . . "

The yellow hours dragged their chains toward noon. Joe joined the flow of prisoners strolling the circuit of the tank. Counterclockwise, according to jailhouse protocol. By traveling in the same direction at roughly the same speed, collisions were avoided with serial killers preparing to enter pleas and gunsels fresh out of Y.A., their secret shivs thirsting for the blood to build an Adult rep. The shuffling feet made a long sad sigh.

A dopefiend named Harold was hanging at the front bars. Spotting Joe, he dropped into the flow. "Save me shorts, Homes." Joe passed over his Camel stub as they fell in walkin' and talkin'. Harold and Joe had capered together on the streets, though petty boosting only; Joe hadn't the nerve for the vet's favored métier, armed to the teeth robbery—"commercial firefights," Harold called them.

Harold picked up his habit in Vietnam and had run with it ever since. A Special Forces paratrooper, he also nurtured an adrenaline jones. Stateside, Harold couldn't satisfy this yen for danger punching a time clock. The capering Life was the closest match to the exhilaration of night drops across the Cambodian border. So he turned in his M16 for a chopped twelvegauge, exchanged his field ampules for twentydollar balloons, and resumed fire.

"I'm just doin what you trained me to," Harold explained his depredations with a shrug and straight face to authorities who wondered how a decorated Marine had ended up a jailhouse veteran—authorities who hadn't noticed that the nation's penal institutions had become bivouacs for middleaged boys home from the war that wasn't.

Joe felt the sickness trembling in Harold, smelled it seeping miasmically from his pores, heard it sizzling his ganglia. Like a spark between live wires, withdrawal leaps from one host junkie to another whose narcotic insulation is wearing thin. Joe felt it welling in his bowels, frosting his extremities. Harold had awakened the demons and they were rattling their cage; sometime tonight they'd be loosed in full cry.

An airbrake gasped and a deputy unlocked F Tank with a large brass key like ones used in morality plays or fairytales as symbols. Consulting his clipboard he wearily cried: "Pierce, Harold . . . Roll em up!"

"I dont believe it!" Harold exclaimed, springing for his bunk to collect his blanket roll. "The bitch made my bail!"

Joe hurriedly borrowed a pencil stub from a card player at one of the long steel tables in the aisle between the bunks. He used his booking receipt flimsy to scribble: *They blew away Rooski and got me for GTA. Please bring money for my books. Well this looks like it.* He chewed his lip seeing the blue effulgence in the shark tank and wanted to scrawl, *I got something big to cash in and make us the life we got coming,* but decided otherwise. No telling if Harold wouldnt be picked up again before he saw Kitty. He wrote simply, *Wait for me. I love you, Joe.*

He caught Harold at the tank gate. "Here. Fly this kite to Kitty. She's still strippin at the Blue Note. Dont let a homey down now . . ."

Harold nodded from the other side of the bars. "Walk slow and drink plenty of water, Homes."

Over the locking wheeze of the airbrake Clovis asked what that meant. Smoothbore explained: "You walk slow so no one mistakes you for makin a fast move. You drink plenny water to keep from gettin hemorrhoids settin on concrete all day."

"Any time you get rhoids, kid, I'll pack em for you," offered another prisoner, grabbing a handful of crotch to dramatize his drift.

Evenings, a half hour after the chow wagons rolled, a TV was positioned in the hallway so as to be visible from the front bars. Which meant invisible to any who weren't black. The hambone majority controlled the front bars where the action was. There to beg phone calls from passing deputies, greet incoming crimeys and vilify enemies trudging down the line with their blanket rolls; hoot and whistle at the transisters swishing to and from the Queen Tank, haggle with trusties for food and cigarets— and control the image connected to the metallic babble ricocheting around angled concrete. Some action.

The cholos crouched murmuring and smoking against the rear wall, beneath a graffitied gallery of names and numbers burned with matches or scored with sharpened toothbrush shivs into the concrete. The white-boys read on their bunks or played cards on blankets spread on the steel tables. Joe played dominoes with Smoothbore and Clovis. The thwacking of the bones punctuated desultory conversation.

The TV was tuned to the local news. The newscaster's voice echoed in F Tank like a man shouting into a toilet. Something about a sixyearold black girl's raped and mutilated body being discovered in a dump behind Candlestick Park. A suspect had been arrested. And here! This tape just in of the suspect being led into the Hall of Justice . . .

"Whoa!" A young blood named Toot Sweet swung out of his hammock fashioned from a blanket tied between bars. "I seen that motherfucker in *here* . . . "

"You smoked too much rock on them streets, be seein things," his crimey Top Dog was sure. "That boy's gotta be in Protective Custody . . . "

"*Nooo*, Doggie boy." Toot Sweet shook his head emphatically while casting wildly around the tank. "He's the nigger the deputy told the Rev needs religion. He's right here in F Tank."

Joe sensed the horror to transpire; a surf began booming in his ears and his neck swelled like a bullfrog's. Jumping to his feet, he propped a foot on a stool and snatched up his bones in both fists, convictstyle. He whacked out the double six to open a fresh domino set, growling: "Big six to the board. Come big or stay home . . . "

Top Dog cried: "Why you think they put that nigger in here, then show us his face on the news . . . " Yet before he'd finished asking, the awful answer unraveled on his face; though it took a third blood to articulate it: "They *wants* Bones to do their justice. Save taxpayer ducats, hold court right here in the tank . . . "

Suddenly Reverend Bones stood among them, rubbing sleep from his emerald eyes, tolling the bronze bell deep in his breast: "Where?"

"Here the nigger be!" sang out Toot Sweet. He'd located the wretch cowering in one of the concrete toilet stalls in the rear of the tank.

Down the line of double bunks rolled the avenging angel. He paused at the box stall's open front, grinning like a cathouse piano. "I have heard of thee by the hearing of the ear," he chuckled, the smooth warm sound of whiskey from a bottle's neck. "Now mine eye seeth thee."

Toot Sweet and Top Dog blocked the opening when Bones entered the stall. It began then, the dull thump of the fists into flesh, the grunts of exertion interspersing biblical denunciations. Joe heard a bone crack and the child rapist scream, a decrescendo wail dying in wet bubbles.

"Rev," cried Top Dog, eyes big as cue balls. "He's out cold."

"He's warm," answered Bones's congested voice. "I gots to have him." The mellifluous pulpit baritone dropped a half octave: "All they that take the sword shall perish with the sword."

The sudden clatter of Clovis's dropped dominoes rang like pistol shots on the steel table.

"Pick em up," urged Joe's hoarse whisper.

"*Aaarrgghh* . . . " It was Bones.

The spectators who had collected at the stall's opening collapsed backward, eyes pinned wide, exclaiming in low disbelief. First one, then another turned and bolted. Toot Sweet rushed to another toilet stall, hand over his mouth.

Joe couldn't stop himself. Softly he set down his dominoes and walked back to the cubicle. Before reaching it, he heard the rhythmic wet plangency in the stall, a sound like a horse trotting through deep mud. His first glimpse of the activity within turned him to stone; his head filled with a sustained silent shriek.

The child rapist was crumpled on his knees at the toilet, orange coveralls bunched around one ankle. Reverend Bones was naked, crouched behind him on the balls of his feet like a baseball catcher. One great hand held his victim's head inside the bowl; the other gathered lifeless loins to his own. His gleaming head flung back, straining noisily through clenched teeth, Bones was exacting the punishment to exactly fit the crime. Blood bubbled, splattering the gray concrete.

Over the synaptic storm in his skull Joe heard Clovis pray, "I sure hope I dont have to do no time."

"The time does itself," schooled Smoothbore. "You jist got to live with it."

SPACE

||||

Rings and Darcie waited after Lights until they heard the other whores snoring before bumping bellies again, quiet as they could beneath the blankets, switching tops and bottoms. They shared a Kool afterward.

"I wish you *could* raise up with me," Darcie said wistfully.

"Yeah. That would be fur shur maximum kasj."

"We could open a tattoo parlor, maybe a bodyfender shop."

"Whoa, Silver!" Rings snapped the Kool through the bars.

"What's with you, girlfriend?"

"Maybe I *can* raise up with you. I just remembered I got info I could fur shur parlay into probation, maybe dismissal."

"You dont mean turn state?"

"*Shhh . . .*" Touching a finger to her lips, Rings peered through the interstitial darkness, searching the surrounding bunks. She saw only motionless humps, heard only the sounds of women meeting children and lovers in dreams. She paid no special heed to one particularly large, wooly shape, a lump with neither lovers nor children awaiting its sleep. In her excitement Rings forgot the bulldagger whose hair she'd knotted through the bars, adding injury to the insult of spurning her advances. But Big Lurleen hadn't forgotten. Lying perfectly still, the dieseldyke held her breath to better hear, swearing vengeance.

Turning back to Darcie, eyes dancing in the dark, Rings related in a whisper the details of Gloria Monday's murder. "I'm callin Homicide in the ayem," she concluded excitedly. "This Humpty Dumpty's got a fall comin."

"Then we *can* get the bodyfender shop," Darcie cried softly, her aversion to snitching squelched once she knew its subject. "But aint you a little afraid of him?"

"Of the Pimp Blimp? Like, totally. But I'm more in love with you."

Purring deep in her throat, Darcie pushed Rings back on the bunk. Unsnapping her jumpsuit and plucking it off, she hitched one of Rings's feet on a crossbar and planted the other on the floor. "You soppin wet, slut," she panted, slurping a thumb in Rings's milky snatch. Next she slid her forefinger up Rings's glomming anus to massage against her thumb the secret membrane separating the channels. Gently gripping the two digits, she lifted Rings closer.

"Whaddaya think I am," Rings chuffed, "a sixpack?"

Sixpack my sweet ass, simmered Big Lurleen's brainpan. *Landfill's what you'll be once the Fat Man hears you fixin to run your bitch mouth.*

MAN DOWN

||||

Someone in the murmurous dark called for Toot Sweet to pop some corn, and he obliged the ironbarred gallery with the Homeric ballad of that badass Dolomite:

> *Now Dolomite hailed from San Antone*
> *Baddest nigger the world has known*
> *Why same day he dropped from his mammy's ass*
> *Dolomite rear up slap his pappy's face*

Top Dog took up the toast:

> *Now one day Dolomite took a stroll*
> *Run up on Mabel, Queen of the hos*
> *Dolomite, he say, Bee-itch!*
> *Had me job in Africa fuckin steers*
> *Fucked a she elephant till she broke down in tears*

A falsetto broke in:

> *Mabel jus say, Dont give a damn where you been*
> *Say, I'm layin to wrap this juicy hot pussy*
> *Round yer badass shittalkin chin*

And so on until that sweet peter jeeter, bad womb beater Dolomite was feeding worms and the jailhouse was bailed out into dreams of hundred-dollar whores and midnight scores.

Alone, Joe listened to the snores mixed with the low moan of the Hall of Justice generators and, deeper still, the city groaning like a gutshot giant. Alone with his heart in solitary, his soul in chains—staring at the luminous freckled face on the Felony Tank ceiling, its jaw clamped comically cock-eyed, the same skewed grimace Rooski aimed down pool cues and pressure bars, saying: "I'd die first . . . " And maybe he would have if Joe had only let him, not murdered him . . . No, he couldn't even credit himself with that courage. No, for the killing he'd delivered the man who loved and trusted him to the police. At last Joe recognized, with the translucent clairvoyance of withdrawal, the one sin within his doing that was commensurate with all his life's unfocused guilt; and knew it was as deeply and irrevocably committed as was Rooski's corpse by now to a backhoed welfare grave. *I'm sorry. Sorrysorrysorry.* Though for whom he wasn't sure.

Then the Big Hurt pushed aside all thinking and Joe could only lie hugging his cramped middle and suffer the agony that gnawed on itself, metastasized, grew like a cold malignant fetus in him. A reeking viscous sweat like cold bacon drippings filmed him. The jailhouse stinks of toe jam and farts and nigger hair and concrete sour with piss and sweat dizzied him with nausea. Orgasm after electric hairtrigger orgasm convulsed his groin. His entire being became the shortcircuiting terminus of a billion scraped and shrieking nerves.

And then came ripping down his intestines that glacial fecal boulder compacted by months of bowel paralysis, and through gritted teeth he cried: "Christ! The Yenshee baby."

He bailed out of his bunk and staggered to a rear toilet where he sat bent double for minutes or hours, he didn't know, trying to pass this bowel monster; until sudden pain flashed the darkness, and he felt himself tearing in two. Blood vomited into the toilet. His sweatslick buttocks slipped off and he was on the floor, shrieks percussing his skull; and from a great distance heard Smoothbore shouting at the bars: "MAN DOWN!"

The armored Mercedes maneuvered nimbly around a cable car and plunged down Leavenworth Street into the Tenderloin. Robes of misting rain swept darkened streets that reflected lights like spilled paint. Quicksilver beaded the long black hood; the tires whispered steelbelted secrets.

Quick was behind the wheel, scarred brows twitching, jaw muscles rippling. Beside him Fabulous Frank's polished nails drummed a nervous salsa on his gabardine knee. Baby Jewels filled the whole backseat, swinging side to side from the straps like King Kong from his chains. He wheezed, "I still dont get it, Quick. How could there have been a witness?"

"The dyke got word to our guy on Vice . . . "

"Villareal?"

Quick nodded. "She told him the cunt was hiding beneath the bed. She saw it all, including the rock. She's gonna try dealing down her charges turning state."

"Who we using? Not you, Quick. If she was there, she knows you."

"I tapped Truck Infante for one of his Teamster torpedoes. Did you know prison guards were Teamsters? That's what this hitter is, a moon-lighting prison guard. Villareal's gonna help him from the inside."

"It's gotta be fast and sure," hissed the Fat Man in imitation of a roach bomb.

"Truck says that's the only way this goon knows. Says he's the best."

"I want to know as soon as that problem is eliminated."

Quick nodded, his washedout eyes never straying from the street.

"Which brings us to the next item on the agenda, Frr*aank*." It was when the doll's voice sounded laziest that the bookmaker knew to watch out. "Run the ripoff by me one more time."

"Like I told you, Jules, it was over before it hardly began," Fabulous Frank explained for the eleventh time. Geez, could he use a shooter of whiskey. That chubby little Darla with her toiletplunger mouth and Hoo-vermatic cunt wore him out this afternoon. Even Mister Fab had to admit he wasn't getting any younger, while his prey yearly regressed in age; until if this perverse inverse ratio continued widening, he'd be birddogging playgrounds. Darla was just fifteen and wore braces that shred the hell out of Fabulous Frank's pubes. And now this KGB routine. The mingled fragrances of lavender and leather clinched his gut; his nerves were un-springing faster than a tendollar whore's mattress. He snapped his fingers. "It happened just like that . . . right, Quick?"

Mister Personality just grunted. Frank wished like hell just this once the man he'd taught to cheat at gin would lend a little support. After all, he was as much to blame as El Fabuloso. Not that Quick would've supported his grandmother if she needed a boost on the streetcar. Of the many fighters Frank had known in his player's Life, most had their brains knocked goofy; in some tank town, Quick Cicero's heart and soul were kayoed.

"So it was unlocked. The safe was goddam open when Ronnie came downstairs and threw down on us. So kill me already . . . " Quick's furious pale glance volunteered his services for just that honor, and Frank's knuckles whitened cupping his knees tighter. "We were playin a hand of gin, waitin for Vinnie to run up from the peninsula and Turo to make it from the East Bay. Another coupla minutes and the shleppers woulda got zilch. It was *that* close . . ." Frank measured how close between a trembling thumb and forefinger.

"I told you guys when the safe wasnt spun, always have a man on point. Armed."

"But Jules—we open that thing ten, twelve times a day. We go playin cowboys each time we're gonna shoot each other."

"Better you had," slithered the doll voice.

"Jeez, boss. It was just a coupla hundred and a lump of blue paste. I mean what are we *talkin* about here? Liberace's *poodle* wouldnt be caught dead wearing that thing."

When this witticism was met with silence, Fabulous Frank began to catch on. Something big was afoot, something big enough to kill for. The hit just ordered on the hooker in the hoosegow proved that. That's why Baby Jewels was laying all the blame on him. Killing machines like Quick Cicero were inexpendable; not so pennyante players like Frank Stutz.

"Dont tell me," he mumbled, "I dont want to know." His lungs clamored for nicotine to soothe his nerves, but the Fat Man allowed no vices in his presence save French lozenges and murder.

For several moments they drove in silence but for the breathing from the backseat, which mimicked the faint swishing of the tires down the rainslick streets. The Mercedes turned left on Market, heading past ninetyninecent movie houses and check cashing outlets and pawnshops whence switchblades and cufflinks winked from darkened windows.

The Fat Man sucked a sudden wet sigh. "Listen close. We're stepping up to red alert. These are the battle plans."

For starters, with things so hot, all bookmaking action had to be temporarily "diversified," laid off to Johnny Formosa, Manny the Wart, or the tracks. When Frank objected that making book with those cheap hoods was something of a status drop, Baby Jewels asked maybe would he like a real drop, like into the bay where he could make book for the crabs. Frank used both hands smoothing back his ducktail and didn't answer.

"And make those runners hop," said Baby Jewels. "It takes a lot of pictures to pay off attorneys and grease the boys downtown, which"—Baby Jewels turned and continued speaking to Quick as if Fabulous Frank had suddenly vaporized—"brings us to the subject of the Blue Moon. We must have it back."

Quick nodded. "Or be bluffing with a busted flush."

"Worse. Even with the singing hooker zipped, the stakes have climbed now the rock's been ripped . . . If the wrong cop finds these punks with the diamond before we do, he'll trace the ice to the shvartze, ask him what it's doing in a pimp's bookmaking safe, and this thing blows up in our faces. The shvartze will be ruined already and wont hesitate giving up our game. Blackmail's a pretty motive. Opens us up to a One Eightyseven."

"Us suspects?" Quick ejaculated. "What about the other evidence. The hair and skin samples, the partials on the crack pipe? . . . "

"Only proves that he was there, maybe that he assaulted her. But that was three hours before we . . . had our little chitchat. The Medical Examiner has her checkout time fixed pretty closely by now, I'm sure."

"So he went out to get a bite to eat before tying her ribbons." Quick was only suggesting what he might do, being a man whose own appetite was whetted by violence.

"*Tch.* Thursday evening, while we were in the apartment, he was attending a reception for some African dignitary at the Pacific Press Club. It was in the papers . . . So you see, Quick, it isnt even just our respect we gotta save, it's our asses." Baby Jewels paused, allowing his impassioned wheezing to subside, then continued: "Everything depends on the shvartze believing he killed her and believing we have the diamond to prove it . . . So get to Rasmussen on Narcotics, Solstein on the Pawnshop detail—we have to keep an eye on the hock sheets, it isnt reported stolen—and our special pal on Vice, Villareal. I want all their arrestees tumbled. Then I want you to start the drums beating on the streets, dangle a reward maybe. I want every character of flipside Frisco watching for the Blue Jager Moon. Sooner or later they have to try downing it and I want that ice hotter than a meteor, harder to move than the Rock of Gibraltar." He paused, then added: "At least they werent pros. At first I thought maybe the shvartze sent them to get back the rock. But pros would never have fooled with the patrons or blown holes in the screen."

"The cops think the stuff out back belonged to the Chinks who did the restaurant party," Quick said.

"I know," said Baby Jewels. "And the zipperheads had alibis. It smells like a switch. Find those ricepropelled punks, Quick. If they wont give up the creeps they gave the masks to, turn them one by one into yellow bars of soap."

Meanwhile Mister Fab, who may have been a fool, but not a big enough one to want to know about any blue moon not over Kentucky, remembered what his mama always told him, that trouble never travels alone; and secretly rejoiced in the Fat Man's multiplying dilemmas. Each new knot in the web entangling Baby Jewels broke another bond tying Fabulous Frank to his whipping post. He'd celebrate with Darla, that's it. Tongue-flicking a bead of sweat from his lip, he could almost taste her toddler trim. To distract himself, he concentrated on translating a fresh bebop rhythm from his bookie bean to twitchy knee, including just for Baby Jewels the timeless player's refrain—*the worm turns.*

"*Tch.* When I get my hands on them . . . " The doll's voice coiled tightly, like a snake about to strike.

IRON BUTTERFLY

||||

It was a cool crisp colorless smell, one addicts relish: fresh bandages, alcohol, astringent medicines—*chemicals*. Voices burred soothingly in his ears. He cracked one puffy lid; everything indistinct, trimmed with foggy white; happy fungus growing everywhere. Ah, surfacing from anesthesia in Sick Bay, lying on an oldfashioned hospital bed, chained to it by the ankle. A barred window overlooked the ruins of the Hunter's Point Naval Yard: sagging warehouses, fragile silhouettes of rustfrozen cranes, hollow ironribbed drydocks littering the mudflats like carcasses of beached sea monsters.

A face swam into focus, smiling slyly; a saffron face above starched white. "How you doin, Joe?"

Joe could only go *pfft pfft*. The mouth of a glass widened upward; a glass straw clattered against his teeth. He sucked the cool apple juice, wet his lips and managed, "Fuh-fine. What happened?"

"C-sectioned your Yenshee baby," the Chinese medic chuckled, going on to explain Joe had been rushed to Sick Bay where a fecal boulder big as a toilet float was surgically removed. His anus required sixteen stitches; he'd lost much blood. He'd remain on Sick Bay until a regimen of antibiotics was completed.

"It was nearly impossible finding a vein for the IV," the medic continued. Finally they drove a twoinch catheter into the artery beneath his collarbone. "That makes it easy to administer this little present. The brothers said it was a down payment, you'd understand."

From beneath his tunic the medic withdrew an antique syringe with a curlicued metal plunger. The glass barrel filled with molten gold.

"An oldtime iron butterfly," Joe breathed as reverentially as any train buff hearing the Erie-Lackawanna hoot behind faroff hills.

Already the Chinese medic had fitted the long shiny needle into a feeder clip on Joe's IV line. It looked so sexy, the graceful gleaming stinger piercing the translucent virgin vein . . .

"No," Joe blurted. It was a decision he'd made without thinking, one sponsored by an inchoate notion of atoning for Rooski by transforming himself. "If I dont get anything else out of all this," he said, "I'm going to get clean."

The medic withdrew the iron butterfly from the clip. "Power to you, homeboy. You have Darvon prescribed for your pain in the ass. It'll coast you off your jones . . . You mind if? . . . " He held the syringe aloft.

"Knock yourself out. Only dose me first."

The medic lifted Joe's head and fed him a handful of brightly colored pills. He fitted the glass straw in his mouth to swallow them. Joe lay back feeling his belly chuckle straining the painkillers into his veteran blood. From far away he heard the painful grunt as the butterfly struck, then that familiar whoosh of wondrous rapture, followed by the medic's whisperly rendition of "I've Got You Under My Skin." Smiling, Joe watched the windowbar shadows build stairways to somewhere warm and bright and still. Then the whiteness closed in from the sides, turning slowly, then gyring faster and faster, sucking Joe down the flossy vortex of a carnival cottoncandy machine.

SPACE

||||

"**M**atron!" Rings hollered waving the slip through the bars. "Hey, matron! This aint no love note, it's a fuckin court order for a phone call. Judge gave it to me at sentencing."

"You tell her, girlfriend," chimed Darcie at her elbow.

The matron dogeyed the tattooed termagant. "No calls until after the lunch wagons roll. Undersheriff's orders."

"You mean Chester?" Rings shouted over the jailhouse din.

The bulky matron stepped to the bars, slitted eyes to Rings's laughing ones. "Undersheriff C.C. Collins to you, bitch. Unless you want to book yourself a rubber cell on the disciplinary block."

"That's him!" Rings cried in triumph. "You know what C.C. stands for? Ole Change Clothes Collins. He was one of my regulars and that's what we'd do. I'd put on his uniform and he'd wriggle into my kinkiest lingerie. Then we'd play My Hammy Vice. You know, like in the pig and the prostitute. *Oink Oink.*"

"No shit," the matron guffawed, hefting her keys off her belt. She shook so with laughter the keys rattled in the big lock. "And here we all thought he was such a hard case."

"Oh he can get hard all right," Rings assured her, passing out of the tank into the corridor's blear fluorescence, "but only in lace bikinis."

Prisoners normally had to place calls from the phone atop the booking desk. But in gratitude for the useful departmental smut, the matron let Rings use the private booth by the mugshot room. It smelled of winy puke and dank desperation; its floor was thick with crushed pills and shredded reefer unloaded by suspects lucky enough to get their phone call before their stripsearch. Rings felt funny dialing 911 from inside jail.

"Lemme have Homicide . . . Homicide? I need to speak to whoever's handling Gloria Monday's murder. Fur shur I'll hold . . ." She looked up to see a black trusty licking the booth glass, leaving a slimy trail like a giant slug. She kicked the door, banging his head, and smiled to hear him howl.

"Hello? Who's this? Well, me Jane. Just kiddin! My name is Rosemary Hooten and I'm in County Two, Female, and I know who offed Glorioski. What? Yeah. It was Baby Jewels, he killed her for her sugardaddy's radical diamond. How do I know? I *watched*. Only he didnt know. Will I testify? Fur shur! Like kasj! But only if I get it in writing you'll get my sentence commuted to time served . . . It's okay you'll need some time. I got a little to spare . . . Okeydoke, kasj . . . Just swing by my tank, ape man."

Opening the booth, Rings saw the chow wagons rolling back from the tanks to the kitchens. "Hey!" she shouted to no one of the milling deputies in particular. "Rack me up, I dont want to miss chow. This health food's gettin good to a bitch."

Back into the tank Rings swaggered, grinning foxily, bursting to tell her newfound love it was a green light for the bodyfender shop. She didn't see Darcie eating with others in the dayroom. Probably so sick with worry about me she lost her appetite, Rings figured, heading down the line of cells to the one they shared. But at its gate she froze, and her grin sagged into a mask of grief. Darcie's roll was gone, her bunk empty, its indentation trembling with abandonment.

"They rolled her out," Rings heard over her shoulder. "They found a halfway house willing to take a broad who killed her own baby."

In a daze Rings turned, facing the grungy grin of Big Lurleen.

"Jailhouse romances," said Big Lurleen, "stay in the jailhouse. Dont break yer heart over Darcie cuz the only thing that could break hers is a dick long enough to reach it up her ass . . . Here, I saved you a tray."

Rings plumped down at the steel table, staring at a stew that would have lost any taste contest with Alpo. This time I've put my life on the line for love, was all she could think. Slowly she spooned up the greasy sludge. Her mouth tasted so much of ashes that she didn't notice the acerbic powder lacing the stew until her stomach cramped so violently she jackknifed to the floor, yowling, spinning in a puddle of her own puke, scrabbling at her belly and seeing through scalding tears Big Lurleen the Sex Machine standing over her, grinning like a sink full of broken dishes, shaking the upended and empty can of Ajax.

"BITCH DOWN!" chorused the hambone hos at the bars. "BITCH BE DOWN BIG TIME."

DEAD HEAT

||||

The mailorder lingerie catalogue that appeared overnight on his desk was just the icing on the cake. Undersheriff C.C. Collins knew his secret was out within five minutes of coming on shift. The dispatcher's blush, the stifled sniggers squeezing each good morning; the cutoff conversations and compressed smiles as he passed the booking desk. Men with a secret to guard keep a keen eye out for any sign of its escape.

It was my picture in the paper last week, he told himself, hiding the catalogue beneath a batch of files on his desk. He attended the Boys Will Be Girls Gala in his Eleanor Roosevelt getup, and just his luck as he was leaving, so was a sevenfoot transvestite celebrated in cheap cult movies. At the barrage of paparazzi flashbulbs, C.C. dropped instinctively in a combat crouch, reaching for his offduty piece. Next morning there he was, on an inside page of the morning edition, squatting by a potted fern in the background, impersonating Eleanor wrestling with her girdle. C.C. was surprised it took a whole week for someone to recognize him. He thought it was pretty obvious, even with the plastic buckteeth.

In a booming bleacher bum voice C.C. ordered coffee from a trusty passing his open office door. If I tried explaining, he reasoned with himself, these cretins would never understand. Hell, let em think I'm gay, he decided—it's chic in this town.

He followed his morning habit and repaired to the staff toilets at ten.

He took along the lingerie catalogue hidden inside a budget folder. Passing through the lockerroom, his neck hairs frizzled feeling the stares that followed him. It wasn't until he was seated with the catalogue spread on his bare knees that he stopped to consider that there were too many deputies lounging in the lockerroom for this time of watch. He frowned down at a young girl sitting on a rock, weaving daisies in her garter. His nostrils spread, smelling something worse than the staff toilets could offer. Hastily he concluded his business there.

The lockerroom smelled of shoe polish and gun oil. The half dozen deputies were gathered around a television playing a tape of *E.T.* They jumped at the Undersheriff's sudden voice from the door. "Where are you men posted?"

"Sick Bay," several answered.

"Then what the hell are you doin here?"

"What did he say?" a deputy asked.

"I said . . . "

"No," the deputy said. "I meant the little space freak."

C.C. stalked across and shut off the television. "You're all on report."

"Sir," spoke up a stocky redhead with eyes like broken blue glass, "we were *ordered* off Sick Bay. SFPD took our places. They put a wired informant in a tank with a suspected killer. They want their own guys on hand if things go wrong."

The Undersheriff's mouth dropped. It was the same cover used the last time. "Who ordered you off Sick Bay?" he asked in a dull voice already sure of the answer, yet no less in dread of it.

"The Comptroller," answered the stocky deputy.

"Mackey?! He has no authority over the ranks. He's an administrator."

The deputies shrugged and traded bored looks. The Undersheriff rushed from the lockerroom.

The executive offices were on a lower floor, beneath the racket and reek of the county tanks. Comptroller Lamson Mackey was a lean, emphatic man whose height of forehead and steelframed glasses gave him a scholarly look. He was watering an avocado plant on his windowsill when the Undersheriff burst in. He turned to look at him in vast burlesque surprise.

"Why, C.C. What has you so worked up?"

The Undersheriff heard contempt in his voice and knew it was grounded in the recent revelation, but didn't give a damn. He stood holding the open door. "The whole Sick Bay watch is kicked back in the lockerroom. They say at your orders . . . "

Mackey set down the miniature watering pail without speaking.

"That's the same story you used to pull deputies off the court detail last month." The Undersheriff closed the door. He crossed the room and set a folder on the edge of the Comptroller's desk. "The Teamsters sent a hitman into the holding tank. He shot all nine prisoners so there'd be no witnesses. No one ever figured out which was his target."

Slowly Mackey sat behind the desk. He picked up a small typewriter brush and began dusting his watch crystal. "You better figure out whose side you're on, C.C."

"I dont follow you, Lam."

The Comptroller set down the miniature broom and placed his hands flat on the desk blotter. "Without a loan from their pension fund, our widows and orphans would be without a health plan . . . Or maybe that doesnt bother you. Not being a *family* man, that is." Mackey's smirking eyes were fixed over the Undersheriff's shoulder.

"I know whose side you're on, Lam."

"Oh, stop with the goodytwoshoes bit. It's a war out there, C.C., and we're losing. We have to accept whatever allies offer themselves . . . Besides, what's one less bag man with a case of the gabs, or one less tattooed streetwalker . . . "

"Tattooed streetwalker?"

Mackey took the question as a signal that the Undersheriff was coming around. He smiled confidentially. "They're scratching a hooker with so many tattoos she looks like the side of a city bus."

So that's how word got out. The Undersheriff lunged for the door.

"Dont rock the boat, C.C. Your position in this department is shaky enough already . . . " But he was talking to an empty door. He rose and closed it, snatched up the phone and dialed Narcotics. "Lemme talk to Villareal . . . "

Waiting for the cop to come on the line, Mackey idly fingered the file left by the Undersheriff on his desk. It flipped open revealing the catalogue within. *Paris Nights,* it was titled. Mackey cringed hoping his wife hadn't ordered one of its numbers before he swiped it off her sewing table.

"Tony? Lam Mackey here. We got a loose cannon on deck."

Joe awoke from a morning nap to a Howl From Beyond the Crypt cranked up by a comatose form bandaged head to foot in the next bed. The cops who chased this thief off a downtown building had yet to ID the mess scraped off the pavement.

Next he heard the familiar *whrr zzz whrr zzz* of a wheelchair. It was Spencer, Sick Bay's quadraplegic gadfly, jockeying close to Joe's bunk. "King Cheops is feeling his Wheaties today," he chirped. Spencer had been a Navy pilot in Vietnam, losing his arms and legs when he was shot down. In the field hospital he contracted an exotic jungle infection through transfusions, a virus attacking his spine like meningitis and rotting his flesh like leprosy. No two doctors had yet to concur on a diagnosis, agreeing only that he was a "medical anomaly."

"Got a square, Joe?"

Reaching for the Camels on his bedstand, Joe held his breath to wince in pain and was surprised instead to feel only a tightness. He was healing nicely. Spencer pinched the cigaret in a preposterous coathanger prosthesis he'd fashioned for himself to smoke against doctors' orders. The quad leaned his strawthatched head to the match Joe held; an elongated head calling to mind an eggplant squashed at the bottom of a Safeway bin. His gown fell open, showing translucent skin stretched over ribs like white silk thrown over a bird cage, against which his heart fluttered like captive wings.

If I had the wings of a turtledove, the lyric lofted in Joe's head, prompting him to ask Spencer if he missed flying.

"Do I? Hell, when they transferred me stateside, from the freefire zone to the Twilight Zone, I wanted to punch the Big Clock. Not because I couldnt walk to the corner bar for a beer or have a woman anymore. I was past those cares. I wanted to die because I couldnt fly anymore. There's no rush like screaming over the jungle with thousands of pounds of thrust between your legs . . . " The talking eggplant flung back, loosing that shrill bird to the ceiling. *"Oh Gawd!* I must've caked every flight suit in my squadron with cum!"

The outburst unnerved Joe. Somehow he doubted Spencer had flown any planes outside dreams. But even allowing that men who lived beyond the law were freed from its moral boundaries of truth and falsehood, the quad seemed more daft than deluded. Drunk on his private mythology, Spencer reminded Joe uneasily of Rooski. It was as if the spiritual alchemy that compensated each for his handicaps had confiscated the common sense needed to survive them. Grown old without the benefit of experience, they shared the hellbent innocence of children playing with matches.

Up to the bars rolled the Pill Cart, its orderly shouting: "Medication call!" Spencer stabbed with the coathanger at his transformer, whining his motor like a hornet, and spun a wheelie shooting straight to the bars. On an impulse, Joe swung his feet off his bed and stood shakily. Rolling his IV stand beside him, he toddled to the bars for his painkillers.

"You're not supposed to be on your feet," the orderly admonished.

"I'm feeling much better," Joe said, dry swallowing the pills handed him in a Dixie cup.

"Dont get feelin too much better, too fast, or it's back to the Felony Tank," the orderly advised with a wink.

The effort weakened Joe, and he stood clutching the bars while the others retreated back into Sick Bay to smoke and play the dozens and swap lies. The Darvon made him hungry and he smiled hearing the tympanic rumble and clash of chow wagons rolling down an intersecting corridor. From the women's Sick Bay echoed a doowop chorus of "Baby Love."

His smile set with perplexity as he heard another sound, a steady metallic scraping. Pressing his face to the bars, Joe peered down to the end of the corridor. There a giant exhaust fan set in the wall opened to the southern sky. Its grill cover was removed, and its giant double propellers paddled slow rubescent shadows down Sick Bay. A white trusty with long hair tied in a topknot was perched on the fan's wide frame. He held one of the threefoot blades, filing its edge with a large steel rasp. He paused, taking a can from his toolbelt to oil the rasp, then swung the blades, grabbing the next.

"Hey, dude!" Joe called. "You wanna loan me that thing to cut through these bars?"

The trusty whirled on Joe and unsheathed a soundless snarl. Square on his brow was tattooed a blueblack swastika, one bent branch pulsing to the beat of a gorged brow vein, likening the emblem to a wriggling black widow. With laughing eyes he drew the rasp slowly across his throat.

"Never mind," called Joe amiably, reminding himself that they put people in jail for *reasons*.

The trusty whirled back to his task, seizing a blade, screeching its edge with the rasp. With a start Joe realized he was stropping the propellers, sharpening them, though to what end he couldn't guess.

Then he heard a warped male voice from the direction of the women's Sick Bay: "Ready?"

The trusty raised a grimy thumb.

"Then crank her up," came a giggle.

Joe scooted to the end of his bars, trying for a wider angle of vision up the corridor, curious who issued this command in a slurred voice as if slightly braindamaged. But he couldn't see.

Without replacing the cover grill, the trusty threw the switch on high. Joe's ears filled with the howl of the twin propeller blades, his gown flapped in the typhoon sucked down the corridor.

"Where you takin me?" Joe heard a girl's voice in the corridor. "They awready pumped my stomach."

"Special surgery," Joe heard the slurry voice.

A gurney drew abreast of his bars, pushed by an orderly Joe had never seen before. His irongray hair was cropped close in a style as militant as a Wehrmacht tank commander's. Down one sidewall streaked a platinum patch, like a lightning bolt. His lips were gray and fat as worms, and he walked with a clumsy limp. A naked girl graffitied with tattoos lay strapped atop the gurney, protesting: "But I aint scheduled for no surgery."

"Kind of a last minute thing," chortled the orderly, handing keys to the trusty who had made his way up the corridor leaning into the tunneling wind. The trusty unlocked a mechanism mounted beside steel elevator doors opposite Joe's bars. The doors thumped open, a halogen quartz lamp above them began flashing.

"We got thirty seconds," the trusty shouted.

Joe knew the girl on the gurney, she was a Strip character. He rifled his memory for her name and found it. "Rings," he called, but his voice was swept up in the roar of the exhaust fan.

"What am I, buffet brunch?" she screeched.

"Twenty seconds," the trusty cried.

"Unstrap me!"

"No sooner said than done," chuckled the orderly, unbuckling and flinging aside the canvas restraints. She tried to climb off but he held her down with a fist on her chest. "Say your prayers, snitch bitch," he slurred.

"Gag me with the moon!"

Moon? Joe's heart dinned with horror.

"Ten seconds," the trusty shouted. "If these doors are still open the whole jailhouse locks down automatically."

Still holding Rings down, the orderly broke into a lurching run, wheeling the gurney down the corridor, toward the sucking blur of death.

The Undersheriff danced between the elevator banks, banging the buttons. A tattooed prostitute in the jailhouse at the same time that his secret slipped? It had to be Rings'n'Things. They were going to kill the only woman in his life who'd let him act out his deepest impulses. For that he'd forgive the fleabrained floozie's motormouth a thousand times. He shook his fists at the ceiling, cursing himself for not ordering the deputies to return directly to their posts. If he was too late, her blood would be on his hands.

He gave up on the elevator and took the stairs two at a time up to the seventh floor. Past the booking desk he ran, crashing into a trio of gang-bangers reciting their vital stats to the sergeant in rap music. Making saucer eyes, they recouped their cool without missing a beat—*There's a*

panic in the jailhouse, THAT'S . . . NO . . . JOKE, Sheriff jukin down the
line like a MAN . . . ON . . . COKE.

Reeling around the corner of the booking tanks, he dashed down the disciplinary block, eliciting taunts and jeers. Several prisoners threw food, the chow wagons must just have passed, and C.C. realized with enough force to redouble his pace that they'd make their move on Rings during lunch hour, when the increased movement would contribute to confusion and assist escape. He was in a dead heat.

Past the federal and extradition tanks he flew. He skidded around another corner, pumping his legs high down the south corridor for Sick Bay. A chow wagon blocked the corridor, one trusty passing trays through the food slot in the tank gate, another stacking cartons of milk on a crossbar. The sight of a half ton of rolling steel reminded C.C. that he was unarmed, that he needed something to even the odds, and he cried out for the trusties to stand aside as he hit the wagon at a full run, capsizing trays, drawing cries of anger and surprise. But he heard none of this over the wagon's mounting rumble as he ground the bones in his wrists and ankles straining to push it up to speed.

Neither did he hear the breaker trip, nor the turbine lift its howl. He became aware of the fan by its shadows spinning down the corridor. Lifting his head over the teetering trays, he spotted the fan cover leaning against a wall at the Sick Bay intersection. He couldn't imagine how, but he knew instantly that the ventilator was being used as a murder weapon. Thirty feet to the intersection, twentyfive . . . Sweat stung his eyes, his breath scorched his throat; he'd wrenched one knee, it's cap jiggled sickeningly . . . Fifteen . . . Then, over the rumble of the wagon and the turbine's windy roar, he heard a strange inhuman baying ringing down the walls, and his limbs flooded with adrenaline. He ducked his head and dug harder, leaning into the wagon, feeling it gain speed, grow lighter. Heaving all his strength from the balls of his feet up his legs, across his back and down his arms, he flung the wagon before him with a cry and fell sprawling to the concrete.

Joe nearly fractured his cheekbones squeezing his face between the bars. The orderly slid to a screeching rubbersoled halt some ten feet from the ventilator. With a maniacal howl, he released the gurney and leaped sideways through the street elevator doors which slammed shut behind them.

The turbine scream eclipsed Rings's own. There was a terrific crash, it had to be the gurney striking the fan blades, though Joe didn't see, having buried his eyes in his arms linked through the bars, unable to bear the horror. But his inner lens captured all: Rings shooting off the gurney into the blades, dancing a spastic fandango before being seized in the centrifugal vortex and spun faster and faster, shooting off bloody pulps—this he heard beneath the roar, a muddy mincing—until just her shredded torso still twirled in the reaping shadows; then it too disintegrated, sucked out the Hall of Justice's tenthfloor exhaust vent in a pink puff, mingling her misted flesh with the night fog blowing off the Pacific.

Something warm and wet splattered his face, chasing his heart up in his mouth, and he squeezed his eyes tighter.

Then suddenly the fan fell silent, the wind died. Joe counted to ten and raised his gaze from its cradle. The elevator doors were shut. The wall opposite his bars dripped bloody globules of flesh, the same gore dribbling down his face.

"Christ!" Joe screamed, sole witness it seemed to the final transubstantiation of Rosemary Hooten from Valleygirl to vapor. "Deputy!"

But the corridor was empty. He whirled, facing into Sick Bay. The other patients were playing cards, pretending to sleep, reading pulp westerns as if nothing had happened.

"Christ!" Joe screamed again. This time King Cheops responded to Joe's cry, answering with a particularly bloodcurdling Howl From Beyond the Crypt.

His mouth was stretched to scream once more when a lumpy rivulet of the offal on his face found his tongue. He seized his throat to hold down his gorge and stumbled for a sink. Then he stopped, pursing his lips quizzically—it tasted like onions and chili powder . . .

It wasn't grief which loosed his next sob. He was filled with reproach that he could find no words of outrage over the murder or find a single serious thought to dignify the life Rings'n'Things had left. Instead his mind was monopolized by a single banality: You really are what you eat.

Zooming down the corridor Rings was shur this was It, as in Big Time. Struggle as she might, the combined forces of momentum and rushing air fastened her to the gurney. Faster and faster the hypnotic blur of blades rushed up; it was like being dropped into a giant Mixmaster. A home video of her loony life fastforwarded between her ears, its highlights freeze-framed: reaching her first orgasm with an electric toothbrush, winning the disco rollerskate competition in the mall parking lot; watching Daddy lowered into the ground to the derision of the Dead Kennedys through the Walkman clamping her ears.

Over the scream of blades she didn't hear the wheels screeching down the intersecting corridor, she saw only a peripheral flash of steel before the gurney broadsided the chow wagon suddenly interposed between it and the ventilator.

Rings did a front somersault, knocking a twentygallon steam tray of sloppy joe mix into the fan. Ground chuck and tomato sauce sprayed the corridor. Gag City, was all she could think lying on the floor, her skull numbed by the collision. Then hands lifted her by the armpits and she heard a familiar voice: "Hurry."

Rings gazed up in the jowly face of her Tuesday lunch special, Change Clothes Collins. "My hero," she gasped.

"Hurry," he huffed again, hoisting Rings around the chow wagon and stuffing her into an empty lower compartment where normally a garbage can was stored. He slid shut the compartment door. From her cramped and clammy sanctuary Rings heard the fan motor die. As her senses returned, her heart began pounding and her stomach went on spin cycle.

The heavy wagon rumbled down the corridor. Through the kitchen doors it barged. Greasy swirling steam seeped into the compartment, clutching Rings's throat. She heard the rubber wheels swishing through shallow water. Her head struck the top of the compartment with a stunning bump, making her howl. "Say what, cap?" she heard a culinary trusty ask. "Just my belly aching out loud," C.C. answered. "You got enough onions and chili powder in that slop to wake the dead . . . What's with the flood?"

"The grease traps in scullery are backed up, sir."

"I want them cleaned. Now!"

"But we got two hundred chickens to clean for dinner . . . "

"No use preparing food under unsanitary conditions. I want every available man on those grease traps. Jump!"

Once the kitchen was cleared, C.C. opened the compartment. Out Rings tumbled, gasping for air. She brushed aside his apologies for the wagon's poor ergonomics, peppering him instead with questions.

"I'll explain later," he said. "They probably believe they killed you, the Sick Bay corridor was empty when I got there. We have to get you out of the building before you're seen alive."

"My radical hero!" Rings jumped up and down.

C.C. blushed and scuffed his shoe.

"How can I repay yu-?"

ZZzzzppp! Frilly lace panties effloresced through his fly, strumming a tumid pink pistil.

The debt retired, Rings climbed off her knees.

"You could suck the dark out of the night," said the undies sheriff.

"Like, major thanks. You can put that on my tombstone if we cant figger a way to get me out of this dump."

"Kitchen elevator. Opens out on the loading docks. No one will notice you."

"Naked? I'm shur! . . . Hey! Why cant you get my own clothes?"

That would attract attention, C.C. was certain. He had a better idea. He told Rings to wait behind some garbage cans and rushed off.

With her hysteria subsiding, Rings's ability to reason returned, one thought fitting into a second, setting a third in motion: *That freak who tried to kill me had to have been sent by the Pimp Blimp—who, if he can get at me in the jailhouse, can reach me anywhere in this burg. I cant count on them believing they mulched my bahakas. If C.C. busts me outta here, I gotta fur shur book a long vacation.*

C.C. loped back with khakis over his arm. Rings blanched. "Dress like a deputy?"

"A *female* deputy," C.C. grinned.

"Kasj! Good ole Change Clothes."

"I'll miss crossdressing with you," he mumbled and blushed again, as brightly as if a bulb blinked in his mouth. Then he whipped a large brassiere out of his hip pocket. "I've only worn it twice. It's a Playtex Cross Your Heart . . . "

"I'm glad you think I still got one to cross," smirked Rings, scooping a tit tattooed like a bullseye into a cup.

Downstairs on the loading docks C.C. asked what she was going to do.

"Beat cheeks down the blacktop," was what.

Down the loading dock steps she skipped, and across the parking lot. Reaching Harrison Street, she flung out her thumb. Several cars slowed without stopping, leery of a hitchhiking cop. Prancing out into traffic, she shot her hip, plucked a kiss from her lips and planted it on her fanny. She ignored the braking Toyota rearended by the pickup, running instead to the open door of a maroon Oldsmobile with outofstate plates.

She never heard the shot or saw C.C. do his halfgainer off the loading dock.

After Lights, Joe heard the *whrr-zzzz* of Spencer's wheelchair maneuvering close to his bed.

"Joe," he whispered, "dont be mad at the others. They already know what you'll learn when you get to the pen. It pays to be selectively deaf and blind. That was no orderly. That was a contractor sent after that girl to keep her from turning state's evidence against Baby Jewels Moses."

"*Moses?* You sure?" Between Joe's cranial precincts flashed neuronic SOS's, warning in manic Morse that coincidences compounded become causalities. Christ! Could the moon on the whore's last breath be the same as the one guarded by the sharks?

"Aint no secrets in a jailhouse, homeboy."

"Christ," Joe prayed to the phantasmal dark.

VENUS DE MILWAUKEE

||||

"**I** came to this town in a hot Studebaker with a stolen hot gas card," Baby Jewels wheezed expansively. "I slept in the Studie three months before I opened my first club, the Blackhawk. My father Izzy said I'd never amount to anything. He spent his whole life slaving in the garment district, keeled over of a heart attack shlepping a dress rod up Seventh Avenue, and he said *I'd* never amount to anything." Again he wheezed, a ventosity vast as a hippo blowing Limpopo mist.

"If he could see you now," Quick Cicero said, sipping customground Peruvian coffee. They were breakfasting on the terrace encircling the Fat Man's Pacific Heights penthouse. Lesser buildings below spilled down to the sparkling bay. The city sighed softly on the breeze ruffling the white linen table cloth.

A black butler in livery ghosted to the table with silver tray heaped with sliced salmon.

"I hope that's Nova Scotia lox, Wesley," clucked Baby Jewels, "not that Alaskan junk."

"Nossir. Aint no Eskimo fish."

Baby Jewels heaped the lox on a halved bagel slathered with cream cheese, wistfully wheezing, "Yes, if he could see me now." Mirth burbled from his baby mouth. "Though he'd probably be ashamed, say I was a cheap goniff. But he'd be wrong, wouldnt he? We're living the primetime American Dream. Horatio Alger doesnt hold a candle to Jules Moses."

"Fuckin A," corroborated Quick, though his voice wavered uncertainly, thinking of a highyaller jazz musician named Horatio who blacksocked parttime for Climax Produxions, and imagining with distaste that his boss was comparing himself to him.

"Hey, Tubby!" called a sharp voice through the sliding glass doors. Lieutenant Rick Tarzon stepped out onto the terrace. One hand held Fabulous Frank by the scuff of the neck, the other jammed a Walther P-38 down the front of his pleated trousers. "I cant understand why you'd go through the expense of installing a private security elevator, then post a drunk to guard it."

"You got a warrant," hissed the Fat Man.

"Doan need no steenkin warrant," Tarzon grinned.

"Dont piss him off, boss," Frank quailed. "He'll blow my nuts off sure."

"He'd be doing you a favor," was the Fat Man's verdict.

A dozen lifesize terracotta nudes composed in various wanton attitudes populated the terrace. Yanking the Walther from Frank's pants, Tarzon cuffed his wrists around one statue so tasteless that it was timeless in its own right, a bustout reproduction of the Venus de Milo, arms and head regrafted to her torso. The arms were arranged in the manner of a game-show hostess gesturing toward a prize La-Z-Boy recliner. The sculptor must have used a photograph of Jayne Mansfield as a model for the baubly head. The blond hair was reproduced in rampant goldleafed swoops.

"Yer stogie's ruinin my appetite," Quick groused.

"I'm sorry. I'll put it out."

Stepping to the table, Tarzon ground the Hav-A-Tampa Jewel into Quick's halved cantaloupe. The expug leaped to his feet, toppling his wroughtiron chair. Tarzon smacked him backhanded with the Walther, cracking his jaw. Quick hula'd drunkenly, then fell.

Tarzon emptied the pitcher of orange juice on Quick's face, partially reviving him, then hoisted him to his feet and cuffed him hugging the nude from the side opposite Frank. He stood back with an appreciative cluck. "I guess you'd call that a Venus sandwich in your trade, huh, you tub of slime."

"What do you want?" the Fat Man spluttered.

"Who was the guy with the limp, Fats?"

"Who you talking about?"

"The one who pureed Rosemary Hooten."

"I dont know any Rosemary Hooten."

Tarzon righted and sat in Quick's chair. "You didnt know she watched you zero Gloria Monday." He took careless aim with the Walther and blasted the head off one of the nudes. "Just like that."

"The city's going to pay for that."

"No, the city's going to pay for your murder trial. I didnt have time to get a sworn statement from the girl before you had her killed, but she told me she watched you ice Gloria Monday and take a diamond belonging to her sugardaddy. Smells like blackmail, Fats. I'm going to identify this sugardaddy and expose it. Then I'm going to bill you for Gloria Monday's murder. You've committed dozens, but I only need to prove one to gas your fat ass."

"You shouldnt listen to jail gossip, Lieutenant."

"Did I mention jail?" Tarzon smiled pleasantly.

Baby Jewels mottled. "The papers said a black killed her."

"A black *assaulted* her. He used a television cord to tie her wrists. When the TV was reconnected, its LED clock read 5:48 P.M. Two hours before the time of death fixed by the M.E. Twenty minutes before she died, Miss Monday called your limo. You forgot that time and charges for mobile calls are logged just like long distance ones." Tarzon blasted another head in a cloud of glazed clay. "That diamond's going to prove your bad luck piece, Fats. It's gonna drop the pill on you." Tarzon laid down the Walther. Boxing his thumbs and forefingers, he measured the elephantine rump squeezed in Baby Jewels's chair. "They're gonna have to build you a custom seat for the chamber, lardass."

"Fuck you," lisped the ancient baby voice.

"I've got a daughter about the same age as these girls you enjoy killing. If anything happened to her . . . " Tarzon trained the Walther between the eyes glinting in the Fat Man's head like tenpenny nails. Suddenly, without removing his stare from Moses, Tarzon swung the automatic and squeezed three times. Steeljacketed parabellums splashed through Venus de Milwaukee's neck and each shoulder, simultaneously recreating Jayne Mansfield's decapitation and restoring the statue to classical verisimilitude. Frank screeched and wet his pants.

"Just cant get good help these days, huh, Fats?"

Tarzon stood, holstering the Walther P-38 beneath his arm. He stared thoughtfully at the table. "I heard you talking about your father, a Jewish garment worker. My father was a Mexican magician. He never graduated from the border dives. They used to squeeze his act between the live sex shows in Tijuana. I'm afraid he wasnt very good, but he taught me a couple of routines. Here, I'll show you the old tablecloth trick."

Sternly Tarzon composed his blueshadowed features and deliberately shot his cuffs. Stepping to the head of the table, he took careful hold of the edge of the linen tablecloth. "Guess I dont get a drum roll," he joked selfeffacingly before violently jerking the tablecloth, launching Waterford crystal, bone china, and silver flatware high into the bright morning, crashing to the terrace flagstones.

"Sorry, Fats. I wonder if my ole man would be as ashamed of me as yours would be of you . . ." He turned to leave and stopped. Facing Baby Jewels one last time, he said: "When they dog down the door on you inside the green room across the bay," pointing to where the jumbled cellblocks of San Quentin across the bay were emerging from the morning mist, "look for me in the front row of witnesses. I'll be the one jacking off . . . motherfucker."

WHISPER MORAN

||||

Spring ushers new hope into the real world; in the jailhouse it only births fresh despair. The same sun brewing life into the earth grills discontent into the concrete tanks. The same breezes nodding flowers in the park and lifting cotton skirts converts the rusted ventilators atop the Hall of Justice into furnace flues.

If warm weather made F Tank's recycled air unbreathable, the crowding of extra lungs effected by stricter sentencing laws and the Sheriff's practice of inflating population for the upcoming fiscal census turned it suffocating. Thirtytwo men were now crammed in F Tank, and the count rose daily, new arrivals lugging in mattresses to spread wherever room remained on the floor.

It was called a prison boom—more Californians doing more time in the largest prison system in the free world, a felony population greater by twenty thousand than the U.S. Bureau of Prisons even; and growing by one hundred and fifty felons a week, fodder for a correctional Chicken Little feeding uncorrectably on itself, bloating beyond control.

Last night Reverend Bones and another hammer dueled over a carton of milk. A storm of oaths; a sudden black blur of fists; then Bones's foe was jackknifed over the front table. The Reverend's coveralls were down, his deadly weapon of a dick out, swelling thick as a radiator hose when the deputies stormed and gassed the tank. A rain of billy clubs beat Bones insensate; they dragged him from the tank by the heels, crashing his skull against the gate in a spray of blood, smearing a bright red wake down the corridor.

All night the Mace eddied through the tank, clinging to coveralls and bedding, threading noxious tendrils through nightmares. Now the sun rose over the East Bay, baking the jailhouse walls anew, reactivating the Mace and inducing a fresh round of streaming eyes and retching.

Naked, the prisoners lined up ten deep for the two showerheads. When Joe's turn came, he stood mouth open in the boiling steam, bellowing his lungs, flushing out the gas eddying miasmically deep in his chest. He turned, letting the hailstorm of spray pelt his back. Languorously, he lathered chest, underarms, belly, and balls. He wore the motelsized soap bar to a sliver, raising a foam everywhere. On the streets, he took no showers: junkies, like cats, hate the touch of water. Joe'd forgotten how good one felt; forgotten how good many simple things felt.

Beneath the other showerhead, Smoothbore was vigorously scrubbing the crack of his withered ass. He looked so droll and vulnerable in the nude: little cannonball tummy, matchstick arms and legs, saggy little tits with gray nipples.

"While you wuz on Sick Bay I got bitched," Smoothbore cried over the crashing water. "Life Without for being a ha*bitch*ual offender." He grinned, dismissing his last years lost with the easy fatalism of a pennyante gambler watching the dealer's cards scoop his last chips off the table.

"All day long . . . " Joe shook his head. A ghostly light suffused the steam enshrouding the drifter.

"You comin outta there any time this week?" came a hoarse whisper at Joe's back. He turned, swiping water from his eyes to look into the subzero stare of a tall, dark man reticulated with tattoos.

"No Hollywood showers in the jailhouse!" crowed Smoothbore. The drifter jumped from beneath his showerhead and grabbed two towels from the steel table. Brows raised meaningfully, he shook one in warning at Joe.

"Dude's got more than whore splash comin," Joe growled, still locked on that impenetrable stare. It took all his heart to pretend he was ready to fight for an extra minute in the pelting spray. Casually he stepped dripping from the stall and took the towel. "All yours, podner," he drawled as if the villain shouldering past him needed the telling.

"Life dont *get* much better," Smoothbore brightly signified to break the tension.

"I guess it dont," Joe mumbled, dogeyeing his successor beneath the showerhead. At least he didn't come off weak, he consoled himself. Losing face was more frightening than fighting.

Smoothbore jigged from foot to foot drying chalkwhite calves filigreed with broken blue veins like old bone china; trying to whistle without his state teeth, making flubbery sounds like a pony stamping for its oats. "Now we *jailin'!*" he laughed aloud.

Jailin' was an art form and lifestyle both. The style was walkin' slow, drinkin' plenty of water, and doin' your own time; the art was lightin' cigarets from wall sockets, playin' the dozens, cuttin' up dream jackpots, and slowin' your metabolism to a crawl, sleepin' twenty hours a day. Forget the streets you won't see for years. Lettin' your heart beat the bricks with your body behind bars was hard time. Acceptin' the jailhouse as the only reality was easy time. *Jailin'*.

"I guess we are," Joe agreed ambivalently, still gunning with a gritty eye and tuck of lip between his teeth the frescoed freebooter in the cone of steam. He had the look of a night manager of a sleazy motel, but was indelibly marked as a hardrock career convict by more tattoos than Joe had ever seen on one man. And not the variety shavetails and sailors select from tattoo parlor walls to look dangerous to their sweethearts. These were prison tattoos, their primitivism alone attested to that; and they spoke a violent legend of the California mainlines.

LOVE and HATE were lettered on his left and righthand knuckles; chains encircled raw, red wrists. A snarling panther clawed blood down one forearm; one the other, a dagger with the words JUST DESSERTS on its blade skewered a rat with X's for eyes; on the insides of his forearms, a forest of criminal commitment numbers, the most faded preceded by the initials Y.A. for Youth Authority; littering his upper body the leitmotifs of the perennial pariah: DEATH BEFORE DISHONOR, LIVE SUFFER DIE, DUST IS MY DESTINY—among swastikas, hangman's nooses, several aspects of the Grim Reaper, dice showing snake eyes, and on his left pectoral a black cat inside an eight ball. Ornately scrolled rocker arms, like the identifying patches on biker jackets, adorned his belly. The bottom arm, or lower banner arch, describing a smiling semicircle beneath his navel, heralded his home county: SAN BERDOO. The upper rocker arm followed the curve of his rib cage and announced the problem: JACK MORAN.

Out of the shower stepped Jack Moran, slinging water from his black mane. Eyes reflecting the jaundiced jailhouse light caught Joe staring at the wrong part of his body. The thick lower lip barely moved making a sound like grinding bones: "You got a problem?"

Joe tore his eyes off the penis with flames inked down its length as if its glans were an engine cowling. Christ! Would the Bearded Clam That Ate San Pedro have met its match in a Panavision version of that nookie nuker!

"I aint got no problem . . . unless you do," Joe parried, rolling his shoulders, praying the hardrocker wouldn't call his bluff.

Moran's eyes blinked once, becoming gun slits. Then Smoothbore had Joe by the arm, hustling him to the front of the tank to exchange his soiled coveralls for one of the fresh pairs being distributed through the bars by a trusty from a rolling hamper.

"You dont know who you woofin at," bumped Smoothbore's naked gums. "That's Jack Moran. They call him Whisper on accounta the police bullet what blew out his voice box. Whisper's back on another murder. He paroled just last week from Folsom, got off the bus here in Frisco and stabbed a dude to death in the station. Jist fer bumpin into him! Whisper told the police he walked the mainline eighteen years and was never once bumped. So he bladed the citizen for not showin respeck. Carved his initials on his heart . . . He's General of the Aryan Brotherhood, too. Check the lightnin bolts and butterfly on his neck, the iron cross on his throat . . . Dont even look crosseyed at that man, Joe. Blood makes him laugh. He *likes* killin . . . the way you like chokin yer chicken."

Joe returned to his bunk with his fresh issue: ripped orange coveralls, a yellowed towel, and threadbare sheet. He made up the bunk and donned the coveralls, which billowed like a parachute, and scouted for a domino game. None were in progress, the rest of the felons being busy showering and dressing. He lit a Camel, casting idly around the bustling tank. And his eye was drawn once more to the man called Whisper.

He stood naked at a rear sink, grooming his hair. With alternating comb flicks and delicate hand sculptings, the General of the dreaded white supremacist prison gang was building a stratospheric pachook pomp that fairly begged for half a tube of Brylcreem. The style was strictly early Roy Orbison, unseen outside Tupelo, Mississippi, for twentyfive years. Joe might have laughed had he not known this man had killed another only yesterday for the imagined slight of jostling him in a crowded public place. And something else too—something ineffably sad suggested by his grave demeanor as he conducted the archaic tonsorial ritual. Career convicts like Whisper Moran were marooned in time, Joe realized, watching this aging ghost of an early sixties punk gone bad.

Not that this detracted from the glory of his dermagraffiti. From the sink Whisper Moran afforded Joe a rear view of his body pictography. More of the conventional loser icons across the shoulders, skulls and scorpions and such. Down his backarm triceps, in vertical Gothic print above spiderwebbed elbows, WEISSE and MACHT, German for "White Power." Similarly, on the back of one calf, BLUT, and the other, UND FEUER, "Blood and Fire," the motto engraved on Nazi SS daggers. A vision of penitentiary apocalypse covered the ganglord's back; a nightmarish prisonscape of medieval crenellated walls and stone guntowers engulfed by smoke and flames out of which a firebreathing dragon reared its fearsome head, eyes rendered glaucous by metallic ink. Scrolled beneath was the legend, "Which way I fly am hell. Myself am hell." The anonymous Mainline Michelangelo signed his work SATAN.

Satisfied with his hairdo, Whisper Moran turned from the sink. On his neck just beneath the SS runes and butterfly Joe spotted the jagged surgical scar marking the wound that left him voiceless.

The A.B. General didnt have to stand in the linen line with the others. A neatly folded pair of orange coveralls awaited him on the edge of the table. He slipped into them; they fitted as if tailormade. Idly Joe wondered if he might join the A.B. and tack on the bolts and butterfly himself. If only to steal their symbolic courage, cheat for himself the respect these badges commanded behind every locked gate in the state. If only to protect himself inside from the powers pursuing the Moon.

Then Whisper Moran fitted an oldtime baseball cap on his head. On its faded crown was stitched a P.T. Barnum letter "B." Once more he caught Joe gawking. The deadly calabash within the tattooed throat rattled, "I think maybe you do have a problem."

"No, no." Joe crisscrossed his palms before him, signaling surrender. "I was just admiring your old Brooklyn Dodgers cap. Never be another team like em."

Something that might have been amusement flashed in the shadow of the cap's bill, and Joe first noticed falling from one eye a single tattooed tear.

BON APPETIT

||||

Sammy Chin appreciated his job as pot cook at Woh Sun's Chinese Restaurant on Washington, next to the cable car barn. Sammy was a chemistry major at San Francisco State, and pot cooking for Woh Sun paid his basic tuition and board. For pin money Sammy did an altogether different sort of cooking. In basement Chinatown labs he produced Methedrine, LSD, PCP, and crack for the Joe Sing gang. And pretty pin money it was, for it kept up the payments on his Datsun 300X and covered his gambling losses.

But when the rivalry between the Joe Sing gang and the Wah Ching erupted into open war, the gang's streetcorner retailers became troops and the labs closed down. War had broken out five times in the two years since Sammy joined the Joe Sing gang, and each new time a shaky truce was forged it was harder for Sammy to rationalize continuing as the gang's chemist. Each time he was so many units closer to the degree, that much closer to the realization of his dream of a career in industrial chemistry. One bust would ruin forever all he'd worked for.

Two days before the Golden Boar massacre, Sammy had interviewed with a campus recruiter for Dow. When the recruiter asked his views on toxic waste management, Sammy answered with the cooking analogy: "You cant make an omelette without breaking eggs." The recruiter found this response practical, realistic. Little could he know just how practical and realistic Sammy truly was when it came to chemical toxins. The recruiter was so optimistic about his chances with Dow that Sammy concluded he'd retire from the Joe Sing gang.

That morning he turned the fancy Datsun back to the dealership; and that afternoon before he went to work called Ah Toy, Woh Sun's eldest daughter, and proposed marriage. Woh Sun was a powerful and wealthy man, Snow Leopard of the Circle of Six, Chinatown's oldest and most powerful tong. Ping Chin, Sammy's father, had also been a Leopard of the Circle until his death. Sammy was confident that Woh Sun would assent to Sammy's union with Ah Toy—and grant a substantial dowry with which the chemistry student might satisfy his outstanding gambling debts. As a bonus, Ah Toy was a stunner of the stripe that Chinese poets liken to celestial phenomena and Western manufacturers award bluejean contracts.

To his proposal over the phone Ah Toy responded with a tintinnabulation closer to birdsong than giggle, a purely ceremonial pretense of chastity. After all, Ah Toy once worked at one of Johnny Formosa's doll shops. Unbeknownst to Woh Sun, of course. She would be as relieved to escape her father's tyranny through marriage as Sammy would be to sever his ties with the Joe Sing gang.

A shipment of arcane spices ordered by Sammy had finally arrived this afternoon, and he was working alone in the closed restaurant, preparing the chicken stock by which a Chinese eatery is judged just as an Italian one is distinguished by its tomato sauces. Sammy didn't know that Ah Toy had slipped out of her home to meet him at the restaurant and demonstrate her personal delight at his proposal in one of the rear banquet booths.

She slipped through the restaurant's front door. If she made a sound it was lost in the shuttlebang of cable cars in the adjacent barn, the whine of turbines turning the fiftyfoot iron wheels that pulleyed the miles of pleated iron cable beneath the city streets.

Stealing through the darkened restaurant she heard Sammy whistling cheerfully from where he stood on a milk crate stirring with a giant ladle his simmering concoction in a vat atop the great stove. "You shouldnt have crossed the road," he scolded the bobbing chicken heads. Sammy's heart was light as the briny breezes wafting through the open rear doors, his prospects bright as the sunlight glancing off the stainless steel pots hanging from overhead racks.

Ah Toy paused at the kitchen's bamboo curtain to think up just the right seductive remark to inveigle Sammy to the lovers bower she'd chosen. She started suddenly at unfamiliar voices. Men had entered the kitchen through the rear doors. She bent close enough to the bamboo to see, yet not so close her shadow could be detected through its interstices.

"Sammy, we're callin in all our markers," said a gangly character wearing a loud sports jacket and too much greasy kids stuff in his droopy grey hair.

"Frank," Sammy said, "aint I always squared with you guys?"

A second man carrying a Belgian FN-LAR automatic rifle sauntered to the stove. Ah Toy watched him roll his shoulders and twitch his neck as if his jacket and collar were too tight. He said, "Look, you fuckin slope. Square is payin yer debts without us havin to come ask. You got three and a half large in yer jeans there?"

"No," Sammy said. He started to climb down from the milk crate.

The second man slapped the back of Sammy's knees with the assault rifle. "Stay up there on your playstool, wimp . . . Now we know you aint cookin dope up there. How you expect to pay us?"

Ah Toy was about to turn away from the curtain to phone the police when she was shocked to hear Sammy blurt: "Lissen. I'm getting married to the daughter of this dive's owner. I'm doing it for the dowry. Soon as I'm hitched, I can pay you off. With juice."

"What's a dowry?" asked the one who looked like washedup pimp.

"Alimony up front," the twitchy one said; then to Sammy: "That takes too long. We got to cover these markers now . . . But there is a way you can square up without cash. We need some information which is worth more than what you owe us."

"What? Anything." Sammy was shaking so violently the ladle clinked inside the vat of stock.

"The masks and guns the Sing brothers used for the Golden Boar massacre. They loaned them to a coupla whiteboys who used them to rob us. Tell us who these characters are and you can put these markers inside fortune cookies."

Sammy's shoulders sagged. "Oh, shit. You gotta understand. When Joe and Archie go militant, they go alone. They keep the rest of us in the dark . . . honest," he spluttered, staring crosseyed at the assault rifle touching the bridge of his nose, "I'm just the chemist. They . . . they dont tell me nothing about the killings and all."

"One last chance, zipperhead," he said. "Either of the brothers mention a diamond in your little gang powwows? Put us on to the diamond those whiteboys robbed from us and you get more than your markers back. I'll give you your life. Otherwise . . . "

"You said you wouldnt . . . " quavered the greasy one.

"Shut up, juicehead . . . Well, Sammy boy?" Now the rifle was poking at Sammy's genitals, making him squirm.

"Please. I never heard of any diamond. But I will pay my markers. As soon as Ah Toy and I are married, I'll pay you first. I'll . . . "

Like a snake striking, the twitchy one swept the rifle behind Sammy's knees, overturning him into the bubbling vat. He mounted the stool and held Sammy's Reeboks until his kicking legs went limp.

The gangly one giggled. Hopping from loafer to tassled loafer, he trilled just like Julia Child, *"Bon appetit!"*

The other hopped off the milk crate and stared disgustedly at him. "Are you finished, asshole?"

"Yeah. Just got a little carried away." He hung his greasy head.

"This is the last time I take you anywhere." Motioning with the rifle, the twitchy one ordered the other out the back door and started to follow. But at the threshold he paused, teased by an impulse. "I'm gettin bad as you," he laughed to the other. He whirled and fired a burst on full automatic, ringing showers of sparks off the hanging pots and pans so that Woh Sun's kitchen cymbaled and gonged like a Chinese concert hall.

Lieutenant Tarzon was among the first police on the scene. While the rest took pictures of Sammy in the vat and suggested ways of getting him out of it, Tarzon led Ah Toy back to the very booth she'd chosen for her tryst with Sammy to question her. Briefly she described the two men. They were trying to discover the identity of other white men, ones the Sing brothers had loaned guns and masks. The last thing they asked before drowning Sammy was about a diamond they said was stolen from them.

Would Ah Toy be willing to come down to headquarters to look through some mugshot books? It wouldn't take long. The dark little lieutenant seemed to know already who killed Sammy Chin.

"Ah Toy know nothing, go nowhere," boomed a voice through the police hubbub. It was Woh Sun himself with his glinting goldframed glasses and seablue silk suit.

The Snow Leopard of the Circle of Six swooped up his daughter and was gone before Tarzon could protest. Not that it would have done any good. Distrust of foreign authority among the Chinese dated back to their enslavement by feudal Manchurian warlords; the bloody persecutions visited on coolies by nineteenthcentury Americans only confirmed their xenophobia. They made Sicilians seem like a race of gossips. If he tried holding her as a material witness, Woh Sun would post her bail and spirit her out of the country.

Besides, Tarzon already knew all he needed. The diamond had been stolen, it was loose on the streets. He had only to recover it before the Fat Man did to identify the sugardaddy and lock Moses behind the green door.

He screwed a Hav-A-Tampa Jewel into a lupine smile. Stolen by whiteboys with the same guns and masks used at the Golden Boar. Lieutenant Tarzon had a strong hunch just which punks those were.

DEAD TIME

||||

Joe wasn't the only prisoner who didn't sleep that night in F Tank. Most felons with weeks, sometimes months between court appearances, reset their body clocks to remain awake nights. Then, in the steelstitched jailhouse shadows, when its stone bowels ceased from grinding, their fantasies were unfettered and their deepest longings released in masturbation and minstrelsy. By day they slept like the dead, rising just for meals; by night they came alive and were free . . . *Jailin'*.

Toot Sweet sprawled in his blanket hammock at the front bars. A newcomer named Champagne sat crosslegged nearby. Toot was running down the further pedigree of that mythic badass Dolomite:

> *Say, Bee-itch! I fucked the cow jumped over the moon*

Joe stared at the sagging bunk springs over his head, mired in a lovelost funk. Why hadn't Kitty visited or written him? She hadn't even left money on his books, as he'd asked in the kite sent with Harold, for cigarets and candy. Maybe she no longer shook a tailfeather over the candycolored lights. Maybe another dude had taken Joe's place. He tried comforting himself that he hadn't told her of the Moon. If she knew and remained true, he would never have known whether it was to him or the promise of wealth.

Champagne was privy to certain details of Dolomite's sex life:

> *Dat ho bee-itch Mabel farted*
> *N dat's when de FUCKIN started*
> *Her pussy do the mojo, turkey, popcorn n grind*
> *Lef ole Dolomite six strokes behind*
> *Nex mawnin dey founded Mabel daid*
> *Wid her fonky drawers wrapped round her nappy haid*

On a top bunk near the front of the G Tank, across the corridor from F, a puttyskinned youth with glasses thick as Coke bottles was ripping and chewing his blanket. Joe smirked. Ruffage was a desirable supplement to the jailhouse diet, but fireretardant wool? Marinated in creosote, sweat, and jizz? Joe decided the dude was going Eleven Ninetyeight, the administrative section number for snapping under the stress of incarceration. Well, he hoped vaguely, if they catch him eating county property, maybe they'll get him the help he needs.

At the front bars Top Dog had switched the toast to the saga of that Ole Signifyin' Monkey always gettin' over on the bigger, stronger jungle beasts like a streetcorner pimp runnin' the Murphy on a gang of Shriners:

> *Now Monkey wore them uptown stitches*
> *Drove a Cadillac fulla dem monkey bitches*

Joe swung off his bunk and stepped to the front bars, lighting a cigaret. Tomorrow he would go to court, where he would plead not guilty but be ready to cop out if their case was airtight. Let 'em give him the book. The max for GTA was three years. Two, with work and good time off. *Short time, homey!* he jollied himself. Do it standing on yer head stackin' BB's. But the time wouldn't start running till he hit the penitentiary gates. County jail was dead time.

"Quicker you get to the pen," he encouraged himself, "the quicker you'll raise up and cop the Moon."

Flicking the Camel stub into the corridor, he noted with alarm that the puttyskinned whiteboy was braiding the torn pieces of blanket.

> *Monkey say, I measures fortyfour cross de chest*
> *My dick scores nine, chicks say it's dee best*
> *I fear no motherfucker twixt God and Death*
> *I wuz born in the Battle of the Butcher Knives*

"Nigger!" hissed Champagne. "Shet up yer signifyin!"
Because now they all saw what the man on the upper G Tank bunk was

up to. He'd tied a noose at one end of the braided blanket. Standing on the bunk, he knotted the other end through a ventilator grill. He settled the noose around his neck, then carefully removed his glasses and put them in his jumpsuit's breast pocket, patting them to make sure they were safe. With a towel he tied his wrists and slipped his feet through the hoop of his bound arms so that his hands were effectively secured behind his back.

Joe's mind stalled. It was a jolt discovering faith's intimation in himself by another threatening to repudiate it to the fullest measure. All he could think was how amazingly agile a desperate man became. It wasn't until the G Tanker was kneeling on bunk's edge, mouthing a silent prayer, that Joe squeezed his mouth between the bars and cried: *"Dont do it!"*

But the G Tanker had already flung himself from the upper bunk. The braided blanket snapped, held. He gagged horribly. His shins remained propped on the bunk from which he depended at fortyfive degrees. His eyes bulged big as eggs, staring in blind bemusement. His tongue ballooned his cheeks, bulging purple, and bloated through his open mouth like the bladder through a tear in a basketball. An erection sprang through the flap of his coveralls. The stink of suddenly evacuated bowels washed up and down the tank.

Only then did the calls begin—"MAN DOWN!"

Joe turned and staggered to the tank's rear. He banged his head against the wall until supernovas exploded in his skull. Through the roar in his ear he heard the deputies cursing as they cut down the fouled corpse; then the gurney's rusty wheels, the tank gates crashing.

Still leaning against the wall, Joe felt a hand on his shoulder and heard a voice like a rusty bucket being hoisted from a deep well: "Man's gotta do what he's gotta do. Once you aint feared of dying, it's easy as steppin through an open cell gate. You couldnt stop him. No one can stop em once they decide to hang it up."

Joe turned. Somewhere in Whisper Moran's black eyes moved a light; and about the lower lip a tremble of compassion.

Much later, Joe looked over at the bunk where Whisper slept curled around himself. The jailhouse night was hot, and the top of his coveralls was undone and pulled down, tied at his lean waist. The faint corridor lights suffused his tattooed torso with a soft metallic gleam. He looked like a sleeping serpent.

CANDY ROSES

||||

Things were different now. Kitty Litter came off the Blue Note stage wringing withdrawal's toxic sweat. She made a beeline for the bar, for another shot of booze to take the edge off her sick.

"Glenlivet straight up, Manager."

Maurice the Manager set down her neat scotch and grabbed the bar's rear bumper. He locked his elbows, hunching up his shoulders like goal posts. Oh no, here he goes with the knowitall head oscillation signaling the managerial oracle about to speak. He sniffed one nostril, then its neighbor, more body language for Dutch uncle aplomb that served the secondary purpose of drilling any vagrant grains of cocaine into his crystallized brain tissue. Aiming fondly askance down the bridge of his nose, he treated Kitty to a doublebarreled view of bored and blown cartilage. Finally, from the infinite deeps of bustout backbar wisdom, he spoke: "Thinkin of the Barker, huh?"

From the buildup Kitty had hoped for the Secret to Eternal Happiness and would have settled for a recipe for Spam casserole.

"Yeah, that boy's restless on muh mind. Howd you ever know?"

"Women." The Manager winked slowly. "I know women."

The jerk.

Music like a fistful of fingernails across a blackboard filled the club.

"Aw no." Kitty threw down her head on the bar. "You aint lettin Desdemona do her infuckintwerpytive number again."

"One last chance, I told her," sniffed Maurice.

"As if a stiff dick hasnt enough on its mind without interpreting," Kitty bemoaned. "She got a sexy caboose. Awta chug those cheeks like a coupla Volkswagens tryin to pass each other round a corner."

"So tell me about the Barker," the Manager said as if he gave a fuck. Kitty could see him nervously watching Desdemona's act from the corner of his eye. Every time he told the ditz to shuck a clam, as in pink, Desdemona babbled with gradschool earnestness that it was what they *didn't* see that turned them on; tap her head and say, "Sex really happens between your ears . . . "

"If it does, it's an empty experience," was the Manager's professional judgment.

Kitty gave him the lowdown on not being able to write or visit Joe because of she was listed as one of his crime partners. "I bet Joe dont even remember it, but we were busted together once shoplifting at Safeway. And I bet that dopefiend vet stole the money I sent for Joe's books." She took a slug, shuddered. "He goes to court tomorrow."

"And the penitentiary the next day," Maurice said.

Kitty nodded, staring wideeyed into her drink. "I just hope that boy's got better sense than to think I quit him."

"Hey! Dont worry bout the Barker. Coupla years off dope'll do im good."

"It's me I worry about. Gettin left behind's harder than goin, dont matter where. Joe's gonna change. I dont know how, but he cant help changin . . . So I gotta change. And hope in most of the same ways or he'll get out and I'll be in love with a stranger." There, she got it out.

"Whaddya wanna change?" the Manager's spread palms wanted to know. "You got yer friends, yer health, yer job. Like, Hey! Cinderella. It's past midnight and you're still at the ball, even if Prince Charming booked."

Some friends, Kitty reflected ordering another drink. There wasnt a girl in the joint who wouldn't steal her last tampoon. As for her health, Kitty hadn't fixed for twelve days but still had the geewillies and was running to the bathroom every fifteen minutes with the Hershey squirts. As for shakin' booty at the Blue Note . . .

"Some job. With Joe, it was fun. A game, kinda. Now it aint even work." She took a slug of Glenlivet. "It's punishment."

"Punishment?" The Manager shook his permed curls at such illogic. "We all should be so punished, the money you make flashin keister."

"Payin' customers!" bayed Bermuda Schwartze. She stood at the waitress station, resting the Continental Shelf on the bar. By some atmospheric quirk, one of the megamams was overinflated tonight, the other shrunk and flaccid. Staggering around the club in her stilletos, Bermuda listed sharply as though an invisible hand tugged her hair.

"Why dontcha start pickin up ashtrays?" the Manager suggested to her, ringing up drinks for the latecoming Joe Colleges. It was only an hour until closing, and only diehard dingdongers still drank at the Blue Note.

"I aint your nigger! Be a mensch! Ask Oblivia Neutron Bomb."

But Oblivia was busy skulling a patron in a back booth. Giving him his money's worth, too, from the looks of it. His head over the top of the booth jiggled like someone driving over speed bumps. Naturally, Oblivia also had a hand patting him down for his wallet. A pro like her never popped a nut until she'd popped the swag.

Kitty drilled her scotch and rapped the glass on the bar.

"Hey Kitty baby," Bermuda purred like a lawnmower working uphill. "If you dont like chocolate, I'll take them preshush flowers."

One sickeyed sweetheart seeker had been in two nights running mooning over Kitty, telling her he wanted to treat her the way she deserved, whatever that meant. He was nicelooking, too. And rich. It was just too tragic. Like, how could Kitty Litter *relate* to a guy who said her eyes reminded him of moonlit pools after Joe telling her for so long they looked like the five ball off the eight, the hard way. Tonight he brought her a dozen chocolate roses with his business card—DANSIGNS LTD., Daniel Graves, Prop. Some overpriced accessory boutique for young urban morons. "No, I *like* em, Bermuda."

"Suit yourself, babykins."

"Where's Dwan tonight?" The Manager still sought an ashtray gofer.

"School," Bermuda said airily.

"Seminar, she means," Kitty said. "Too many leather boys been showin up dead, so the Coroner's holdin safe bondage seminars."

"Dwanny took an apple," Bermuda added.

"Take it off, take it off!" the latecoming collegiate mafia began razzing Desdemona. She was fluttering around the stage in what looked like a hospital gown; with the faraway look of a patient traipsing up and down a psych ward. She styled her "art" after Martha Graham. Maurice said learning to strip from a bimbo named Martha was like learning to drive an eighteen wheeler from a guy named Timmy—so skip the grahamcracker bit and git *down*. And she would for a couple of numbers, stoically betray her ideals flashing tush; then, before you knew it, be at it again: transcendental striptease. As if these Blue Note bozos came searching for anything deeper than six, *maybe* seven inches.

And the music! Those raghead guitars like sick cats.

"This joint's goin downhill," Kitty proclaimed on sound authority.

"Bare nookie!" One of the Varsity Squad yelled their common wish; another waxed even more poetic: "Hair pie!"

Each segment of Desdemona's routine was introduced by her own deadpan voice overdubbed on the soundtrack. Now she was launched into something called "The Excruciating Tightness of Being," which seemed to consist of her impersonating a twisted pipe cleaner. In the middle of a contorted pirouette, with the keening sitars reminding everyone of overdue dentist appointments, the largest of the frat boys, the King of the Kampus Kulture Klub, slung his drink at her. Her face blanched, then was quickly suffused with a martyr's beaming beatitude as she writhed on like Joan of Fuckin' Arc at her stake.

"Dee, get on stage!" hissed the Manager down the bar. But nothing doing. Dee Brie had just come off before Kitty and was done for the night. The triple Cutty Sark in her fist attested to that.

"Bermuda! Show those boys what we stand for here at the Blue Note," Maurice tried summoning the old school spirit.

"Ixnay, Maurice! My bwests is out of balance."

"Kitty . . ." Pleadingly.

"Shitfire, Maurice! Why not Eartha Quake?"

You didn't have to ask that natural disaster twice. Eartha reached behind the bar and ejected the sandnigger music with an earsplitting screech as if someone had thrown scalding water on the sick cats. Desdemona was just beginning her "Life Sempiternal, Life Evanescent" blooming lilac shtick, all scrunched up in a weird ball meant to represent the sleeping flower. Up sprang her mousy head, eyes squinched in the colored lights.

"Whom ceased my music?" she quailed. Maximum tragic.

"Yo mama!" Eartha had her know from the top of the runway. "Now get off my ramp, tramp."

To a saxophone coiling like smoke around a fat bass pulse and panting snare, Eartha glided down the ramp cupping her long skinny tits and tweaking their rusty horned nipples. Around the stage she slashed those big long legs. She halted at a post and slowly hunched it while her slitted eyes clearly doubted any face behind the candycolored lights was man enuff for *her* bad stuff. Then she resumed her prowling march, clawing at her belly, sneering. Suddenly she stopped and yanked aside her G-string. She jammed a finger up her quim, wiggled it with a snarl, and, after passing the fouled digit beneath the college boys' noses, sucked it clean. Class.

"Now *that's* what the boys eat up," cried Maurice, all smiles.

"Gross." Kitty's tongue was fuzzy with scotch. "For an encore she'll smoke a cigaret up there."

"So gross is what they pay for." The Manager was right: the Varsity Squad was reaching up, tucking sawskis in her garter belt.

"She's . . . dead, Maurice. Just aint no one told her to fall over," Kitty surprised herself saying. But it wasn't just the booze; she meant it. Something behind Eartha's eyes was shut like steel shutters. Dead. "Gimme anudder Glenlivet, Manager."

He poured it, saying, "You should be so dead."

I *will* be, was Kitty Litter's bustout epiphany.

The big one, the Kulture King, refused to tip Eartha. She crouched at the edge of the stage, wringing her squashlike tits in his sodden face, and sneered something Kitty didn't catch. His face reddened, he lurched to his feet and stumbled to the mensroom. Eartha stood hands on hips watching him with open disgust. Then she reached under her G-string and, wincing, yanked out a cunt hair. Reaching down and picking up his halfempty beer bottle, she pushed the fat black hair down its neck. Before returning it to the table, she held the bottle up to a light. *Yrrgghh!* You could *see* the hair floating in its very own miniature oil slick.

"I dont believe it," mumbled Kitty. "She makes me feel like Nancy Drew."

Eartha put her finger to her lips and winked, joining the other collegiates in the conspiracy. In a moment the big one returned. He took no notice of the others stifling their hilarity, doubled over, choking. He chugged the beer. They burst out screaming and laughing and shouting at him what he'd done. The Kulture King barfed beer froth across the stage apron.

"That's it, Maurice. I'm hangin up my G-string," Kitty announced in a clear voice.

"And all over the nice clean stage," wailed Bermuda.

"Clean, my ass," cried Dee Brie. "I've been having yeast infections ever since I come to work here."

"Girl, you were born with terminal vaginitis."

Desdemona blithered about the excruciating nausea of being.

"You guys take your friend home, he's had enough," cried the Manager. He turned to Kitty, his face screwed sideways. "What're you talking about?"

"I'm outta here," she declared, heading for the stairs.

"Dont come snivelin to me when you want your job back!" the Manager called up after her.

In the dressingroom Kitty peeled out of her cheap peignoir and kicked off her stripper heels. Into her jeans she shimmied and laced on her sneakers. God! the smell up there of curling irons and weekold Aqua Net and something else that might be mistaken for a tunafish sandwich rotting somewhere.

Her eye fell on the chocolate roses. Funny thing about heroin with-drawal, you developed a tragic sweet tooth, a real sugar yen. Probably all the lactose in the cut: you were shooting ten times more sugar than junk. She stuffed the silly things in her gym bag. The perfect souvenir of the bustout Life devoted to the cynical cheap synthesis of All Things Beauti-ful, the rustling of lonesome dreams.

Danny boy's card fluttered to the floor. She frowned down at it, deciding she'd probably need it. She shrugged, blowing a curl off her forehead, and scooped it up. She might have to let Mr. Dan Graves have his way and keep her. Tragic.

She collected her few bottles of scent and tubes of mascara and tossed them in the gym bag. She was about to leave when Detox, a stray cat adopted by the Blue Note girls, hissed and spit. He crouched before the mirror baring his wicked little fangs.

"What's the matter, pussy . . . One bent chick flying the coop? There's more where this one came from. *Oceans* more . . . " Detox screeched. She hurled a can of hair spray at him. He jumped clear. The mirror smashed into a hundred broken Kitty Litters.

Downstairs, all hell had broken loose. Oblivia's trick had tumbled to the rip and run: he was staggering in circles, pants around his ankles, screaming where the fuck was his wallet. Bermuda was bonging him over the head with her tray, hollering for Maurice to call the cops, they had a weenie waver on the premises . . . *Bong! Bong!* And the Ultimate Grossout: Eartha Quake sitting on the edge of the stage beside the big kid's head lying passed out in the sudsy beer puddle, with another kid's head clinched between her legs, eating out her raunchy box.

While Gene Pitney's adenoidal bleating over blown speakers put a philosophical spin on the scene by reminding one and all that it wasn't very pretty what a town without pity *cannn deeeewwww.*

Before Kitty could hit the door, the Manager took time out to scream: "Better not have any Blue Note G-strings in that bag!"

Sure. So he could sell them to the next tragedy off the bus.

The jerk.

SILENT BEEFS

||||

"**I** remember your case," the Public Defender said, reading from the topmost file on his arm. "A Grand Theft Auto. You were hospitalized and I pled you not guilty in absentia at your arraignment. The Assistant D.A. is unwilling to cut any sort of deal. I tried to budge him, but no soap. You've got an ugly silent beef . . . "

"What kind of beef?" Joe cupped his hands to his mouth to be heard over the din in the Muni Court bullpen, a concrete box the size of a cheap motel room crammed with forty felons furiously smoking, breaking starchy jailhouse wind, and shouting all at once.

"*Silent* beef. When the authorities believe a man guilty of a crime or crimes which they cant prove and must settle for a conviction on a lesser charge, they attach memoranda to the man's record stipulating the uncharged offenses. These memoranda ensure he is punished to the fullest legal limit of the lesser offense."

"Damned American of them. What crime are they convicting me of without a trial?"

The P.D. smiled wanly. "Murder during the commission of a felony."

For appearances, Joe cursed. Inwardly, he rejoiced that he was being silently beefed for the pharmacist, not Rooski. Tarzon hadn't made good the veiled threat near Twin Peaks. The felony murder might mean harsher treatment by the Man; the snitch jacket would have spelled swift death

at the hands of his fellows. Believing himself shielded from the consequences of his own moral dearth by Tarzon's helpless surplus, Joe flushed
with the coward's historic vanquishment of the brave.

"I recommend you change your plea to guilty at this Preliminary Hearing and throw yourself on the mercy of the court. The judge might take
this as evidence of contrition and modify your sentence accordingly. He
might throw out the narcotics paraphernalia found on your person at the
time of arrest."

Joe said cool as a quart of beer, "No, I think I'll take it to trial. Yup,"
tugging his ear ruminatively, "twelve in a box."

The P.D.'s nose twisted oddly at the end as if smelling sideways at an
illusive bad odor. Plainly it irked him not receiving the awe customarily
accorded the mysteries of his profession by the indigent. "I wouldnt do
that. They're going to max you on the Four Eightyseven GTA anyway,
but if you force it to trial, they can run an additional year consecutively
for the paraphernalia. Even though it's only a Health and Safety Code
violation, they can bump it up to felony for your numerous priors . . . and
will, taking the silent beef into account. Copping out might save you a
year."

"What's another bullet, wild or bowlegged . . . Anyway, they have to
convict first."

"If every case went to trial the system would . . . "

"I know. Gridlock and collapse. But case crunch isnt supposed to be
your concern, Counselor—my rights are. And chief among those is the
right to a trial by my peers. No wonder they call you guys Penitentiary
Dispatchers. Maybe I should act in my own defense. At least then I'd have
a principled fool for a lawyer."

Court was a dim looming chamber smelling of stale floorwax and inartic-
ulate despair. Nary a breath of fresh air to wash the jailhouse stink from
Joe's nose. The prisoners were ushered in a dozen at a time and seated in
the unused jury box.

In the carved wood galleries ornate as RKO poopdecks perched that
hardcore squad of spectators who stayed each day till closing, seeking relief
from their own misery in that of others: brighteyed little old ladies in crazy
hats beside shopping bags stuffed with rubbish, papery lips fluttering
around mad mute maledictions, frail fingers flying around unseen guillotine knitting; shabby old men, faces suffused with the same stupefied
rapture panned by televangelists' cameras and lit by the Blue Note's
runway bulbs.

Excepting this Senior Jurists' Auxiliary watching the wheels of justice
grind human lives, court was nearly empty. Several black mothers huddled

in shadows of their own desolation, wringing handkerchiefs and mouthing silent prayers when they spotted their babies in the docket. In the last row slouched an emaciated whitegirl who looked as if she'd been up for a week alternately shooting speed and getting gangraped—and now was being forced to appear by her new pimp to testify against her old one.

No Kitty Litter.

"Manuel Echeveria, line fourteen," called the bailiff.

A small mustachioed Mexican stood uncertainly and shuffled to the rail. The ones who couldn't speak English fidgeted and looked frightened. The language barrier compounded the terror of alien and hostile proceedings.

Judge Trepanian, presiding, leaned on one elbow, hand scrunching dewlaps above ruddy ears attached to what was presumably the tenement of his jurisprudence, intent on a document before him. He leaned back, furrowing his brow, sucking his pencil. Removing it from his mouth, now he used its wet eraser to tick off the digits on one hand, counting.

"Your Honor," the P.D. began, standing at the defense table and gesturing in the defendant's general direction. "Mr. Echeveria is charged with a violation of Penal Code Section Three Seventeen, to wit, Forcible Rape. As per agreement reached in discussions with the office of the District Attorney, it is Mr. Echeveria's intent today to enter a plea to the lesser charge of Aggravated Sexual Battery . . . "

Bang! Bang! The judge glared at the docket where another Mexican was excitedly waving his cuffed hands. "Bailiff! Have that man come to order or remove him from court."

" . . . and be sentenced according to the recommendations of the State . . . " The sallow P.D. looked up at the bench and smiled three prim millimeters.

"Does the State have any objections to disposing of this matter in the manner indicated by defense counsel?" The judge still stared at the docket, where the other Mexican was talking volubly in the bailiff's ear.

Up shot the shavetail Assistant D.A. and rapped out, "None, Your Honor. Not so long as it is understood that the State must seek law prescribed owing to the plethora of sexual battery priors . . . "

At the word "plethora," Judge Trepanian started. Quickly he recounted his fingers, then lunged forward, scribbling frantically. Slapping down the pencil, he leaned back with a fatuous smirk.

Why he's doing a fuckin crossword puzzle, Joe almost laughed aloud.

"Manuel Echeveria," Judge Trepanian charged the pachook. "Are you aware that in entering a plea of guilty today you are waiving your right . . . What *is* it, Bailiff?"

The bailiff trotted to the bench; motioned the judge to bend closer. A fervent whispered exchange ensued. The judge's face mottled; his eyes popped. He motioned the bailiff away, leaned back and addressed the P.D. sternly: "I have been informed that the defendant at the rail, Señor Echeveria, is charged with nonpayment of child support and driving without a license. The accused rapist to whose charges you have addressed the court is named Manuel Escobar. Señor Escobar is currently standing trial in another court for the subsequent murder of that rape victim!"

The P.D. gulped, fell back in his chair and began frantically shuffling through his threefoot stack of case files. Joe regretted giving him a hard time in the bullpen. The practice of overloading Public Defenders with every kind of case from juggling expense accounts to human heads was as unfair to them as it was unjust to their clients.

The judge turned back wearily to the docket. "Señor Echeveria. Do you speak English? No? Well, is there an interpreter in court? Okay, you'll do"—as the other Mexican rose to his friend's side—"Bailiff, let the prisoner stand . . . Señor Echeveria, do you promise to make the payments to your child ordered by the Court?" He waited for the translation; lots of enthusiastic nodding and doffing of invisible sombreros. "And go to the Department of Motor Vehicles and obtain a driver's license? Good. Case dismissed." More excited gestures of gratitude as the judge measured the wounddown clockwork of the municipal soul with three weary bangs.

"Call line fifteen, Joseph Holly Speaker"—the judge gunned the P.D. an arch look of scorn—"unless Mr. Speaker is already domiciled on Death Row." This witticism drew a crop of ghoulish cacklings from the Senior Jurists' Auxiliary.

The Assistant D.A. read the police report into the record, including Tarzon's narrative of apprehending Joe with the Porsche, then presented its sole witness, one of the parking valets. A regular rattailed Romeo with padded shoulders and pointy sideburns. He identified himself as Horace Desmond, a drama student working his way through the winter and spring quarters parking cars at Rossi's Famous Seafood Restaurant. He mumbled it in an embarrassed way as if admitting to changing linen at an X-rated motel.

"Mr. Desmond, could you recognize the man again who was loitering across the street from Rossi's Famous parking lot the night in question?"

"You bet!" sang out Horace. The judge cleared his throat, and Horace hastened to amend himself. "I mean, I can . . . I *could.*"

"Kindly confine yourself to answering the questions," the judge gently admonished, "with a direct yes or no."

Horace nodded, studying his folded hands.

"Mr. Desmond!" The shavetail prosecutor paused dramatically, bouncing on his toes while Horace prepared himself for the Biggie. "Do . . . you . . . recognize that man in this courtroom?"

Horace slishslashed a shiverish eye around the court. He gave the Senior Jurists' Auxiliary a onceover in case the culprit had sneaked in disguised as an escapee from a geriatric ward. The speed moll returned his thoughtful frown with a snarl that plainly communicated her impatience to get back to chasing the American Dream counting ceiling cracks. He looked askance at the weeping mammy contingent, redoubling their rockin, wringin, and *LawsyLawsy*in. At length Horace's bright censorious eye traveled across the prisoners' docket, where Joe stood grinning at the rail. He did a convulsive doubletake. He pointed a trembling finger.

"That's him! Oh yes, that's him. Only he didnt have that . . . awful beard."

Horace would've identified the Pope were he standing at the rail in Joe's stead.

Joe asked loudly, "But can you dance?"

Judge Trepanian banged his gavel with a force that wished Joe's tongue lay beneath it.

"Counsel for the defense?"

"No questions." The P.D. didn't even look up from the file open before him; the next case, a juicy kidnap-murder, the sort of celebrity capital case which presented a P.D. with his only chance of promoting himself from court servitude.

Not that Joe couldn't have thought of several germane lines of questioning. Like had the witness picked the defendant out of a lineup? Or made him out of mug book? Or had the police just had him memorize Joe's face—not that it was necessary from his position in court. And how, across a crowded twilit street, and most likely under the influence of whatever might be a valet's drug of choice, could he be certain of the ID? Not to mention what loitering was supposed to prove. But that kind of Darrowesque defense cost money.

When the State rested with the motion that the defendant be bound over to Superior Court and requested a date for Pretrial Hearing, Joe sang out from the docket, "Your Honor, on advice of counsel, I'd like to withdraw my previous plea of not guilty and enter a new one of guilty. I have been fully informed that by so doing I am waiving my rights . . . "

Trepanian whacked Joe with the expected maximum of three years for the GTA and at the State's recommendation dismissed the narcotics paraphernalia charge. The bailiff was guiding him back to the bullpen when he spotted a mane of coarse mestiza hair behind the mammys. Kitty! She must've come in late. The courtroom began carouseling to a slow waltzing calliope pumped by his heart, and for a dizzy instant he tasted her cunt, all ocean spray and wild fruit.

The head tilted up then, showing a strange Latin face, and Joe's heart dropped to his stomach.

The bailiff thrust him into the bullpen. He stared around, wildeyed. A black jumped back and hollered—"Whoa! *I* dint sentence yuh, homey."

Back in the tank, Smoothbore was showing Clovis how to fold and weave empty cigaret packs into a picture frame. It was an indigenous jailhouse art, as sacred as lying. Smoothbore was more adept with silver foil than what he called his silver tongue.

"The real trick is closing the square, tucking the last pack into the first," the drifter schooled the punk.

Joe stood nearby, staring at his image in a metal jailhouse mirror. His bentnosed reflection further bent by the warped sheet of steel was the only proof he had that time didn't stand still. The beard he'd grown in jail served an unexpected function—it measured time. It became a living standard of change in the dead changeless world. The slow attenuation of jailhouse days first flossed his cheeks, then trailed mosslike tendrils; now he could curl it around a forefinger.

"Here, kid." Smoothbore handed Clovis the finished frame. It should have held a picture postcard of the Virgin over the washbasin of an Ensenada whore.

"Thanks!" gurgled Clovis. Rapture lit his face like a Christmas ornament. Wondrously he ran his fingertips over the interlocking foil tiles; he held it up to the light to adore its true geometry.

"Now when yer girlfriend sends in her pikchur, you got someplace to show it," Smoothbore told him.

"*I* aint got no girlfriend," Clovis came clean.

"Then whut pikchur you aim to stick in there?" Smoothbore scowled, suddenly suspicious. An artist, after all, has a right to know what uses are made of his work.

"Mama's," Clovis declared, quickly stashing the frame beneath his bunk, lest the dexterous drifter turn Indian giver.

Smoothbore borrowed the cholos' traditional gesture of disdain, shaking invisible water from his fingers. He grinned, rolling his eyes at Joe.

But the grin Joe returned was slack and queasy. The conversation reminded him again of mistakenly ID'ing Kitty in court. As much as he resented her for not being there, for being so indifferent to his fate as to ignore its moment of decision—he resented her even more for resembling the strange chicana in court. He blamed her for the misidentification as much as if she had deliberately perpetrated this hoax.

"You still thinkin on yer girl," Smoothbore guessed.

Joe nodded. A thought swirled up in his mind, sudden and chill as a winter wind through a hidden crack in the wall. Had she guessed the truth about Rooski, did she know Joe's most silent beef? Had killing Rooski killed whatever in Kitty hoped to love him? . . . No, that was impossible. Kitty would understand why he had to do it. It was nothing more noble than a stiff dick that kept her away.

Concern luffed Smoothbore's toothless lips. He'd seen the symptoms enough times to know they were best addressed gently but directly.

"Jody's gonna get him some leg," the drifter said.

Jody was the moniker all prisoners christened the anonymous lovers inevitably taken by their wives and sweethearts. The sated shadow in the female glance across a visiting room table, the invisible writing between the lines of censored letters, the unknown eye behind the camera at which women smile knowingly and children stare in mute confusion. The cholos called him Sancho.

"Dont pay bein jealous," Smoothbore further advised. "Jist cuz you gonna be slammed up three years dont make her a nun."

"Jealous?" Joe guffawed. "I used to *pimp* that bitch."

"You cant let Jody live rent free in yer head, Joe," the drifter continued in the same tone, having seen the act before. "That's hard time. If you cant shine him on, you gotta cut her loose . . . Unless you too hard in love."

Joe arched a blasé brow. "Not me. Love's too dangerous. It needs victims."

After Lights Off Joe lay on his belly gripping the bars at the head of his bunk, feeling their cold travel through his bones. Of course, another man; Smoothbore was right: a woman had her needs and had to do what she must to get by, too. Shine it on or turn it off. Accept or reject, that simple, he told himself. But he couldnt sleep for all their memories replaying with the stagy innocence of home movies in his head. He tried to think of other things, of being processed through the system like a hunk of meat through the packing plant he once B&E'ed, of the things he might do when he raised the streets and recovered the Moon. Yet his mind was drawn back to her like a metal filing to a magnet; no abstraction could displace the visceral anguish of her big ass and chichis wrapped in another's arms. Just the thought of it set those longgone lost and lonesome blues howling down the canyons of his heart.

Whore!—that denunciation dampened the selfpiteous echoes. Furiously scolding himself, *You're beating up on your heart for another just like her!* Your mother, yes. Doubledamn that bitch for sucking and fucking the nameless legions of pachook lettuce pickers, cotton stompers, and tomato sorters, while he watched with baby hands clutching playpen spindles the way the grown ones now gripped cold steel bars; condemning the undefended infant heart to hunt forever her unregenerate ghost.

While down the restless jailhouse line a solitary black voice skitskatted just for Joe:

> *Aint no use in lookin back*
> *Jody's gotcher Cadillac*
> *Aint no use in feelin blue*
> *Jody's gotcher girlfriend too.*

WRITING ON
JAILHOUSE WALLS

||||

"**S**olly on Pawnshop says Tarzon's been checking the hock sheets for a diamond," Quick Cicero droned through clenched teeth. His jaw was wired shut to set the cheekbone fractured in the terrace pistolwhipping.

"So he knows we lost it," Baby Jewels wheezed. "The Hooten bitch couldnt have told him, she didnt know."

Quick winced rolling his neck and hitching his shoulders. "He's also scanning the computers nationwide for diamonds missing or stolen."

"*Tch.* I heard Tarzan was king of the jungle, I just didnt know the asphalt kind . . . "

"Tar-*zone* . . . "

"I know, shmuck! You ever heard of a joke maybe?" The ringed fingers drumming the desk trembled gaudy lights. Seeing the hurt clamped on his henchman's mouth, the Fat Man relented. "Never mind, I'm a little tense. Why dont you fix me a bromo?"

Quick ran a glass of water at the wet bar. Though the parlor upstairs remained closed following the raid, the downstairs office was restored to working order. The filing cabinets ransacked by Faria and company had been neatly rearranged against the velvetflocked wall. The babyspots jiggled askew by trampling police boots were retrained on the framed photographs. All that was missing was the staccato of highheels from above, the cynical tinkle of whore mirth, the throbbing juke measuring the pulse of ejaculant members. Yet these sounds, as much music to the twat trader's ears as stuttering tickertape to other brokers, would soon resume. Baby Jewels didn't expect the Tender Trap to stay closed long.

Quick tore open a foil packet, dropping a pill in the glass, and handed his boss the fizzing beverage.

"It's no wonder he knows," Baby Jewels gurgled between gulps. "We've got half San Francisco helping us look for it." He drained the glass and belched daintily into a fistful of bright lights. "You got the line on this guy yet?"

Quick produced a small leather notebook from his jacket and flipped it open. "Rick Tarzon. Homicide lieutenant. Widower, wife murdered . . ."

"What?" eructed the Fat Man.

"Murdered," Quick repeated. "Got zotzed by burglars she surprised on their boat . . ."

"*Tch.*" Baby Jewels wagged his head and popped a lozenge, which he sucked ardently, like kissing a holy relic. "*Tch . . . tch . . . tch.*"

"One daughter," Quick went on. "Whereabouts unknown. Remember he mentioned her?" A menacing waggle of lights spurred Quick to get on with it. "Came up through the ranks in San Diego. Transferred here laterally to fill one of the vacancies created by the police corruption probe two years back. Lives alone near the Presidio. No known vices, unless you count two packs of Hav-A-Tampa Jewels a day. Works strictly solo. When he needs backup, uses State Police Tac Squad. Rogue all the way. Word is his superiors wont buck him. Maybe he's got goods on them . . ."

"No," the doll voice wearily wheezed. "If he had goods, he'd turn them over. They just dont want him to start looking. You just gave the classic profile of the supercop." The fingers resumed drumming the desk, a miniature bank of neon. "Exactly the kind I didnt want dogging my heels after the Moon. Or am I dogging his?" He wheezed mountainously. "We got anyone in Homicide to copy the Monday file for us? It would help knowing what he knows."

Quick twisted his mouth, narrowing dead eyes that awaited only a bullet between them to close. "Homicide aint got her jacket. Tarzon dont trust SFPD. He had the Attorney General flag the Monday case *California Security*. The jacket's locked in the State Police barracks vault in Sacramento."

"He's leaving nothing to chance." Lavender wafted across the desk as it always did when Baby Jewels sucked hard in thought. Then he smiled, pink brow fat swallowing his eyes like snails gulping pebbles. "Maybe he knows we've lost the diamond, but he cant know *what* diamond. If he did, he'd already have braced the shvartze and billed us for zipping his squeezy toy. So we're still in this hunt."

"We'll beat him, boss."

"*Tch*. Alone he thinks he's gonna do what all the powers in the state cant—bring me down."

"Sick mother's dreamin."

"It's one dream I cant have come true . . . Now listen. Supercops like Tarzon always got secrets. Call them chinks in their armor, Achilles heels, whatever. They spend their lives trying to make good for some wrong of their own. They bluff every hand never to show that hole card, reveal their guilt. But you have to know which hand to call or they'll beat you every time. You got to follow him, Quick. Find his weakness. Study him, *feel* him . . ."

"Check."

"But dont try secondguessing him or calling him out. The best cops, just like the best crooks, got crystal balls for brains. A sixth sense. Just tail him, see who he visits. Then you visit them, find out what they told him, only make *sure* he doesnt find out."

This carte blanche for carnage so elated Quick that he forgot his jaw was wired. The sudden smile forking his mouth suck whistled pain through his teeth. Carefully he resheathed the tiny gold pen in its nifty leather scabbard along the notebook's spine, imagining it was an icepick he was sliding at fortyfive degrees up the base of Tarzon's skull.

"You got a line on the chink brothers, what's their name?" asked the Fat Man.

"Sing. And that's just what they'll do as soon as I strike up the band. Only, ever since we drowned their chemist, they've been slippery as hell. Maybe it's all the eels they eat."

"*Find* them, Quick. *Talk* to them. You can be *so* persuasive when you want," cooed the Fat Man, liquidly as a lovebird.

This time Quick remembered not to smile.

Joe sat tracing the crudely engraved outline of a cunt on the gray steel table. It looked like a halved prickly pear. Etched beneath it was the legend PEDRO DE TENTH Y HIDALGO, 203 P.C., 2-10.

There came over his shoulder a sound like wind rushing through dry weeds: "Those were the good ole days of the indeterminate sentence. Mayhem's a flat four now. No room for play."

He turned; saturnine Whisper Moran, a smile playing in the shadow of his cap, the sourceless glimmer of a cave pool.

Joe said, "Why dont they paint over these things?"

Whisper circled the table and sat opposite Joe. Laughter dry as a sack of beans shook in his throat. "*Cant* paint over them. Dudes write their names on jailhouse walls so they can come back through and read them . . . Or so the superstition goes."

"You dont seem the type to truck with superstition."

"Stare at one long enough and it gives up some truth . . . How about a hand of casino?" Whisper produced a deck of cards from his coveralls' breast pocket. Fanning them north and south, he sprang a rainbow flourish between his palms, shuffled them twice in midair, and slapped them down for Joe to cut. "Hear you pulled a trey. We'll be on the same penitentiary chain Monday morning. They violated my parole. That's Life Without. They want to bury me so far under the pen they'll have to pump in daylight." He chuckled, the creaking of a rusty gate, *arrchh arrchh.* "Unless they can gas me for this fresh homicide . . . Cut."

Tapping the cut deck with his forefinger, Joe started at the thump of a ventilator down the line. The nightmare returned: again he felt the threshing suction, heard the meaty flutter, stared once more into deepset eyes beneath a crooked cross. Maybe telling Whisper of the Sick Bay slaughter would end its terrifying reprises. Edging up to it casually, he said: "I hope I make it inside. Shit comes down I dreamed of, and I've been around some corners."

"You'll make it," Whisper said, his voice like the svelte snicker of the cards he dealt. "Just remember, never take any shit that comes down to the Man."

The unexpected enjoinder woke Rooski's ghost, a guilt tugging Joe's guts, a need to confess swelling in him with the pressure of orgasm. He asked, "How about another con? One I trust?"

Whisper shook his head. "Not unless you trust your worst enemy. You dont front off friends with secrets they dont need to know. I seen bocoo dudes shanked for being talked to out of school." Whisper slapped down the deck, scooped up his hand. "Just remember, homeboy. Do your own time, hold your own mud. It's simple, just aint always easy."

Joe resigned himself to living alone with the horror of Rings's dismemberment as he must live alone with his own iniquity.

Through the second hand Whisper schooled Joe on the secondary commandments for staying alive in the penitentiary:

"Dont fuck with sissies, they'll put you in a cross every time. Dont gamble, you end up unable to cover your losses and stone cold dead. Same for narcotics, you'll dig your own grave. Ditto borrowing. I've seen dudes gutted for a pack of cigarets paid back a day late. Then, if you're lucky enough to hit that gate, dont look back . . . "

By the time Whisper blitzed him for the third straight hand, Joe suspected the killer was using conversation as a diversion while he dealt seconds. The ironic glimmer in the cap's shadow when Joe cried uncle, refusing a fourth hand, seemed to confirm it. Whisper boxed the deck and returned it to his breast pocket. He folded his hands and said:

"There's one last rule, maybe the most important. I noticed you staring the other day at these . . . " Whisper touched the tattoos clustered at his throat, the SS runes, the iron cross, the delicate blue butterfly. "Aint no security in clicking up. If you got a problem inside, joining a prison gang only gonna worsen it."

"But you—?"

Whisper laughed like a ripsaw. He swept off the Dodgers cap, smoothed back the pomp, and refitted the Ebbett's Field relic even lower over his eyes. "Yeah, I'm A.B. A charter member, so to speak. Now General. Head chingaso in the Aryan Brotherhood. But before you get impressed or anything lemme put you wise . . . "

The way Whisper ran it down, before the midsixties, there were no racial gangs in California's penitentiaries. Every joint had its tips for controlling dope and prostitution and gambling. But they weren't coordinated throughout the system, nor racially based. Yet within prison populations, blacks protected blacks and Hispanics looked after their own. It was an instinct brought out of the ghettos and barrios. The whites, accustomed to their majority in the real world, lacked this instinct. No white stood up for another simply because he was white.

"That's the way it was when I first came in on a burglary. They carried me to the Glass House, the old L.A. County jail. The second night they brought in a pretty young whiteboy. Right at the gate, the niggers took his cigarets. He asked the other whiteboys for help, they told him to cover his own ass. When he made the canteen cart, the beaners ripped off his zuuzuus and whamwhams. The rest of the whiteboys just watched. That same night the niggers and chilichokers dragged that boy back to the showers, gagged him with a sock, and ran a train on him all night long. Left him half dead . . . And what did the other whiteboys do? Pretended to sleep through it. I was a firsttermer, young and scared, but half them guys were career cons . . . And here's the kicker. Along about dawn, this Arkie bohunk named Hutchinson actually got up and went back there and helped himself to some of that boy's butthole. Actually stood in line with niggers and chokes to rape his own kind.

"Well, I guess you could say the Aryan Brotherhood was born that night in the Glass House. A group of us who'd been there went to Quentin together. Including Hutchinson. We got together, just a bunch of lowlife bikers and white trash, and decided something had to be done. Whites had to start watching white backs. The Black Muslims and Mexican Mafia were already on the line . . . We caught Hutchinson in the Auto Shop and I run a tie rod through his heart . . . " Whisper paused. Deep ironbarred shadows leaned through the shallower shade eclipsing his face. "I was a fool kid then. A punk gunsel out for a rep. I put on a big front, but underneath I was scared shitless. You'll meet the type inside. Brave enough to die but scared of the dark . . . I didnt give a fuck about protectin whites. I run that tie through Hutchinson to make my bones, to belong. I was too scared to stand alone. I'm tellin you that just in case you think I was bein fuckin noble or something . . . " The laugh rattled in his throat like dice in a cup. Again he touched the bolts and butterfly. "These tacks. They mark me as A.B. for life. Aint no divorce cept dyin. I'm locked in my role now, too old. If I go back to the pen, I gotta play the role on the Mainline or some punk gunnin for a rep, some punk like that one in the Glass House who killed Hutchinson, is gonna read me for weak and send me to the Clinic with a bellyful of steel . . . "

Joe was beginning to see the bolts and butterfly more as marks of Cain than badges of honor. "What do you mean *if* you go back?" he asked. "I though we were on the same chain Monday morning."

Whisper tipped back his head, studying Joe. "Never mind . . . Just remember, if you join a prison tip or click, you'll never fit in out there again. You'll just keep comin back in with more and more time till it runs out on you."

Whisper dropped his head, staring down at his folded hands as if they clasped the memory of his lost youth when glory could still be bought on the tip of a prison blade and the time he did was still on his side; and for just that instant Joe imagined the frozen blue tear fell for the Mainline years that couldn't be turned back like usedcar miles.

The ganglord sighed then, a sound like wind soughing through ragweed; his shoulders sagged. "I know, you see. My name's written on every jailhouse wall in the state."

ARSE ARTIS

||||

The Plexiglas sign creaking in the cold gritty wind blowing off the docks read, in jagged red letters like lightning bolts, CLIMAX PRODUXIONS. Beneath, studded to the rolling warehouse doors, a placard warned IF YOU ARE NOT EXPECTED, YOU ARE NOT WELCOME. It was signed with an unequivocal skull and crossbones.

Within the rolling doors, a vestibule furnished with blue vinyl couch, coffee table, and dusty plastic palm. Above the couch a poster of a daisy alongside child's print proclaiming TODAY IS THE FIRST DAY OF THE REST OF YOUR LIFE! In the far wall was a locked fire door operated by an electric buzzer, controlled by a receptionist; she was stationed behind a sliding frosted glass panel window, like those found in dental offices. A tightlipped overweight old lady of implacable mien who could have easily been a hatchet murderess or a bingo caller. The electric buzzer admitting one to the inner sanctum whined like a wicked lowspeed drill.

Through the door and down a passageway between tall black panels; sharp left, angle right, the stream of air blew chiller—out into the looming warehouse interior, a vast hollow darkness swirling with the scents of new rubber, lightly scorched oil, astringent emulsions. Thick black electrical cables snaking everywhere, a muted rockenroll pulse; from somewhere a generator's insistent hum.

To a visitor unfamiliar with the Fat Man's operations, the guillotine standing at the center of the warehouse might be mistaken for a lighting scaffold. The oblique blade was drawn up high in the echoing shadows on runners clustered with klieg lights.

Today the bluewhite beams were trained on a makeshift schoolroom scene with blackboard and desk. On her back across the desk lay a naked girl. A young man stood over her wearing nothing but a mortarboard. She was giving him an upsidedown blowjob.

The girl disgorged the long thick penis with a slurp and squalled: "Hey, I'm gettin a crick in my neck awready!"

Behind the smoking lights a collective groan rose and fell, and the cameras chattered dead. Out strutted a squat figure in leather puttees, jodhpurs, and a maroon beret. He crossed his arms over his chest and flung them wide, crying: "Cut!"

"Antoine," whined the starlet. "I'm here to tell ya Muley's too goddam big to be suckin upside down!" She shook the penis in question.

"Stella!" brayed the Mule with primal anguish.

Antoine stared at his star with fresh eyes. "You'd be *perfect* for Stanley Kowalski!"

"Yeah! Only a Polack pansy could love *this* whammer." Stella flung it aside; it sprang back, slapping her face. Eyes agog, she spread her claws for an allout attack.

"*Sugarpeachespumkinpie,*" Antoine wheedled desperately. "We must get this loop into the can. You know how much I need this for my serious film endeavors, projects in which you'll figure prominently. Remember, we artists must take *risks.*"

This shrewd appeal to Stella's higher muses averted porno mayhem at the last second. She lowered her lacquered claws and took a deep stoic breath which as much as said, "The show must go on."

But Antoine pushed his advantage, pettily reminding her, "We need total envelopment, dearie."

"I still got my tonsils!"

"Oh, silly, we could have had Horatio here."

She splayed horrified fingers across her breast implants. "Antoine, my contract says no nigras. I dont . . . burn . . . coal. A girl's gotta stand up for somethin or fall for everything. My agent told me that." Her face softened, she pouted coquettishly. "Why dint you get the lil midget, lil whosits?"

Antoine stamped his foot. "Rigoletto! And he's a dwarf. And he isnt here because your *aa*gent attached a rider to your contract stipulating no more freak fucking. So just hold your breath and take it to the cojones. We havent time to argue, this isnt Hollywood, in case you havent noticed. We're operating on a tight budget."

"Well I'm operatin on a tight neck, Myrtle!"

"You better behave, we have a *visitor*," Antoine said, freighting the word with portent. He rolled his eyes at the guillotine looming behind the set. "So let's not lose our heads."

Stella looked up to the control booth high in the shadows. A faint ruddiness tinted its smoked glass. It was the truth, Antoine wasn't bluffing. Baby Jewels was on the set this morning. And Stella would rather get a stiff neck for the birdie than a severed one.

"Awrite, Muley!" she cried, all professional trouper. "Lets play some serious hide the salami."

Antoine backed away still bowing over clasped hands until he reached the dollied camera. Frantically he waved it forward, yelling, "Action!"

Above, in the smokedglass combination sound booth and editing room, the Fat Man had eavesdropped on this artistic exchange over wall speakers banked beneath television screens that monitored the simultaneous video-taping for VCR distribution.

"*Tch*. She's getting spoiled, starting to think she can pick and choose the dicks she sucks."

Quick Cicero leaned on a panel of meters, gauges, and sliding switches. The blinking electronics underlit his battered features, producing the Spooky Effect. He said, "Next she'll be wantin a dressingroom."

Baby Jewels snorted. "Yeah. To change from nothing to nothing. Call whatever agent she's yakking about n tell him to back off or he'll be booking flea circuses . . . "

"Check."

"And Quick . . . " Baby Jewels shifted in his custom Stratolounger. "I've been thinking. The most likely way Tarzon found out we lost the rock is by one of the guys on our pad telling him. What do you think?"

Quick shrugged. His brain had absorbed too many subconcussive blows to bother with anything his boss had already thought through.

"So I want you to tell our boys on the force we found it. Tarzon may believe it and back off. I'd rather it stay lost than have him find it. But we'll keep on dragging the streets. Anything new there?"

"Blanks everywhere so far. But it's just a matter of time. Street punks cant sit on something that big. They gotta try movin it soon."

"What about the elusive Sing brothers?"

"I got a bead on the younger one. I should take him down any time now," Quick promised thickly, his head bobbing in sync with the bleached one he watched below.

"Dont just keep promising me the Moon, Quick. Deliver it."

The phone built into the Stratolounger's arm tweeted. Baby Jewels screwed the receiver into his ear and wheezed: "Speak."

The hurried crackling was Sidney's voice. The Grand Jury had come in an hour ago and handed down twelve indictments. Ten Pimping and Pandering, a False Imprisonment, and a Grand Theft Person. Sidney hadn't read them yet, but the D.A. had issued warrants, so it was best if Jules surrendered before he was arrested. Sidney already had the bail up; they could settle the collateral later. The media had the Hall of Justice front steps staked out waiting for Faria to publicly announce the indictments. Jules should enter through the basement police garages and take the jail elevator upstairs. Sidney was already at the Ninth Floor booking desk awaiting him.

Listening to his attorney, the Fat Man's jowls began quivering and his eyes sharpened to icepicks. He hung up without speaking. His face mottled like a planetarium's production of Martian storms.

"What's wrong, boss?" Quick patted himself down to make sure he was carrying the pills.

"Look!" Baby Jewels squeaked horribly, pointing.

Stella had tried to deepthroat the Mule. Tried for Antoine, tried for *art*. The second she felt his dork start its final spasm, she reached behind him and pulled her mouth down over its entirety. She made it, too. Clear to his stones. Then, for the cum shot, quickly started working it back out. But it clogged in her throat like one of the hero sandwiches it was her habit to eat before shoots as a sort of warmup stretching exercise. The pepperoni, onions, olives, and anchovies rose volcanically up her gullet, spurting first through her nostrils before the pressure built to a force that blew Stella's head off the Mule's dong like a faulty pipe fitting.

"Cut!" Antoine wailed. "Someone get some towels."

"Dumb cunt!" spluttered Baby Jewels. "She knows better than to eat before a shoot." He started gasping, slapping bright lights on his breast.

Quick Cicero bounded over and prodded two of the tiny nitroglycerine pellets in the Fat Man's gasping mouth. In a moment the gelatinous blob overflowing the Stratolounger was wheezing normally.

"Help me up, Quick. We got an errand to run."

PENITENTIARY BOUND

||||

The penitentiary chain announced itself with a big brass gnashing of keys and bellowed names and steel slamming down the line. At each tank state commitments were picked up and handcuffed to the thirtyfoot length of casehardened links. Loaded, the chain impersonated a drunken centipede; whenever it halted, those in the rear didn't hear the command and stumbled into those in front. Twice before it reached the elevators, it collapsed in a kicking, cursing confusion of arms and legs.

With a smile as big and bright as a Vegas casino greeter, Sergeant Nanu, the hulking Samoan transport officer, held open the doors as the chain wound into the elevator cage. Noting Joe's idiotic grin he guffawed, "It's the penitentiary you're bound for, not the Promised Land."

The elevator plunged to the basement police garage. The doors groaned apart revealing a black immensity blocking them, and Joe's grin fixed like a skull's. The cloying scent of lavender turned his heart to a lump of cold fat. There stood the Fat Man and Quick Cicero.

"One side, gents," rumbled the big Samoan. "State property under escort."

Baby Jewels moved like the parting of a vast black curtain, revealing the garage behind. Quick stepped to the other side. Joe could have sworn the pale furious eyes narrowed minutely, spotting him.

Then they were past, the chain wending through the blackandwhites and unmarked units and cars impounded for investigation. Chained beside Joe, Whisper Moran felt him sag and cupped his elbow. "I shoulda warned you. Fresh air'll make you sick after a coupla months in the tanks . . . Just breathe deep and slow."

Joe nodded weakly. He knew the effects of prolonged tank dwelling from experience, but was grateful to Whisper for supplying an excuse for nearly fainting. The sight of Moses and Cicero momentarily seized him with the certainty that he'd been set up for assassination. He glanced over his shoulder in time to watch the elevator shut the mismatched pair from view. Just a coincidence, he chided himself as they approached the transport van. They're only here to bail out one of their McBimbos.

The second transport officer cracked the van's rear doors while Nanu released the convicts from the chain and cuffed them in pairs for loading.

"Moonpie," Nanu marveled at a hammer huge with irondriving Big Yard muscles. "Every time I turn around I'm truckin you back from Frisco to the pen. Why dontcha at least give another county the chance to commit you?"

"San Francisco's my home," Moonpie replied indignantly.

"No, the joint's your home," Nanu returned.

Moonpie jingled like a giant tambourine shrugging. "It be secure at least. Maximum, like it's advertised. Twentyfourhour armed guard. Folks out there work their whole lives to buy theyselves into a high security community. And all they gets is their visitors announced. I dont care how many millions you gots, yo visitors aint gonna have their asses stripsearched and warrant checked like the Pie's. I breathes a sigh comin home, Sarge. Out there . . . " Moonpie shuddered at the mere thought of the parlous bricks. "It be a jungle out there."

The van vroomed up the ramp, bursting into the racketing glare of the Bryant Street forenoon. Joe choked a cry and flung his free arm over his eyes. His head throbbed like a stubbed toe; behind his lids rings exploded within blazing rings of light. Again Whisper apologized, this time for not warning him of the effect of daylight after months without sun.

Gradually, Joe could tolerate the whitehot splinters of light glancing off the glass and chrome. Through the steel mesh covering the van windows, he harvested his last free memories—the sights and sounds of a city he knew intimately, but which seemed already strangely unfamiliar.

The smallest details stood out, pinning themselves like tiny bright flags on the map of his perceptions. A bay window framing a jungle of houseplants behind the reflection of the Transamerica Pyramid; a fourfoot wooden wingtip shoe swinging over the doorway of Pepo's Shoe Shop. The bright brass concentricities of a streetcar bell; the fungic musk of rising dough and big brown smell of roasting coffee; the way a young girl in lederhosen flipped long hair over her shoulder while bending to unlock her car, a mother who couldn't help laughing as she scolded a child for spilling ice cream down the front of its sunsuit; the shadow of a solitary cloud turning windows bottlegreen and indigo; a west wind shivering newspapers in the hands of old men on park benches.

Crossing the Golden Gate Bridge, Joe exclaimed softly at the Pacific, rolling blue and free forever. With his free hand he gestured beyond the mesh screen. "It's so strange. Like a déjà vu . . . "

Whisper husked, "Nice place to visit, but I wouldnt want to live there."

On they highballed north to the Northern Reception Center at Vacaville, the freeway singing to the rhythm of the tires bumping over its seams. The twelve riders were oddly subdued; gathering memorabilia, perhaps, of the world they were leaving—or implanting it with grudges to one day square.

Joe watched the passing cars, trying to read lives in the blank faces behind the windshields. He thought of his mother's face under the casket glass. Funny, it was the only time she really looked like a whore, that drizzly morning at the cutrate funeral parlor behind Grand Auto in the Merced Plaza Shopping Center where the mortician had used gobs of cheap makeup to disguise the bloated scars from the fire started in her trailer by the Chesterfield she was smoking when the aneurism bubbled up and blew out her brain. They glued a cheap wig on her, not even her real color, and painted her lips redder than a strawberry sucker, pursing them in a sulky heartshaped moue, shaping the syllables forever branded on Joe's brain: "Short time, sugar?" He spat on that face beneath the glass and the Juvie officer took him out back and busted his nose and hauled him back to the detention center where it was left unset and he still could smell the rough state blanket wool soggy with warm tears and hot blood.

Past subdevelopments and convenience stores and filling stations they rolled; blossoming groves stretching to the hills, feed sheds and grain silos and roadside fruit and produce stands; gimcrack motels and fastfood stations ringed round with cars like feeding sharks; past oil wells like giant mosquitoes, steel suckers dipping deep, drawing the lifeblood of the newborn earth.

Moonpie was holding a seminar on the Northern Reception Center. Having left only a few months before, he was the van's foremost expert on Vacaville. It was there all the felons committed to the state from northern California counties were dispatched. They'd receive medical and dental exams, psychological and aptitude testing, vocational skill assessments, and counseling. These results would determine to which of the satellite penitentiaries they'd be shipped to serve their time.

"Course all that be bullshit," a hammer called Red for his rusty Brillo hair tossed in. "They send you wherever a pen be short of niggers. Democratics or somethin . . . "

"Demographics," another voice corrected him.

"Them too. Sounds scientific, dont it?" Red said. "Not that it matters. Joints all the same, gladiator schools."

Now the van was shuddering down a rutted twolaner past chainlink fences bordering a moribund orange grove. Through the naked stunted branches Joe saw the low squat sunbleached walls ranked with barred windows that stared into the lowering light. At regular intervals along interior fencework guntowers on iron stilts bristled with antennae.

They halted before tall rolling gates beside a concrete tower marked ARMORY. A large sign warned in stark red letters: IMPORTATION OF FIRE-ARMS, DRUGS, AND OTHER CONTRABAND ONTO PENAL RESERVATION IS PUN-ISHABLE AS A FELONY UNDER SECTION 844 OF THE CALIFORNIA PENAL CODE. In the light of the dying sun the tower looked swollen and red, as though about to spurt stone seed.

A group of guards loitered by the Armory. They wore forestgreen jumpsuits and laceup hobnailed paratrooper boots. Each carried a threefoot riot baton. The sinking sun flamed their helmet faceshields.

"Goon Squad," Whisper rasped.

"Who?" Joe asked.

"Search and Investigation . . . The guards of the guards, you might say. They make a practice of harassing Frisco commitments." Whisper's manacled hand gestured at their leader, a heavyset brute with sergeant's chevrons. He carried a teargas launcher slung negligently over a shoulder that pitched with his each yawing step, tripping Joe's memory, pinning his eyes wide. "That's Rowdy McGee. Dont never cross him. He's meaner than a boot fulla barbed wire."

Nanu and the other transport officer alighted from the van. A key was lowered from the Armory tower. Nanu used it to unlock a door. He took the other's sidearm and checked it with his own inside. Relocking the door, Nanu jerked a thumb over his shoulder at the van and said something. Rowdy McGee wrenched off his helmet and bellowed with laughter, and certainty hammered Joe's heart like an anvil: he was staring at the freak who launched Rings'n'Things into the dicing fan blades.

"See that patch of white?" Whisper's finger waggled, indicating the jagged swatch of dead hair slashing the brushcut Joe could never forget. "Underneath's a steel plate they put in after we threw him off a third tier at Quentin. That's how he got the limp, too. We meant to kill him but just left him meaner. Like I say, that's one motherfucker you dont want to cross."

It was Joe's turn to whisper. "I already figured that."

"Welcome home," husked Whisper.

Nanu remounted the van alone and silent. The gates rolled open, they passed within. With glazed eyes Joe stared at the bonewhite blocks of stone as if they might yield some portent of things to come. Yet the walls behind their veils of chain spoke not at all.

NOT JUST
ANY CAP

||||

Lieutenant Rick Tarzon frowned fingering the Ziploc evidence baggies on his blotter. The tags identified their contents as the inventory of the stolen Porsche. Italian sunglasses, two Pentax camera lenses, road maps, an operator's manual and maintenance log, various receipts, pens, the parking stub from Rossi's Famous Seafood Restaurant, a pack of prophylactics, souvenir matchbooks, a Fort Baker brochure, a blue ticket stub bearing the imprint of a leaping blue dolphin.

All these items the Porsche's owner, an aerospace engineer, had more or less identified as his own. After all, who keeps track of the minutiae accumulating in one's car? The only articles at which he expressed puzzlement were the rubbers and blue dolphin ticket. This Tarzon ascribed to embarrassment: the guy was married.

He slipped the Ziplocs in a buff envelope marked AUTO DETAIL to be returned this morning with the Porsche. The insurance company was raising hell at having to pay for a replacement vehicle.

"What rathole did you stash the rock in, Speaker?" he asked aloud.

He stood and cramped his hands backward on his hips and arched. His spine cracked, pushing a groan up his throat. He crossed to the office door and snatched up the venetian blinds. The slapping rattle startled several homicide cops dozing at their desks. Shaking his head in weary disgust, he plucked the packet of Hav-A-Tampa Jewels from his shirt pocket. It was empty; he crumpled and lofted it through the miniature basketball net fixed to the wall over the trash can, whispering *swisshhh*.

Reseating himself at the desk, he yanked open its bottom drawer and plucked a fresh packet from a case of Hav-A-Tampa Jewels. He started to shut the drawer when his eye flared like a horse's about to bolt. He reached slowly behind the stash of stogies and withdrew a crimson carton, a video-cassette seized in the Tender Trap raid. He set it on his blotter and stared as he had a dozen times before at the sticker photograph.

She was clamped by the wrists and neck in a chromium hightech pillory, gorging on a penis long and black as a nightstick. Her neck was twisted, aiming sideways at the camera that profound and distracted gaze of hatred Tarzon could recognize even through the eyeslits of the leather mask. The penis bulged her cheek, the same cheek that in a snapshot on his dresser bulged merrily with dulces knocked from a piñata he had hung for her fifth birthday.

It was his fault, his sin, it all began with his lie. He snapped the cheroot to his mouth, biting its plastic mouthpiece like a handgrenade pin. All along she'd known her mother hadn't died as he had told her. Even when so many years had passed, and so much of his life was constructed on the lie that he almost believed it himself, *she* knew, denunciation and damnation ever trembling in her eyes. Everything that followed that monstrous event and the falsehood invented, he believed, to protect himself, was infected with perversity. It was a disease, progressive and fatal; the cassette, had he the stomach to play it, would bare the depth of the rot.

If only he could have faced it earlier he might have saved her, saved them both. Pregnant at eleven, addicted at thirteen, a dozen prostitution arrests before she could vote. All her life she sought to prove the truth by provoking him to repeat it; she craved exactly the fate he'd provided her mother. She couldn't help it; her own destruction was all that could balance the scales, rationalize her universe. And when instead he mutely suffered her transgressions, she was forced into the streets in search of a surrogate.

And now her search was over. The cassette seized in the Tender Trap raid proved it. It's label read in jagged red letters like ones warning of high voltage, CLIMAX PRODUXIONS. Now she made bondage movies for the Fat Man. It was only one step further . . .

He must find her. Find and tell her the truth that he was at last desperate and frightened enough to acknowledge. Until he found her he must press with every resource to destroy his awful surrogate, Baby Jewels Moses. Destroy the Fat Man before he destroyed Belinda Tarzon. And for that he needed the diamond.

Firing up the Hav-A-Tampa with his Screaming Eagle lighter, he reached for the phone and punched a Sacramento number.

It was time to have another talk with Speaker.

Kitty sat nude before the bathroom mirror, knotting a towel turbanstyle around her head. The mirror was veined with gold and misted with the scented steam of the bath from which she'd just emerged. With the heel of her hand, she wiped a circular space to see her face. She frowned. Not at herself, but at the ornate bathroom. The golden fixtures in the shapes of mythological birds, the fluted blue marble seashell sinks, the sterling silver tub with lapis lazuli clawed feet, everywhere busy mosaics building geometric migraines.

No wonder Dan's wife, Melissa, took the kid and booked. Only a whore could love this Turkish bellyache. Dan must have built it with just that fantasy in focus, to keep some bustout bimbo with a big ass and chichis in a style befitting Little Freakin' Egypt.

"Shitfire," she called through the partly closed door. "It must cost plenty to make a crapper look this cheap."

"Come again, dahling?"

"Skip it, bozo!" she hollered. Jesus, what a lop. "El *Paso.*"

If there was one thing Kitty hated it was being called *dahling* like some highsociety floozie. Especially the way Dan did it, honking the *a* like a failed Hollywood actor. She knew just what he was doing lying in there on his Danslumber bed, wearing his silk monogrammed Danjammies beneath his chamois Dansplash robe—watching a kraut film classic on the VCR and reading a critical tome, copping egghead comments to drop at the upcoming San Francisco Film Festival. The fraud had been at it for a tragic week. Not that Kitty minded him boning up on his phoniness. Just so he didn't practice on her. When he did she'd remind him, "If you wanted an undergraduate soulmate, you shoulda birddogged Berkeley, not the Blue Note . . . *dahhh*ling."

She made a face, scooping a hand over her tummy; the wall was building. She tweaked a nipple. Ouch, but was it sensitive. Before it started showing she'd have to tell Dan . . . tell him it wasn't his. She reached for the hairbrush, but before she could lift it from the sink it blurred in warm, salty water.

Okay fella, I've gone all day and havent thought of you once, she credited herself, *then it just comes over me like a chill. And each new time I think of you, I have a harder time remembering you, like a dream. Oh, I remember the little things, like your voice so tough but pudding underneath and the*

*way the tip of your tongue sticks out when you concentrate on things like
tying a shoe or jacking a shot, the way you got about sex. I just cant put
you all together.*

"What's in my belly proves you aint no dream, fella," she said aloud,
cocking and aiming her finger pistols in the mirror. "I used to say I didnt
know where I left off and you began. Well I do now. Inside me, growing,
where we both end and both begin."

"Ah, the Cubist nightmare of post-Versailles Germany," she heard Dan
working on his Leslie Howard imitation through the door. "I can feel it
in my . . . my . . . my *viscera!*"

"Girl, I dont know how much more of this you can take," Kitty's mouth
muttered back from the goldveined mirror. She snatched a handful of
Kleenex and dabbed the hurryhome drops from her cheeks. Next she
slapped her face with a loaded powder puff. The sudden explosion of
perfumed particles practically smothered her. Frantically she flapped her
hands, choking in the pink dust storm. Then suddenly she was still, staring
agape into the mirror.

The powder and steam still wreathing the bathroom recalled the swirling chaff in that ramshackle East Texas barn so long ago. She'd choked
then, too, on the dust and her own impotent selfdisgust. Nate Winder was
the name of the boy she made take her up there that brassy August
afternoon to do what Papa had taught her to want, but from no other; and
Papa caught them, it was like he was laying for them, though they hadn't
seen him—caught them before it could happen even and stamped back
out to wait, roaring in the sunblasted yard with Mama trembling in his
terrible, long shadow; roiling the leaden air with whiskey fumes and fulmi-
nations, cracking his tongue like a whip until Nate came out like a man
and said he'd marry her as a man should; though Papa still backhanded
him like a woman, bitchslapped him to his knees; and none knew but the
girl that his rage was not the blameless red that sprinkled the dust, but
green.

Least of all Nate, who got up. Got up and did the Christian thing and
married Katherine Quintana without asking her even (knowing if he did,
she'd say, You neednt, you didnt, what's swelling me isnt yours) in the
clapboard church on the bluff overlooking the Gulf; then went off like the
others to the war that wasn't and did his duty, and got his fool head blown
off on a tropic upland plain for reasons he would have understood less than
Kitty even, who could no more pronounce the name of the province pasted
on the Army telegram announcing her widowhood at fifteen than give a
damn. She was wild.

They brought Nate home and buried him behind the church overlooking another summer's Gulf; folded the flag like a tragic napkin and lowered

the knottypine box into the grave beside the tiny one of the infant Mama and Papa had made her carry to term against her will. Nine months she felt the horror growing in her, crying to Mama it was wrong, a sin; and Mama crying back, *What sin?* She and Nate were married legal, a family. Behind, Papa stood scowling drunk; and when she smothered the newborn in her breasts and they called it crib death, none knew but him to whom it was son and grandson both . . . *Damn you, Papa, but not before you see proof that this second bloom is blessed of the womb whose first you poisoned* . . .

Joe learned the meaning of hard water in the Receiving and Release showers. It was like standing beneath the tailgate of a truck dumping gravel. Stepping out, an inmate fumigator frosted his pecker with a nozzle blast from the delousing canister strapped to his back like a scuba tank.

"Dont touch it, fish," warned the fumigator, using the handle for new prisoners. "Might snap off."

"Maybe it'll give it longer shelf life," Joe hoped.

Naked then, the fish were paraded past desks manned by twofingered inmate typists who recorded their physical descriptions, next of kin, religious preference, educational and medical histories. Through the barred windows Joe watched the day being squeezed down to an angry red line beyond the fences. R&R was a halflit dream of Purgatory, peopled by antic shadows who spoke in echoes. The din dizzied him, the reek of leaking adrenaline made him queasy. The absurdity of being checked into the zoo by the animals tempted him to pinch himself awake.

Once he was fingerprinted, Joe was pointed to a long table where he was issued his fish roll: blue work shirt, denim pants, brogan shoes, socks, underwear, toothbrush, and sack of state tobacco. Gratefully, Joe dressed and took his place on a bench to await his prison mugshot. Beside him Whisper sprawled, legs straight out and crossed at the ankles, arms folded across his chest, cap pulled low. He might have been dozing but for his catlike aura of quiescent vigilance.

Joe rolled and fired up a state cigaret. "Tastes like yak dung."

"You gonna lay up on the state tittie," Whisper shared some cellspun savvy. "You better get used to its juice."

"I hope I dont have to get used to guards like Rowdy McGee." Joe shuddered, wondering what fate the Goon Squad leader might devise for him if he recognized his face from Sick Bay.

"May as well. You gonna find Gooners in every pen takin numbers and kickin ass . . . "

"Not like him," Joe was sure.

"Nooo, that I'll give yuh."

"What if he recognizes you? From Quentin, I mean. From throwing him off the tier."

Whisper tipped back his head to study Joe. "He's already recognized me. By this . . . " He touched the cap's faded bill; something glinted in its shadow. "Only he's scared of it. As long as I'm wearing it, he wont touch me."

Joe asked what was so scary, it just looked like any old baseball cap to him.

"Only it aint . . . See, when the Dodgers moved to Los Angeles the general manager donated the old caps to the state. We had a baseball team at Quentin, nine of us, that old Glass House gang I told you about, and we each got one. The 'B' stood for the Brotherhood. We were wearin em that day when we came in from practice on the Yard and caught McGee alone on the third tier and flipped him over the rail. Ever since, when he sees one of these lids he spooks, like he's smelling the flowers on his own grave."

"Wish you killed him."

"Stop worryin bout McGee. You'll ship out to another pen in a coupla weeks."

Joe snorted. "Sure. Just whistle on off to gladiator school . . . "

"They aint all gladiator schools."

"But they're sure to send me to one. I'm doin a GTA with a silent murder. I heard you gotta grab a bunkframe member for a spear and a garbagecan lid for a shield to survive in gladiator school."

"Like I say, they aint all so bad. And it aint up to *them* where you go." The dice shook in Whisper's throat. "Remember who really runs these joints."

"Jack Moran!" called the photographer's assistant.

Hearing the name, the convict photographer ducked from under the hood attached to his antique camera. Already Joe had discovered convicts usually looked young for their age, as though the rancor of prison years was spent grinding down souls, sparing physiognomies. This coot was maybe sixty; tall and stooped, with a beaklike nose dropping in a straight line from his high liverspotted pate. Owlish eyes completed the impression of an old predatory bird. Eyes of two colors, Joe noticed when he turned a long face unraveling in smiles—one pearl gray, the other gunmetal blue.

"Well, I'll be snakeeyed, yeah, if it aint Whisper Moran!" The shutterbug's accent skipped lightly over his words like a flat stone across smooth water. He and Whisper gripped and shook forearms like longlost brothers. He asked, "This time whatcha in for?"

"Forever," Whisper scowled.

"Yeah you right," breathed the old bird, his gray eye dilating above its pouch of penitentiary secrets.

While the assistant dogged down the stool in the plywood booth, Whisper and the man he called F Stop cheerily reminisced about old times on prison yards. Whisper took the stool then, and the assistant swung a pegboard with his name and number beneath his chin, and Whisper swept off the Dodgers cap and smoothed his baroque pomp and even laughed at something the old con said from beneath the hood the instant the bulb popped.

Leaving the booth, Whisper said something in the coot's ear, jerking a thumb Joe's direction. The old convict slanted Joe the bright blue eye and nodded tightly.

Finally Joe was on the stool himself, directing his best deadpan at the camera.

"Amigo, look like Dillinger or Daffy Duck," the old con said. "Only remember this mug will be stapled to the jacket that goes to the Parole Board, yeah?"

With a bat of his eye, Joe changed his look from Billy the Kid to the kid next door.

The pegboard the assistant swung beneath Joe's whiskered chin read: SPEAKER, J CALIFORNIA PRISON B-83478—"Memorize your number, dude," an R&R clerk had instructed him. "You left your name hanging on the gate."

The old con finished fussing around inserting a new plate into the contraption Mathew Brady might have used and disappeared beneath its black hood. A large hand with half of the second and third fingers missing reached in front to swivel the lens delicately.

Suddenly the hand froze. It reached back flinging off the hood. The photographer's pale face rose behind the camera like an elongated moon. Wide unhooded eyes stared fixedly and confoundedly at Joe as though the camera lens had revealed some awful truth invisible to the naked eye.

"What's the matter, Pops? I aint a ghost. Not yet."

"Is the 'J' for Joseph?" Dread leadened the photographer's voice. Absurdly Joe was reminded of Professor van Helsing starting from an empty mirror to stare back at Count Dracula with a terrible new comprehension.

"Just plain Joe is fine," he said amiably. With the wild hope of escaping the gladiator schools just hatched in his heart by Whisper, Joe wanted to remain on good terms with any friend of the A.B. General. He grinned crookedly, asking: "Why? What's the big deal?"

"Oh . . . not a thing, amigo." The photographer shook his head with a peculiar diffidence. "There was a baseball player once . . . "

"Tris Speaker! Not many people remember him. He died the same year I was born."

The long face quickly rehooded itself. The flash exploded a hundred colored balls, the induction process was complete; Joe was a convict.

When Kitty entered from the bathroom, Dan was watching the kraut flick with the whore in the top hat again. She was singing with her foot on the chair. The butchy tuxedo whorefit reminded Kitty of Bermuda and Eartha and their bustout ilk.

"Ah!" Dan gasped when the Professor flapped his arms and crowed. "She's weaning him off his sanity."

"Cuttin his lil weenie right off. Shitfire."

Dan hardly gave her time to pin up her hair before he started with the sexy stuff. Lunching on her chichis was his favorite pregame warmup. Joe used to suck and nibble them like big gum drops. Dan had to scissor them in his teeth like tearing open cellophane potatochip sacks. It was tragic, like nursing a piranha.

Kitty yanked him up by his layered hair to read her lips.

"Stop."

"Stop?" His eyes were untracked.

"Like in cease and desist, buddy. My jalobies are too sensitive."

"Ja-what? Oh, nipples. I wish you wouldnt talk that way when we . . . What's wrong with them?"

"Nothing's wrong . . . Havent you noticed I've been puttin on weight, eatin goofy things like Top Ramen for breakfast?"

"Pregnant?" His eyes said such biological inadvertencies weren't Danstyle. "Have you seen a doctor?"

"Danny boy, I dont need to snuff no rabbits. I know I'm pregnant just as sure as I know I'm a woman . . . Hefty muchachas like me can tell early."

"Then I'll marry you." He might have been volunteering to go into a burning building.

"Dont want to marry you. Aint yours no how, buddy."

"You mean . . . it's *his?* But he's been gone . . . "

"It took the last time we did it." She snapped her finger. "Rang my ovaries like church bells."

"Oh Jesus." Dan buried his face in his pillow. But after a minute he lifted it from its satin grave, and it shone with a zeal as if running into burning buildings, not Danstyling America on the Make, was his true calling. "I'll *still* marry you."

"You dont get it . . . "

"Oh, you're going to abort it."

"Shitfire! Flush *my* baby to San Pedro? Say that again and I'm outta here. I'll go home to Galveston n have it n wait on Joe to raise up."

"But you cant go home again."

"Home's where all the good girls go before the credits roll."

"But him? Wait for *him*? That deadbeat?"

Kitty set her mouth hard, holding back telling him how he stacked up against Joe Speaker.

After a moment he gave in as she'd expected. "If your mind's set on it . . . At least let me take care of you. You dont want a welfare baby."

Kitty's shrug wondered what difference such labels made, not that Dan noticed, he was getting all sexy again, and she let him have his way. For the baby's sake, she needed Dan a little longer. Galveston was only a threat; the last place she'd go broke and pregnant was home to Papa's brutalities. Alone, she'd take her chances on the streets, but she couldn't gamble with the life within her.

To avenge the crack about Joe, she grudgefucked Dan. Doggystyle, she wrung expert snapper muscles slamming it shut like elevator doors, so he went limp trying to push in. An old hooker's trick to keep the little boy in every man strapped to his psychic trainer toilet.

In the dark she patted his sobbing shoulder and told him it happened to real men too, take it from a whore; and with a cheery nite nite she turned over, punching a saddle in the pillow, and hihoed off to sleepy pastures.

Joe's was the last school of fish through the inner gates onto the Vacaville midnight Mainline. Their steps echoed down the tall stone hallway, halting at each cellblock, dropping off the fish assigned to each. Joe was deposited at the last. A First Watch sergeant keyed him through and checked him in at a small desk lit by the only light in the cavernous cellblock. Overhead the tiers loomed up into a stonechambered blackness animated by myriad sounds of sleep merging into a restless hum like a phantom dynamo.

Joe followed the beam of the sergeant's flashlight up three flights of ringing steel stairs to the uppermost tier. Then all the way down the narrow catwalk to one of the last cells. He looked down once at the desk light far below and got dizzy and had to grab the handrail.

Alone, he stood in the black cell listening to the sergeant's metal steps descending the steel stairs and crossing the rotunda to the lockbox. He heard the faraway airbrake levering the doublelock thunking home in his cell gate.

He tossed his roll on the bunk and crossed to the window bars. Across moonlit folded fields shone a cluster of lights, the brightest one blue. Blue as the mysterious photographer's eye, he mused. Blue as a rock called the Moon. He clutched himself to the bars as tightly as he clung to that image of all that was left for him to believe in.

FENCE PAROLE

||||

The Interview Room was as naked and cold as the surmise narrowing Tarzon's eyes. Strewn on the table between them were the betting slips found in the house on Treat Street, some blackened and curled with blood.

"Look familiar, Speaker? That's your crimey's blood."

Joe's nostrils flared smelling death; he shook his head tightly.

"Soon as I finished booking you, I had these compared with slips seized around town by Vice. They matched those of a flyweight named Frank Stutz. Fabulous Frank makes book for Baby Jewels Moses. That's how I knew you and Rooski took off the Fat Man. The revolver and masks found behind the theater confirmed what I already suspected finding Rooski with the Mossberg, that you'd pulled a switch with the Sings."

Joe swallowed hard and fingered one of the slips. "Your thing crystal channeling or just an oldfashioned Ouija board?"

"Is being an asshole a fulltime job or do you take a day off now and then?"

Trying to screw up a grin half as enigmatic as that encasing the Hav-A-Tampa Jewel, Joe succeeded only in looking sick.

Dentalwork flashed brightly to the side of the Hav-A-Tampa Jewel. "Didnt expect to get the diamond, did you?"

Joe crushed his lower lip between his teeth to still its trembling. "You better send that seegar to the lab for analysis."

"I'm as sure you got it, asshole, as I'm sure I'm goin to get it back." The seegar erected like a Minuteman in his wintry smile.

"You may be playin with a full deck, only with an extra joker."

"It aint just a diamond you stole, Speaker. You stole the key to lock the Fat Man in the little green room . . . I'll put my cards on the table. All fiftyfive of them, asshole. Give up the diamond and I'll have your sentence modified to time served."

Joe spread a grin that would have dripped canary blood had it been a cat's. "You shouldnt lay your cards on the table until all the bets are down. Supposing I had the diamond and gave it up. What's to keep you from giving me up to the Fat Man? Let him do what you and the state cant, execute me."

Tarzon's badge was displayed from the wallet tucked in his breast pocket. He tossed it on the table. "I swear on my shield."

Joe puffed his cheeks and gunned the cop a chary sidelong. "I've had such a wealth of sanctified oaths broken right over my head, you must be kidding . . . Besides, it might be against my principles to give up Moses. Maybe I'd rather walk the Yard a man than the streets a punk . . . "

"You didnt have any qualms about snitching off Rooski . . . "

"So say you."

From an inside pocket Tarzon produced a cassette player; set it on the table and pushed PLAY. Joe heard his own voice muffled by the dragon jacket: "183 Treat . . . Chakov . . . armed . . . wont be taken alive . . ." Tarzon punched STOP and tucked the player back into his jacket. From another pocket he pulled out two short rolls of graph paper. He laid them side by side before Joe. Each was marked with parallel jagged lines.

"As you know, all 911 calls are recorded. I also recorded our first interview. These are voice prints. Perfect match."

Christ! This guy's a one man police state!

Tarzon leaned back and laced his fingers behind his head. "Lemme explain my feelings, Speaker. I know it was Rooski skulled the gook. You may be a chickenshit, but you're too crafty to panic. I'm sworn to enforce legal technicalities like the felony murder rule. But they dont govern my personal morality." He paused, blinking thoughtfully. "As for what you did to Rooski . . . what you made *me* do . . . I think you're sensitive and bright enough to suffer all you should for that without my help. You've got that idiotski's ghost on your bedpost the rest of your life. So I got no personal problem with you . . . But *Moses*"—he hunched over hands folded so tightly their knuckles glowed red and white—"he's a whole other breed, a stone killer. He gets his cookies dusting whores. They've been showing up dead in motel rooms and under wharf pilings and in car trunks for years.

There's talk he uses them for . . . weird movies. And they'll keep on showing up dead if you dont help me here."

Joe's eye was caught by a photograph behind cracked plastic in the wallet on the table. It was the same girl from the first communion portrait on the Lieutenant's desk, several years older, in cowgirl togs atop a Shetland pony. Her broad mouth, button nose, and black bangs reminded Joe of someone . . .

Tarzon's hand snapped up the wallet, returning it to his breast pocket. "Did you hear me?"

"Yeah. Girls who work for Moses have a way of dying for him."

"Then help me put this monster away."

Why? Joe wanted to ask. To save the whores who sign on as his victims? No, I gotta protect what future is possible before all that's left me is a past. He noted a strange light playing in the cop's eyes, a tic wriggling on his brow. Tarzon's got more than just a professional interest in this thing, Joe told himself. He's obsessed.

"You shouldnt take Moses so hard," he said. "As long as the world has stones, his type will crawl out from under them."

Tarzon's temples stretched tight as drums. "It's personal. More personal than you could imagine, judging from your jacket."

The phrase echoed teasingly, like the first two bars of a song whose third trembles just beyond recall.

"I beg you, Speaker. As a human being. Give up the diamond."

The desperation wringing his voice gave Joe heart. "I cant, Loot. I dont know anything about any diamond."

"You seem pretty goddam sure you're the only person alive who knows you stole it."

As he had a hundred times since the Kama Sutra caper, Joe reviewed the cast. The Sings were standup, having the Golden Boar goods on them was superfluous insurance. Belly Blast was gone from her crib when he laid the drawings out to Rooski. And Rooski, well, unless they raised him in a séance . . . That left only Tarzon.

"You keep forgetting. For the record I dont know any more about a diamond than I do a gook pharmacist or fancy sports car."

The homicide cop's eyes sharpened to gimlets; he screwed the cheroot into a rictus snarl. "You're the one forgetting. When I offered you your freedom, I meant from the grave, not just these walls. Because dealing with me's your only chance of survival, Speaker. When Moses finds you you're dead."

Joe smirked at the empty scare tactic. Baby Jewels couldn't find him out unless Tarzon gave him up, and Tarzon couldn't betray him and still hope to recover the rock himself. Only if he surrendered the diamond was Joe in danger. He couldn't count the number of characters he'd known who'd believed police promises and divulged evidence and been thrown to the dogs. The same way that crooks scorn citizens who fall for their schemes, cops scorn crooks who succumb to their enticements. And that contempt compounded with the hatred Tarzon must already feel, despite his denials, for being set up as Rooski's executioner . . . No, Joe must keep the timeless blue tear a secret; it was his only protection.

Yet he felt no security in this, instead he suffered a bitter selfmocking despair. He deserved to die for what he did to Rooski, something deep in him cried out for annihilation; but now his worthless breath was preserved by a lunk of crystallized carbon. Christ! Sentenced to survive! A black hilarity seized him like an ague.

"Funny?" The cheroot was slung low in a frown. "Where's the comedy in dying?"

"Not dying," Joe giggled. "Living's the joke."

"You'll be calling me when Moses runs you to ground."

"I sure hope to fuck not." Joe rose to knock on the door for a guard. "Watch your back in there . . . motherfucker."

Joe made Yard with Kool Tool Raoul. A Mission District dopefiend, Tool was also jefe of the Guerrero Caballeros, lowriding rivals of the Mission Dukes with whom Rigo La Barba was affiliated. The tattoo on Tool's shoulder read MI LOCA VIDA, the cholo version of BORN TO LOSE. This scrawny pendejo wheeled a mutant '65 GTO which he claimed could outjump *Crystal Blue Persuasion*, though the Imp and Goat had never showed down.

Tool and Rigo were bitter enemies on the streets, but in the pen, both being members of urban barrio gangs, they automatically became members of La Eme, the socalled Mexican Mafia, and were now sworn carnales, the Hispanic term for homeboys. Sworn blood brothers, allies to the death against La Nuestra Familia, or Nesters, whose membership represented California's rural chilichokers.

Hence Kool Tool spoke civilly, if not eagerly, of La Barba on the prison yard. *Si*, it was correct that La Barba was in la pinta. But he fell in SoCal lifting from a San Diego gutter drain a kilo of chiva floated under the border through the Tijuana sewer. So La Barba was at Chino now, the Southern Reception Center. Hearing these institutional euphemisms, Joe had to guard against imagining they'd all been admitted to some exclusive resort colony.

"And you, *ese?*" Joe invited the cholo to tell his own Tale.

Tool launched into a convoluted mestizo curse on the next thirteen whorespawned, doggysired generations of el jooge who took such a dim view of converting Detroit's finest into fourthousandpound steeljacketed jumping beans that he whipped twelve bowlegged Receiving Stolen Properties on the Guerrero Caballeros' spiritual advisor and sidewalk jefe for the twelvevolts in the Goat's trunk.

Making simpatico noises but only halflistening, Joe gave himself over to the sensory banquet offered by the Yard. The shouting softball players, popping handballs, jingling barbells, the June zephyr purring through the cyclone fencing—all tonic to ears long trapped in stone echo chambers; the smells of turned earth, new grass, and, faintly from the orchards across the highway, orange blossoms were giddy elixir to nostrils long stuffed with dirty socks and dayold farts; and after months of cornered inside horizons, even the featureless fields surrounding the prison seemed spectacular scenery. Joe plucked a blade of grass; chewed it and wondered when he'd tasted anything so sweet.

Kool Tool suddenly clutched Joe's shirt and pointed across the Yard, crying: "*Mira!* Dude's goin for a fence parole!"

Joe shaded his eyes and squinted into the sun. A lone convict was scrambling up the twelvefoot inside fencing. The Dodgers cap was turned backward in the flight or fight configuration.

"Ees suicide!" Kool Tool yelped.

Five hundred convicts stood stunned by disbelief. Then the silence was shattered by a cheer quickly joined by many: "Go for it!" "Git gone like a turkey through the corn!" "Hondele! Corre como el diablo!" "Hoo-*whee*, lookit whiteboy climb! Guddum spiderman what he is!" They whooped and jumped; they shucked their shirts to snap in circles around their heads, whipping on the con with the heart to hit the fence.

A warning shot rang out from a guntower. Instantly the Yard was littered with prone men in blue. Kool Tool yanked Joe down beside him. Through the broken crab grass Joe saw Whisper still climbing, his weight swaying the the fence. Reaching the top, he slung his shirt over the razor ribbon and concertina wire and scrambled over. He dropped to the access road between the inner and outer fences. Across the dirt road he sprinted and leaped halfway up the outer fence and started climbing again. Two, three more shots cracked the air. The guntower bulls had switched their shotguns for Ruger Mini-14 carbines. Whisper slumped, a groan swept the yard; he was hit. It was impossible to tell how badly. He clung spreadeagle halfway up the outer fence.

The baseball cap spun lazily through the warm spring air.

"Tack another deuce on that loco's time," Kool Tool muttered. Two years was the standard sentence for escape attempts. "Beats a tag on beeg toe though."

Joe said dully, "Deuce dont matter. He got all the natural day."

"Joo know heem?"

Joe didn't answer. He rose to one knee, preparing to run to where Whisper hung.

Tool snatched him down by his shirt. "Doan move unteel pinche tower say, *ese.* Bust cap at joo."

A pickup truck was speeding around the access road between fences to where Whisper hung. Joe saw his head move at the sound of the engine. At least he was still alive.

The truck braked to a halt beneath him. Momentarily it was obscured in the dun cloud of dust catching up with it. When the air cleared, a solitary figure in forestgreen stood by the front bumper, looking up at Whisper. Joe saw the greasy gleam of the shotgun barrel slung carelessly over the green shoulder. He was sure they were talking. Whisper's bare head was turned, looking down. Even at a distance there was no mistaking the streak of dead hair. It was Rowdy McGee.

Whisper shook his head and McGee lifted his arms and lewdly rolled his hips. He tossed back his head, laughing, and threw down the gun, tromboning a shell into its breech. It was a curious flat noise like a cough that blew a hole the size of a hubcap in Whisper's back. The impact of the blast strummed the fencing clear around the Yard.

Rowdy McGee calmly got back in the truck and drove away, leaving Whisper hanging lifeless on the fence. For what seemed an eternity there was no sound on the Yard save the harping of the wind through the fences. Maybe the others like Joe occupied their minds with inanities to forestall shock. All he could think was what would become of the Dodgers cap lying in the access road.

Then its nerveless fingers loosened, and the corpse slid down the bloodied fence, crumpling at its base on denim knees.

On the Yard's far side, a convict jumped up and screamed an unintelligible obscenity. Before the tower guards could trade their Rugers back for shotguns with birdshot loads and draw beads, the whole Yard was on its feet shaking fists and howling. Cons witnessing the murder from cells overlooking the Yard joined in the uproar. They yelled and screamed and raked tin cups across window bars. The Yard P.A. whined and popped but couldn't be heard over the tumult. Now they were dropping burning paper and bedclothes from the cell windows.

Suddenly convicts were babbling a different tune and pointing toward the Yard gates. A platoon of guards was pouring through and forming a flying wedge. They were outfitted in full riot equipment: helmets with Plexiglas faceshields, flak jackets, gas masks; they wielded yardlong riot sticks. Two jumpsuited Gooners armed with fortymillimeter grenade launchers led them in jogging lockstep.

At an unheard order, on went the guards' masks. "Gas! *Gaassss . . .*" the warning spread like wildfire across the Yard. Pop! *PopopopPOP!* They were firing the canisters pointblank into the thickest crowd of convicts. The phalanx raised its forest of long sticks and charged.

Joe bolted willynilly with the rest. The yellowish clouds billowed across the Yard. There was no haven from the gas, a saffron pall enshrouded all. Joe's eyes boiled in their sockets; his breath licked up his throat like flames. Ripping off his shirt to cover his mouth helped not at all. Now the only sounds were the guards' oaths and the choking and retching of convicts. The P.A. ripsawed through the gangrenous fog: "Face down, spread your arms and legs. Down or we fire! *Down!*"

In short order all the convicts were spread belly down on the grass where the gas was thickest. The masked guards patrolled among them, clubbing any who spoke or moved. One by one they were ordered to rise and proceed to the gates. There they were stripsearched and passed naked down a gauntlet of jeering guards.

"Awrite, you pukus delecti!" a towheaded Gooner crowed jubilantly when Joe's turn came. "Bend over and crack yo daddy some redeye, punk!" Joe bent and reached behind and spread his buttocks. The Gooner spotted the stitches and windmilled his arm for the other guards to come have a look. "We got us one's been *tampered* with . . . *big* time!" "Tampered hell," Joe heard a voice younger than his own. "There's been so much stick pussy shoved up that Hershey road they could rent it out for a convention center . . . " "Why, rub a little anchovy on that button n I might jist believe it was real pussy . . . " On and on, an anal liturgy fouling the balmy June air with a drone like typhusladen mosquitoes.

It was twilight before the Yard finally was cleared. Joe watched from his cell window the last con being searched and run inside over the bodies of those who'd fallen beneath the gauntlet's clubs. Stretchers had to be called to collect these as well as the several bodies still lying on the scrabbly grass by the pitcher's mound. From the shrieks and bright splintered bone sticking through prison blues, Joe surmised they'd been hit by deliberately aimed canisters.

Finally no sign of that afternoon's atrocity remained, save the shape still kneeling where it had dropped at the base of the outer fence. Whether it had been left purposefully on display or simply forgotten, Joe didn't know. While every P.A. in Vacaville blared over and over: "Lockdown, Lockdown . . . Remain standing by your bunks for count . . . General Lockdown . . . " Joe stared at the corpse genuflected in the mud of its own blood and marveled that his dream of the man he might have been had taken flesh just long enough to denounce itself by dying, as if to expose Joe's own delusions. On he stared at the crumpled form merging with the gloom, stared until his eyes burned as though some avenging specter of Whisper Moran conjured by the sheer force of Joe's outrage might yet arise from the dim ravening dust.

THE GRAY GOOSE

||||

The transport dock faced west where the last stars were melting on the coral lip of dawn. It had rained the night before; inky pools reflected a sky darker than the one above, filled with rosecolored clouds. The Vacaville cellblocks were trimmed with bright runnels of water tinseling in drains. The cold wind cracked Joe's cheeks.

Alongside the dock idled a converted Greyhound bus. Painted battleship gray, its windows were welded shut and screened with steel mesh. Black fumes growled from its diesels.

"I'm just glad my mother didnt live to see this day," cooed a familiar voice beside Joe. "She'd never understand why I couldnt come home weekends."

It was Oblivia, who had arrived at Vacaville a week after Joe. She was hardly recognizable without her tinsel wig and warpaint. Surprisingly, she hadn't fallen for the old rip and run at the Blue Note. Turns out she had some side action the Manager didn't know about. During the day, Oblivia would dress up as a nurse, sashay into hospitals, and loot their pharmacy stores. Until the day the security guard caught her. She had the rentacop half convinced she was looking for a job application in the narcotics box when the real heat arrived. The sergeant was writing her a summons for simple trespass when out of her pocket fell a forged Dilaudid prescription. So it was down to the station for a full booking. The sergeant called for a matron to conduct the stripsearch. That's when Oblivia said, "Cmere, buster. I got something to confess." "I already know," said the sergeant. "You're not a nurse."

"This Gray Goose stops at Quentin, Soledad, and Coldwater, Barker," said Oblivia, shaking her chains at the idling bus. "Where you tagged?"

"Coldwater," Joe said. He'd discovered this just an hour ago from the owlish convict photographer who was also under transport. He was waiting at the head of the cellblock while the guard woke Joe and told him to roll it up. By now Joe knew his name was Earl Fitzgerald, and the convicts called him F Stop. Coldwater, he told Joe in a musty mutter, was no country club, but it wasn't a gladiator school either. At this favorable turn of fate Joe felt that familiar bitter blend of joy and grief. Whisper must have fixed it. With a smile he remembered the ganglord's assurances that it was the animals who ran the zoo. Why else would the convict photographer be shepherding him? Whisper's old friend was the executor of his unwritten will.

"Goody!" trilled Oblivia, jumping up and down, jingling her legirons. "That's where I'm going. It's just like camp!"

F Stop stood shackled in front of Joe, holding a cardboard orange carton elevated like a monstrance. He turned and frowned at Oblivia.

"Oh, Barker," Oblivia gushed on. "You dont know how long I've dreamed of being on a desert island with you . . . but prison will do in a pinch." Like a debauched Gila monster she vibrated her tongue at him.

Over the rumbling diesels Joe heard a fourth convict warbling "Witchcraft." He smiled recognizing Duck Butter's felt falsetto. It was the same ditty the highyaller hophead would sing to signal he held junk for sale as he strolled down Eddy Street, trailing dopefiends like the rats of Hamlin.

His smile turned up full wattage when Duck Butter emerged onto the transport dock carrying Spencer in his arms. "Small world," Joe said.

"Got a way of shrinking inside these felony spas," Spencer chirped. He looked even frailer out of his wheelchair, reminding Joe of religious pictures of the dead Christ lifted down from his cross. "State's gonna give me a new one," Spencer answered Joe's query about the absent wheelchair. "That's why I'm going to Coldwater. It's got the biggest hospital in the system."

"Which is how come I be headed there," put in Duck Butter. "Where else they gonna make good use of my bedside manner, my deft shooter's touch."

Gates crashed behind them, and a hoarse bawl rang around the tiles of R&R—"DEAD MAN WALKIN!" The cry was meant to protect a condemned man from the other convicts as he was escorted through their midst. No killer behind these walls was as implacable and jealous as the state. Joe and the rest parted as silently as smoke allowing the Death House detail to pass. It was a slight Filipino teenager carrying more than his weight in chains to his date with the gas chamber. He wore white transit coveralls like their own, only on his back was stenciled DEATH ROW. The two guards escorting him looked in need of the same tranquilizers slackening the boy killer's jaw and leadening his feet. He stumbled on the dock steps, and they gripped either elbow, lifting him to the bottom, then dragged him across the gravel, his lifeless toes plowing wobbly furrows all the way to the station wagon marked DEATH ROW, SAN QUENTIN.

"Load em up!" halloed the transport officer once the death wagon had departed with a wet surge of gravel.

Joe and the others chinked down the steps and boarded the Gray Goose by its front passenger door. The last two rows of seats had been removed and a widemesh steel screen erected, turning the rear of the bus into a gun cage. A transport guard armed with an autoloading shotgun climbed into it through a special door cut over the rear wheelwell, which was locked by another guard from the outside.

The Goose had landed at Susanville and Folsom to the north during the night and was half filled with sleeping convicts. Oblivia woke several she knew with little shrieks. After Spencer was deposited up front by the driver, she and Duck Butter took seats together in the middle, where they'd be least visible having sex. It amazed Joe how seamlessly Oblivia made the transition from street to prison, scarcely missing a beat.

He and Earl chose two seats nearer the front. Joe tripped over his legirons and somersaulted upsidedown into his window seat.

Earl chuckled, the sound of a straw sucking drops from a glass bottle: *"Errp errp.* Usta to have a sooner Catahoula, every time he run up on an armadillo hole he get his head stuck down there, yeah. Legs wavin in the air like you . . . "

"What's a sooner Catahoula?" Joe asked untangling and setting himself upright.

"Hound he grows only down the bayou and jist as soon as he do something, that's how soon he in trouble."

Joe rolled his eyes. "Earl, you said you had something of Whisper's for me . . . "

Up flew a rooty finger to the steep spotted nose. "Not till we on the road, no."

Joe shrugged: all he had was time. The old bus crashed its tired bones in gear and roared out the Vacaville gates. One last time Joe looked back at the vast stone warren, saying a silent farewell to Whisper Moran.

Down Interstate 80 the Gray Goose flew, then skirted the northern rim of the bay. Joe watched a flock of egrets stepping with infinite cautious grace across the mudflats. At the howl of diesels they took sudden flight, beating slow wings in unison, stopping at once to glide long and smooth ten feet above the gray ruffled water, solemn with memories of prehistory.

"There she is," Earl pointed. "The Big Funhouse."

San Quentin's storied walls shone salmonpink. The massive cellblocks and looming battlements reminded Joe of fairytale illustrations. Through the yawning portcullis the Gray Goose wheezed on aged airbrakes, into a court walled high with stone. At its center shivered a bed of dahlias, brave and incongruous. While they unloaded prisoners and took on others, Joe peered through the mesh at gray convict faces that might have been hewn from the same granite that yielded the silent walls.

Two of the convicts boarding at San Quentin took seats across the aisle from Joe and Earl, a hambone and peckerwood comprising an impromtu saltandpepper traveling band. All the way back around the bay, south through Pinole, Richmond, and Oakland they entertained the Gray Goose with a spirited rendition of "Working for the Man." The black hamboned on every available body part, using limp hands to thrash on thighs and arms a rebop rhythm, knuckles to knock a backbeat on kneecaps and skull, fingers to strum a melody on the flexing diaphragms of throat and tautened cheek. The pockfaced white with a frog in his throat yodeled the lyrics. Their stamping legirons and clinking cuffs punctuated phrases, and at the end of each chorus the peckerwood let rip a rebel yell dying in a lovesick yowl while his sideman knucklerolled his nappy skull, grunting "Gud Gawd Awmitey!" Then, shaking their chains like tambourines, they were off again.

Joe meanwhile leaned his cheek against the cool steel mesh and closed his eyes. The throbbing diesels made him feel peaceful and sleepy. His mother and he always traveled by bus, maybe this very one before it became a Charon's ferry for the state. She would be anxious and snippy before they embarked. Other people looked wistfully back at what they would miss; she craned dreadfully over her shoulder at what she was escaping. Neck tendons leaping, chewing her lip, she boxed Joe's ears for being such a whiny brat. But once the bus was under way, her face softened and she stroked his hair and whispered how different things would be in the next town where always a brandnew uncle awaited. No matter that they ran always into the same old trouble they'd always been through, while on the bus anything seemed possible.

They never reached Soledad proper. A contingent of guards in riot gear halted the Goose at the outside perimeter gates marked CALIFORNIA TRAIN-

ING FACILITY. There had been a double shanking on the Yard the day before and the joint was under General Lockdown like Vacaville.

Earl shook Joe awake with this prophecy: "Things keep up this way the whole damn system's gonna be locked down."

It took Joe a minute to fist the sleep from his eyes. The tense roadside guards distributed bag lunches to the Goose's riders, then herded aboard five bandaged and beaten cholos. The driver and gunner remounted front and back and the Gray Goose coughed, grumbled, doubleclutched stripped gears, and headed back to 101, backtracking north. When the running noise was loud enough, Earl gestured with his chained wrists where the new riders were seated and said, "See the skinny one with the glass eye? That's Flaco de la Oilslick, a Nester General. One evil choke, yeah."

"Dont like his looks," Joe said. "But the Nesters go with the whiteboys if shit comes down, right?"

"Yeah you right. The barrio cholos band natural with ghetto blacks. Their country cousins, like that crew, become our allies in a riot or war."

"Why they moving them out of Soledad?"

Earl shrugged. "The Department moves in mysterious ways, its blunders to perform . . . My guess is that Flaco's been ordering hits and they cant stop it. So instead of containing a problem, they spread it."

Glancing back at the startlingly white cellblocks against the azure mountains, Joe wondered if a face in one of the slit windows was offering a thanks to a God of his comprehension that the circle of blood was broken this time.

He leaned back in his chains. "Spread it where?"

"Coldwater. It's this heap's last stop."

The Gray Goose hooked off 101 onto 152, heading east, rocking . . . Through sleepy towns the Goose downshifted, where drugstores still had soda fountains and barbershops striped poles outside; where movie theaters showed double bills and old men played checkers in shaded courthouse squares.

That such burgs existed heartened Joe. On the hurtling freeway he had the disquieting sensation of being spirited away to some desolate spot where time would pass him by. Riding down these dusty streets where cars parked perpendicularly still, the way horses once were hitched, it seemed he was being transported back to a time patient enough to wait for him.

Or so he daydreamed as the diesels howled climbing the Sierra foothills, and a chill wind rattled the windows' steel mesh, and Earl began humming a tune Joe recognized, "St. James Infirmary." When Earl reached the last bar, Joe sang it softly to a close—"*So cold, so bare, so fair* . . . Thinking of Whisper?"

"Yeah you right." Earl chuckled *errp errp*, slanting Joe the bright blue. "I guess I can give it to you now. I got it when they sent me to mug his corpse."

Earl rummaged at the bottom of the orange carton between his brogans. It lay beneath ancient reams of legal papers, yellowed correspondence smuggling memories across the years, frayed postcards, a number of cracked and faded photos the old con took pains to shield from Joe's view, several bulging manila folders marked ARMADILLO. Right at the very bottom, its crown neatly tucked and folded: Whisper's Brooklyn Dodgers cap.

Earl's gray eye clouded abstractly handing it to Joe. "I bet he would have wanted you to have it," he said.

Joe slowly turned the cap in his chained hands, studying it minutely as if it held some clue to the enigma of his fate. A glowy chill suffused him, raising gooseflesh, and he would have wept were he alone.

"We're home, amigo," Earl said, pointing toward the vaulting Sierras. "The California Institute of Medicine at Coldwater."

Joe stared at the monstrous gridwork of cellblocks clamped to the purpleshadowed plain. Without thinking, he put on the cap, yanked it low over his eyes, the way Whisper Moran once wore it. Suddenly the light shifted, spreading shafts like a Japanese fan. Then clouds blotted out the sun and the fields blackened and crows cried.

PUNKS OUT
FOR REVENGE

||||

"**O**ne more dirty test, Miss Batista, and you're off the methadone program," warned Belly's counselor, a dowdy old dame who couldn't find a husband to badger and had to settle for addicts. "You've yet to give us one that hasnt been full of marijuana, cocaine, methamphetamine, and what have you."

"Dont worry, Miss Aspinwall," Belly said.

"I'm not the one who must, Miss Batista," handing Belly the plastic sample bottle and pointing to the clinic bathroom. "You are."

Fine by Belly, who had just that morning figured the way to beat this system. "Booze dont count, huh, Miss Aspinwall? I had a beer or two last night."

"Alcohol isnt a controlled substance, Miss Batista."

Good, because it was a wino Belly bribed with a shortdog to piss in the douchebag slung hidden under her arm where it would stay warm. Cold sample bottles were dead giveaways.

She waited at the bathroom door for the previous client to finish. It amused her that the clinic called its addicts clients, the same term massage parlors used for its tricks.

Inside the tiled room she went straight to the only stall, regretting that it had no door to latch. She yanked down her Levi's and sat on the bowl. Here was the tricky part: she had to reach with both hands between her legs, one holding the sample bottle, the other groping for the douchebag's tube swinging down her ass. She caught a glimpse of herself in an opposite mirror and laughed. There, she snagged the tube. Holding its end over the bottle, she popped the clip. Her smile rose with the burble of urine in the little bottle.

But at the crash of the bathroom door, her smile turned green. Miss Aspinwall and a male clinician blocked the stall opening. "That's a twoway mirror, dearie," smiled Miss Aspinwall. The male clinician grabbed Belly under her arms, derricking her off the bowl with her Levi's twisted at her ankles, to snatch the douchebag from beneath her arm. Only the prospect of an assault and battery charge restrained Belly from whipping a Missouri mule on the geek and using his head for a toilet plunger.

Triumphantly, Miss Aspinwall held up the douchebag. "Miss Batista, never darken this clinic's door again. You're going in the dead files."

Outside, dark ragged clouds wrung dirty water onto the sidewalk. Ducking her head, Belly hurried down the line of clients waiting to be dosed and crossed the street to the Early Bird Cafe. There, in a dimness tiered with grease and tobacco smoke, the clients congregated afterward to trade drugs and gossip at the chipped formica tables.

Belly spotted Gino the Pick at a front table. Gino was dispensed juice at clinics in two counties and always had doses to sell. For a jackson Belly scored an eightymilligram jug, half her normal dose, but enough, she prayed aloud, to give her the nerve to ask Aldo Tortoricci to let her back in the ring.

Gino was eager to help. Getting eightysixed from the methadone program was every client's nightmare. He asked, "Hey! Why get beat up for a buck? Why not make loops for the Fat Man?"

"Shit," hissed Belly, shaking a Marlboro from Gino's pack. "Last time Gordo had me use a rubberspiked dildo to cornhole this kid couldna been more than twelve. You gotta draw the line, know what I mean?"

"Hey! If I dont, who does?" Gino was from New York. "But at least with the Fat Man you get to pee in guys' mouths instead of bottles."

Belly screwed her mouth sideways. "You're a hoot and a half, Gino. Really a fuckin riot . . . "

"Hey." Gino spread his palms.

"But you got a point. Plus the Fat Man pays good."

"I'll say. You heard about the reward he's got out on the streets?"

"Reward?"

"A kilo of dope for the character who can finger the dudes who took down his theater."

News to Belly. Quickly, to change subjects, she asked, "You got a Valium to kick in the juice?"

"Hey! I got better, babe. Two Tylox." Gino cartwheeled the pills across the table and Belly used his cold coffee to swallow them.

"Gotta book," she said. She had to get alone to think this one out.

Splashing along the pavement, oblivious to the rain guttering down her neck, Belly believed that the way her life was going, she was due a reward. And it was hers to collect. The Barker never knew, but that day when he thought he was alone with Rooski in her crib, she was eavesdropping at the front door. She got back early from running the credit cards in the Troll's wallet—wouldn't you know they were already overcharged. Just as she was putting her key in the lock, she overheard him telling Rooski how they were going to rip the Fat Man. The Barker sounded just as crazy as the caper. It was one conversation she wasnt about to walk in on. So she tiptoed back down the hall and didn't return to her crib until after she heard Rooski was blown away.

Chica, she put it to herself, how much closer to heaven could you get than holed up somewhere with a kilo of heroin? Rooski was dead, the Barker was slammed up with nothing much more to lose. And it wasn't like he wouldn't give her up. But wait—she pulled up short in the blinking yellow neon of a barroom beer sign. That aint no reward, chica, it's *bait*. Sure, Gordo wants the info. But he aint gonna pay no key of junk once he's got it, not when all he's gotta do is off a bitch's bahakas. And you know how, too. For the dirty birdie.

A passing man mumbled something and Belly turned. "What?"

"I asked if . . ." He smiled shyly, stepping close to hold his umbrella over them both. "I asked if you maybe liked to party."

"Long as you pay the band," Belly said, hooking his arm and steering him down Mission toward the nearest motel she knew with hourly rates. The Tylox was kicking in the methadone now. She felt its warm petalfall in her tummy, its soft kiss on her brain. Playfully she skipped from beneath the umbrella, turning her button nose and bangs to the sky. The rain splashing her face was sweet and warm as blood.

Joe walked the Yard alone. It was the first time he'd been outside unchained since Whisper's slaying. The Dodgers cap felt momentarily tight when he reflected what tumult of desperate ideation had seethed within its band to vault Whisper Moran onto the Vacaville fences.

The Coldwater Yard was larger than Vacaville's and scenically grander. To the west the vast valley swooped up like an immense purple wave, trailing webs of bluegreen foam, cresting where the jagged high Diablos met an electricblue sky. To the east the sky was blocked and boxed by the white geometry of prison walls, which seemed to emit as much as reflect the lemongold light.

It was Sunday, and the Yard was fairly crowded. Five hundred or more convicts lifting weights, playing softball, pitching horseshoes, languishing on the grass, idly strolling. Joe passed among them with a strange sense of invisibility, as though either he or they were phantoms. He felt secretive but not alien. Looking around, he realized he knew none of the men on the Yard by name but all by heart. His and their hopes and fears were commingled in some pool of mutual need. They were his tribe.

It was the same with the prison. Joe had never heard of Coldwater before, he'd received no preparation or orientation. He was simply thrown into General Population to sink or swim. Yet he knew the currents, the prison's moods and rhythms; he was instinctively prepared. He was home.

He found a spot in the center of the Yard and sat. He looked around him at the hundreds of the Yard; looked toward the secretive white walls, imagining the hundreds more scurrying around their assignations like ants in a hill. Each in his own time had been born into this violent new world within a world. And the trauma of each had been reduced to something distant and insignificant like a cyclone on Saturn, like Joe's.

Home is where they can't throw you out, he decided, gazing at the walls. Home is also what doesn't change while you do. He was looking at a kind of living laboratory, a time machine almost, from which he must emerge finally and irrevocably changed, a stranger to his self that sat on the Yard; yet another fish that future day sitting where he was now would stare at the same enigmatic white geometry against the same too blue sky and be visited perhaps by the same thoughts.

"Life dont get much better," he caught himself repeating aloud the phrase he used to buck up Rooski when things could always be worse. And once more arose the seventh wave of grief, rolling his heart among stones. Sadly he was reminded that this was Rooski's home before he ever found it. If only the carrottop kook were hunkered beside him on the grass. *If only* . . . the phrase choked him with a bile of remorse and pity, the one for betraying Rooski, the other for condemning himself to live and remember.

A crowd of convicts clustered around the handball courts attracted Joe's attention, and he rose to investigate. Approaching the courts, it appeared some sort of ceremony was taking place. Two men stood together on the court facing a third with his back to the tall concrete backstop, reading aloud from a book. The rest of the convicts stood in a solemn semicircle, heads bowed.

It wasn't until he reached the crowd's fringe that Joe noticed that one of the men was wearing a dress. Well, not a dress exactly. A sheet swept over one shoulder and gathered around the waist like a sari. He also spotted Oblivia. Dipping his shoulder through the crowd to her, he felt angry stares like tentacles clinging to his back.

"Oblivia!" he whispered.

"Shhh!" she held a finger to her lips, lips which were newly daubed with orange crayon. Her hair was also freshly bleached and curled, and her workshirt knotted beneath her hormone titties, flashing a belly glistening with baby oil.

"Christ! What have you done to yourself?"

She turned an arch look of affront on Joe. "A girl wants to look her best at a wedding, Barker. Suppose I catch the bouquet?"

"Wedding? I thought this was a prison."

Oblivia lifted a plucked brow that wondered what difference that made. Over the silence floated liturgical mumbojumbo from the convict with the book. Noting Joe's stark stare, Oblivia said, "That's Swami. He's so spiritual I dont think he knows he's in the joint. He's New Age and all, but he's being a perfect dear doing a Catholic ceremony, otherwise Magdalena couldnt go through with it, her religious upbringing was too strict."

"Strict," Joe repeated dully. At a sudden gust of wind the bride turned to flick a strand of hair from large green eyes. She looked like the young Sophia Loren. The strong nose and wide cheeks, the broad compulsive mouth; the sheet's loose front baring . . .

"Christ! He's got tits as big as Bermuda's."

"The best money could buy, Barker. Maggie was two weeks from her tuck and roll operation when she fell. She was tricking Arabs in Bel Air for the rest of the money. The courts have ordered that any felon undergoing hormone treatment for a sex change operation at the time of his arrest be allowed to continue such treatment in the pen. They send them here to Coldwater. They got enough hormones in Y-1 Clinic to turn the Jolly Green Giant into Tinker Bell."

"You get free rubbers at the Clinic or do you have to buy them at the Commissary?"

"Why, Barker!" Oblivia gurgled. "Thinkin of comin out? . . . *Relax,* I'm just funnin you . . . No, condoms are contraband, like dope. A rubber'll cost you two packs of smokes."

"But AIDS? They turn men into women just to . . . watch em die?"

"You aint heard there's a little population problem?"

With a shudder, Joe turned his attention back to the ceremony. The groom was having trouble repeating some words Swami was reading to him. A hunky honcho, he wore his best starched and pressed prison blues, his boneroos, and a blue wool watchcap pulled menacingly low over his eyes. "He plays the male," Joe guessed idly.

"That's what he'd like you to think," Oblivia said in her most tired voice. "Billy Skaggs would like you to believe he just pitches and Maggie catches. But lemme put you wise, it's all baseball."

"Then why the big macho act?"

"Billy overplays the hardrock role because he's angry at being a weenie woman. The Mainline's swarming with them, punks out for revenge."

Faintly the words "pronounce you man and wife . . . " wafted up on the warm air. Swami made a sign of the cross as energetically as a football coach signaling in a play. Simultaneously a flight of pigeons rose from the nearest cellblock's roof, a pale liquid brushstroke against the chinablue sky. Billy Skaggs and Magdalena grappled in a swooning silverscreen liplock, the wedding guests whooped and cheered; from a boombox balanced unaccountably atop the concrete backstop Elvis wailed the wedding march:

> *Number fortyseven said to number three*
> *You're the cutest little jailbird I ever did see*
> *I'd sure be delighted if you'd bunk with me*
> *Cmon and do the jailhouse rock with me . . .*

Joe hadn't expected prison to be an MGM Big House where Wallace Beery and Jimmy Cagney called the guards "dirty screws" and dug tunnels with their spoons, but neither had he quite expected all of this.

"Recall, recall," the Yard P.A. scratched the pellucid light. "Return to housing for count." Joe and Oblivia joined the rest of the wedding party herding their shadows through the Yard gates.

"Christ, Oblivia. It's bad enough without you crying."

Captain Reilly's office in the Admin building faced west and was thus deprived a view of the Yard nuptials. One of Reilly's obligations was the final approval or disapproval of new guards. In former days, this was a rubberstamp process. Candidates who didn't come up to Departmental standards had already been weeded out by the rigors of Correctional Academy.

Then the doubling of inmate population within ten years coupled with a skyrocketing turnover rate among correctional personnel created an unprecedented demand for new guards. At first, accelerated academy curricula and minimal training criteria were implemented. But these quickly collapsed under the sheer weight of numbers. By now the Department was one step away from hiring directly off the streets.

That one step was represented by Reilly and the system's other line captains; their desks were the last checkpoints between the streets and the mainlines. Captain Reilly was CIM Coldwater's sole guarantor that it wasn't hiring back its paroled felons into the cellblocks as guards. And recently, even that authority was being abrogated. Last week, his decision to reject the application of a refugee officer of Somoza's *Garda Nacional* was overruled by Sacramento; the week before, it was the human cannon-ball from a bankrupt circus.

"The Department spends 1.6 billion a year," Mrs. Reilly had noted more than once. "It costs as much to keep a man in prison for a year as it would to send him to Berkeley. Why cant they raise basic pay so you could attract a better class of guards?"

And the Captain would reply: "It's the same as the Pentagon, honey. All the dough goes to decorating the generals' jets."

So, all things considered, this wingnut sitting across his desk today wasn't all that bad. He had one big plus; he was a hometown boy. That alone excused a plethora of faults in a nepotistic institution. His name was Raymond Savage.

"So, Ray, after you failed the Madera County Sheriff's exam, what did you do next?"

"Got drunk."

"I mean after you got drunk."

"Got laid. At least I *think* I got laid. I oughta do it the other way around so I could remember."

That was pretty much the tone of the interview. Savage's cornyellow hair was brushed straight back and fixed by some grooming gel with the consistency of Verathane. His overbite and folded eyes the color of watered milk bespoke recessive foothill genes. After he was unable to get hired as a mercenary through the classified in *Soldier of Fortune*, Ray told Captain Reilly, he decided, What the heck, how about prison guard? All his buddies from Coldwater High lugged prison keys.

During Captain Reilly's explanation of guard responsibilities to attend In-Service Training, Ray Savage spotted the desk nameplate and interrupted. "Is your wife Mrs. Reilly?"

"Of course my wife is Mrs. Reilly."

"Usta deliver her pizzas from Forget Domani."

"That's nice, Ray."

"Then, when it changed owners and was Pizza Pizazz, I *still* delivered her pizzas."

"Ray . . ."

"She liked em when you worked nights. Usta order extra sausage. Extra *hot* sausage!"

Captain Reilly took a deep breath and counted to three. This yoyo must eat plant food for breakfast cereal; it was the only explanation for the shiteating grin. Better wrap this interview up.

"Ray, in your own words, what is it you hope to get out of a career in corrections . . . You may take a moment to consider."

"Dont need it. Action. A-K-S-H-U-N. Ack-*SHUN!*" Ray convulsively smacked a fist into his palm, jerking halfway out of his chair. "When do I get a *gun?*"

Captain Reilly explained that guns weren't used inside the prison, but that as soon as Ray qualified on the range he could put in for tower duty.

"Cant wait!"

"Ray, I'm going to start you on a probationary status. When you've passed an exam on the material in this training packet and have two hundred online guard hours in, your appointment will be made permanent . . ."

Ray gulped, leaving his mouth open.

"You're hired."

"Hooray!" Ray grabbed for the badge inside the plastic training packet. He started looking for a place on his Pennzoil windbreaker to pin it.

Captain Reilly told him he had to wait until he was in uniform and pushed a button on his desktop intercom. There was a knock on the door and a big blond inmate entered.

"Ray, this is inmate Sonny Hauser. Hauser will escort you to Personnel Lockers and help get you dressed in." Reilly turned to the inmate and rolled his eyes. "Sonny, next take him to Control for key issue and then on down to a segregation wing, make it X, and give him a little training on grille gate operation and proper cell unlock procedure."

Ray snapped up to attention and saluted smartly.

"That's not necessary, Ray," Reilly said wearily. He watched the inmate and recruit leave the office and picked up the phone to call his wife.

"Honey . . . I just hired someone through the front gates any judge would have ruled incompetent to enter the back . . . Another Savage, yeah. This one's Raymond. You guessed it, like Bucky Beaver with per-oxided hair . . . What's so funny? . . . So he delivered you pizzas for ten years . . . Upside *down?*"

TRICK BUNK

||||

The dripping spoon of Mocha Monsoon stalled halfway to Kitty's mouth. "What kind of note you layin on me? What's the game?"

"It's not a con," Tarzon insisted. His hand snaked toward the cheroot lying dead in the ashtray. Her widened eyes shot daggers pinning it to the table. Not until she looked away did his hand withdraw, reluctantly. "I'm trying to save Joe because if he dies, so do my chances of nailing this monster."

This scene stinks even without the stogie's help, she huffed to herself. What did you expect? He's a cop. It's like you keep thinking you're gonna find one different. Your ass.

"How'd you find me?" she switched topics.

"Got your place of employment off an arrest report. Went down to the Blue Note. This girl with . . . with . . . " His hands zoomed in and out from his chest.

Kitty narrowed her eyes to take a big fat guess. "Milk trucks for tits?"

Tarzon nodded energetically. "Like *water*wings. She told me you took up with Dan Graves."

Who else but Bermuda was stupid enough to run her mouth to the heat? You could blow in one of that Twinkie's ears and the other would whistle. Kitty needn't have bothered asking. Same as she needn't have bothered trying to remember this cop from that longago night at the Blue Note.

From outside she spotted Tarzon through the Chocolarium's plateglass windows. Who else would wear a shiny black Sears Roebuck suit and sop a paper napkin between his coffee cup and saucer and pollute the lushly confected icecreamery air with one of those cheapass little cigars with white plastic mouthpieces?

The creep.

Though meeting in Ghirardelli Square was her own bright idea, that she had to confess. She should have suggested some bowling alley bar. Some dive named the Eleventh Frame, where Orkin exterminators and satellite-dish installers made passes at hairdressers in stretch pants named Sonja. Tarzon would fit right in; they'd take him for a pet undertaker.

"You havent answered my question," he said sharply.

Kitty flinched at the sudden flash of gunmetal in his eyes.

"Why dont you ask Joe?" she parried.

"I did. He denies having it."

"Shitfire, that's good enough for me." Kitty decided to soak the taxpayers for another sundae, a Banana Boomerang this time. Hurriedly she killed the Mocha Monsoon and signaled for the waitress.

"He's lying. He believes he can do his time then cash it in and live richly ever after."

"Good for him."

"No, dead for him. Believe me when I tell you this. The person he robbed is very resourceful. No way can Joe Speaker survive this term without being found out."

"I still dont get the point in askin me. I didnt see that boy after the night you cut him loose."

"I thought maybe you hadnt. He was moving too fast. He had to find Rooski before I did . . . "

"I guess you aced him there."

Tarzon took a deep breath and said, "If Joe helps me, I can get this killer behind bars forever. Maybe I can get him in the chamber. In exchange, I'd set Joe free. You two could be back together . . . If I arranged it, would you speak with him in prison?"

Kitty pushed a spoon of ice cream in and out of her mouth, lips shaving the softening mound smaller and smaller. Noting his eyes fastened on this oral occupation, she noisily sucked the spoon clean and laughed deep in her throat, a gamin croak.

"No," she said. "I wont talk to him unless he calls and asks me to. If he's holding his tragic mud, he's got reasons."

"If you dont help, when this monster finds Joe, it'll be too late. I cant protect him inside."

Kitty's wandering eye spotted through the window a bird perched on the terrace rail. She heard its moist whistle. It fluttered to a sheetmetal rain gutter and sang; flew on and sang. The eye strayed back and homed in hard with its companion on the lean blueshadowed face. "You heard of the whore with the heart of gold? Well, you're lookin at her, hoss. Sure it's been dipped in plenty shit, but it aint no less gold. You can give up tryin to get to Joe through me."

Tarzon began blinking too fast and brightly for Kitty's taste. "I'm not trying to *get* to him, I'm trying to save his ass. He's not just throwing away his freedom, he's forfeiting his life. It's almost as if he knows it, *wants* it. As if he's letting the circumstances abet his own suicide . . . "

"You belong on a talk show."

Tarzon shook his head, brushing the crack aside. "Just give me a hint about the hiding place. I swear he'll never know we've spoken . . . Most couples have secret places. My wife and I used to, where we'd leave notes and presents and go together when things were bad . . . There were cherry blossom petals pasted to the Porsche's fenders and shell chips in its tire treads. Can you think where they might have come from?"

"I'd say cherry blossoms and shell chips are about as meaningful in San Francisco as cow chips and cactus burrs would be where I come from . . . Say, why you shakin? You gotta try and not take your work so personal. What I gotta try is a Strawberry Serenade . . . Waitress!"

Tarzon dropped his stare to his twisting hands. Kitty heard a knuckle crack. Then he reached inside his jacket, shrugging black shoulders together like trying to close a book, and withdrew a yellowed *Chronicle* folded to the last page of the entertainment section, where the dog shows and sheriff's auctions and porno theaters advertised. Slapping the paper on the glass table, he stabbed with his finger at a promotional photo of two broads kicking and pulling each other's hair.

"Do you know this girl?" he asked in a thick voice.

Kitty cocked her head, squinting in the silver slants of light stippled with the shadows of hanging ferns. "Inga, She-Wolf of the SS? . . . " She checked the date at the top of the page. "This paper's six months old, hoss. Now she's Natasha, She-Bear of the KGB."

"No!" The finger jabbed angrily. "*This* one."

"Belly Blast," she read aloud. Kitty vaguely knew this chicana, they'd met once coming and going through a connection's kitchen. It was said the wrestling was only a warmup for the real action filmed in an Embarcadero warehouse; info Kitty wasn't about to share with the Man. "No," she said, "that one I never seen or heard of."

"Are you sure?" he asked, his voice coiling like a bullwhip.

Kitty ducked her head and drew back her thick mane like a curtain to smile. "Well sakes alive," she exclaimed, stretching out her Texas drawl. "So that's what's so personal. Here I thought you were trying to help my boy out and all you've been after's a date." She arched her brow, aiming one askance down her nose at the paper. "Roughhousin trip your trigger?" Seeing the blood drain from his lips, she smiled with false solicitude, "Hey, Lieutenant. *I* dont mind. Whatever floats yer boat, hoss."

"Keep on fuckin with me," he said, "and maybe I'll just let Mr. Dan Graves know how many B cases are on your sheet, let him know where you come from . . . "

Kitty curled her lip. The down and dirty hole card was only further proof that a cop is a cop is a cop. As if she needed it.

"Where do you think he *found* me, creep?" she seethed. "Where do you think he went *looking?* The same places your kind of pervert oughta look for scumbags like Belly Blast. In the sewer."

Tarzon shot to his feet. "Crosseyed bitch!"

He stormed from the Chocolarium. Kitty cursed seeing he'd left her the check.

The creep.

Joe stood shaving in the showerroom at the head of the dormitory block. He was ducated to the Handicrafts Department for the following morning and wanted to put on his best, if bent, face. Clerking for Hobby, other cons in his dorm had told him, conferred a license to hustle. Drugs were smuggled into the institution secreted in hobby supplies, hidden in handicraft items returned by visitors for modification through the Admin Building store, in the hip pockets of guards needing a leathertooled belt for junior or a cherrywood jewelry box for the little woman. All contraband traffic required the clerk's cooperation, he had only to quantify his cut.

Joe wished Earl was around to thank for encouraging him to take the typing tests at Vacaville which qualified him for this juice job. But the old bird had gone straight from R&R to the Hospital Wing, where his gallstones were removed, and from there to V Block, the socalled Hole in the Wall Wing, where the old cons housed together, a sort of penitentiary retirement community. Joe had passed him on the Mainline once, but Earl was too busy to stop and talk. With a bolt of fabric stolen from Occupational Therapy over his arm, he was rushing to Q Wing where one of the queens had promised to hem him cell curtains. This was Earl's third stretch at Coldwater, it was just like reopening a household after a vacation.

Watching his whiskers swirl down the drain was like watching four months of his life washed away: each separate hair could almost have been a day. Joe wished the suffering of those days might be so easily whisked away, leaving his memory as virginal and smooth as the face he stroked before the mirror.

He returned to the dorm with his gear. Halfway down the aisle between the bunks when his mouth fell open and he froze in his tracks.

His bunk was moving! Wildly, he looked around, but he was alone. Midafternoon on a weekday, and the worker dorm was empty. He looked back at the bunk. Now Bunk Twelve was *groaning!* Moving above the waxed floor in an undulant fashion, doing a kind of slow hula, and *mooing* like a sick calf! With a start he noticed the blankets he'd tucked in making up the bunk were hanging to the floor. Was there an earthquake, a localized tremor right beneath Bunk Twelve? It was *shaking!* He stood transfixed watching his bunk gyrate faster and faster to the accompaniment of grunts and groans building in pitch and acceleration to a crescendo that rigidified the slack amazement on his face into a mask of revulsion.

The grunts and groans at last exploded and died in a wet rattling, and the bunk was still. A moment later a balding, middleaged convict rolled out from beneath it. He stood pulling up his trousers, and brushed past Joe on his way out of the dorm without so much as a look.

Joe's eyes stayed fixed on the bunk. So that's what the dorm tender meant warning Joe that he'd been assigned the *trick bunk*. Of course—it was the furthest from the door, least visible to passing guards, best suited for the quickie clandestine cigaret date.

With a squeal, the second convict slid out, this one unmistakably the one just married on the Yard, the strict Catholic called Magdalena. Lying flat on her back, she wriggled up her jeans, then pushed herself upright on one slender arm and greased Joe up and down with penciled crib puta eyes, husking: "You new, eh buster? You wan stir it up a little? Half n half five packs, short time onny two."

Joe stood rooted to the spot. Her T-shirt neck was deliberately stretched, baring brown shoulders in a décolleté effect. He stared at the loosely hammocked breasts. Then a sudden fume of feces mixed with petroleum jelly jolted his senses like ammonia salts. Clumsily he spun and stumbled from the dorm, her gurgling laughter dripping like spittle down his back.

BUTTERFINGERS

||||

"**W**hat the fuck you mean you havent been able to follow Tarzon?" the baby voice was pitched at tantrum decibels.

Quick Cicero swung the big Mercedes around a stalled bus and reached to adjust the rearview. He wanted to monitor his boss's temper. But all he could see was a jiggly morass of talced blubber. The Man in the Moon's face would fit in that little mirror before Baby Jewels's. What Quick needed was one of those convex jobs like truckers use.

"It's like he knows we gonna try n tail him. He uses a coupla state police cars for screens. But now with the election just a few months off, the Governor and Attorney General need every state unit for their campaigns. No way SFPD is going to cover him, even if they could keep up with that crazy motherfucker . . . No," Quick shoved out his lower lip to nod with a confident grimace, "he's naked now, boss. I'm on his spic *ass* . . . And another thing, I got a date with the younger zip brother this evening."

"That's good news indeed." Baby Jewels settled back with a wheeze as pressurized as a leaking tractor tire. Shortly he began drumming his fingers, dangerously blinking his rings, reminding Quick in the rearview of gumballing police lights. The baby voice lilted with wheezy coquetry: "We've fallen behind, Quick. Now we must play catchup. You know how to play catchup, dont you?"

IIII

Hands clasped behind his back, Captain Reilly rocked on his heels, scowling out his office window. The flagpole at the center of the Admin lawn was naked. It was the third time he'd come on watch this month and the colors weren't flying. The younger officers couldn't comprehend his vexation. Whether or not the colors were raised with the sun every day seemed of small consequence to them. They couldn't understand what it had to do with institutional security. They didn't see that something is done the same every day because it's supposed to be. They couldn't grasp that when basic procedures weren't followed, a general breakdown in order followed. It might be gradual, a slow erosion of attention to detail, a rotting of security consciousness; but, however trivial and slight the individual lapses might seem, their cumulative result was always cataclysmic.

Captain Reilly had picked up a term for the malaise at a recent penology seminar. The speaker, an oldline captain like himself, called it "correctional anomie." Captain Reilly thought this was something that grew in the ocean until he looked it up and found it was something growing right in the Coldwater Muster Room.

The desk intercom buzzed; he yanked his eyes from the slender white portent of chaos and angrily punched the button. "What?"

"It's your wife, sir, on one . . . " came his clerk's electrific lisp. "And C.O. Savage is waiting to see you."

"Tell that yoyo to cool his heels, I'll be with him in a few minutes." Captain Reilly lowered himself in his chair with a deep, composing breath and pressed the blinking button.

"Darling!" the receiver trilled in his ear. "Who *is* inmate Oblivia DeHavilland?"

Arthur Gottlieb, the Captain grumbled, and he wasn't supposed to be using his drag name. He promised to put a stop to it.

"Dont be silly darling. Those central switchboard gals are so dreary. No harm having a hoot."

Captain Reilly told her men weren't sent to prison for laughs, though he agreed the central switchboard was a depressing lot. Marsha was always about half right, which meant she was consistently half wrong. There's a lot to be said for all wrong, the Captain often thought. All these years Marsha never grasped that prison wasn't some kind of dude ranch with him head wrangler. And the trouble, as usual, was she was half right. Reilly had to admit, when he retold the average day's happenings over cocktails in the sunroom they did sound comical. In the retelling, the horror mixed with the absurd acquired the farcical dimensions of a Grand Guignol, a ball and chain bouffe. Of course that was the deadly illusion. Behind each jest snickered the secret shiv.

"Mel, I'm just calling to remind you of dinner at Warden and Mrs. Gasse's home. It's pot luck, what absolute *fun,*" she croaked miserably, "and I want to stay ethnically *honest* so I'm picking up a German potato salad at the deli because you know Mrs. Gasse, whatshername? . . . "

"Hedwig."

"That's the Valkyrie. Well you know how she always whips up those kraut things, cabbage and schnitzel and pancakes and God knows what else. I wouldnt want to be out of *step* . . . Have you had your haircut?"

Captain Reilly explained that Chico Del Rio, the staff barber, was in AD SEG. As he spoke he twirled the silver hair where it curled at his neck and flipped up in winglets over his ears.

"'Release him, Mel! You look like an aging hipsidoodle."

"I cant release a man from lockup because I need a haircut."

He heard her stamp her foot. "But he made you look so distingué, like Stewart Granger. Oh please darling *every*one will be there tonight."

Captain Reilly hung up on the tinny arfing just like her lapdog, Alfie. He focused his eyes on a greasy scrap of paper at the center of his blotter. Forcethree storm clouds blackened his visage as he reread the clogged pica type.

MEMO   CDC FORM 1823

TO: Melville Fenton Reilly, Captain
         Commander, Second Watch
         California Institute of Medicine
         Coldwater, California

FROM: Raymond Carl Savage, C.O.
         Gym Activities Detail, Second Watch

RE: CAL. ADM. 3016, Cal. P.C. Sec. 4600, Cal. P.C. Sec. 4574

AT APPROXIMATELY 1345 HOURS WHILE SUPERVISING "COLDWATER COLD CUTS" PRACTICE IN GYMAZIUM OFFICER OBSERVED VISITING MUSIC INSTRUCTOR, MR. TIEBOLD TURNER, BEHAVING IN A SUSPICOUS AND FURITIVE MATTER. INSTEAD OF "BEET THE DRUM" HE SAID "GEE-SEET GEE-SUM." ALSO HIS EYES WERE RED AND SPEECH SLURED. OFFI-CER FERTHER OBSERVED SUBJECT MONROE DELIVER INMATE JOHN "MOONPIE" MONROE, B-42572, IN A SUSPICOUS MATTER THE TRUMPIT

WICH HE HAD RETURNED FROM OUTSIDE THE INSTITUTION FOR RE-
PAIR. POSESSING PROBABLY CAUSE, OFFICER SEEZED AND SEARCHED
TRUMPIT AND DISCOVERED GREEN LEEFY SUBSTINCE IN FINGER VALVE.
OPEN BEING ADVISED OF HIS RIGHTS PERSUANT TO MARIMBA SUBJECT
TURNER STATED "I ONLY GIT THE AX FIXED." SEEMILARLY MIRIM-
BIZED, MONROE STATED "I DONT NOW NUTTING ABOUT NUTTING."
SUBJECT TURNER REMINDED TO CUSTODY OF MADERA COUNTY SHER-
IFFS. INMATE MONROE RUMPED TO MAX A HVP AND TRANSPORTED TO
AD SEG X-213.

CC: Madera County Sheriffs
     Superintendent G. Gasse
     Search and Investigation
     Donner Unit Offices   *Raymond C. Savage*
     Inmate File   RAYMOND C. SAVAGE, C.O.

Captain Reilly stabbed the intercom. "Is that yoyo still out there?
... Yeah, send him in ... And Gottlieb? Use your real name on the outside
line at least. Save all that queen stuff for Q Wing."

Savage entered, snapped to attention and saluted.

"Put your damn hand down, Savage."

The salute stayed parked beneath the cornyellow crewcut. Savage's
tightly tucked chin squeaked his voice like air through the pinched neck
of a balloon. "Officer rules sez we gotta hold the salute till the superior
officer returns it."

Captain Reilly wasn't about to play tin soldiers with this yahoo. "Put
the hand down and sit, hotshot. That's an order."

"Yes, *sir!*" Ray Savage took the chair facing the Captain across the desk.
Reilly ignored the supercilious gleam in his eye claiming victory in round
one.

"Savage, I havent had a chance to talk to you about writing Del Rio a
One Thirteen for sexual misconduct. How do you think the rest of the
officers feel about you throwing the joint's only barber in the hole who
doesnt make them look like Parris Island gyrenes?"

Savage loosed an incredulous, gasping laugh. "It was my *duty*, sir. Del
Rio was giving those convicts blowjobs! The other guards on the gunrail
thought he was crouched at the bars talking to the men in the cells. They
were fooled by Del Rio wearing the dozer cap sideways on his head. They
actually thought he was smoking the cigar stuck in his ear. What he was
smoking was convict bones."

"Did it ever occur to you," Captain Reilly asked with an icy smile, "that the other guards werent fooled, that they were turning a blind eye to Del Rio's activity? Or hadnt you noticed that they all call Del Rio by his drag name, Dolores, after the actress? Blowjobs are good corrections. They pacify General Population."

The force of his gulp bulged Savage's eyes; he might have been swallowing a medicinal toad.

"But even the stupidity of Del Rio's writeup is eclipsed by this piece of shit." Reilly snapped a blunt forefinger at the disciplinary on his desk. "What do you think is going to become of the Coldwater Cold Cuts now that you've socked their leader, Moonpie Monroe, in the Hole?"

Savage shrugged. "Hadnt thought of it. Guess they wont be no more jazz band."

"That's right. Does that bother you?"

"Nossir. Never cottoned to jungle music nohow."

He was actually smirking; his IQ couldn't exceed the speed limit. Reilly wanted to rip his yellow head off.

"Well, it's gonna bother the fuck out of the Warden, asshole! Now there's no one to play at his dinner party tonight."

Savage found unexpected diversion thumbwrestling with himself.

"What now, sir?"

Captain Reilly leaned back. "Madera will *nolle pros* Turner's case, the marijuana will be 'lost' at the lab. Not that it matters. I wont be able to get Moonpie released in time for his gig tonight . . . You, I'm transferring to First Watch Culinary."

The rookie's mouth dropped. "The graveyard kitchen shift?"

"Until you learn not to write up the cons we depend on to run this institution. You will write up no one in the kitchens, I dont care if you see them hump out a side of beef."

"I was only tryin to do my job."

"I believe you. You just werent trained to know what job. I hope our discussion has helped."

"You bet, Captain! Is that all, sir?"

"No." Captain Reilly swiveled his chair and pointed out the window. "See that flagpole? It's naked! I cant make it understood that not a daylight hour should pass without the stars and stripes flying. So I'm making it your duty. You're a oneman color detail. See to it you raise the flag at dawn before you go off watch." He turned and looked solemnly at Savage. "Do you read me, mister?"

"Yes sir!" Savage's eyes were bright with the sound of faroff bugles. "Should I raise Old Glory now?"

"No, it's closer to dusk than dawn. And you're off for two days. Start Monday."

"Yes, sir!" Ray Savage snapped out of the chair to attention and smartly saluted. This time Reilly returned it. Savage aboutfaced and sprang out the door.

Captain Reilly shook his handsome head, staring at the closed door. He could think of no inmate who could present the same clear and present danger to institutional security as an ignorant, untrained guard. Yet that's all they'd been hiring lately, and it was playing hell with Custody morale. Remembering the term he'd picked up at the seminar, he growled aloud, "Goddam enema's what it is."

Archie Sing always came the same way to Chinatown Park, across the causeway connecting it to the Chinatown Hilton. The damp spring breeze tugged his pantlegs and sang soothingly in his ears over the bicker and bustle of rushhour traffic. Behind the steep tiled roofs and gilded tiered pagodas of Chinatown, day's last warm winy afterglow drained down the western sky. The red paper lanterns hung in the park trees lit all at once and Archie saw Firecracker sitting where he always did, at the last checkerboard pedestal. The angle at which the old Chinaman's porkpie hat sat atop his pigtails signaled that the fist in his overcoat pocket was fat with cash from that day's drug sales.

Archie didn't notice the stumblebum wearing sneakers bound with duct tape, leaning back with his elbows atop the causeway parapet. Not until he was staring at the shield and hearing: "You're wanted for questioning."

Gripping Archie under the arm, the undercover cop frogmarched him to the end of the causeway and down the steep stairs to Kearny Street. He saw Firecracker start halfway up from his seat and knew that his brother would be alerted and have his bail up before he reached the booking desk.

The undercover cop flung Archie on the hood of the unmarked beige Plymouth and cuffed him without shaking him down. He threw him in the backseat and climbed in front behind the wheel. Next to him sat a silent man with scarred brows and ears twisted like ginger roots.

The Plymouth pulled out into traffic and headed up Kearny. When it failed to make the first turn heading back toward the Hall of Justice, instead turning left onto Columbus, Archie said evenly, "I want to see my lawyer."

"Which brother are you?" asked the driver.

"I'm Archie . . . This aint the way to the Hall. I want to see my lawyer."

"Fuck you," said the driver, pressing his taped sneaker to the pedal. The Plymouth shot right on Grant and started winding up Telegraph Hill.

The parking lot at the base of Coit Tower was ringed as usual with cars admiring the panorama. Teenagers sat on hoods, drinking beer and listening through open doors and windows to thumpity rockenroll, fathers fed quarters into the binocular meters and held their children up for a look, lovers exchanged murmurs in hopes of igniting passions half so grand as the view. Even were the snubnose not snuggled in Archie's ear, no one would have heard him cry out as he was trundled out of the Plymouth.

The art deco megalith was closed, but the one with the taped sneakers had a key to a side door. They rode the elevator up to the cupola in silence. Then they were alone high in the night with the lit city hills spread around like a jeweled gown wantonly discarded.

The one with taped sneakers asked, "Who did you ricepropelled motherfuckers give the guns and masks to?"

Archie waited a beat, then said again: "I want the advice of counsel."

Archie saw the one with ginger ears flinch. He was knocked cold before he ever felt the fists.

He came to swinging by the scruff of his neck over the railing. The city lights swung dizzily, like the view from a Ferris wheel bucket. He heard the voice ask once more: "Who did you give the guns and masks to?"

Archie tried to speak, but the neck of his shirt was gathered in the same grasp holding his jacket, shutting off his windpipe.

"Once more, you gook punk. Who got the guns and mask to rob the theater while you and your puke brother set up alibis to cover your asses for the Golden Boar massacre?"

Archie could only snarl. He gagged and tried again and managed a growl. Then his arms flew up and he was freefalling through black air gemmed with lights, yelling: "Jo-*whoaaah* . . . "

Ginger Ears stepped to the rail. The decrescendo wail was swallowed in slashing branches as Archie Sing crashed down the wooded hill.

"I didnt mean to drop the little zipperhead," Detective Sergeant Villareal of Narcotics said. He held up the empty jacket, adding as if it were Archie's fault: "He slipped."

"Who's Joe?"

"His fuckin brother." Snorting disgustedly, Villareal tossed the jacket flapping into the night. "Musta called him by instinct. His big brother saved his yellow ass every other time he was . . . "

"What? At loose ends?" chuckled the other. He drew back from the rail. "A pudpuller at the movies that night said one of them called the other Joe . . . "

"Whoever worked the switch made a point of dropping Joe Sing's name. But Joe Sing aint got the ice. He's alibied for the time the theater was hit, just like that one."

"So we find him next."

"After Joe Sing hears about this? Shit. He'll be harder to find than a virgin in Nevada." Villareal pulled a radio from a deep pocket on the pantleg of his camouflage trousers and telescoped its antenna. "Unit 64 to Control. This is Tango Charlie Niner. Present location Powell and Union. Just spotted a header off Coit Tower. Am proceeding Code Eleven to secure tower. Over."

"Ten Four, Tango Charlie Niner. Meat wagon rollin. Over."

"You better book," Villareal said, pocketing the radio. "Downstairs door opens from the inside. Tell Mr. Moses I'm sorry I dropped the zipperhead."

"He'll understand. You're only human . . . " Quick Cicero turned on his heel and stabbed the elevator button. Awaiting its arrival, he started giggling.

"What's the joke?" Villareal asked nervously. "Jesus, you sound like that idiot Frank Stutz."

The elevator sighed open and Quick Cicero stepped within and turned around, still giggling. His gloved hand stopped the doors just long enough to say, "Catchcha later, butterfingers."

SHE SELLS
SEASHELLS

||||

Kitty sat legs folded beneath her, elbow propped on the back of the loveseat in the baywindow. Her chin in her hands felt cool, her hands warm; she reached out and touched the window pane sparkly with dust: cold. "Shitfire," she sighed.

It was the kind of apartment—*condo,* excuse tragic me, Dan—that let you know you were alone in it. The sleek gray furniture yawned emptier, the shadows stretched colder, the chrome tubing everywhere shone ghostly as coffin rails, the digital clock in the foyer italicized the silence with hollow measured tocks like a designer time bomb.

"Shitfire," she muttered again, regretting that she'd agreed to stay with Dan for the baby's term. It made practical sense; he had the money for the doctors and all. He'd given up trying to marry her, said there were no strings attached. And she wanted to believe him the way she'd believe in Santa Claus, for the kid's sake. But shitfire, she ragged herself, you've heard enough men protest no strings to know that's when the web is woven thickest. If only she could get her hands on enough of those sourpussed dead presidents to cut and run.

The phone on the end table bleeped and blinked. Kitty chewed her lip staring at it. She knew it was Dan, he was down in L.A. opening a new store and was calling trying to talk her into taking a vacation. Belize, Capri, Rio, Ceylon, a Nile cruise—the exotic brochures littered the smokedglass coffee table. Dan couldn't understand her reluctance to leave San Francisco. He couldn't guess at her need to cleave to the memories of the man whose image largened daily in her belly.

On and on bleeped the phone, panicking Kitty with its manic insistence. Impulsively she decided then and there to leave Dan immediately. She'd hock the jewelry he gave her down on Sixth Street and hop a Greyhound on Seventh. Pawn shops and bus stations operate in the same neighborhoods for just such getaways.

She jumped up and ran to the bedroom and dumped her jewelry box in her purse. *I dont like doin you like this Dannyboy but fuck it, a woman's is a tragic tough lot.* She rushed out of the condo and into a waiting elevator. *I'm sorry, Danny. In that significant way you're always talkin about, I'm shitfire sorry, but I got no choice.* She pushed B for the underground garages and blew a curl off her forehead, thinking *fuck it, aint no Christian way to go about these things so fuck it.*

She was halfway across the garage, her heels stabbing the concrete *fuckityfuckityfuckity,* almost to the Rolls, when she halted. She couldn't doublepark and abandon a hundredthousanddollar automobile in front of the bus station. Get a handle on yourself, girl. She started to turn back when something black flickered at the corner of her eye and she whirled.

There was the Corniche, mauve and stately gray. It was just her damn nerves. DanNerves, she tittered to herself, sold in the Designer Angst aisle.

Wait a sec! She heard a rasp of shoes from the Rolls's blind side. She'd surprised a tragic car booster, that's it. Probably someone of her bustout acquaintance.

Wraithlike, Lieutenant Tarzon rose from behind the Corniche.

"Good morning, Miss Litter."

"What the fuck you doin snoopin around that car?"

"Bored. And when I get bored I get to wondering and wandering."

"This is private property," she said evenly. "There's laws . . . "

"Guess what I found in this land yacht's tire treads?" His gloved fingers unfolded, revealing a handful of pearlescent chips. "Seashells . . . And here . . . " His other black leather hand gently picked several pink petals from the windshield. He smiled taking the Hav-A-Tampa Jewel from his mouth and blew them swirling in a verdigris cloud of smoke across the gleaming hood, saying in the artifically drawn voice of a magician, "Cherry blossoms."

"They're from the parking lot of the Hai Ginza," Kitty said. "It's a zen cuisine dive on the peninsula Dan practically lives at."

"You did see Joe that night. And he told you the hiding place. I could hold you for obstructing justice. I might even get the D.A. to go for an accessory charge."

"You're fuckin bananas."

"Or maybe you've told Graves. Yes, he'd have the connections to down the diamond discreetly. You sold Joe out . . . "

"Diamond? What tragic diamond?"

It was as if he hadn't heard. Starting around the car, a queer light fluttering from his eyes, he began singing—*"She sells seashells by the sea shore . . .* That gives me an idea. I could tell Joe you were doublecrossing him with Graves, then have him released. He's killed twice, a third time would be . . . " Tarzon snapped his fingers. " . . . that easy."

Kitty had backed up to the elevator. Blindly she reached behind, stabbing the buttons. She heard the doors opening and threw back her hand, cocking its finger pistol. "You're a lot sicker than Belly Blast can cure with whips and antifreeze enemas."

He was lunging for the elevator when the doors closed.

Back in the condo she rushed to the phone and punched out the L.A. number Dan had left beside it on a pad. Thank God he picked up. "Never mind which flight. Just meet the next three planes into Burbank . . . "

A '65 Sting Ray was parked at a hydrant down the street. In it Quick Cicero was jotting notes in his leather pad. Tarzon emerged from the building first and drove off in his doubleparked unmarked. Quick was about to leave his car to bribe the doorman to tell him which apartment the cop visited when a girl ran out waving her arms for a cab. Quick's flat eyes narrowed. This bimbo he knew. She worked the Strip. Some whore who knew Glorioski, that's who Tarzon had questioned.

Quick followed the cab all the way to the airport, to one of the commuter lines. Shootin to Vegas to sling highstakes pussy, Quick entered in his pad. Tarzon was probably wasting his time with her anyway. Wasn't no bimbo stole the Blue Jager Moon. But Quick would pay her a visit anyway when she got back. Just to make sure. He wondered if she'd hold the bow while he tied her ribbons. She couldn't be gone long, he concluded pulling the Sting Ray out of the departure zone. Bitch didn't take no luggage.

Breakfast was the convicts' favorite meal. Fresh from dream furloughs, hearts renewed and hopes replenished, their voices clamored the Chowhall with a roar like many waters, brightened with clashing metal trays and utensils. Mist swirled off the steam tables, billowing orange and yellow in steep ramps of barred light through high windows. Joe shoveled grits onto his fork with a wedge of Wonder bread.

Across the fourman table, Earl was disputing the allegation of a rawboned Indian giant named Horsekiller. "No one ripped off yer fifi bag,

Johnny. You just wore the sucker out and threw it away and dont remember. So turn that frown, yeah, upsidedown."

But the crease in the jowls the color of baked clay only deepened, the scowl trained on Joe now, trampolining his gut. He set down his steaming cup of chicory to swear, "I dont even know what a fifi bag is, pal."

"*Errp errp . . .* " spluttered Earl. "Fifi bag's a phony snatch. They take orange juice cartons from the Commissary, yeah, cut em in half and stuff em with a baggie loaded with hand lotion. That's your basic fifi bag. Every con has his own touch, yeah. Johnny"—pointing with his fork at the ponytailed hulk still staring at Joe—"stuffs his with dirty drawers for that backdoor aroma. Johnny likes . . . "

Horsekiller interrupted, "I like Boston Red Sox." He snapped his red suspenders as evidence.

Joe grinned snapping the cap's brim in turn. "Thanks. Only it's this belonged to the Dodgers when they still played in Brooklyn."

"Brooklyn? Where's Brooklyn?" the Indian asked suspiciously.

In the midst of Joe's geography lesson, Horsekiller stood abruptly and left the table.

"Dont mind Johnny," Earl assured Joe. "He's cellshocked. Done so much time he can only concentrate long enough to tie his shoe . . . or kill. But he's harmless, yeah, less you call him Chief."

Joe made a mental note to guard against that gaffe.

Earl said he had a favor to ask and he bet Joe knew what; and Joe said he hadn't consulted his Magic 8 Ball but would take a stab anyway—"You want to borrow more cigarets."

Earl bobbed his head for unseen apples, grinning as if Joe had just solved the riddle of life and death.

"You already too far in the the hole, F Stop. Ever since you learned I've been getting over at Hobby, you've been putting the arm on me. Besides," Joe concluded, "I need motion lotion myself to bribe a oneman cell."

"Trouble with a cell," Earl pointed out, "is you never know if you shittin in the bedroom or sleepin in the shitter."

"I'll take that confusion over the madness in the dorm."

Earl ducked his face to glower at Joe from beneath scraggly gray brows. Behind him convicts in the food line jerked by like tinstamped shooting gallery targets. "Malec and Irons wouldnt be dealing with you if it werent for that cap on your head, no. And you owe that cap to me."

Joe narrowed his eyes. Rudy Malec was Captain of the Coldwater A.B. tip, and Gerald Irons its Sergeant at Arms. Joe's first day at Hobby, the pair joined him in a sophisticated and lucrative smuggling scheme involving bogus jewelry supply houses, double invoices, and falsebottomed delivery crates. Nearly two pounds of drugs were being funneled through this pipeline into the penitentiary each week. Joe enjoyed imagining his savvy demeanor earned his enlistment, that Whisper's cap was only a strong reference. Discovering now that the cap was his sole qualification would have pained him more were it not for the greater wound inflicted by Earl's exploitation of that truth to extort him. He was about to scratch an itch to slap Earl's face with the cap when a fluty voice piped suddenly over his shoulder: "Hey, got a square?"

Joe spun on his stool to face mischievous eyes level with his own, Spencer in a wheelchair. Laughing, Joe shook out a Camel, which Spencer seized in a twisted coathanger fixed to his arm stump, a replica of the prosthesis he had used to smoke AMA on Sick Bay. A cough wracked the quad, a sound like an engine trying repeatedly to start and failing. Lighting Spencer's cigaret, Joe asked casually after his health.

"Sucks," pronounced a daunting blue cumulus. "They cant wait for me to shuffle off so they can cut me open and see if there isn't a publishable paper they can write on my condition. If the postmortem yields no enlightenment, they'll hide my death in the AIDS stats. I'll catch the plague sooner or later anyway. I get weekly transfusions and all the plasma's drawn from CDC population." He shrugged armless shoulders at Joe's look of alarm. "You gotta go sooner or later."

Something happened inside Joe like falling down stairs, something that dampened the Chowhall's din to a roaring silence out of which echoed Rooski's words: "We all gotta go sometime." Christ, Joe remonstrated to a god who went unacknowledged until a scapegoat was needed—Is heaven so desolate, so lonely that you must martyr all its hostages?

Spencer's voice returned him from the void. "Joe, meet Roy." Between the wheelchair's arms stood a gaunt convict, his eyes in their deep sockets rolled up, his stubbled skull tipped back, swaying to silent music. He extended his hand to Joe in slightly the wrong direction. "He's blind," Spencer explained needlessly. "I'm his eyes and he's my limbs. We go everywhere together. Siamese twins, only by choice."

Joe pumped the bony hand, mumbling something about any friend of Spencer's.

"Medication call in ten minutes," rumbled Roy.

"Sounds like he's your conscience, too," Joe said.

"Dont be fooled," piped a fresh blue cloud, "he's only looking out for numero uno. When I croak he goes back to licking stamps for the chaplain."

The swaying head stilled.

"By the way," Spencer smiled, "I hear you're hustling down at Hobby hard as a onearmed bookie on Derby Day. Watch out."

"What are they gonna do?" Joe spread his palms. "Put me in jail?"

"Worse. Z Block . . . Home, James." Roy spun the wheelchair and the bizarre convict symbiosis trundled off between the thronged tables.

"That's a helluva pair to draw to," Earl submitted.

A Chowhall guard stopped at their table and ordered them to hook it up, the bell for the second shift was about to ring. Earl jabbed his thumbs at his crotch. "Hook this up, Gomez." The guard glowered and slouched off.

Watching Earl slurp down his pineapple ring, Joe saw he was avoiding his eye and knew the old coot regretted his manner of requesting a loan. They stood together and wended their way to the bus station by the Chowhall doors. There they scraped and stacked their trays and dropped their forks and spoons in the suds bucket beside the cage where a guard slept with a shotgun across his knees.

It was morning rush hour on the Mainline. Up and down the corridor bowled convict voices loud as thunder trapped in a narrow canyon. Clerks with reading glasses and pens in their pockets, toolbelted telephone technicians, hardhatted roofing crews; cooks in white, nurses in green, plumbers in grimy overalls—the fortress citystate of Coldwater was going to work.

"I'm sorry how I put the arm on you, amigo," Earl said as they stood aside for a team of electricians wheeling copper spools on a handtruck. "I just cant seem to help myself, no."

Joe dipped his shoulder, reentering traffic. "Dont worry about it, F Stop. I suppose a cell can wait. I'll have your smokes at the head of the dormitory block at lunch call . . . By the way, what's Z Block?"

"Psych unit. Only you dont need to be crazy to end up there, no. Hit a guard or fuck with his action, you get gaffled up to Z Block. They straitjacket your ass with Prolixin and lock you in an iron box."

"How long?" Through the Mainline's eastern windows Joe watched the sun spear up behind the Sierras, bloodying ribbed clouds.

"Just as long as you survive. Aint no gettin off Z Block, no. It's the terminal unit."

DESPERATE MEASURES

||||

Captain Reilly stood gazing out the Warden's office windows overlooking the town of Coldwater, parasite of the beast on the hill. Where the sycamores shading town hall still held night in their branches and Toby Ellis tossed first editions from the tailgate of his daddy's stationwagon onto lawns jeweled with dew; where Ernie took time out from hosing down the islands of his Texaco station to help a kid put air in his bike tire, and Art Phelan's pickup was parking at the Morning Call Cafe. There the 6:10 Amtrak was just pulling into the station by the feed lots, its diesels chugging white puffs as perfect as those puffed by a toy locomotive Reilly bought his son years ago. Indeed, from the prison's elevation, the town itself had the look of a collection of scale structures designed for a model train set. Reilly imagined he could reach out and lift each to read its price tag.

"Sorry I'm late, Mel!" cried Warden Gasse, slamming the door behind him. A small man, Gasse did everything in a big way. He crossed to his desk, gesturing to the wingchair facing it. "Cop a squat."

Reilly sat and crossed his legs. For several minutes Gasse noisily shuffled and boxed papers, made faces at memos, wiped inmate janitor germs off his telephone receiver with a handkerchief. With his bald peaked head and complexion like cold oatmeal, he looked more like the manager of an allnight checkcashing center than a maximum security prison. Reilly emitted a sigh, signifying polite impatience.

Gasse leaned back in his chair, delicately holding a pencil between the thumb and forefinger of either hand. The rising light painted his bald head orange. "I received a phone call late last night, Mel. After the party broke up. It was my source from Department offices in Sacramento. More exactly, it was my friend on the Director's staff." Gasse paused to let his wellconnectedness sink in; Reilly made an appropriate little O with his mouth. "He informed me, Mel, that I'm about to lose my job."

"What in hell? . . . "

"They feel Coldwater is experiencing a security crisis. As evidence they cite the fact that not one homicide occurring behind these walls in the last five years has resulted in a conviction. Coldwater is the only prison in the system without a delegate on Death Row."

"Makes it sound like a beauty pageant."

"Ha! In a sense it is. The more homicides a prison successfully prosecutes, the sexier a warden's bonuses and prettier his commendations. My string of goose eggs makes me look soft, Mel. No . . . muscle . . . *tone!*" The pencil broke. "What drew attention to us was that kid who got killed last month on R-2. Turned out the little snot was a state senator's nephew doing time for cocaine sales . . . "

"A routine penitentiary killing, sir."

"They dont see what's so routine about getting your dick sliced off and rammed up your ass with a mop handle."

"They would if they knew his wife brought her child from a previous marriage on a visit. Her husband was black, the kid was highyaller. The other whites had to take him out for having a redheaded stepchild."

"Well . . . the fact remains, Mel, that they dont rate a warden's effectiveness on the peace he keeps but the butt he kicks. So we're gonna have a crackdown here at Coldwater. I'm bringing in a new commander for Search and Investigation. We need to shore up our Custody image." Gasse snatched up the transfer order tucked in his blotter. "This hardass made his bones the oldfashioned way, by breaking them, including a few of his own."

"Crackdown? Sir, have you read my memos, weighed my arguments?"

"Yes, Mel. Following your advice is what's got me in this fix. We cant operate any more on the theory that if we treat convicts nicely they'll return the favor."

Reilly rose heavily and crossed to the window, looking down once more at the town in the prison's shadow. All along he'd considered the town a symbol of all that was protected by the existence of the prison. Now he wondered if it wasn't the prison that needed protection.

"Warden," he said, "every day this prison is becoming more crowded, and every day one inmate program or another is being axed, removing their incentives to preserve order. We only control this human toxic waste dump because the convicts view us as reasonably fair and just, people they can somewhat trust and understand. When we resort to coercion and violence, they'll respond in kind. When we say, 'Hey, fuck you, scum—we got you behind bars and we got all the keys and guns and clubs . . . ' we're lost."

The Warden wasn't listening; he'd heard the spiel a hundred times before. Reilly was a relic of the rehabilitation age. He couldn't grasp that prison was a business and the convicts were its inventory which must be *controlled*. Again, as Reilly spoke, he examined the transfer order. Yes, this ballbuster was a blowback to days of yore when men were men and prison guards kicked any ass that needed softening. Just the Custody fanatic to prove to the Director that Warden Gasse appreciated that desperate times called for desperate measures. He'd fax it out as soon as Reilly left the office. He cleared his throat. "Mel . . . "

But Reilly was on a roll. Turned from the window, hands spread, looking around the walls, across the ceiling, an eerie tremolo mystifying his voice: "You've been here long enough to know, to *feel* this . . . place is theirs. It was built for them, it stands for them, it's their home and right by birth almost. We only control it because they allow us to. Otherwise, it's theirs any time they want it."

Gasse stared at his oldest, most decorated line captain with alarm giving way to wary pity. Maybe it was time to put Reilly out to pasture. At least then Gasse wouldn't have to look at that luxurious silver mane every day.

"Hey!" the Warden shouted suddenly. "What happened to your hair? Who cut it?"

Grinning abashedly, Reilly rubbed the stubble around his neck and ears. "I had to go to the barber in town. Del Rio got sent to the Hole by the same rookie who gaffled Moonpie up."

"Savage! I want to kill him!" Bloodlust rocketed Gasse to his feet. Reilly could hardly blame him. When the Cold Cuts didn't show, his wife put on polka records and the dinner party couldn't have been gloomier than a soiree with Adolf and Eva at the Berghof.

"How are you disciplining that imbecile, Mel?"

"Graveyard Culinary. Also, he's assigned color detail every morning. In fact . . . " Reilly again turned to the window and chuckled with satisfaction. "There he is, right on time, raising the flag . . . I always say that there's hope for a man who knows how to follow an order."

Gasse joined Reilly at the window. With approving smiles, they watched the solitary figure on the Admin lawn pulleying the flagpole lanyards. The flag reached the pole's summit; a gust of wind snapped it flying . . . and Reilly's eyes bulged in horror. Blunt fingers scrabbling the thick glass, he let go a terrific howl. Warden Gasse sprang like a mongoose to his desk. He grabbed the institutional line and ordered Tower One to fire warning shots at the moron with orange hair saluting an upsidedown Old Glory.

HOTSHOT

||||

Day broke like a wine cooler smashed suddenly on the curb of the sky, splashing the derelict building with lemon and peach, drenching its concrete crevices cherry, inking the lacework shadows of exterior catwalks and ladderways in grape.

Quick Cicero alighted from his '65 Sting Ray. His washedout gaze scanned the tall pocked face of the abandoned brewery and locked just beneath the cracked blue globe that once revolved this legend girdling its equator: BLATZ, A BEER TO CHEER THE WORLD.

From broken davits beneath the globe a derrick boom swayed above great iron doors frozen half open on rusted tracks. The climbing sun widened a wedge of light inside. Quick glimpsed the smooth arcs of the giant oak beer barrels hooped with rusted steel.

On slithered the expug's kid leather gloves, slick and thin as wet membranes. He popped the Vette's hood and used a pocketknife to carefully scrape the corrosion from the battery terminals into a glassine envelope. He held the tiny opaque square to the light, shaking it, fluffing the white powder with its yellowish tinge like urinestained snow. The hotshot glittered as genuinely as the capped teeth flashing from his forked smile.

Pocketing the envelope, Quick quietly closed the hood. His Nikes scrunched quickly across the empty gravel lot to the loading dock beneath the boom. Catlike, he zigzagged up the ladderways to the iron doors and slipped through, ducking sideward into the shadows to look and listen.

And *smell*. Once these horizontally ranked barrels big as cement mixers were redolent with hops and barley. Now the reeks of piss and pigeon shit dankly streaked the air. The aisle separating the oaken barrels was choked with rotting garbage rustling with rats. Faintly he heard a woman's ragged moaning, either dying or getting fucked; rockenroll from somewhere else; a raucous shout of laughter suddenly sliced off.

Quick began picking his way down the aisle through the clutter of refuse redolent with human feces. He grimaced, betting Tarzon fired up one of those Hav-A-Tampa Jewels to camouflage the stink of these catacombs. Several wraiths darted between huge round shadows, urgent knuckles warning barrel dwellers of his approach. From the darkness above, pigeons cooed like bubbling poison. Something swooped by screeching, the rush of leather wings raising his gooseflesh. A fat rat slouched across his path, dragging a piece of blackened flesh in its bared yellow teeth.

Quick stopped at the last barrel on the left. Like the others, its hatch was ajar. He cocked his head at a steady hissing from within. He pulled the winch wheel, creaking open the circular iron hatch, and stepped over the bulkhead into the barrel.

The hissing was a kerosene lamp's jet. By its blear light a naked girl crouched on her haunches. Her thin body was blued with welts, lumped with abscesses, studded with scabs. Her hands were so swollen with infection that they resembled surgical gloves filled with water. By the lamp's side lay the square lid of a Vaseline jar filled with a silty white substance like wet sand.

So absorbed was she in her occupation, she didn't hear Quick enter her barrel or note his long arched shadow. One ulcerated hand held aloft a fat syringe filled with a cloudy solution, the Codeine coldcooked and strained from the multiple tablets crushed in the jar lid beside her; the other's bloated fingers frantically squeezed her scaly skin, hunting for a pinch of unscabbed flesh to plunge the shot.

Veins were just another entry on Fay DuWeye's lengthening list of the Life's bustout ustabe's.

"Hey, baby. Squirt that shit out. I got the real thing." Kid leather fingers waved the glittering glassine bag.

The dark eyes flying wide were all pupil like a dayold corpse. She said, "Quick . . . How did you find me?'

"The same way Tarzon did." He grinned watching those zombie eyes attach hypnotically to the plastic envelope swinging like a shingle in the hissing light. He said, "What did the murder loot want with a nice girl like you?"

"You brought me . . . "

"Pure China white, baby. Remember, you worked for us once. Kinder like family. Mr. Moses looks after his family."

"You're an angel, Quick. Lemme slam it. These Codeines dont touch my kind of sick . . . "

Quick held back the bag and shook a finger at her. "Ah ah . . . No talkie, no junkie. What did you tell Tarzon?"

She had crawled to him now, looking up into his flat face with those eyes like rainslick tombstones. "He wanted to know about Gloria. You remember Gloria . . . "

"Sure. Gloria was family too. What did he want to know?"

"He found a motel manager up in Tahoe remembers she and I checking in with a coupla dates . . . "

"*You?*"

"Yeah, *me,*" she declared, surprising him with an unsuspected reserve of defiance before resuming a tone of tender banter: "It musta been a year ago. I dont usually do blacks but Glori's friend was one and he had a friend, so as a special favor to her . . . Anyway, Tarzon asked did I know who Glori's sugardaddy was. I told him no, Glori kept it a secret and he didnt exactly introduce himself . . . Only Glori did mention he was some kind of bigshot, like a politician, only not like in elections. I knew he had to be someone you'd recognize."

Quick cocked his head like a bird at a worm. "How?"

"Like I told Tarzon, the bonenose wore big cheap shades and a heavy trenchcoat and bigass cowboy hat in July . . . and a phony beard . . . Now?" She lifted a bloated hand.

"What did Tarzon say?"

"Please lemme get straight . . . I'll do ya . . . "

Quick slapped away the swollen hand groping for his zipper.

"Sex is a deflated currency in my world." It was one of the Fat Man's lines.

"Maybe I can *in*flate it . . . " Her lips cracked a smile like lifting a sewer manhole.

Quick snarled, "What . . . did Tarzon *say* when you told him that?"

"He asked would I recognize this nigger if he brought down his picture with . . . What did he call it? . . . a composite layover sheet for the beard."

"Anything else?"

"Yeah. He asked if I'd seen that Belly Blast. I told him no."

"The spic rassler makes loops for Mr. Moses? Where does she fit in this?"

"He didnt say."

"When's he coming back?" Quick dangled the glittery bag closer.

"Said a coupla days. Said the cops wouldnt have the mugs he wanted me to see, he'd probably have to go to the newspaper morgue . . . I was gonna lie, even if I did recognize the bonenose. That's what Mr. Moses would want, isnt it, Quick?"

"Sure, baby. Sure."

"Can I have it now? Please, Quick?"

Quick handed her the glassine envelope.

"You tell Mr. Moses he can trust me, hear?" She squirted the Codeine solution in an arc like milk squeezed from a tit and cast around for a cooker for the China white.

"It's pure, baby," chuckled Quick. "Just pour it in the barrel . . . then shake n shoot."

While she did so, her demented twittering echoing in the barrel, Quick looked around, nodding, his lower lip stuck out. "Lifestyles of the broke and bustout . . . You come a long ways, Fay."

"Old hookers never die," she giggled, burying the needle deep in her hip, "they just fade . . . " A strangled shriek cut off her voice as the sulphuric acid struck through her veins like lightning, melting her universe white, blasting her cerebral cortex to a stump the M.E. would later be unable to distinguish from number nine coal.

Quick stood hands in pockets enjoying her spectacular death spasms. Trying to claw open her chest, Fay DuWeye tore off one of her flaccid breasts. A swollen hand wrung blood from its pulp, then was still.

"Sure I'll tell the Fat Man he can trust you . . . now."

In the charcoal light of 0435 hours a state car passed in the gates and deposited an ungainly form on the Admin Building steps. The great prison stirred in its sleep with a gnash of steel and stretch of stone and grumble deep in its belly of chained souls.

SPACE CADETS

||||

The neon hand of stud circling the big sky outside Laramie showed bullets over deuces. Beneath, a scrolling digital sign promised vittles, lodging, and diesel fuel at independent prices. A soothing sight for bloodshot eyes squinting through the flyblown windshields of Kenworths and Freightliners cresting the Medicine Bow Range and slipping into sweet Georgia overdrive for the long downhill coast to the honkytonk oasis called Aces High Truck Ranch. And how those citizens bands would sizzle—

"Cmon cmon, Prairie Dog callin lot lizards, got financin for romancin . . . " and "Manitoba Blue haulin pipe that needs tight fittin, lust or bust, need a fillup filly, *come* back . . . " and more and more these days "Gypsy girl dance round my truck, Gypsy girl I want to . . . "

And Gypsy would come back, hawking her bahakas on a band beneath the hearing of ICC or Smokey: "Gypsy could, Gypsy would, Gypsy do what she oughtna should. Put one foot on the wheel, the other on the floor, and if a trucker dont get enough I wont let im back for more . . . *kasj!*"

She'd been ranching peckers at the truck plaza most of the summer. Where seldom was heard a discouraging word and the action was seven twentyfour—round the clock every day of the week. The handle Gypsy went with the new cover for the tattoos and rings. She'd been kidnapped as a baby by the gypsies and raised as their queen until she shot the whole camp one night in its sleep. It was the sort of hardtime fable that appealed to the highwaymen.

"Gypsy's had it rough," they'd shake their heads over coffee after roughing her up some themselves in their cabs. "But she's got heart still." "And she could suck the grain out of a twobyfour and spit toothpicks." Talent, after all, will out.

If she wasn't watching MTV in some trucker's cab or issuing her siren call over his CB, Rings could be found in the truck plaza's video arcade feeding quarters from a styrofoam cup in her favorite game, Space Cadet. So accomplished a cadet had Rings become that she could pulverize each malevolent meteor, disperse the intergalactic herds of dragoids, blast every last Hell Ship to electrons, and still retain forty cents' worth of gamma rays and photons with which to vaporize the Space Blob, last protector of the Cosmic Cube, the space cadet's holy grail. Many a weary trucker, seeking peace in a game of Pac Man, was startled by her cackling as she depressed both triggers, really pouring the beams into that pulsing glob of hyperspacial puke that had become in her febrile imagination the Fat Man. The Cosmic Cube, of course, was the diamond. Like, fur shur.

During the night the heat washed up from the valley floor, awakening the prison in a brass grip squeezing the breath from the walls, wringing sweat from the bars. Career cons demonstrated cellmade airconditioning for first termers, draping wet towels over the electric fans that ticked in the cellblocks by the hundreds like caged locusts.

It wasn't the heat itself that maddened Joe, but the claustrophobia it sponsored. He had to get outside. Finishing his paperwork at Hobby early this afternoon, he headed down the Mainline to the Yard gates blazing bright as furnace doors at its southern end. The heat dragged down the faces of passing cons into masks of agony.

Fingers nipped his sleeve. "Wait up, Joe." Benny Rizzuto, a Hobby potter, fell into step beside him. "We got trouble right here in River City," announced the side of his mouth.

"What trouble?" Joe laughed. "Other than it's too hot to even bop my baloney."

"I'll tell you on the Yard," Benny said darkly.

Control's riveted iron door swung wide in their path and a fourman escort of guards marched onto the Mainline with a chained convict in white overalls in their middle.

"Z Blocker," Benny whispered. "Come back from a parole hearing."

"Man walkin," hoarsely cried one of the escort. Joe and Benny pressed their backs to the wall with the other convicts on the Mainline.

The Z Blocker was in full body restraints, legirons and a bellychain to which his wrists were cuffed. A football helmet was strapped to his drugged head to protect it in collisions with floors and walls. In its shadow Joe glimpsed the dull sheen of lidless glassy eyes. The wretch twitched and trembled as though afflicted with Parkinson's disease. Waiting for the escort to shut Control's door and form up, his feet pawed at an invisible doormat and his hands yoyoed thin air.

"What'd he do?" Joe asked.

Benny shrugged. "He's so fulla Prolixin he dont even remember himself. That's what he's doin there, the Prolixin shuffle . . . A little step we may be dancin ourselves before long."

"What?" The security detail passed; they started walking again. "For Christ's sake, Benny. Quit jerkin me off. What trouble are you talkin about? Something about Hobby?" It was the only connection Joe could think of between the lifer and himself.

"Please, Joe. Dont rush me. I'm sorry I'm so squirrely. Maybe it's the heat, maybe I'm just scared. Seeing that Z Blocker didnt help. Let's bump some iron. Maybe I'll calm down some then and be able to think straight enough to tell you."

Murderers are usually the most easygoing convicts, their biggest problem having already been eliminated, and this cherrycheeked wifeslayer was no exception. But today Benny was pulling hard time. Joe only hoped the remitless heat wasn't driving him stir crazy.

"Take all the time you need, Benny."

The sun was hottest during its descent when it seemed stalled atop the cellblocks. Only two other cons were mad enough to be driving iron on the weight pile beneath Tower Three, Moonpie Monroe and Dr. Raggedy Mouth. Dr. Raggedy Mouth was a selfproclaimed voodoo witchdoctor from the Atchafalaya swamps of Louisiana. He greased his long dreadlocks with pork fat and crayoned circles around his protuberant eyes and flew into frenzied trances several times a day when he'd yap in Creole gibberish. Dr. Raggedy Mouth was Coldwater's black response to Swami.

No heat could burn out Moonpie and Raggedy's enthusiasm for iron. If they could, Joe was sure they'd eat the Olympic plates like pancakes. Moonpie was benchpressing six fortyfive kilo plates like feather pillows, grunting joyously to the meter of Raggedy's chant:

Pie yous a covershaker . . . TWO
unna slick slatbreaker . . . FOUR
one sweet babymaker . . . SIX

yous a binder Pie . . . EIGHT
a shonuff grinder . . . TEN
unna weak spot finder . . . TWELVE

Moonpie finished his set with a titanic groan and Raggedy took his place on the bench. The three hundred pounds flew off the stanchions as though Moonpie's conjuration suspended gravity:

Raggedy yous a sweet peter jeeter . . . TWO
one chilly womb beater . . . FO
cradleshaker . . . FIVE
whoretaker . . . SIX
lovefaker . . . SEVEN
yous a buckbinder Rag . . . NINE
a cold womanfinder . . . TEN

John Henry was a wimp next to this pair of ironheads.

Silently Benny loaded the bar with six twentyfive pound plates. Joe benchpressed it fifteen repetitions. Not bad for a whiteboy who'd never lifted more iron than a U-100 syringe, he kidded himself. At the end of three sets, his pectorals were inflated like hotwater bottles. Next they did military shoulderpresses, one hundred pounds behind the head until Joe's deltoids bunched tighter than lover's nuts.

He took a break while Benny burned out his last set, staggering in circles, hands on his slippery hips, in the trapezoidal shadow of Tower Three. The oxygenated blood foamed through his torn muscles, flushing him with an exhilarating sensation of depletion. Driving iron was the best means of dissipating the sourceless rages swirling on the Mainline like tornadoes out of neutral skies.

Two chicanos had joined them on the pile. Joe watched them working silently and earnestly through their routine. Neither could be over twenty; both wore the regulation cholo razorcut hair, spitpolished Santa Rosa hightops, sharply creased denims rolled just so at the cuff—*Zoot!*—the ubiquitous bandannas low over black eyes. The tattoos slithering on their sweaty torsos illustrated their romance with La Madre and La Muerte. On one back the Virgin was installed on a jeweled throne; she wore ermine capes and a riot of jewelry and looked more like an overcompensated puta than the Mother of God. On the other's back Jesu Christo rolled up weeping eyes beneath his bleeding thorns; below was a lengthy Spanish prayer in Gothic scroll. Each on his shoulder displayed the lowrider legend, MI LOCA VIDA; from one eye apiece flowed the frozen inkblue tear.

One of the ironhead carnales caught Joe staring and issued a mute challenge with a roll of gleaming shoulder muscles. Joe turned to watch Benny wrap up his set.

"You'll be musclebound in a coupla months," warned Joe. "You wont be able to toss any pots."

Benny flung the barbell down. "If I'm around in a coupla months," he gasped. "Cmon. Let's do the stroll before we cramp up."

They crossed to the cinder track circling the hundredacre Yard next to the double row of fences festooned with razor ribbon and concertina wire. Joe puffed his cheeks and said, "All right, Benny. I'm not trying to rush you, but if this thing involves me I think I've got a right to know."

Benny studied Joe's face with a sad slantendicular. "You're right. You got that right . . . Two weeks before you got here, Joe, a kid was murdered. It was a racial thing. His killer cut off his dick with an X-acto knife, then crammed it up his . . . "

"Hey! Cmon. I dont need *this* noise."

"Yeah you do, Joe. Cuz X-acto knives can only be ordered through Hobby."

"But still, if I wasnt here even . . . "

"Wait. Just listen . . . Night before last the Warden brought in a new ramrod for S&I. A regular Conan the Gooner. His first order of business is to crack that murder." Benny bit a nail, spit out its quick. "To do it he's playin the snitch game."

"The what?"

"Snitch game. It's just as simple as it's deadly. They coerce information from convicts by threatening to falsely expose them as informers. It's a no win game for a convict. Either way, whether he snitches or not, he's branded one. He's as good as dead unless he locks up. Maybe even then."

A frisbee fluttered across their path, coming to a rest on the sixfoot strip of grass between the fence and track. Joe made a reflexive move to retrieve it.

"Wave!" Benny warned him. Convicts weren't allowed on that strip of grass; it was no man's land. Tower guards could assume they were making for the fence and fire. To retrieve balls and frisbees and such, they had first to wave to the closest tower and receive an answering wave acknowledging their innocent purpose.

Joe waved. Nothing from Tower Two. He lifted his cap and waved again and shouted into the still heat. After a moment, in the shadows behind the smokedglass window, a shotgun described a lazy arc. Joe crossed the strip to the fence. For a fleeting, manic instant he wanted to follow Whisper. It was the same hypnotic exaltation he felt in high places that made him want to leap. Death as liberation, death as instant redemption. Instead, he stooped, picked up the frisbee, and fluttered it back to its waiting convicts.

"Because the X-acto knife was a Hobby requisition," Benny continued as they fell once more in step, "S&I is ducating inmates with lead Hobby positions. That includes me . . . and that includes you. They know it was whiteboys who thrilled that kid."

Joe laughed disbelievingly. "How can they ducat me? If I wasnt even here, how could I have any information on the killing?"

Benny shrugged. "You might have heard something. Besides, the Hobby clerk is always worth putting the screws to. He has his fingers in enough contraband pies that he's sure to give up something. If they got an inkling of your A.B. action, they'll lean on you to turn that over. Whether or not you do, they'll make sure the brotherhood believes you did. You're finished on the Mainline then . . . "

"Christ."

"Just remember, if they take you in, hold your mud. If they try jacketing you, lock up. You're a short timer, Joe. You might last in Protective Custody."

Joe jumped at the shriek of the Yard whistle. Reentering the prison with its stench of huddled flesh and hollow echoing noises revived a childhood memory, of coming out of a hot summer day into the primate house at the zoo. Once a baboon hurled a pawful of shit right smack between Joe's shoulder blades. A woman behind him screamed. The boy only turned and looked with the briefest astonishment into the atavistic replica of his own defiance, then laughed.

"What about you?" Joe asked. "Can you pull life in the Hole?"

Benny didn't hear him; his eyes were widened down the Mainline. He grabbed Joe's arm. "Here come the space cadets."

Approaching the Yard Sally Port down the Mainline marched in lockstep the most menacing military detail Joe had ever seen off the silver screen or outside comicbook covers. They were uniformed in a synthetic quilted armor like black polyester chainmail. It flowed from the bottom rim of their conical helmets, giving them a scifi samurai look. They wore heavy studded gauntlets and kneehigh metalnailed boots that rang sparks down the Mainline.

"Christ! They look like they're policing a nuclear meltdown."

"AIDS armor," growled Benny. "Kevlar, the stuff they make bullet-proof vests from. Director's finding said that Coldwater was an AIDS greenhouse. Wearing the armor they can kick ass and not worry about the blood . . . Look, there in front, that's the new captain playing dragons and dungeons for keeps."

"How do you know?" Joe asked. Their black Plexiglas faceshields were down.

"His *limp* . . . "

Christ! It cant be! Even in my direst imaginings of Hell . . .

The convicts shrank to either side, hugging the walls as this band of futuristic guards approached. Joe and Benny followed suit. Joe kept telling himself over and over again it couldn't be true . . .

Until the blackmailed squadron halted right before them and its leader reached under and lifted off his helmet and Joe was staring at the lips like bloated worms, the veinburst nose and bleak bloody eye of Rowdy McGee.

Another of the detail removed his helmet and stepped forward. He held a clipboard. "Inmate Rizzuto, Benjamin A-00893 . . . " he cried in a loud voice obviously calculated to spread the news to all of General Population. "You are under escort to the offices of Search and Investigation for questioning in the matter of the homicide of Billy Joe Girod . . . Inmate Speaker, Joseph Holly . . . "

"Take the other puke in," McGee slurred. "I want a word with this bowelbaby in private."

It's the cap, Joe flashed. He's too frightened of it to take me in. Whatever fate awaits Benny, this old rag on my head has spared me. From the corner of the eye Joe watched the potter being swallowed into the black phalanx, which aboutfaced and marched back up the Mainline in gunfiring lockstep.

McGee lowered his voice to a gaseous croak redolent of beer and tacos. "Where you get the . . . *lid?*"

Joe didn't answer. He had no wish to reduce McGee's pathological terror by explanation. McGee had been rendered outwardly by Whisper's baseball team what he'd always been inwardly, a monster. Now he associated the cap with that metamorphosis. Any mystery attached to the cap could only deepen and enlarge his paranoia.

"Okay, Speaker. Play it chilly. But you saw what happened to the last man who wore it." McGee cocked his head, stretching a pink eye at Joe. "You did see, didnt you?"

Joe nodded tightly, remembering suddenly that the cap had flown off when the first bullet struck Whisper, that McGee shotgunned him bare-headed.

"That's *good*, " gloated McGee. "Having something to look forward to helps pass the time."

McGee's howl could have won him a job in television hosting latenight horror flicks. Tucking the helmet beneath his blackmailed arm, he turned and lurched back up the Mainline. The head with its jagged streak of platinum tipped back, laughing. The way he laughed at Whisper on the fence before blowing a hole big as Dallas in his back.

LA MORDIDA

||||

The waiting room of La Infirmia de la Nuestra Madre smelled of chloroform and humid limestone and dense, wet jungle rot seeping through the single windowless aperture overlooking a greasy calm Pacific. The adobe hovels of Boca Prieta tumbled down to the beach; the lights strung on naked wires through the streets had just come on. The tinsel slab of the Hotel Fiesta remained a dark megalith against the indigo ocean, like a giant transistor radio with batteries gone dead. A wind snuck up the arroyo, bringing the smell of frying tortillas and the tattered thrash of wild palms.

They brought Dan in before light; Kitty arrived at dawn and had been there since. They said the jeep flipped several times falling down the fiftyfoot cliff to the beach and Dan was lucky to breathe. The girl, sadly, was dead.

"Shitfire," Kitty muttered trying to straighten the pleats of her wilted dress. "Silk," the label read; cornsilk, she suspected. Already ruined and Dan had bought it at the Hotel Marejada's gift shop just the day before yesterday when they arrived from Mexico City. He'd selected the prim dress to accompany the ring he bought to masquerade as a wedding band. Just for appearances, he quickly explained to allay any suspicion that he was trying to pull a fast one. Provincial Mexicans were deeply prejudiced against living in sin, he said. Dan was some kind of big expert on Mexican culture.

Kitty lit a cigaret and resumed pacing the waiting room. Her heels clicked on the sandstone tiles, slow sad castanets. If that dufus were conscious, she bet herself, he'd wish our marital status was his biggest headache. It never rained but it poured, and Dan's clouds broke yesterday twenty minutes before the skies over Boca Prieta divided like clockwork at quarter to four to loose their quotidian deluge.

"Telegramo para Señor Graves," hawked the bellhop in the seedy monkeysuit who doubled during the day as cabana boy in appropriate costume. From the way he eavesdropped Kitty suspected the twerp spoke perfect English but was operating on the theory that the native lingo fattened gratuities. If so, Dan, who overtipped by habit, did nothing to disprove it.

They were sitting in the hotel's gloomy stucco lobby giving on to the ocean. The fronds of a potted palm drooped over their heads. They were yellowed and pitted with black. It seemed to Kitty that everything in Mexico was slow and sensually dying.

"Damn!" Dan was trembling, chattering the pastiche of teletype tape in his hand. He slapped it on the table to snap his fingers at the departing bellhop. "Muchacho! Bring me a double . . . no, make it a triple Lonely Bull."

"What is it?" Kitty asked. Dan didn't normally drink. Whenever invited, he'd tap his bean and say "Mens sano," which sounded like a urinal cake to Kitty.

Dan didn't answer. Rereading the telex for the third time, his lips whitened and his brow blackened like the thunderheads marshaling above.

The bellhop delivered the drink in a water tumbler. Dan drilled it in three gulps. "Otro!" he croaked, paying with a large note like a printed party napkin, waving away the change, turning on Kitty as if she and not the bellhop should be killed for bearing bad news, blurting: "My wife has filed charges against me for . . . for . . . " He emptied the next triple down his throat as quickly as he could have tossed it on the floor, reordered, then turned to Kitty with a queer, quizzical halfsmile, as if she might burst out laughing and tell him it was all a joke. "She's charged me with molesting my own son."

"Your son?" And she did laugh, though not the way he wanted or even the way she wished she could. She laughed in the same trembly way he smiled, the laugh of a person praying a joke has run its course. "I dont understand . . . Why?"

"She wants custody, of course. Or should I say child support." His voice assumed a catty lilt. "It's all the rage now. Its faintest suggestion creates a sensation."

"Aw, chin up, hoss. You'll straighten it out. Shitfire, I'll testify you've been too busy molesting me."

"It's no joke." He peered wobbily at her in the gathering gloom. Thunder muttered on the horizon. "Even if the allegations are discredited, the stink will cling to me. My image will shrivel, my business go bellyup. I'll be a pariah. Ruined."

"You're overdoing it, good buddy. Tragically. A little breath of scandal gives business goosebumps, its the American way."

"A little *breath?* We're talkin typhoon here . . . "

Kitty flipped her hand. "She's just jerkin your chain, Dan. The way you jerk hers every time you subpoena her checkbooks or demand an inventory of her jewelry. Shitfire, the two of you fight over that kid like a dinner check. Neither of you want him, you just dont want the other to have the satisfaction."

"How can you say that? I live for my son, he's all that matters." It sounded sappy, like a life insurance commercial.

"Then you should be more concerned about him than your image, your fuckin business."

Then thunder cracked the sky like a hammer striking a gourd, spreading electric branches overhead; and the rain fell in fat drops, plucking silver nipples from the flagstones without. Kitty took a grateful breath of suddenly lighter, fresher air. Dan drilled his drink and ordered another.

"Easy on the hootch, good buddy. Remember what the immigration boys said about humidity and alcohol."

"Good. I cant get a plane out of this dump until tomorrow. I'd appreciate getting twice as drunk twice as fast . . . Muchacho! Otro!"

Kitty laughed. This dump had been primitif chic an hour ago. It was she who suggested Acapulco. It might be overbuilt and spoiled and all that crap, but at least there were doctors available if something went awry with her pregnancy. No, Dan said. They must go somewhere wild and natural to correspond with his feelings for her.

You dufus. Guess who needs the doctors now?

To make matters worse, they arrived to find that La Fonda del Luna, the only hotel in Boca Prieta where iguanas didn't share the bathroom, had gone bankrupt. So Dan booked them a moldy suite at this crumbling relic frequented, as far as she could tell, by Eurotrash with black socks and sandals and six out of the Ten Most Wanted Mexicans, all in mirrored sunglasses.

"Rickie gave a statement," Dan was saying. "It's not every day your own kid accuses you of diddling him."

"Your wife made him . . . Imagine the pressure on the poor kid to make him lie . . . He might be so mixed up he actually believes you been boffin him."

Dan sneered. "What does a whore know about child psychology?"

It was the first that he'd ever called her that. "I'm just tryin to help," she said evenly.

"Gimme some pesos. That's alla help I wan. Wanna nudder drink." Over Dan's shoulder the bellhop cocked his head and grinned at her.

Kitty upended her purse on the pigskin table, dumping out all its beaner play money. She watched with scorn as he stuffed an indiscriminate wad into the bellhop's monkeyclaw.

"If Little Lord Fauntleroy can tell anyone with a straight face I've abused him, fuck im . . . "

Kitty flinched. The phrase was so startlingly out of character as to carry utter conviction. In that instant she couldn't be sure the charges weren't true. Hearing Dan deflect his venom from his wife to son, she flashed on Papa blaming his life's every woe on her while Mama neither heard nor saw nor once spoke the evil and Kitty suffered the outrage in silence.

No, not Dan, she quickly changed her mind—he's just drunk. You got a baby in your belly and Papa on your mind, girl.

"I wish you could hear yourself takin out your lousy marriage on a defenseless kid," she said.

He swiveled facing her with eyes suddenly bright and sober. The rain was subsiding, individual drops hissing on the flagstones. His voice was carved in ice. "Marriage? You whore! What do you know of marriage? And where do you get off lecturing on parentage lugging a convict's bastard in your gut . . . "

Kitty shot to her feet. "I aint got this comin."

"While you were out sucking twelve dicks a day to keep you and that dirtbag loaded, I was working twelve hours a day to send that kid to the best schools . . . "

She dug in her jeans for a coin. Swinging around the table for the tall narrow stairs, she flipped it to him. "Here's a peso, dildohead. Call someone who gives a fuck."

Halfway up the stairs she paused. Below Dan was lurching to the rickity bamboo bar. The mongrel bellhop set the bottle of tequila before him. "Bes fren a man has," she heard Dan slobber; obsequiously the bellhop hissed "Seguro qui si" and winked up where he knew she stood in the shadows.

She locked the door of the suite's bedroom and napped. She awoke to Dan's pounding the door, bleating apologies, begging admittance. He was very drunk, very loud. She listened to his fists slide down the door, pound the floor abjectly once or twice, then fall still. She went back to sleep.

It was night when she next awoke. She heard mariachi music. It was a

song that she'd heard the night before at dinner and asked the band to
repeat when they came around her and Dan's table. It was called Las
Ombras, "The Shadows," and was darkly romantic and moody and, yup
. . . tragic.

She rose and went to the window. Party lights were strung around the
verandah over the ocean. Evidently some big local cheeses were in attendance: a couple of fat guys in military or police uniforms, their women in
outdated American styles. There was Dan regaling a knot of spics, gesturing grandly. She caught snatches of his voice shouting about *la mer* and
el cielo. Bombed wasn't the word for his condition.

The band struck up some sexy tango or other. Everybody started strutting and strolling and dangerously dipping. They looked ridiculous from
above: overage, overweight revelers aping svelte youthful passion and
bumping into crappy lawn furniture. Dan was dancing with the greaser gal
with orange hair who waited on their table in the diningroom. Her name
was Concha. Her movements were languorous and full of abandon. Probably thought she could replace the gringa upstairs, be carried back to the
land of washing machines and takeout chicken.

Dumb cuchafrita.

The music stopped. The band packed up its instruments and the local
couples called *Buenas noches* and *Hasta luego* and weaved away laughing
in the dark. Kitty watched Concha supporting Dan toward the parking lot.
He'd rented a funny little Volkswagen jeep thing with a candystriped
awning to show Kitty some sea caves. She heard it start, watched it careen
out of the lot.

It was just another shouldaknown.

"Señora Graves?" The little doctor with patent leather hair stood in the
waitingroom door, small hands joined, their fingers steepled beneath his
pursed lips.

"Yes?" She stepped on her cigaret and smoothed the Mexican prom
dress.

"The inside bleeding. It cannot be stopped." He spread his hands.

"Then he . . . "

"Yes. I am sorry. Soon he must. There is nothing we can do."

"Does he know?"

"No. We have not told him. We thought you . . . We have given him
morphine for the pain, but he is conscious."

"May I see him?"

"Of course, Señora." The little doctor stepped aside with a sweep of his
arm as graceful as a toreador's paso.

She didn't know why, but she expected IV's and bleeping video monitors and everything like in an American hospital. That a man whose life had been defined by gadgetry should be deprived its benefit at death struck her as tragic. Beneath a naked cross in a naked whitewashed room lay Dan, clutching the sheet that would soon be drawn over his face.

"Well I did it this time," he mumbled when he saw her. He looked like hell.

She pulled a straightbacked chair to his side and sat. "Yeah. Here's another fine fix you've got yourself into."

"I'm sorry."

"Dont be. That news was a jolt. And I dont guess I helped."

"I know I said some things I didnt mean."

"Ssshhh." She laid a cool finger on his puffed and fevered lips.

"I'll mend, dont worry. Be a better man, too. Sometimes it takes a brush with death to bring you to your senses." She only smiled. "There was someone with me . . . What happened?"

"She bought it . . . " The purple eye blinked and Kitty's chichis rivaled great powers rising and falling, taking a big one. "The police here are a little worked up about it, ole buddy. Say either her family's compensated or you go to La Mesa. That's the penitentiary down here. But it can all be fixed with a bribe. La mordida, they call it. The death bite. I've brought one of your checks already made out." She reached in her purse. "You just sign it and I can take care of this business toot sweet so you can concentrate on getting better."

"Say, this dope's gettin me sleepy . . . I cant see . . . How much?"

"Few hundred," she flashed bright teeth lying. She fit the Mark Cross in his slack fingers. The effort of signing left him gulping raggedly.

"Guess I'll mosey along." Kitty stood. She fluttered the check to her lips and blew him a kiss across it, drying the ink.

"I'm gonna get better," Dan repeated. "Be a better man, too."

"Then I'd say you're doin the right thing, good buddy."

Back in the suite she wrote Joe a letter laying out her drawings. She chewed her lip wondering whether to mention Tarzon and decided not to. *Till the wheels fall off,* she signed it.

When Kitty called the next morning the little doctor said Dan had died during the night. She called down to the desk to switch her plane reservations from California to Texas. She had decided to go home to Galveston to have the baby. The ten thousand she scored off Dan would pay the doctors and buffer her from Papa. She packed in a hurry. They were sure to freeze his accounts shortly; she couldn't waste any time cashing the check.

The tickets were ready when she got downstairs. The bellhop with a face like a wasted coconut was playing desk clerk this morning. She handed him the letter and asked him to call a cab, as in *pronto*.

"One's already sittin at the curb," he answered in a flat SoCal accent. "Idling," he added with meaning.

Kitty returned his last collusive wink.

AN AMERICAN
ORIGINAL

||||

Mondays prison salaries were credited to the convicts' books, and Tuesday mornings they made store, thronging the Mainline in front of Commissary's three steel shutters an hour before their opening at 0930. Boisterously as children besieging an icecream truck, they jockeyed for position in one of the lines, playing the dozens with their homeys, finetuning their Tales, catching up on cellblock scuttlebutt.

The Hobby clerk made twentyfour dollars a week, the highest pay level in the joint. Joe jostled in the middle of his line, using Earl's back to complete a shopping list. He'd bribed a cell for himself the week before and was eager to provision it. The most expensive freezedried coffee, the biggest bars of chocolate, stationery unstolen from the state—he housed in T Block now, on the first floor power wing, where the pen's most influential convicts celled. Appearances must be maintained.

Several places in front of Joe stood a scurfy young con whose face showed the scars of pitched battle with acne and now challenged the world to reveal its next adversary. He was holding an impromptu rape seminar, instructing a couple of fish on the finer points of booty banditry: "Always use a rubber. They cant prove it forensically that way." It sounded technical enough to appeal to the fishes' ignorance; they turned wily eyes on one another, nudged out lower lips to nod. Joe coughed to disguise his laughter. How absurd was the popular notion that prisons were colleges of crime.

It made as much sense as going to Alcoholics Anonymous to learn how to drink. Prisons were home to the social fuckup and criminal flunkout; the only thing to learn there was how to keep on fucking up, keep on returning to stand in Commissary lines.

Up crashed the shutters like betting windows. The singing labels, the swirling plastic colors, the airconditioning sweet with icecream and candy—Eden was never paradise until it was lost and once remembered.

"F Stop," Joe said shuffling forward with the line, "what are you doin makin store? You've fucked off all your ducats gambling."

"I sent off for a free text, yeah. The *Dasypus Novemcinctus*."

Joe said that he knew Earl was Catholic but wouldn't have slotted him for a missal reader. In a hollow, oracular voice Earl intoned: "It means arma*dil*los. Which is good as a prayer to me."

"Ah *ha!*" Joe frowned and plucked his chin repeating it, "Armadillos."

Earl trained his ambiguous gaze on Joe, gray eye like a spoiled oyster, blue like a core of flame. "Know what that means in Spanish? Thought not. Little . . . armored . . . things. Spics got a way with words. Words and knives, yeah . . . When I raise up I'm gonna have me an armadillo ranch in west Looziana, Texas maybe, yeah."

Joe thumped the heel of his hand to the side of his head to dislodge whatever was making him hear things.

"Gonna ranch the little fuckers for dogfood. Best dog meat God in his wisdom created. They lowfat, nutritious, yeah, tasty as pork. And with enough Dixie Beer to keep em amorous they multiply faster than Tijuana cucarachas . . . Plus"—Earl raised a bony finger—"they sperm cure baldness, yeah."

"F Stop, I dont know what's eatin your brain worse, Alzheimer's or weisenheimer's . . . "

"Did you know the female lays nine eggs and they hatch into nine eye-dentical baby armadillos she cant even tell apart? Yeah you right. I bet too you had no earthly idea that the armadillo got two choices when faced with danger. He can run, and I guarantee them fuckers can make *time*. Or he can burrer hisself, yeah, completely underground faster n you can zip yer fly. I talkin about sunbaked East Texas *scrabble*ass dirt that's harder n yer dick gonna ever git."

In exchange for this zoologic arcana, Earl felt entitled to ask Joe for another loan. He owed six cartons to Big and Little Casino, Coldwater's bookmaking kingpins. Joe assented on the condition that Earl fasten his obsession on a team other than the Dodgers, whose bullpen, in Earl's words, was "sucking a big one, yeah."

"You gotta dance with the one that brung you," Earl said, shrugging high bony shoulders like arranging folded wings.

"Not after that one's broke both your feet, F Stop."

But the coot wasn't listening. He'd hooked the arm of an ovate hairball rushing from the Commissary windows with a paper sack of groceries. "Lay some of them chips on me, Ramsey. I'll tighten you up, yeah, once I got my own zuuzuus and whamwhams . . . "

"Dont hold your breath," Joe advised.

"That's barbecue flavored," the hairball made sure Earl understood before surrendering the bag of potatochips. Cyril Ramsey was a U.C. Davis animal husbandry student who'd taken his major too far to heart and was doing time for a Crime Against Nature as represented by a lamb. He was also a compulsive writ writer, his most celebrated being a petition to allow him to import a blowup sexdoll into the institution for worship. The court, being disinclined to such a broad view of religious freedom, slamdunked it.

When he wasn't decrying the California Gulag, this Custody clerk enjoyed mourning the rape of the Constitution. "May as well use that noble charter for shitpaper." The convicts of Coldwater, who understood the Constitution's abstract freedoms about as well as the Dow Jones Industrial Average, took to bleating his name, thus: "Rahmsey. Baa Baa *Rah-ahhhmmm*sey."

Sweat formed a twitchy dewline on the sheep shtupper's lip this morning.

"What's eatin you, Baa Baa?" sprayed potatochips from Earl's mouth. "You nervous as a longtailed cat in a room fulla rockingchairs."

"Got sixteen Protective Custody lockups to type . . . I'm late, I'm late . . . " Baa Baa marchhared down the Mainline.

"Who P.C.'d?" asked Joe, reaching for some chips.

Earl sighed, rubbed his nose, and lamped Joe with the sympathetic gray. "I was waitin to tell you later . . . A bunch of cons locked up on the First Watch. Benny Rizzuto was one of em. Laundry workers found a note from Benny to S&I with love in one of McGee's tunic pockets. Already there's a dozen cigaret contracts on Benny's ass."

"Benny wouldnt kite the Man. It's a forgery!"

"Yeah you right. But how many handwriting experts work in prison laundries?"

Joe cursed. "How does McGee get away with it?"

"Because it works. General Population aint caught on he's playin the snitch game, no. They believe one or more of them boys turned over. They see lockin up as proof."

"Proof of what? They havent braced Girod's killer."

Earl nodded sadly. "Gooners picked up the killer last night. Some kook they call Tin Man, yeah, for the Chowhall trays he used to slide under his blues in the Soledad race riots. He's a leatherworker, too. That's what I was waitin to break to you slow. Gooners trashed Hobby big time and found the X-acto knife he used on that kid in his supply locker. They gonna shut Hobby down."

The potatochips in Joe's mouth became peeled paint. He turned and stared out a nearby window. Silver mists flowed fast as whitewater torrents over the high Sierra passes, fanning icy fretwork down the slopes. The air through the open panes was cooly scented with ponderosa pine and chaparral. Nature's grand indifference to the squalid inventions of its creatures enraged him, the way a negligent parent might.

"I'm sorry about Hobby, amigo. But maybe it'll discourage you from believin that cap's a lucky charm. I tell you true, I'm almost sad I give it to you. Yeah McGee's scared of it, but scared jist makes him hate harder. You say the cap saved you from goin with Benny. I say, saved you for what? . . . If Whisper hadnt wore the thing, McGee would never have recognized him, no. Think on that."

Fabulous Frank slumped elbows propped on the cushioned ledge of the bar at the Silk'n'Spurs feeling lower than whale shit.

Darla had packed and gone—that led off the list of reasons for the triple Dewars clutched in his vibrating fist. Mister Fab came back to their hotel the night before, shitfaced and still wearing the Ruger Redhawk .357 Magnum in the Kwikdraw holster Mr. Moses made him wear ever since the theater robbery. Darla was in the bathroom fixing her face and Frank collapsed in the chair before the TV. An old John Wayne flick was on the late show, *Los* something spic or other. And here came the Duker himself down Main Street, gundueling some desperado. El Fabuloso lurched to his feet, stood spreadlegged like Wyatt Earp, poised to slap leather. He *thought* the Duke went for his iron first, but couldn't say for sure. *Ka-*POW! Fabulous Frank rocketed a slug right through the screen. The cops came and everything. Darla said that was it, she was gone if she had to use the fire escape, and Frank better get some help with his drinking.

The real pisser was he lost his tweety twat without even finding out who was faster, the Duke or Mr. Fab.

"Anudder!" he hollered at a shape in the backbar shadows. "N leave out the ice . . . jus gets in the way."

A hand tugged his sleeve. Frank turned blearily. It was Ollie O'Conner, a beat cop out of North Station.

"Frank, here's two hundred on account."

Fabulous Frank frowned thumbing the greasy bills in the envelope.

"But, Ollie. You're into us for five yards. And you know the Fat Man's callin in all his markers now with the heat up."

O'Conner slanted both ways to make sure they couldn't be overheard. "I got a coupla items that's worth maybe more than a few hundred to the Fat Man." From inside his sports jacket he withdrew a microcassette and a plastic baggie filled with slips of paper. "I know he's lookin fer leads on who knocked over the Kama Sutra bank. These come out of Lieutenant Tarzon's office safe. They was tagged for a homicide jacket."

"Tarzon," Frank repeated. His groin squirmed feeling again the steel muzzle nuzzling his cojones. He stepped to the juke to examine the baggie by its fizzing lights.

"Those are your own betting slips," Ollie illumined him.

"I can see that, asshole. Only why they covered with blood?" Frank swung demented eyes down on the short cop. "And what are they doin tagged for a homicide jacket? Werent nobody killed in the theater . . . And what's on the tapes?"

O'Conner shrugged. "You guys figure it out. Just tell the Fat Man who give the stuff to yuh. See if he wont let me off on what I owe . . . Now, today, I want to get down on Top Bubble Gal in the third . . . "

"You aint gettin down on shit till I see the boss . . . Check with me tomorrow." O'Conner turned to leave. Frank halted him with a last question. "Whose homicide jacket?"

"Some hooker named Gloria Monday. Got iced six months ago on Nob Hill."

Frank regained his barstool unsteadily. How had his slips gotten mixed up with a murder? Suddenly the loss of his teenage Hoovermatic paled next to the paranoid fantasies blooming in his bookie bean. He filed the baggie and cassette inside his sharkskin doublebreasted, wrinkling his brow as his wet brain sloshed in search of where he'd heard the name before. He said it aloud, quizzically—"Gloria *Monday?*"

"Wrong bar," purred a blowsy blonde perched three stools down. "But I was called Stormie Monday in my . . . stage days. Among other things."

"I like women with a cute patter," Frank drawled, all parimutuel prophet once more. He shot his cuffs and smoothed back his gray ducktail. "The gift of gab turns on Mister Fab . . . Why dontcha slide on down here and touch asses . . . I mean *glasses* with an American original."

DEVILSTONE

||||

The pronunciamento was posted on the Mainline outside Custody:

> BY ORDER OF THE WARDEN THE HANDICRAFTS PROGRAM HAS BEEN
> CLOSED AS A THREAT TO INSTITUTIONAL SECURITY.
>
> LT. ROWDY MCGEE, S&I

Passing convicts gave the military stencil the briefest and most sullen of looks. It was only the latest symptom of the pen's transformation into a human cold storage facility. The junior college program had been canceled, the prison newspaper shut down; the Band Room was turned into a dormitory for population overflow, and every week inmate ironworkers welded second bunks into the cells of another wing.

That morning Joe overheard at a table behind him in the increasingly quiet Chowhall a black electrician whistle low and soft: "Neighbor back home had a kennel and when his wife got sick he had to take in more dawgs than his pens could rightfully hold. To make her medical bills, y'unnerstan. Just kept packin them in until those dawgs could hardly turn around. The night his wife died, he spent at the hospital. We heard them dawgs yappin and snarlin all night, raisin unholy hell. Mornin half them was dead. Jus tore to *shreds*. Dother half was chewed up so bad our neighbor had to shoot em once he buried his wife."

A certainty of Armageddon was settling like a chill onto the Mainline.

Joe had to stop by Custody for a special ducat admitting him to Hobby to clean out his desk. The guard keyed him onto the Activites Unit at Work Call, and he rushed down to the Handicrafts section and picked his way through the ransacked office out into the shop area. There he stood with mouth agape. It looked like ground zero at Santa's workshop.

The Gooners had smashed ceramic molds, slashed artists' canvases, dumped leather dyes and paints. They ran sheet metal through the table saws, chipping and bending the blades; they jumpwired the kiln's thermostat, cranked it up and blew it out. The inmate lumber cage had been looted. The doors hanging open at the loading docks left no doubt how the lumber and innumerable inmate tools, artifacts, and other possessions had left the reservation. Via every guard's preferred private vehicle, the 4×4 pickup, the better to haul off the tonnage of foodstuffs and materiel stolen weekly from the institution.

When the Gooners finished their pillage of the shop, stealing not only state hardware, but inmate drugs, cash, cigarets—even condoms to be resold at a discount to restock the mensroom machines in Coldwater's bars—they clogged the drains of every sink and left the water running, flooding all. An earthquake might have caused similar wreckage, assisted by a tidal wave.

Joe slogged through the kneedeep dirty water, turning off the taps. At last just one loud drip remained that he couldn't find, a solemn plangence like an echoing clapless bell measuring the deep, silent truth tolling in his heart: that more than these men's pastimes and hobbies lay ravaged; it was their selfworth, the last facsimile of identity represented in their artifacts. Down his face streamed tears loosed by the spilled gallons of toxic fluids; inside fell an acid rain of gall, corroding but not consuming.

Not knowing how else to be useful, he began a spot inventory of what remained. Jailhouse lawyers and writ writers would file suits no doubt; the cons took some consolation in their access to the courts. That decisions were made at their behest was mark enough; it little mattered whether favorably or not.

He passed the potter's wheel smashed to bits and the leather workers' area where several of Dr. Raggedy Mouth's gris gris bags stuffed with sawdust and snippets of his dreadlocks bobbed atop water swirled with bright acrylic paint; past the artists' section where one of Horsekiller's airbrushed paintings floated, ripped in half, a rendition of an Indian maiden astride a Harley, her attitude suggesting sexual congress; past the ceramic shelves hurled to the floor, the hundreds of smashed molds, the carpentry bench where a couple of birdhouses remained intact—anything as eyecatching as one of Irons's jewelry boxes was atop a Gooner's mantel by now. He paused at the blownout kiln, thinking sadly of Benny and wondering how he fared in the Hole.

"I'll send him some zuuzuus and whamwhams," he promised aloud before remembering he was wiped out. Whatever he hadn't loaned to Earl he had hidden around Hobby. All Joe had left was in his cell.

Making his way through the detritus back to the office, he winced passing the jewelry section. Here he knew the Gooners had found the richest booty stored in padlocked lockers. Opals, sapphires, emeralds, gold, and silver—material these men had spent years accumulating for their craft. Rudy Malec's locker on the end had been jimmied with a crowbar; at a glance Joe saw he'd lost not just his gems and precious metals, but all his sophisticated drills, their bits, precision torches, and grinding devices. He was cringing with pity for whatever target of opportunity was afforded the AB Captain's wrath when a colorful pamphlet floating in the filthy water caught his eye. He stooped, picked it up, and dried its cover with his sleeve.

It was titled *Celebrated Diamonds of the World.* Idly Joe thumbed its soggy pages, staring at the photographs of the fabulous stones above brief descriptions and histories. Examining amid such desolation this compendium of boundless wealth both sickened and mesmerized him. Faintly he heard Work Call ring from the Mainline and was about to toss the brochure aside when his heart skipped a beat, then clogged his throat and bulged his eyes. No mistaking the teardrop shape, the blue scintillance against the black velvet backdrop. He was staring at the blue diamond he stole from Baby Jewels.

His eye flitting back and forth between the text and its subject, Joe read:

THE BLUE JAGER MOON   This spectacular sixty-nine carat fancy blue was discovered in 1834 under peculiar circumstances at the Jagerfonstein Mines in Bechuanaland, now Botswana. An underwater sulphur spring of exceptional strength and velocity was accidentally struck at the bottom of the site's deepest shaft. Of the sixteen Kalahari bushmen drowned in the mishap, the corpse of only one was recovered when it floated days later to the top of the flooded shaft. In its mouth was found this extraordinary fancy blue. The bushmen christened it the "Devilstone," linking it to an evil deity of the desert tribe, associated with mirages and poisoned springs. The Blue Jager Moon's subsequent history tended to support rather than debunk this superstition.

The diamond's first owner, Dutch explorer Balthazar Zutger, disappeared with it on a search for the source of the Nile, circa 1857. The

Blue Jager Moon next came to light in the possession of Egyptian potentate, Khedive Ismalamud, at the close of the century. He sent the diamond aboard a treasure dhow as part of the dowry due a Persian sheik for his marriage to his daughter, Fatima Tezreh, a girl of fabled beauty. She and the dhow were lost without a trace in the Red Sea in 1902.

Here the diamond's history becomes indistinguishable from its legend, which has it that a fisherman in the Strait Bab el Mandeb recovered the Blue Jager Moon from the belly of a fish. From there it traveled through the Ottoman court, across the Balkans, in and out of the hands of Ferdinand, Tsar of Bulgaria; was rumored to have been briefly a bauble of Mata Hari, gift of an obscure Swabian prince, before appearing verifiably at auction in Paris in 1912. There it was purchased by representatives of Viscount Wm. Waldorf Astor, who dispatched it in the company of Lady Astor to his American cousins aboard the *Titanic*. Mysteriously, the Blue Jager Moon was not secured in the purser's vault to be lost with the rest of the ship's valuables when the *Titanic* struck an iceberg and sank. The diamond was rescued from the North Atlantic in the possession of one of Lady Astor's maids. Subsequently, the Blue Jager Moon was sold in 1922 to Barrisford Rhiordan, the California sugar tycoon. As part of his estate it now belongs to his granddaughter, Daphne Riordan-Bell, wife of California State Supreme Court Justice Lucius Bell . . . Over its hundred and fifty years above ground, the Blue Jager Moon has been Magna, Marquis and Brilliant cut. Against the advice of gemologists, who argued that a further cutting would rob the diamond of carats and quality, Barrisford Rhiordan ordered its current Pear Cut to eternalize one of the many tears he shed when his wife, Marguerite, drowned in a freak yachting accident while wearing the Blue Jager Moon. Her body was never recovered, only the scarf in which the diamond necklace was entangled. Once again the Devilstone resurfaced from the watery grave to which it had doomed its possessor.

Reading this fantastic biography of a rock, Joe wandered blindly back to the office. Christ! He hadn't stolen a precious gem, he'd invested himself with a curse. The diamond had won riches for none and brought death to all who held it. Whose watery grave could the shark tank be but Joe's should he try to retrieve the Blue Jager Moon? He tossed the pamphlet on his desk. For the first time he recognized, in the face of a menace more terrible and absolute than any of his own contrivance, that he wanted to live.

Yet if he wasn't going to recover the Moon, what should he do with it? Nothing? Leave it in the tank, a sort of private joke on fate? No, that still left him in jeopardy. Somehow Baby Jewels might uncover Joe and order his assassin, Rowdy McGee, to take him out. He snapped his fingers. Of course, he must turn the power of the Moon against the Fat Man, tell Tarzon its hiding place. And at the same time, by disclosing what he saw on Sick Bay, destroy Rowdy McGee. Kill two birds with one stone, save his own ass and avenge Whisper . . .

An alarm sounded suddenly on an upper floor, followed by stampeding guard boots and more alarms and klaxons, then Hobby's siren kicked in, a hellish ululation with teeth of steel that picked Joe up and smashed his skull from wall to wall. The P.A.'s of Coldwater fried like fast fuses: "Lockdown . . . Lockdown. Return to your units for Emergency Count . . . Maximum Lockdown . . . "

Tucking *Celebrity Diamonds* under his shirt, Joe bolted from the office and joined the rest of General Population thronging like a routed army down the Mainline.

JUST ANOTHER
FAT MAN

||||

The wigs were Sidney's idea. He said the jury wouldn't believe Jules was really bald, they'd think he shaved his head.

"Why would they think that?" the Fat Man demanded. He imagined himself something of a specialist on human nature, but this one stumped him.

"Because *bad* people shave their heads. To look dangerous, Jules. Ghengis Khan shaved his head, Pontius Pilate. *Pimps* shave their heads. That's what you're on trial for, remember?"

"I suppose Elmer Fudd's a bad guy," Quick grumbled.

"Why dont you ask Bugs Bunny?" Sidney invited him.

"How about cops, Sidney?" Baby Jewels pointed out. "Look at Kojak."

"Kojak's a TV cop, Jules. TV and movie cops are bad *people*. Believe me, Jules. Bald is nasty. Bald is . . ."

"Sexy," snapped the Fat Man. "It means you're virile."

"As in well hung and full of cum," Quick added with authority.

Sidney rolled his eyes and wrung his hands. Jules was enough trouble without his punchdrunk peanut gallery.

"Jules, trust me. Inside you're a beautiful person. *I* know that. Everybody who *knows* you knows that. Except with the skintop you *look* like a double Y chromosome serial killer . . . But in a wig, hey—you're just another fat man. And all the world loves a fat man."

Grudgingly Baby Jewels agreed to at least try on a few and see if he couldn't find one to fit his personality. Sidney left and an hour later a messenger arrived at the Tender Trap with a half dozen wigs from Adonis Hair Systems. Quick carried them down to the basement office. They came in individual boxes, attached by Velcro to styrofoam heads. Quick unpacked and ranked the heads on the Fat Man's desk. Bleakly surveying them, Baby Jewels really did look like Genghis Khan, inventorying his decapitated enemies.

"*Tch.* They even got names, Quick. There's the Executive, the Tennis Pro . . . How about this one?" He peeled a wavy blond one off its mount and held it aloft. "It's called the Casanova."

"That's you, boss," Quick said. He cocked his head. "There's the bell again, Frank's ring. Be right down."

Baby Jewels shrugged. He read the instructions first. Wheezing resignedly he squeezed several drops of Scalptite adhesive cream inside the hairpiece and slapped it atop his ovoid cranium. It felt funny up there, like a dead animal. It was also much too small. He seized the sideburns and yanked them like earflaps on a cap, wrestling it lower. But the wig wouldn't stretch to accomodate his outsize skull. He yanked harder and the sideburns tore off in his twinkling fists. Meshuga wig! He reached up to snatch it off. It was stuck! "Quick!" he screamed.

Quick tumbled back into the office. "Yo, boss!"

Spluttering, Baby Jewels pointed with both hands at the clump of blond waves clung to the peak of his conical head.

"Looks a little tight, boss," Quick observed. In truth it looked like a canary trying to hatch a dinosaur egg. "You should have tried the Man About Town. Those Casanova types arent known for big brains, you know. They gotta fit em in their dick heads."

Baby Jewels was wheezing too stertorously for speech. Frantically he pantomimed that he required Quick's assistance detaching the wavy pomp clutching his bean. Quick finally succeeded in tearing it off by grappling his boss's head in a half nelson. It left an angry red welt on the Fat Man's scalp. Two Bromos and a nitro were required to reduce his wheezing to a level approximating a small locomotive.

"Fuckin Sidney!" the Fat Man rainbowed spit. "He forgets he's just a lawyer. Thinks he's a drama coach and makeup artist and image consultant rolled into one. Just to show him I think I'll wear . . . You ever seen a pimp in a propeller beanie?" He didn't even give Quick time to think that one over. Suddenly noticing the baggie on his desk, his rings trembled gaudy lights flicking disgustedly at it as if Quick had delivered a cockroach. "What the fuck's *this?*"

Quick relayed Frank's account of acquiring the baggie and microcasette.

"*Tch.*" It was the doll's voice again, all business. "Frank's sure these are his slips?"

"Yeah. Only he dont know how they got blood on them. Thinks maybe on of the thieves had a nosebleed."

"If Frank had gunpowder for brains, he couldnt blow his nose."

"He wouldnt have to worry bout his nose if I just blew his whole head off," Quick offered helpfully.

"Down boy." Baby Jewels popped a lozenge, pursing his rosebud mouth, sucking hard in thought. The waft of lavender stirred emetically with the resinous reek of scalp adhesive.

"First Tarzon learns we got the diamond off the hooker. Then he learns we lost it. Then somehow he figured it was ripped off from the Kama Sutra. That's the only explanation for the slips being tagged for the Monday file. I must say he's methodical . . . leading me step by step to the chamber. Incidentally, I thought you said the Monday file was under seal in Sacramento?"

"It is. For some reason Tarzon was keeping these two items in his office safe."

"Loose ends arent his style," the doll's voice simped. "And the blood. I wonder if it means he busted the thieves, maybe killed them. For something else. No, then he'd have the Moon . . . What's on the midget tape?"

Quick rolled his neck. "Frank said he couldnt make it out."

Baby Jewels yanked open his top drawer so abruptly it slammed into his stomach, loosing an *oommph.* He slipped a microcassette player on his desk, loaded the tape and punched PLAY.

"Take this address, 183 Treat . . . " A porklink pinky punched STOP, a fatty brow bowed upward.

"An empty lot, boss. A house burned down there."

On the tape hissed: "Chakov's holed there . . . Hopped up . . . " Again the Fat Man stopped it.

"What jackoff?" demanded the doll's voice.

"Whatever jackoff boosted the Moon," Quick's spread palms guessed.

Lieutenant Tarzon hadn't wasted any time. The instant he walked into his office and saw his safe standing open, he knew of all the documents and items stored there that the microcassette and betting slips were gone. And he knew exactly where—the Fat Man.

Cursing himself for leaving such sensitive evidence within reach of corrupt cops, in a niggerhead safe any moron could crack with a stethoscope, he leaped around the desk and grabbed the phone. He'd removed the betting slips and microcassette from the Monday file at the State Police barracks as aids in questioning Speaker at Vacaville. That he'd been so busy between then and now tracking both his daughter and the diamond was no excuse for neglecting to return them to safekeeping. It was the tape that was most damaging. On it Speaker used Rooski's name. A simple check of police computers would yield the information that Rooski capered with Joe Speaker, identifying him as the diamond's thief. He had to warn Speaker—fast.

He canceled his appointments for the day and dialed the Department of Corrections in Sacramento to ascertain where Joe was pulling his stretch. As he listened to the clerk clack Joe's name into the computer, a ironic grin lifted the Hav-A-Tampa Jewel. This mishap might just be the motivation Speaker needs to give up the diamond.

He didn't reach the Coldwater gates until late afternoon. Storm clouds were boiling up over the serrated peaks behind the cellblocks. A forbidding stillness was settled on the place, a quiet so immense and immanent it nearly breathed. He parked in the visitors lot and walked to the Gate House. The only movement he noted were several crows quarreling along the concertina wire atop the fences.

"The institution's locked down, sir," the Gate House guard informed him. "No visits until further notice."

"Police business," Tarzon said, flipping out his shield. "I have an inmate to interview."

"Have you a firearm to check?"

"No. I locked it in the trunk of my vehicle."

"Oh." The guard seemed momentarily confused. He leaned closer to the shield. "One moment, Lieutenant. I'll have to phone Custody."

Tarzon fired up his cheroot while the guard made the call. Yes, just maybe he could bring this thing to a head right now.

The guard hung up. "Your escort will be down in a minute."

Tarzon nodded and stepped outside the Gate House. He stood on the cement walk beneath Tower One. Through double rolling gates he could see his own diminutive reflection in the tall glass doors at the head of the Administration Building steps. Then the smokedglass swung his image aside, replacing it with a heavyset man with short, thick butcher arms uniformed in synthetic black mail that shone with an oily luster like snakeskin.

What are these guys playing, Star Wars? he inwardly sniggered. But his amusement was quickly replaced by queasy incredulity. A patch of platinum blazed the side of his escort's militant brushcut. Slowly Tarzon removed the cheroot from nerveless lips. Descending the stairs, the costumed guard swung one leg stiffly wide.

Holy Mary Mother of God, breathed Tarzon. No two men could match the description of the man seen fleeing the Hall of Justice in white orderly ducks. His escort was the Sick Bay killer.

He wasted no time wondering how it could be; he racked his brain for an excuse for being there. Calling Speaker out would identify him as the diamond's thief, single him out for slaughter. He only prayed it was a coincidence that the Fat Man's assassin was posted at Coldwater.

Lurching down the walkway, McGee waved to Tower One and the gates rolled open. He passed through, unsheathing a hand from its studded gauntlet to shake Tarzon's.

"Rowdy McGee's my name. I understand you need to parlay with one of our . . . guests." He spoke in a moany voice Tarzon associated with the retarded, yet a shrewd light flickered in his small mean eyes. "We're always anxious to be of help to outside police agencies . . . Which inmate might it be?"

They stood together in the lengthening tower shadow. Tarzon stalled, slapping his Zippo in his palm and refiring the cheroot. He blew a long stream directly into McGee's face, shading the eyes a deeper shade of pink. If only he could get this freak in a lineup, he thought.

"Well?" McGee coyly coaxed. "I take a vital interest in which of our guests are the subjects of ongoing police investigations."

Fatal's more like it, Tarzon guessed. He jutted his jaw, aiming the Hav-A-Tampa between McGee's eyes. To its side flashed his teeth in a snarl, "Rosemary Hooten."

The swift scowl denting McGee's pocked cheeks confirmed that Tarzon had the right, very wrong man.

"Did I hear you correctly, Lieutenant? *Rosemary?*"

Curtly Tarzon nodded.

McGee coyly tipped his head. "This is a male institution. Someone's made a . . . booboo."

Tarzon furiously sucked his cheroot, then snapped it from his mouth and stutterpuffed smoke in McGee's fleshy smirk.

"What the—?" coughed McGee.

"Smoke signals, asshole. They spell *fuck you.* And I will."

With that Tarzon spun on his heel and stalked back through the parked cars. A slow fat rain began to fall, muddying splotches of oil here and there on the concrete. It was growing dark. Over his shoulder he heard the uneven fall of McGee's boots. He reached his car, unlocked it. He climbed in, snatching the harness over his shoulder. Before he could close the door, McGee grabbed it.

"This is a state reservation, Lieutenant. Not only aint you got jurisdiction, you aint got no right to verbally assault a correctional officer."

Tarzon regretted not retrieving the Walther from his trunk. He'd have liked blasting McGee's kneecaps, the fate he reserved for those for whom killing might resemble a favor.

"I got your number, pusbag. That's all I needed."

McGee snatched away his hand the instant before it was amputated by the slamming car door. The rain quickened then, droplets big as bullets dancing on the hood, and the highpressure sodium lights ringing the fencing blazed, staining the rainbullets gold.

Tarzon pulled away. He looked back once at a curve in the drive. There McGee stood, staring after him, oblivious to the downpour, looking in his shimmering skin of scaly goldblack like something half man, half reptile. Before the road swept McGee from view, Tarzon saw him in a flash of lightning throw back his head and laugh.

Captain Reilly couldn't trace which one, Reyosa or Mendoza, was the culprit. The orders weren't logged; the paperwork "lost." But he was sure it was one of those Custody taco tenientes who called the Kwik Fixx market Ray Savage listed on his application as his home. His real home was a freight container in the parking lot, where the clerk went to get him. The clerk rapped the secret code on the box's side waking him up to come to the store phone. Then whichever bean dip it was told that calamity awaiting its occasion to doubletime it back to the pen, he was needed for Second Watch tower duty.

The alarms had tripped just before noon; wild rumors of gunfire on the Yard swirled through the penitentiary; General Population was recalled and locked down for Emergency Count. Once in motion, the juggernaut of emergency procedure was hard to arrest. It was two hours before it was established no riot or mass escape or guerrilla attack on the penitentiary was in progress. It took another hour to identify the gunfire's source. It wasn't until late afternoon that Captain Reilly finally had C.O. Raymond Savage in his office again, this time with Outside Sergeant Fortado.

"At oh eleven hundred," Sergeant Fortado delivered his narrative of the incident, "I collected C.O. Savage at the Rear Sally Port and transported him by institutional pickup along the access road between fences . . . "

"Gene, save the officialese for your report. Just tell me what you know." The Captain was Fortado's brotherinlaw.

"Officer Savage and myself got to the tower about eleven fifteen. Halliday lowered the key. I opened the tower door and admitted Savage. Halliday descended and exited. I secured the tower and reattached the key to its line, which Officer Savage raised. I drove Halliday to the Rear Sally Port . . . Next thing I heard was *BOOM!* I looked across the Yard. Debris was floating from the top of the tower. There was a hole blown in its roof." Fortado shrugged and darted a chary look at C.O. Savage in the chair beside him.

Captain Reilly transferred his gaze to Savage. "Hello, Ray."

"Hello, sir."

"Ray, did you know that almost singlehandedly you've driven me into early retirement? This is my last watch."

"El Bummero! You're like a father to me."

Reilly closed his eyes slowly and reopened them. "Ray, how did you blow a hole in the tower roof?"

Savage slitted his eyes in the manner of a professional indignant that his judgment has been questioned. "Sir, there's a sign on the wall up in the tower. It says all guards should check to make sure their firearms are in working order."

"And?"

"So I checked the shotgun first. I looked it over, pumped a shell in the chamber, and pulled the trigger . . . "

"Aannnd?" Captain Reilly's voice rose cracking with horror.

"And *what,* Captain?" Savage spread his palms in frustration at having to belabor the obvious. "Sucker worked!"

Alone in his cell, Joe turned on his radio. Some prairie punk with a bushwhacked heart twanging his inflamed adenoids about a hightone twat from Tucson who was weekends at the Ritz while he was pork cracklings and grits—she was Moët and Beluga, this cowpoke was Thunderbird and Bugler. Sometimes Joe felt just as grateful as Moonpie for the guntowers and double ranks of lethal fencing.

On the dark plain beyond the town's claptrap outskirts, bonfires were lit along the baselines of the Little League diamond. A night game was about to be played. Headlights snaked across the plain and halted facing inward, their beams crisscrossing the field.

Joe enjoyed watching the Little League games from his cell window. The distant shouts and blaring horns, the regular and orderly rotation of miniature players, the march of numbers down the scoreboard assured him that human values endured beyond this place of stone, passed from fathers to sons through their enactment in innocent pastimes.

Beside the bleachers a stakebed sound truck was parked. Faintly Joe heard an amplified guitar torture the national anthem. At its blatting B-flat conclusion, trucks and cars blew their horns for the Land of the Free and Home of Baseball.

But before the first side could take the field, the breeze quickened and thunder grumbled high in the Sierras, and the rain began, great heavy drops splashing on Joe's cell windowsill.

Joe started to turn from the window when his eyes popped wide, spotting two familiar figures crossing the visitors parking lot. He hugged himself to the bars, straining his eyes until their sockets ached.

There was no mistaking McGee. But the other, smaller one in black . . . He turned then, opening his door, and Joe saw the cheroot. Christ! It was Lieutenant Tarzon! Joe's sweatslick hands slipped down the bars. He wiped them on his pantlegs and gripped the bars once more. Now Tarzon was driving off, with McGee looking after him. *Laughing.*

Christ! Moses and Tarzon were in this together. And he'd been on the deadly verge of trusting the cop, surrendering the diamond, giving up his life.

Joe shrank from the window until the wall stopped his back. There he stood in the raindeafened cell, transfixed with the certitude that now he must guard the secret of the Devilstone with his life.

Sluicing through the rain past the Coldwater Chamber of Commerce's meretricious lawn, Tarzon radioed for McGee's jacket to be on his desk when he returned. It had to be a coincidence that McGee was posted to the same prison where Speaker was doing his time. If it weren't, Speaker would already be dead. Hanging up the mike, he slapped his palm on the steering wheel. It was still a damn ominous coincidence.

Passing the Little League field where players and parents were rushing to their cars with newspapers over their heads, Tarzon's mind clacked like an abacus, adding his options against their consequences. With McGee at the prison, he couldn't warn Speaker of the imminent danger, he couldn't even communicate with him without becoming an accessory to his murder. Could he segregate Speaker? Hardly. Even were it possible, were the Department of Corrections not a bureaucratic fiefdom with closed borders that only complied with outside police agencies under court order, putting Speaker in Protective Custody would have the opposite effect, it would offer him up for assassination.

Okay, so he could have a judge release Speaker for time served. But then the crafty thief would smell a rat, he'd know Tarzon was setting him up to lead him to the diamond, and he'd go to ground. And Tarzon would lose his chance of recovering the diamond, bringing down Moses, and saving his daughter.

No, he realized on the edge of town, the only way of protecting Speaker and getting the diamond too was to arrange for Speaker to be released and believe it was his own doing. Tarzon would have to recheck the penal administrative codes, but he thought he knew of a way already.

But it would take a little time. And a little time could become eternity for Joe Speaker. Tarzon would have to recruit an agent inside Coldwater to warn if Speaker's life was in jeopardy, whereupon Tarzon would release him immediately. He couldn't sacrifice Speaker. Not even for Belinda's life.

On the highway outside town he passed a cutrate gas station, its pennants snapping shiny in the rain. At the pumps he saw a red Corvette, a '65 Sting Ray he thought. The same car in which he first made cramped and clumsy love to Rosa at the drivein. Shamefully he recalled the movie more clearly than the sex. It was *Desire Under the Elms*. "Phew!" Rosa gasped rolling down the windows when they finished. "Desire under the arms is more like it." Her tongue then still was servant to a nimble mind. He proposed to her before dropping her off that night.

Rosa's memory conjured that of the child she carried in her to the altar, the child conceived in the red Corvette, perhaps the very one tanking up back there. Guilt gripped his chest. Where was she? Somewhere, slapped the windshield wipers. *Some where some where* in that hazy haunted zone where the private Rick Tarzon converged with evil.

He jammed the accelerator to the firewall, harrying his fate down the highway, so intent on what lay ahead that he didn't note what fell in behind, the red Corvette, keeping careful distance.

THE STROLL

||||

Evenings after chow the Mainline became a promenade. What duties hadn't been discharged that day could wait on the morrow. Full bellies were a repletion of one sense; the other could await the furtive stairwell rendezvous, the quick blanket curtaining cell bars, the clammy reaches of sleep. For now all anyone had on the Mainline was time. Time to play the strap and run the rap, lay the note and twostep the Tale.

Joe leaned with Earl against the wall, hands thrust flat in his pockets, Whisper's cap pulled low, shading his gaze. One avoided eye contact on the Mainline unless one wanted to fuck or fight. Lamping a statuesque black queen with orange Frenchbraided hair, however, Joe thumbed up the bill, saying, "Man, that's a pretty nigger switchin her stuff there. She lets her walkin do her talkin . . . "

"You dont want no part of Nefertiti. She's plagued, yeah."

"Why dont they blood test her, yank her off the line?"

"Even if they observe the symptoms they cant make em give up blood. Unconstitutional without their consent. N them gal boys wont do it on their own, no. They know if they test positive, it's straight to Quarantine until they roll out the back gates in a body bag. Nefertiti there, she havin too much fun to go wait in lockup to die."

"Christ, some people'll ride their rights right to the grave."

"N take some others with em, yeah. Not just convicts neither. Every day plaguers are bein paroled to spread it in the real world. We livin in an AIDS incubator."

Locking on Joe's stare, the black queen veered out of the Stroll to stand before him with her weight on one leg, hand on its shot hip; pinning him to the wall with icebright eyes that traveled down his body to halt, dilating, at his crotch. A long tongue studded with cysts snaked out to search crayoned lips that lisped, "Wanna burn some coal, whiteboy?"

"Hook it up, Nefertiti," Earl said with unmistakable menace.

Nefertiti started with mock innocence, and Joe first noticed the polished wishbone through her ear. "Who dis ole man," hissed the viral tongue. "Yo dingdong *daddy?*"

Joe found his mouth too dry to answer.

Laughing deep in her throat, the black queen swung her haughty hips back into the Stroll.

Joe turned and looked westward across the institutional acres lying barren and black beneath the August halfmoon as though the prison walls were leaking their poisonous effluvium, blighting the surrounding soil.

"I think I'll head back to my house to read," he said. In the falling distance he could see the lights of the town, a revolving gas station sign, a dingy motel, headlights blinking between buildings.

"Not yet, amigo. You got a letter from your gal today."

"Wha—?" Joe swung on the old con. Earl's right eye flared gasblue in the dusky halflight.

"Custody intercepted it yesterday, yeah. Katherine Quintana's listed as one of your crime partners. Correspondence with crime partners is contraband."

"What isnt?" Joe turned back to the window. The wind between the cellblocks picked up the dust and swirled it, reminding him of the way she tossed her hair.

"Butthole, yeah."

Joe tittered looking up at the nervous evening sky, seeking escape. He tried to project himself into the fleeing clouds, far away from this concrete box filled with other men and their noises, smells, filth . . . and disease. Something inside Joe was broken and leaking blood the way the walls leaked their misery, paroled their plague.

"Dont you want to know what she wrote?"

"You read it?"

Earl shrugged. "It was lying on the Captain's desk."

"No, I dont care what she wrote."

A sharp urgency honed Earl's voice. "Well I'm purely bound to tell you.

Letter was postmarked Mexico. She said she's pregnant, yeah, with your baby. She's headed to her people in Galveston to have it."

"*My* baby? That's close . . . Earl, put a blindfold on that bustout and spin her around with her finger out in the middle of Market Street and whichever swingin dick she pointed at would be as good a bet as me. She's a whore."

"The right whore holds more mud than a nun . . . "

"Fuck it." Joe looked back to the darkening sky where the moon like a silver scimitar sliced a ragged cloud.

"You wouldnt be so upset if you didnt believe her, amigo."

How could he tell the old man it was purely the notion of his rogue seed multiplying its heartache and misery? Its own plague?

"Earl, what's the word of a whore?"

Earl's right eye arced a blue spark. "The word of the right whore's good as a guvmint check. I learned that comin up in Nawlins. Folks referred to socalled good women as women of character. Well, I learned it was the other way around. It was the socalled bad ones, the whores and strippers and all who had the market cornered on character, yeah. Good girls was plain as grits, it was the bad uns had the gumption of gumbo. Only they understood when you down and out, when life's laid you low, your word's all that's left to save you. The others, the ones who never had to fight to keep their souls, they never learned they had em to lose, and their word aint worth the breath they spend on it . . . Show me a gal who's scuffed and scratched to save her heart and soul and I'll show you God's best version of a woman."

Joe snorted.

"What in hell's she got to gain lying to a convict?" Earl spit through the window. "Your heart aint no bigger than a mustard seed."

"I dont want no trick baby!"

"What in hell you think *you* are?"

Thunderstruck, Joe whirled from the window. "How do you know . . . *that?*"

For a long moment Earl regarded him without answering, his ambivalent gaze melding irony and affection.

"I asked you a question, you old fart."

Earl lifted his bony shoulders, letting them fall with a resigned exhalation. "It's all in your Central File," he said softly. "Up in Admin."

"So you dont just read my mail, you memorize my jackets."

Earl pinched his beak, hiding a sad smile. "Thought I was doin you a favor, amigo. I scratched your silent murder beef."

With that the old con shoved off the wall and was quickly swallowed into the Stroll, leaving Joe in a tumult of gall and grudging gratitude.

IIII

Tarzon closed the interrogation room door and returned to his chair. He fixed a Hav-A-Tampa Jewel in a blueshadowed smile and nodded to the other chair across the small table. "Have a seat, Joe Sing."

The lanky Chinese youth remained standing, black eyes beneath a red bandanna staring implacably at the Homicide lieutenant. A mop thunked the wall, metering the riverbottom bellyache moaned by a trusty janitor.

Tarzon said, "I have no interest in your current charges. I'm not here to harrass you. You may return to your tank any time you wish. But I'd be obliged if you'd hear me out. I'm here to make a mutually beneficial proposition. In return for your cooperation, I'll avenge Archie."

Without removing his frostbit gaze from Tarzon, Joe Sing sat. His lips barely moved: "How?"

"I'm sure you know it was Baby Jewels Moses who zipped Sammy Chin and Archie. You also gotta know that he's after you now. But maybe you dont know why . . . " Tarzon cocked his brow; Joe Sing's eyes narrowed. "He wants the identity of the jokers you loaned the guns and masks to caper his bank and cop a diamond that just happened to be in the safe."

Joe Sing inspected his nails, elaborately.

"Dont worry. I cant prove the switch and bill you for the Golden Boar. I dont even want to, I have no interest in gang warfare."

Joe Sing shifted in the wooden chair and tilted his head to study Tarzon. Softly he said, "I've heard about some ice."

"The diamond ties Moses to a One Eightyseven. That's why I'm trying to get my hands on it before he does, to drop the pill on him."

"I cant help you there."

"Only the character who's got the ice can help me, and so far he wont." Tarzon paused a heavy beat. "Speaker's holding his mud."

"So." Joe Sing nodded slowly, then said, "I'd do the same. How could I trust you? See, street characters and cops are flipsides of the same coin. Trusting a cop's as dangerous as trusting yourself."

Tarzon frowned rolling the ash off his cheroot on the edge of the table. "Doesnt it steam your pumpkin that Archie and Sammy Chin would be alive if Speaker had given up the ice?"

"How could it? The Barker didnt know Moses had a switch figured any more than I did."

Tarzon nodded. "Good. Because I'm going to ask you to watch Speaker's back."

"I thought *you* had it in for him?"

"I did. He's done . . . terrible things. But the same as the rest of us, he's doing life without parole behind the same set of eyes with his conscience for a cellmate . . . But Moses has no conscience. He's wrong on the rocks. He's killed many times before and will kill many times again until he's stopped. For greed, for revenge . . . for fun. I need Joe Speaker because I need the diamond. If I lose him, I lose the chance of bagging the Fat Man."

"I'm going to the pen," Joe Sing pointed out. "How'm I supposed to help the Barker?"

"You're going to CIM Coldwater. That's where Speaker's at."

"Oh? You fix that?"

"No. I could have, but it turns out that's where all Oriental felons are being sent anyway. They think it's safest to concentrate the smaller minorities in individual institutions. Something to do with rising racial tension because of overcrowding. Strength in numbers."

"Great." Joe Sing's lips hinted at a smile. "I'm going where all my enemies are. Maybe the papers were right. Maybe Sammy and my brother were done by the Wah Ching. If so, I'm in bocoo trouble."

"You're too smart to believe what you read in papers."

"But dumb enough to believe a cop?"

Tarzon laughed. "Next you'll tell me the Wah Ching run you off the streets."

"What gives you the idea anyone beat me off the bricks?"

"Your uncle, Woh Ping, owns the biggest liquor distributorship in Chinatown, right?"

Sing shrugged.

"And you get popped boosting a case of Hiram Walker from a mom n pop store? Cmon, Joe Sing. It doesnt take a rocket scientist to figure you're P.C.'ing from the streets. Hauling your ass out of the Fat Man's reach. And I think it's a smart move."

"I feel better already . . . So let me get this straight. You want me to watch out for the Barker . . . "

Tarzon nodded leaning back, rolling the cheroot in his fingers. "Dont mention the diamond. He's gotta be paranoid by now and he'll suspect you're in cahoots with me or the Fat Man. Just keep an eye on him. Let me know if he's getting into trouble he cant handle. There's a guard at Coldwater named McGee, Rowdy McGee. If he gets on Speaker's ass, let me know immediately. He's all the way wrong."

"Rowdy McGee," Joe Sing repeated. "That's one with a rep on the streets even."

"I bet." Tarzon slid a business card across the table. "This is an attorney in Sacramento. You can send uncensored letters to attorneys, make unmonitored phone calls. If anything comes up . . . "

Joe Sing stood. His hand snaked the card into his hip pocket. He knocked on the door for a deputy.

"Sing, you'll be on a pen chain by next week. Meanwhile dont let Vice or Narcotics call you out of the tank. Not without an attorney present. They're also all the way wrong."

Joe Sing's eyes disappeared. "Thanks."

QUARANTINE

||||

HELP. BRING BLEACH, SPENCER . . . The desperate kite was penciled on a candywrapper, folded three times and tucked into a triangle. Joe found it on his bunk when he returned to his cell for 1630 count. He stopped to think how long it had been since he'd seen the quad. Months, he realized, glancing away through window bars where other kites of life and death spun golden in distant trees, about to fall. It came then, a thought as cold and still as eternity itself—a first frost soon would turn Rooski where he slept to stone. A shiver shut Joe's eyes.

For three packs of Camels he scored a gallon of Clorox from Laundry the next afternoon and humped it on his shoulder down the Mainline to W Wing, the Hospital Unit. He hesitated at the gates, peering through the bars into the crowded rotunda. The inmate patients sat at tables playing desultory cards, they moved in slow circles; they leaned motionless against walls, staring into nothingness. The cellblock smelled of unchanged bandages and stale medicine and loose bowels. Through the high windows in the block's rear wall ramped steep, greasy light writhing with motes the size of gnats.

Joe took a deep breath and rang the gate buzzer. A Medical Technical Assistant keyed him onto the block and offered him a pair of surgical gloves and mask. "The screened upper ranges," he answered Joe's questioning stare. "Plague quarantine."

Joe asked what about the men in the rotunda, why weren't they gloved and masked? The MTA explained that Administration wouldn't pay for the number of gloves and masks needed to protect the unit's other tenants twentyfour hours a day. Only visitors rated. Joe elected not to exercise this dubious rating, yet declined to enter the cellblock either. He dispatched a runner—actually a onelegged man who used a crutch much like a vaulting pole to hurtle himself down the cell gates, chattering like an organ grinder's monkey—to page Spencer.

While he waited, Joe leaned as warily as a man over a pond of piranhas from beneath the gate area's corona, peering squeamishly upward. Cyclone fencing had been welded on both sides, from the second tier catwalk clear to the high ceiling indistinct from its shadows. The incessant squeak of crutch tips, the shriek of rubber wheels, the shrill flightly echoes—in Joe's heated imagining it became a surreal human aviary, where scavengers of infected carrion were shackled to their roosts. Convulsively, he ducked back beneath the overhang.

Finally he saw Roy's unmistakable monster gait approaching out of the cross stitched stygian gloom. When he'd come close enough Joe asked, "Where's Spencer?"

Roy turned in slightly the wrong direction and Joe craned his neck, guiding the blind man's head around with his voice: "How is he?"

"Oh it's you, Joe . . . He only gets worse. They upped his meds today and he's crashed." Roy stood just outside the shadow holding Joe, his haggard head backtilted, swaying to his silent music. His head still suddenly, and his empty eyes narrowed as if hearing an illtuned instrument in his ethereal orchestra. "What's wrong, Joe? Spooked by the carrier ranges?"

Joe felt himself pulled forward again by that loathsome fascination which slows rubberneckers at freeway accidents. Once more he stared up the cyclone fencing disappearing into the noisy shadows crowding the cellblock's high reaches. Hooked everywhere through the links were white, brown, and black bony knuckles.

"How many they got up there?"

Roy dipped his stubbled head, fixing dead eyes on Joe's breast. His voice rumbled up from somewhere deep. "Couple of hundred." Joe whistled softly. "That's nothing. Another two years every swingin kickstand in the system'll be contaminated. There'll be just one sentence left—death."

"Here's the bleach." Joe slung the gallon jug into Roy's outstretched fingers. "What's Spencer need it for?"

"Not Spencer. He asked for the plaguers. They catch any germ flying around this hospital unit. They use bleach to disinfect their cells. The guards wont give em any. Claim they're using it to flush syringes."

"What else wont they give em?"

"Caulking guns. They need them to seal their window cracks. When the cold nights come in another month, the winds'll blow in all the pigeon shit on their window ledges . . . Also surgical gloves for tending to each other. The MTA's wont give em any."

Joe quickly explained that the Clorox and caulking guns would be no problem. In a matter of days he'd be working where these supplies were bountiful. Rudy Malec, the lead convict on the welding crew, had arranged for his assignment to the Maintenance Yard where Joe could be of assistance in contraband hustles.

The surgical gloves, Joe assured Roy, he could obtain in plentiful supply from the Y-1 Clinic. Y-1 was run by the Chinese the same way the Maintenance Yard was run by whiteboys. Whiteboys also ran Custody and the Library, with the same tightfisted sovereignty that the Mexicans ran the Chapels and Laundry, and the blacks, the Kitchens and Gym. None could say how long these territories had been staked out. By the time Joe came through Coldwater, each sphere of operations was under the immemorial domination of a racial click.

Joe's contact in Y-1 was Joe Sing, who had just arrived at Coldwater. When they first met on the Yard, something in Joe Sing's voice sounded strained; and when Joe extended his condolences for Archie, the Chinese gangster just lamped him with a freezedried smile. Joe wrote it off to Mainline mores. Interracial relations that were tolerated on the streets were taboo behind prison walls.

"Look, Roy," Joe blurted on sudden impulse, "if Spencer could afford it, could he have competent outside medical help and obtain his transfusions from streetside blood banks?"

Roy nodded, facing up into the high shifting panes of greasy gray light, bathing his face with a gentle back and forth motion in his music, basking in its still and silent sorcery.

"Tell him I'll be calling," Joe said with emphasis, forming a plan already.

That evening Joe and Earl made Yard. Before they even reached the Sally Port, Earl apologized for dipping in Joe's business about Kitty. Joe told him never mind, scratching the silent beef more than made up for it.

"You just lucky, yeah, yours aint written in blood," the old coot said sententiously.

Out the Sally Port they passed into the indolent crepuscular yard. Joe felt queerly as if he were walking onto a stage production of someone else's Indian summer night's dream. Fireflies blinked softly in the taller grass along the fencing; blue nightlights blurred from the guntowers. Like bit players in a shadow play, convicts glided heads bent in hushed conversation; here and there laughter burbled. The Sierras might have been cut out of black cardboard; the sky could have been indigo silk pinpricked with stage starlight. A polished silver moon hung from wires. The prison walls throbbed banana yellow and acrylic magenta from an inner source. The tableau seemed to Joe too vivid, like a Disney cartoon. He decided it must be a distortion of his atrophied perceptions, an exaggeration of his starved sensibilities. The scene discomfited him the way beef bourgignon sickens a new parolee, the way simple bread may convulse the malnourished.

They walked slowly along the perimeter track while Joe related his visit to W Wing and discussion with Roy. He was going to save up to pay for street doctors and plasma, he said, and Earl could no longer count on Joe subsidizing his gambling jones. Earl nodded now and then and grumbled deep in his throat, indicating he was listening and thinking at once.

"I'm proud of you, amigo," he said when Joe finished. "And dont worry bout me, no. I've placed my last bet."

Joe puffed his cheeks. "Good idea, with your track record."

"It aint whether I win or lose. It's a habit either way."

"Just so you know you cant count on me any more. I gotta do this. For myself as much as Spencer . . . I knew another dude once who counted on my help and I stabbed him in the back instead."

Earl used his gnarled halffingers to squeeze the bridge of his nose.

"See," Joe said, "I got my own silent beef that's written in blood, and I got to wash it away."

They walked on in silence save the esophageal grumblings of Earl's lungs turned into leather bags by emphysema. They wandered off the track and climbed the bleachers. They sat on the top row. The Yard was streaked with nebular blur like a fallen sky. From below Joe heard the moist oomphy sounds of two men fucking. The sound used to disgust him, then lately it had become merely a distraction. This evening he actually welcomed it, found it soothing. The strenuous, cyclical pulsations old as the cadences of the sea rooted the Kodachrome gloaming in reality.

Earl lapsed into half growling, half humming the bluesy dirge "Saint James Infirmary" again.

"Earl," Joe asked presently, "tell me about it down there."

"Nawlins?" Earl softly spoke the city's name like that of an old lover; then told again of her French Quarter until Joe could almost smell beignets and chicory, see Creole painted pigeons swinging sweet toottoots down leaning streets of rainslick cobblestone, hear the ragged sob of a Dixieland horn, the harlequin hoot of a riverboat's steam calliope, the threshing of the paddlewheels in big muddy waters; then Earl conjured steamy bayou nights until Joe saw moonbeams splashing in mason jars and felt through a gingham dress a slender back supple as tupelo stripling swaying to a Cajun waltz dreamed on pearly accordion keys.

Joe laughed suddenly.

"What's so funny, amigo?"

"I was just thinking that the aim of prisons is to correct criminals, make adults out of overgrown children. The first object you'd think would be to force them to stop living fantasy lives. But that's all prison is, fantasy finishing school. I never learned how to direct my dreaming until I got here."

"Yeah you right."

"I wish they'd hurry up and lower my custody so I could get to work in the Maintenance Yard," Joe said. "These Mainline ayems and peeyems got me doubleparked in the Twilight Zone. Instead of me doin the time, it's startin to do me."

"Hurry up and wait," Earl repeated the timeworn institutional shibboleth.

High overhead a lone nocturnal hawk gyred in a thermal chimney, leaning into its windy sinews. It screamed twice suddenly and flashed toward the darkling Sierras. The Yard whistle blew. Below the lovers climaxed simultaneously, as if by practice.

"Guess they're cured for the night," Earl said arising and taking the first rickety step down.

"That might be all this joint cures," Joe cracked, starting down behind him, "heterosexuality."

SUNNY DEELIGHT

||||

Miss Kranz asked Sunny to dress demurely and please go easy on the vampire makeup and for godsakes leave the punk jewelry wherever she called home. The Moses jury was going to have a hard enough time believing her without the miniature handcuff earrings and slave fetter bracelets and padlocked necklaces. It didn't matter that these items were all the rage, the jury was concerned with *truth*, not trends. Miss Kranz promised to pay personally for the hairdresser to rinse out Sunny's tangerine cockatoo and, once the jury was sequestered, redye and style Sunny's tresses in a titanium Mohawk—*if* Sunny promised in return not to chew gum on the stand. For the trial, she wanted Sunny to look like a Bible *student*, not burner. Miss Kranz was about a hundred and fifty years old and worked for the D.A.'s office.

At their last session she bit her lip thinking up a role model, then asked hopefully, "Do you know *Rebecca of Sunnybrook Farm?*"

Sunny shook her head no; but she had known an Anne of a Thousand Cuts, worked the S&M and bodyworship trade out of the classifieds. Miss Kranz squeezed shut her eyes and shuddered to make something go away. She asked Sunny next if she'd seen *The Wizard of Oz*, which was like asking a hobbyhorse if it had a hickory dick. No American had been spared multiple viewings of this flick unless he'd been comatose for fifty years. Even then the treacly strains of "Somewhere Over the Rainbow" would have seeped into a dead head, sweetening puddled gray matter sufficiently for the coroner to pour over his pancakes.

"Sure. I'll be Dorothy! Only where are my ruby slippers?"

Right off Sunny regretted this crack intended to show the old biddy how cultured she was. Not only did Miss Kranz have a hunched back and dentures that clacked every other word, she wore orthopedic shoes. They were gussied up to look like sensible townandcountry doggers, but Sunny had some experience with foot freaks and recognized them for what they were, spaz pads. She was glad when Miss Kranz dismissed the sensitive subject, saying, "Your feet cant be seen in the witness box . . . Just try and dress the way Dorothy would testifying against the Wicked Witch of . . . " Miss Kranz harumphed something stuck in her throat and waggled her finger in a circle trying to get her compass bearings: "of the *West.* Remember, I'll be there in court so if you get nervous, just look over and think of me as Glenda, the Good Witch of the . . . North."

Sunny stamped her foot. "I like Auntie Em better," whining over and over just like Judy Garland, *"Auntie Em, Auntie Em . . . "* until Miss Kranz clapped her hands over her ears and screamed, "All *right!* I'll be Auntie Em . . . " Though truthfully she looked more like a bag lady in remission than either Auntie Em or a witch from any direction.

"I figured you might," Sunny said smugly.

But she was anything but smug when the Big Day came. Her insides sloshed like laundry in a washer. Sunny had been in court on numerous previous occasions, but her longest line to date had been "Not Guilty." Today reminded her of that awful morning at Olema High when she forgot the lines to "Hiawatha" and the whole school howled in glee at her humiliation. That was before Sunny found what she did best, which happened not to be Longfellow.

Luckily, Sunny had dropped a couple of purple Xanax laid on her by another working girl with a potable handle, Cherry Schnapps. She got to court early and hid in back with the media types while everyone filed in. Gee willikers, this was some kind of celebrity trial, judging by the fancyass looks of the people. It was drawing out the freaks too, the hags in crazy hats and old farts in motheaten period costumes. Sunny figured these kooks were too cheap for long distance phone calls and were taking advantage of the trial's national TV coverage to disappoint distant relatives with proof that they were alive. Boy, was Sunny glad Cherry purpled her down. Xanax was made for days like this.

But all the tranquilizers on Walgreen's shelves couldn't have deadened her horror when Baby Jewels sailed into court like an evil planet trailing its pale cold moon, Quick Cicero. She shrank behind a *Chronicle* reporter to escape the Death Ray the Fat Man's ballbearing eyes swept around court to include any state's witnesses before sitting at the defense table.

When she heard her name called she rose and marched woodenly to the stand without a sideward look, lest the horrorshow Humpty Dumpty sap her resolve. She was already in the box when she remembered the Juicy Fruit in her mouth. She stuck it under a strip of oak molding.

Obviously D.A. Faria had been coached on *image*. With his fresh razorcut hairdo and doublebreasted nautical blazer, he looked like a waterbed salesman answering a swinging singles ad.

"Please state your name, address, and occupation for the record." Hands locked behind his back, rocking gently on his Florsheims, smiling brittlely at her.

Sunny had been through all this a zillion times with Miss Kranz, but it was still so different in the flesh, just like old Longfellow.

"Sunny Dee—" Faria's desperate goggle froze her tongue. "Karen Cowley, Mars Hotel, 1544 O'Farrell, Physical Therapist . . . Unemployed," she raised her voice over the soft lapping of laughter.

"Miss Cowley, were you formerly an employee of Mr. Jules Moses?"

"Baby Jewels, you got it." She couldn't yet bear looking at Fatso, even if she wasn't blinded by Faria's highvoltage glare. Mechanically, she said, "I was employed by Mr. Jules Moses at the Bunny Hutch at 526 Vespucci, since closed."

"And was not your nominal job that of masseuse?"

"You coulda called me a brain surgeon, but that's not what I did."

Faria hid the slitted look he gunned her. "In fact, Miss Cowley, you were employed as a prostitute."

The Fat Man's lawyer leaped up as if his seat were springloaded. He whipped off his glasses to pinch the bridge of his nose. "Objection. Counsel is leading the witness."

"Sustained." The voice was female, prompting Sunny to look up at the judge for the first time. All in black, she *did* look like the Wicked Witch of the West, right down to the wart on the tip of her nose.

"Miss Cowley, what was the nature of your employment?"

Goody, she knew this one. "Prostitute."

"Were the customers at the Bunny Hutch expecting to get massages?"

"If they were, it was just one muscle they wanted massaged. The same one on all of them."

Laughter rolled around the court. Sunny looked at Baby Jewels for the first time and smiled triumphantly. His eyes streamed back stilettos.

The Wicked Witch banged her gavel. "Miss Cowley, this is a court, not a cabaret. You're here to testify, not entertain. Answer directly."

Sunny shot her an affected little girl smile of contrition.

Faria smiled indulgently toward the jury to show he had a funnybone too. Smile pasted in place, he turned back to her and repeated himself.

"No, they were not expecting massages. They . . . were expecting sex."

Faria turned again to the jury, brows arched and mouth agape as if the news shocked him as well.

"Now, Miss Cowley. Who did they pay for this sex?"

"They paid me."

"And where did the money go?"

"It went to Mr. Moses, the man sitting over there." She pointed without looking.

"Let the record show Miss Cowley identified the defendant, Jules Moses . . . " Faria opened his jacket, sank his hands deep in his pockets, and turned to scowl at Moses. Next he treated the jury to a stern prosecutorial frown; then, facing Sunny once more, managed to purse his lips with what appeared to be genuine concern. "Miss Cowley, did the sex for hire always occur on the premises?"

Now the ball was rolling, Sunny was losing her jitters and remembered her sessions with Miss Kranz better. She smiled across court at Auntie Em. "No. Some men, highrollers usually, wanted the girls up in their hotel rooms . . . " She turned and told the jury confidentially, "I bet they were sorry later."

The other lawyer loudly cleared his throat and groaned, "Objection." He made a pained expression standing up as if spraining his back in the effort. He held up the glasses to the light, inspecting for dust. "Irrelevant. Conjectural."

"Your Honor," Faria spread his hands.

"Overruled in this instance."

"Exception." The other lawyer had his hankie out, cleaning the specs.

"Noted. Proceed, Mr. Faria."

"Why do you say that, Miss Cowley?"

"Because they got ripped off."

"Do you mean robbed?"

"That's what I mean. We girls robbed them."

"Who instructed you to carry out these robberies?"

"Who else? My boss, Mr. Moses."

"Can you give the court the details of these instructions?"

"When we got to the rooms, we'd say one little drink first. Then we'd slip little pills in the booze and they'd be out like lights. Then we'd rob their cash and jewelry, whatever was in the room."

"Why rob them, Miss Cowley, when you could simply perform the service for which you were hired and be paid?"

"You kidding? A trick's only a hundred, maybe two. These bozos were totin thousands. They also wore Rolex watches and solid gold ID bracelets and expensive cufflinks. One even had a diamond stud earring."

While she spoke, Faria had stepped to the D.A.'s table and returned with an orange plastic vial. "I show you this bottle of tablets. Are they the ones you used?"

"Shake one out . . . Yup, that's them."

"I move to enter this vial as People's Exhibit G and further stipulate for the record that the tablets contained therein have been analyzed by the police laboratories as containing the powerful hypnotic chloral hydrate . . . " Faria held out the vial for the defense lawyer to inspect. Sidney Dreaks waved it away without looking up from his notes.

"Miss Cowley, how many times did you personally participate in these robberies?"

"Ten, twelve times. Maybe more."

"And to whom did you give the proceeds, the cash and jewelry you robbed from the unconscious hotel guests?"

"I gave the loot to Quick, over there beside Mr. Moses."

"You mean Robert Cicero?"

"Yes. He was always waiting in the hotel lobby in case there was trouble, and we'd call down when we were done. Quick gave the stuff to Mr. Moses, who gave us back our cut."

"One last question, Miss Cowley. What happened to the girls who said no . . . " He turned to the jury and raised his voice. "What happened to the girls willing to prostitute themselves but who drew the line at Felonious Assault and Robbery?"

"Objection. Counsel has not laid foundation for either assault or robbery."

"Overruled . . . Yes, Mr. Dreaks. Your every exception is being noted."

"Miss Cowley?"

"They were beaten. Or worse. Girls usta tell me . . . "

"Objection. Hearsay."

"Sustained . . . Miss Cowley, you may only testify as to what is your firsthand personal knowledge. Not what other people said."

Faria cleared his throat and stared at her from beneath his brows exactly how Miss Kranz said he would for the wrapup. "Miss Cowley, I ask again to make perfectly clear for the jury. Were you a prostitute in the employ of Jules Moses for over three years?"

She tried to put a quaver in her voice the way she'd rehearsed.

"Ye-*eesss!*"

"And during those three years did you commit multiple thefts and robberies at the behest of the defendant?"

"Yaaassss!" There, that was closer.

"Would the witness like a glass of water?" asked the Wicked Witch. Oops! overdid it. "No thank you, I'm sure."

"Thank you, Miss Cowley," Faria bowed from the hips. "You've been most"—he turned, rising on his toes to peer meaningfully across the jurors' faces—*"illuminating* . . . Your witness, Mr. Dreaks."

What? They told her there'd be a break before crossexamination. In a panic Sunny looked to Miss Kranz, who shrugged helplessly. Some Auntie Em. She might as well have been in Kansas. The Xanax was wearing off, she had cotton mouth; she glanced covetously at the gum stuck beneath the lip of molding.

Mr. Dreaks didn't look up until he'd made one last notation. Then he leaned back in his chair and folded his hands across his little paunch and said: "Well, Miss Cowley, that was a nice performance . . . "

"Objection. Combative and immaterial."

"Comment withdrawn." Dreaks draped a complicit smile over the jury. "Miss Cowley, were you assisted in the preparation of your testimony?"

"Jeepers."

"For the purposes of clarification, does 'jeepers' mean yes or no?"

She looked to Faria, who nodded tightly. "Yes. But they just helped me tell what I already knew to be true."

"Ver-ry *good,* Miss Cowley. But that's the answer you're supposed to give when asked if the D.A. actually *fabricated* your testimony . . . I hadnt gotten to that yet." He shook his head, chuckling, and rose. He started walking toward the witness box, looking at the floor. "Miss Cowley, when the D.A. asked your name, you began to give what I believe you call your 'work' or 'street' name . . . What is that name?"

"Sunny Deelight. It's an orange juice drink."

"An orange juice drink. Why are you called that?"

Sunny did a little burlesque for the court, making an innocent O of her mouth and pointing her forefinger into her cheek. "Because I taste good?"

Dreaks nodded knowingly at a fat female jurist in a doily dress who looked like she might write greeting card doggerel and repeated the line: "Because she *tastes* good."

He whirled on her then, scowling accusingly. "Isnt it true, Miss Deelight, that you have multiple arrests for prostitution, for grand theft, for vagrancy, for . . . "

"Objection. Immaterial. Miss Cowley is not on trial here."

"Overruled. Miss Cowley's criminal record can be considered by the jury in evaluating her character. However, the court would remind the jury that the mere fact of prior convictions on other, unrelated charges has no direct bearing on her credibility in the matter at hand."

"Exception. This is an improper time to instruct the jury."

"Noted. Get on with it."

"Miss Cowley, I submit you engaged in prostitution while in the employ of Mr. Moses on your own initiative and with neither his approval or knowledge. That you robbed massage customers in hotels for your own profit . . . *And*"—Dreaks raised his voice over Faria's objections—"that you are testifying today, weaving this web of false accusations about my client in exchange for a deal offered you in regards to a criminal complaint in Las Vegas."

"No. Vegas is where they found me, but it aint got nothing to do with me being here. I'm *glad* to be here. To testify so other girls . . . "

"Come now, Miss Cowley. In exchange for your testimony today, hasnt the D.A.'s office arranged with Nevada authorities to have charges identical to the ones you're leveling at my client dropped? Charges of hotel room grand theft in circumstances suggesting sexual enticement and involving knockout drops? Isnt it true you go from state to state robbing unsuspecting johns?"

"No! I'm an honest whore."

"An honest whore," Dreaks repeated the apparent oxymoron for the jury, gesturing disgustedly toward the witness box.

"Yes, an honest whore!" she screamed. "I'm testifying so Fatso and his sidekick dont hurt no more girls. I heard the office beatings, seen the cuts and bruises and broken hands and feet. Oh none of them reported it, not unless they wanted killing."

Dreaks sneered, "Miss Cowley, did these girls wear doggie collars like the one about your neck today? And if so, werent those cuts and bruises the willing fruits of their sexual orientation?"

"This collar belonged to my Yorkie. His name was Pard. Your client cooked my only friend in his office microwave. Because he thought maybe, just *maybe* I held out on him. That's the kind of scum signs your check . . . "

"Your Honor, I move the witness be dismissed. She is overwrought, her imagination is running away with her."

"Imagination, huh? I suppose I imagined *this*!" Sunny jumped up and ripped open her blouse exposing a shriveled breast shiny with burn scars. "It's called a Moses boobjob. Some are done with butane torches, others with an iron. Quick Cicero did this baby with a hotplate ring. For telling a customer I'd meet him for a drink after work."

The court recoiled in horrified silence. Then the voices gathered, rising in an irresistible wave, drowning out the judge's furious gaveling, the bailiff's shouted orders; drowning out everything except Sunny's piercing cry from the box: "But that aint nothing! Others who wouldnt flatback for him died for the birdie. Got fucked and blown away. On film and video. He made em star in their very own snuff movies. Welcome to *This is Your Death*. Snuffers shipped to every sick corner of the earth by his company. He used to make the other girls watch em just to know what they had comin if they crossed him . . . "

Then even her tirade was drowned as the wave of noise crashed and chaos erupted. Baby Jewels was on his feet screaming threats, shaking fistfuls of rings at the witness box, Quick was pummeling the father of a preteen milkcarton model who'd charged the railing to get at the Pimp Blimp; the fat female jurist in the frilly dress fainted. Extra bailiffs poured in through side doors, adding to the melee. One young reporter, in a frenzy to reach a phone, catapulted himself atop the churning surf of arms and legs clogging the center aisle to bodysurf out of court on the seething human tide.

Unconscious of the tumult, Sunny Deelight sat with wide glassy eyes watching the snuff flicks projected onto the back of her skull: the red and white brains splashed on yellow motel wallpaper, a knife opening a wound like an eager pink mouth, lolling dead heads atop bluing shoulders shuddering again and again under the assault of posthumous intercourse.

She shrugged sadly. She hadn't meant to say anything. Mr. Dreaks shouldn't have doubted she was an honest whore. She really and truly was until Baby Jewels nuked her naynay. After that the Murphy was the only game left Sunny Deelight.

She screwed her mouth sideways. Gee willikers, was it dry. She reached under the oak molding and retrieved the wad of Juicy Fruit.

MAINTENANCE YARD

||||

The Maintenance Yard was a collection of corrugated tin sheds facing each other across a narrow enclosure surfaced with cinder chips and gravel. The sheds abutted the cellblocks on the inside and the perimeter fencing where it ran closest to the prison on the outside. The biggest shed belonged to Crew Five, headquarters to Joe's fellow T Wingies Rudy Malec and Gerald Irons, their base of contraband operations since Hobby was shut down. The Paint Crew, Electric Shop, Carpentry, Plumbing, Glazier, and Institutional Locksmith occupied the other sheds.

At the head of the enclosure tilted a prefab construction with CHIEF OF PLANT stenciled on its door. The Work Order clerk's office occupied its front, a single room reeking stalely of blueprint ink and packing grease. On one wall was impaled the motheaten head of a bull elk, binoculars hanging from the broken antler opposite the missing glass eye. Beneath its scraggly whiskers a bluefaced Belfast Water clock told the wrong time.

Joe's beatup desk faced out the first unbarred window he'd seen in nearly a year. The Typewriter Shop had "secured" him an electronic Olympia typewriter, and Moonpie Monroe a Mr. Coffee purloined from the kitchens. Everyone was eager to propitiate the Work Order clerk because his bribed blessing was required for all building and maintenance work.

Joe picked up Work Requests from all sectors of the institution each morning from the Chief of Plant's box in Custody. His job was to type these into Work Orders, obtain or forge the needed signatures, and route them to the appropriate Maintenance sectors. But Work Requests had a way of getting lost, never to become Work Orders. Displease Joe and that toilet might never get unclogged, refuse to kick down the ducats he demanded as juice and those shelves would never be built, thwart his contraband enterprise and forget having your cell lights fixed. No use trying to go over his head to his Supervisor, Chief of Plant Homer T. Chubb. Homer was drying out at a fidget farm on his state medical plan.

Over his boneroo new coffee machine in Joe's office hung a *Playboy* calendar X'ed off to the date of his predecessor's parole, two months earlier. Joe didn't believe in counting days to freedom, on the theory that a watched pot never boils. Neither was he partial to this month's Miss November impersonating Pocahontas in buckskin lingerie. So in seeming defiance of the cold wind whistling down the Maintenance Yard and the peajackets and woolen watch caps issued to the outside convict workers (his cap fit nicely over Whisper's legacy), he kept the calendar turned to his favorite of the twelve pinups, Miss July, reclining in her wraparound shades on a poolside chaise, shrugging humongous oiled udders to an L.A. sun.

Except on days when he yearned for some strange. Then he spread the calendar on his desk to flip through and abuse whichever month he chose. Joe wasn't serving time, he was fucking it.

Yet this gritty gray ayem there was a better show than ole Hef's boys could stage five yards outside Joe's window in the lumber cage. Magdalena and Billy Skaggs had already started swapping passionate spit when the phone rang with Earl on the other end.

"I got some news might give you a rise, amigo . . . " Joe was only halflistening, so rapt was he on Magdalena sinking to her knees, unzipping and digging out Billy's thickening whammer to plop in her mouth, reaching behind for two fistfuls of denim to drive him. "That shemale friend of yours from the street's drivin McGee crazy. She organizin weenie women for safe sex the way he recruitin guards for Teamsters . . . "

Earl was talking about Oblivia, recently dubbed the Rubber Queen for her contraband heroics. She'd been holding AIDS prevention seminars in desperate secrecy, like conclaves of early Christians. McGee was wild to bust Oblivia, it had become an obsession with him, but she was too slick. To thwart his snitches, she held her sessions extemporaneously on the Yard, in individual cells, in empty dorms and classrooms. The transformation of the bustout Blue Note B-drinker into Coldwater's very own Mother Teresa inspired Joe as profoundly as it infuriated McGee.

"That's one chick with a dick I'm proud of," Joe said thickly. Billy had grabbed Magdalena by the hair and lifted her around and slammed her up against the cage's wire mesh, which he clutched to facefuck her for all he was worth. The cage shook as though it held wild animals. Joe wondered if Magdalena's imminent parole loaned the sex added piquancy.

"Why you breathin funny, amigo? You spankin yer monkey?"

"Sure, F Stop. Just keep talkin dirty . . . "

And damned if the old coonass didn't start pumping Joe's ear full of pornographic minutiae concerning armadillo reproduction in captivity—"They shy, yeah. Only respond to that hands *on* approach."

Ballooning his cheeks, Joe interrupted with a plea to be allowed to return to work and hung up.

He cursed rolling a Work Order into the machine backward. He wished Billy would wrap up the show; he couldn't wrest his eyes from the lumber cage. Finally, the big con sagged, staggered backward and socked her in the mouth. Must have been good. Magdalena swished the cum oyster from one cheek to the other; her adamsapple bobbed like a toilet float swallowing it. She chanced to catch Joe's eye and licked her bruised chops with a sexpot sneer just for him.

To his horror and dismay, Joe was harder than a hanged man. That weenie woman doesn't even characterize feminity, he tried castigating himself, she rebukes it. But his moronic member would not bend, much less cave in, to such abstractions; and Joe had to mount a commando assault on Miss September, nude bowling at the Playboy mansion. She stood at the line, eyes predatorily slitted, lips hungrily parted, cupping the shiny globe aloft between polished knockers of like mass and mold; becoming in Joe's fisted rapture a tripletitted Tantric manifestation in Lucite by Mattel, at once terrible and tacky—Barbie, Destroyer of BMW's, Devourer of Active Assets. At length selfsated and disgusted, he rolled in a fresh Work Order right side up.

That evening Judge Harriet Innes-Brown held in camera proceedings in chambers to review new disclosures made in the Moses case and determine the advisability of declaring a mistrial. Present were Judge Innes-Brown, District Attorney Faria, defense counsel Dreaks, Homicide Lieutenant Ricardo Tarzon, state's witness Karen Cowley, and a court reporter.

Having stipulated for the record that Miss Cowley at her own request, and under the City and County Medical Examiner's direction to forestall traumatic shock, had been administered tranquilizers; and having further stipulated that said tranquilizers impaired the witness's mental acuity, Judge Innes-Brown inquired of both counsels if, in the interests of justice, they had any objection to the continuation of the proceedings; and both counsels acceded with the exception by both recorded that any testimony heard must be later reheard in open court under oath.

JUDGE INNES-BROWN: Mr. Faria, would you care to open this inquiry?

D.A. FARIA: Miss Cowley, why didnt you tell us earlier about these things, these . . . snuff movies, as you call them.

KAREN COWLEY: You want to know why? I'll tell you why. They snuffed my best friend, Peaches Supreme. All Peaches did was stuff a tip in her twat . . . vagina, I mean. Quick Cicero caught her. They made a snuffer of her. I saw the video. Mr. Moses played it for all the girls on his office VCR. Afterwards, they rented a motel room on Lombard Street and left the body there. I remember reading about it in the papers. The police called it murder-rape . . .

D.A. FARIA: Just a minute, Miss Cowley. Lieutenant, do you—

LT. TARZON: Real name Nancy Hoffstedder. Her body was discovered with its throat slashed and a bullet through its left ear in Room 234 of the Cablecar Inn in the first week of February last—

D.A. FARIA: Please continue, Miss Cowley.

KAREN COWLEY: Her folks came down from Oregon to get the body. Nice folks, Christmas tree farmers. They held a little memorial thing in Golden Gate Park. In the Japanese Tea Gardens. All us girls came dressed like I was in court today. See, they thought she was a PBX operator, so we made like secretaries and stuff. They were just country, didnt know the difference. Her mother showed us pictures of when she was a kid. On a bicycle. At the state fair with a stick of cotton candy bigger than she was. Her father read a stupid poem about death taking the brightest and best in the middle of life. At the end her mother couldnt quit crying. We tried to comfort her and all, but she wouldnt stop bawling. Then her father said she was crying for joy because her daughter had such a fine bunch of friends and knowing her life was so enriched made losing her a little easier. And here we were a bunch of cheap whores. It was sad. But it was sweet, too, with the shallow ponds full of fat goldfish and the cherry blossoms blowing everywhere—

D.A. FARIA: Cherry blossoms? I thought we were talking about the first week in February?

LT. TARZON: The cherry blossoms bloomed early last winter. I know in connection with another case.

KAREN COWLEY: So now those nice folks are going to read about her in the paper and maybe even see the snuff flick. Just like I had to. Watch some twisted son of a bitch bust a nut up their baby's cunt and a cap in her ear at the same time . . . Blew her brains all over the front of the camera. I didnt want Peaches's folks to have to see that or even hear about it. That's why I didnt say nothing about it. Not till I lost my head in court. And now I dont want to say any more about it. Only this. I hope you're proud, Mr. Smartypants Lawyer.

COUNSEL DREAKS: No, I'm not proud, I want the witness to know I regret this as much as she does.

JUDGE INNES-BROWN: Mr. Dreaks, am I correct in assuming you are making a motion for mistrial at this juncture as the jury has been hopelessly subverted with inadmissible testimony.

COUNSEL DREAKS: I have so advised my client. However, he insists I make no such motion. He understands his rights have been compromised, but wishes the matter to proceed with this same jury.

JUDGE INNES-BROWN: That is highly irregular. I hope that it is an indication of nothing more than his faith in the system. The District Attorney is to take under advisement this Court's recommendation that new charges be investigated and, should grounds be found, referred to the Grand Jury . . . In closing, I offer you all my thanks, you in particular, Miss Cowley, for your cooperation at this late hour after an extremely trying day. Good evening.

NO PAIN, NO GAIN

||||

Three walls of the YMCA weight room were painted a soothing powderblue; the fourth was entirely mirrored. That way fitness devotees could see the immediate fruit of their labors on the sixteen gleaming exercise machines ranked like medieval torture engines across the rubber-matted floor.

State Supreme Court Justice Lucius Bell was strapped in a Nautilus pectoral fly machine. Not to appease such vanity as drove the strutting Adonises and ardent Artemises in spandex activewear, empty heads clamped by Sony Walkmans, gushing holistic hocuspocus about highfiber diets and higher colonics and Highest Selves. Judge Bell was there for a *reason*. His doctor told him his ticker was clogging and he'd better lose some weight. What the doctor didn't mention were the lesions on Bell's heart, damage typical of cocaine abuse.

Bell could have opted for swimming. But he hated getting wet and could do nothing more dignified in the water than a flailing doggie paddle. Then there was raquetball. The trouble with raquetball, he told his cronies at the Black Friars, was it was too *white*. Once he'd seen a film of colonial India where the Sikh officers played cricket. That's how he felt playing raquet-ball, colonized. He said. Secretly he wanted to control every symbol of New Age ofay doodadism. He already had his own vineyard in Sonoma, a twelvemeter yacht, a son in school in Switzerland, and a seat on the Sierra

Club Board. And it was hard imagining anything whiter than a white wife. The true trouble was, Bell's archrival on the State Supreme Court, ultra-right superwhite Chief Justice Kingsley Crowder III, was also senior state raquetball champion. It wouldn't do to have their perennial judicial joust-ing decided symbolically with a hard rubber ball. He'd like to see Bill Cosby act so twofortennis cool if he knew his next time out on the court he was going to get thrashed like a house nigger by Jesse Helms.

Bell breathed out at the top of the fly where his arms in the pulley levers were fully extended above his chest; inhaled deeply, spreading them wide into a rigid cross. Today he'd boosted the pin to the fortypound plate. *No Pain, No Gain* read the cute computer sign on the wall. His muscles burned . . . *seven* . . . spots danced in his eyes . . . *eight* . . . his arteries throbbed . . . *nine* . . . blood boomed in his ears . . . *annnd TEN!* He released the levers high; the weight plates crashed on the pulley rack behind the incline bench. His lungs exploded breath like a blown tire. He leaned back, eyes closed, tasting the sweat at the corners of his mouth. He thought of how he'd look in swimming trunks at the country club this summer. He opened his eyes, flared the lids to rinse away the spots; tested his vision looking into the mirror. Immediately his eyes bulged.

Across the room a solitary figure in old gray sweats and black wool watchcap was working out on the heavy bag. He wore no gloves, only tape. A staccato flurry of jabs signed off with two lightning left hooks and an explosive right uppercut that could have launched the Space Shuttle; shuffle back, feint north and south; then into the bag again with a stutter-ing highspeed jab. He stopped and dropped his arms and rolled his neck and shoulders. He turned, chugging both fists low, skipping an invisible rope. He grinned from across the room into the mirror. None other than Quick Cicero.

That psychotic slug has sent his hachet for a meet. They're getting desperate, and desperation breeds stupidity.

Lucius Bell unstrapped and hopped off the Nautilus bench and rushed from the mirrored room. On the way to the lockerroom, he passed the juice bar. Usually he stopped there for a Kharma Krush or Chakra Frappe.

"Astral Smoothie's today's special," the girl said in a purr that could just as easily have offered a half and half. Her name in this life was Bambi and she taught jazzercise and always wore a T-shirt imprinted with the YMCA logos. As usual her nipples protruded like thumbs. Once Bell had over-heard one of the bodybuilders ask why they were perpetually erect. Those boneheads interpreted a mutual devotion to fitness as a license to pose with impunity any anatomical question. "My eyes"—she'd pointed to her baby blues—"are the windows of my soul. My nips"—she tweaked them—"its antennae. I keep them tuned to life's potentialities. I used to be into rage, now I'm into growth . . . Like in bioenergetics, awareness through body movements. It's all in this totally astral book of consciousness out-takes . . . " She held up a shiny paperback spread on top of the juicer. It was titled *Just Bring Your Body, Your Mind Will Follow.* On its cover a nude couple stood holding hands facing into a sunset so pyrotechnic it might have been an H-bomb explosion.

But this morning Bell was too addled by Quick's unexpected appearance to even ogle Bambi's satellite dishes. Rushing into the lockerroom he nearly bowled over another member in his frantic search for his locker. It was always hard remembering which of the identical three hundred lock-ers, each fastened with an identical combination padlock, was his. This morning it was nearly impossible.

What the hell was Cicero *doing* here, where Bell was known? All his other contacts with Baby Jewels had been by public phone. On a weekend Black Awareness Seminar in San Francisco, Bell had noted the numbers of a dozen pay telephones in open, crowded places. When his secretary received a message from a Mr. Moss from the California Association for Convalescent Action, or CACA, a fictitious lobby for resthome residents, Bell phoned the Tender Trap's machine from a Sacramento pay phone and left a message instructing the Fat Man to be at a certain pay phone at a certain time to await his call. That way he was reasonably sure of not being recorded and witlessly adding further blackmail ammunition to the formi-dable smoking gun represented by the Blue Jager Moon. But now the stakes were climbing, the papers were full of the latest snuff movie revela-tions, and Baby Jewels was acting recklessly.

Judge Bell was half out of his gym clothes before he found the locker. Skip the shower today, he decided in a flash—beat Cicero out of the Y. But when he was nude he had a better idea. Quickly he stuffed his shorts and tank top into the locker and spun the combination dial. He grabbed a towel off the stack and ducked into the steam room.

The first lungful of wet heat reminded him of why he never used the facility. It was like being lowered down the stack of a steam ship. Come to think of it, he never saw any blacks use it. It was always the flabby old white men. He wondered if a taste for steam heat was acquired by genetics or environment.

Never mind. Today he was just grateful no one was using the steam room. He took a seat on the woodslat bench furthest from the door and forced himself to breathe deep and slow. He had to last in there long enough for Cicero to figure he'd flown the coop and leave himself. He'd just remembered his Aston Martin in the lot when he saw through the swirling steam the wiry figure with a towel around its waist.

"How you, Yonner?" Smiling, Quick took a seat on the opposite bench; stretched out his legs and folded his hands over his corrugated belly.

"This is insane! We could be easily spotted."

"You fergittin. You's the only one hurt if we get tossed."

"Oh no, if we're uncovered, I cant help you any longer."

Quick Cicero shrugged and rolled his shoulders. Then the little son of a bitch stepped over and turned up the thermostat. Returning to his seat he said, "Mr. Moses dont figger you've been such a big help anyhow."

"I was doing all I could . . . " Jesus, to have to grovel at the tail of *this* snake. "First I approached HYENA, the prostitutes' union. They traditionally support independent working girls and take a dim view of kinds like Mr. Moses, whom they see as exploiters of women. I convinced their leadership, however, that Mr. Moses was quite the opposite, that he protected these girls from the perils of plying their trade unprotected in the streets. I had them convinced his motives corresponded with their own, the preservation of these young women's welfare and dignity, and that now he was being singled out for persecution. I lobbied hard behind the scenes in this portraiture of Mr. Moses as the protector of the working girl. Once won over, HYENA used their influence to persuade the ACLU that issues of civil liberty were at stake here. The ACLU took up the cause largely on their faith in my record and integrity."

Quick rolled his eyes and began mining lint from his navel.

"The ACLU roped in the NAACP and local black civic organizations. All of these parties had already informed the Mayor and D.A. that they were withdrawing their support in the upcoming election unless the witch-hunt against your boss was called off. Faria was about to give in, his case against you was faltering anyway . . . when these . . . *horrible* new allegations were made."

Quick started a series of stage yawns.

Bell's glistening face contorted like an Ashanti war mask gulping steam. "Five days before the election! What timing! All the leverage I'd worked so hard to build blasted to thin air . . . Overnight the Mayor and D.A. of San Francisco were household names across America. The case became instant grist for newspaper editorials, the sensation of morning talk shows . . . Stop that!"

Quick performed one last elaborate yawn like a silent Indian war whoop before returning his attention to the ceiling tiles, counting cracks, *break this mother's back* . . .

"No way could Mancuso and Faria lose the election, with or without the support of the groups I just mentioned. Not that they were making a peep any longer. Murder, Mr. Cicero, doesnt qualify as victimless crime."

Quick turned slitted eyes on him and drew back his lip. "Yours would be, Yonner. You *need* killing, you earned it. If I clipped you, you'd be your own victim, no one else's. And you'd be canceled. So your murder would be the perfect victimless crime. Not that it's worth the effort." It took a moment for Quick to recover from this feat of logic, then another to find the lost thread. "Mr. Moses says if he falls, you fall."

"Oh?" An addled grin creased Bell's jowls. "But I dont see what I can do to help now. The election's in the archives. The D.A. and Faria are snugly back in office due to the *outstanding* publicity you guys gave them. Such good publicity that they cant back off your case, as they normally would with another four years sewed up. They've got to keep after you now. Nailing you's more important to the electorate than cutting taxes . . . What's the Grand Jury going to hear? What are the police going to discover? . . . " The war mask turned witchdoctor. "How could you *make* those movies?"

"Who said we did but a burntout whore? But never mind that. We got that covered. Her word's gotta be backed up with evidence and they aint gonna find any . . . " Absently Quick began tweaking his nipples. It was hardly the titillating spectacle offered by Bambi, and the judge shut his eyes in disgust. "But we've already been convicted in Superior Court on the pimping and pandering and grand theft. Naturally, we're gonna appeal. We got a clerk in the Appellate Division who can have our case assigned to whichever judge we name . . . So what you gotta do, Yonner, is tell us which judge you got the most influence with. We wont settle for anything less than reversal."

Judge Bell's steamironed lungs wrung out, "So . . . *that's* why you didnt go for an easy mistrial . . . "

"You got it, Yonner." Quick Cicero stood and rewrapped his towel—breathing easy, the little bastard. "You got five days to get us a name." Quick Cicero turned to leave.

"The Moon," gasped Bell. "When do I get it back?"

"You gotta talk to Mr. Moses about the ice, Yonner. Which reminds me. The boss says no more spy stuff with the phones. When Mr. Moses calls you, you call back on his personal line. You remember—the one you used to order girls like pizza pies?"

THEM JONESES

||||

Joe leaned on the counter at the Law Library, awaiting a clerk who was assisting an aged pachook word a writ of *a certiori*. He glanced again at the ducat he found on his bunk the previous evening. It was the first such summons he'd ever received from a convict, and its presumption annoyed him. It was signed CRABBLE, GENERAL COUNSEL. Joe had heard of this character. The highest paid jailhouse lawyer at Coldwater, he first gained acclaim by winning his own release from the Hole on a writ of *habeas corpus* presented to the court on toilet paper.

The clerk sauntered down the counter and Joe asked just where this legal luminary might be found.

"Down at the Mailroom."

"Point him out to me when he comes back," Joe said.

The Law Library was in the corner of the regular Library. Joe sat at a long table beneath tall iron windows and leafed through a *National Geographic*. Rain streamed down the pitted glass, making a cozy shushing sound, flooding the Library with a wavery gray light. "Yard down," faintly fizzled the Mainline P.A. Like fog, rain obscured the guntowers' lines of fire. Too bad, he thought idly. It was the kind of raw autumnal rain he remembered from his youth, its stinging pelt against his face, its smell of faroff snow and dank dark dying things becoming earth again. He would have liked to have gone for a walk in it.

The Library itself awakened another of the childhood remembrances that lately were evoked by the slightest stimuli, as if imprisonment was purifying the pool of his perceptions. The smells of old pulp and print, the soothing sense of refuge, the dense hush numinous with knowledge . . . When he and his mother went to town and she got to slinging down shots at the Red Dog or passing quarts of beer in the park, Joe would slip away to the public library; there to wander the looming aisles, slack lips shaping the titles like exotic ports of call, finger running down the bindings like a stick down a picket fence . . .

Joe started at a tap on his shoulder. It was a trim, middleaged black with a neat mustache and nervous smile. "Scuze me, man," he murmured. "But I gots two packs of cigarets if you could help me make a letter to my bride. See, I cant write."

Joe nodded. The black sat beside him. He passed Joe a sheet of lined paper, a pencil stub, and two packs of Camels, the most popular brand in the pen, the ones used for currency.

"Dont need the squares," Joe said, pushing them back and taking up the pencil stub. "Shoot."

Dear, Joe started writing—"Is that an E or a U in Irlene?" The hammer shrugged. "I," Joe decided a little loudly, drawing a savage slantendicular from another convict at the table writing a letter, his tongue stuck out sideways.

Dear Irlene, How are you? I'm fine. Did Mama get you that job at the Rib Hut? Look out after Mama. Irlene baby, I sure do miss you. I hear they have—"No, no," Joe laughed. "It's conjugal, not conjure visits." *That's you and me alone in a trailer for a weekend. I know you got no car. Maybe ask Hank next door. I swear I'll make up for this. Seems I hardly knew you. We were married only a month . . .*

The hammer's voice trailed off. Joe was anxious to be done with the letter, it only summoned thoughts of Kitty, but when he turned he saw Irlene's husband was bent over the table, head cradled on his crossed arms, shoulders trembling with silent grief. Then, suddenly, he jumped to his feet and bolted out of the Library.

Joe stared after him in bewilderment.

A skinny convict with bushy white hair and a banana nose approached the table. "That's one letter that would never be delivered," he clued Joe in. "Alonzo there caught Irlene gambling with their food stamps and cut her head off with a roofing hatchet."

Joe tore the letter slowly in pieces.

"Every day he comes to the Library and tries to write her."

"Why didnt you tell me before I started," Joe groused.

"Because I just got here. The other law clerk said you were looking for me . . . "

"You're Crabble? Well . . . " Joe stood and snapped the ducat from his shirt pocket. "What the hell's this? I got no law business."

Crabble led him back to the Law Library, chuckling.

"I routinely review the jackets of cons who can afford my services," he explained. "You'd be surprised at the number with unexplored legal options who dont know it. I pay particularly close attention to T Wingers. Look at it as professional solicitation."

"I look at it as pure pesteration."

Crabble hoisted conspiratorial brows. "Wanna go free?"

Joe cocked his head, slanting Crabble a suspicious eye.

"I see from your jacket, Speaker, that you're a candidate for a coffee break parole."

"A what?"

"A Special Circumstances release. They call them coffee break paroles because that's about how long they take." Crabble produced a business card from under the counter and slid it across. Joe picked it up. MARVIN MAAS, ATTORNEY AT LAW. Joe recognized the office address as being on the same street as the Department of Corrections complex.

Crabble leaned across the counter. "You've heard of Maas. Sometimes they call him No Maas, as in no *mas* time.

"I've heard him called Maas Dinero."

The convict counsel chortled. "Oh, he costs, but he delivers. He and the Director are tennis partners. Hell, they probably switch wives. For two large you hit the gate."

"But I dont even have a parole hearing scheduled."

"Dont matter. A Special Circumstances release doesnt require a hearing. It's all very informal and discretionary. Maas just has to make a case that your rehabilitation would be best continued in the community. All the members care about is whether they'll get any backlash. You know, like they couldnt cut Charlie Manson loose. In your case I dont think there'd be a public hue and cry . . . Once you get Maas the dough, he'll walk you in three, four months. Just keep your jacket clean."

Joe pocketed the card. "Before I thank you, what's the freight?"

"Pro bono, baby."

Crabble watched Joe leave the Library, then picked up the institutional phone. The convict he dialed was doing time, a Murder Two for tying his coke connection by the heels to the bumper of his Audi 5000 and dragging him cowboystyle through the streets until they needed dental records to ID the remains.

"Donnie? . . . The D.A. wont make a peep if we enter a motion for retrial on a reduced charge of Involuntary Manslaughter . . . Diminished capacity, what else? . . . What changed their mind? You remember that homicide loot in the crinkly black suit? . . . Yeah? Well, I just did him a favor . . . "

Joe went straight to his Maintenance Yard office and typed a letter to Maas. He also typed a withdrawal slip authorizing Accounting to forward the attorney five hundred dollars from his inmate trust account. Enough, he guessed, to bring the parole specialist to Coldwater for an initial interview.

It wasn't until after he slipped Maas's letter into the Legal Mailbox on the Mainline outside Custody that he remembered the promise he'd made to Spencer only three nights ago. The quad was playing checkers in the Chowhall at Evening Activity call, pushing the pieces with a pencil wired to an elastic headband, the same clumsy rig used to scrawl the Clorox kite.

"No more convict plasma," Joe pledged. "We're goin to cop blood that's already been tested. Plus we're gonna send for a free specialist so you're not at the mercy of these sorryass state sawbones."

Spencer chuckled, wistfully it seemed. He jerked the coathanger prosthesis in Joe's direction, as if to shake, a ghost reflex of the departed arm; then laughed at both his physical and emotional helplessness.

How could Joe pay both for Spencer's medical needs and his own freedom? To which was he more obligated?

He made Yard alone to think it through, crossing the baseball diamond to the weight pile beneath a fall sky scattershot with clouds. He bench-pressed until stars burst in his eyes and his jugular bulged. Aerated blood brimmed his brainpan, surcharging thought with optimism. I can do both, he felt certain. Save Spencer and liberate myself. I've got a few hundred left from my Hobby scams; I'll spend that on Spencer, then scare up some fresh hustles, not such a tall proposition in the Maintenance Yard. Exploding breath copperish with blood, Joe had himself convinced that he had everything under control—when two shapes joined their shadows across his heaving chest.

"Whaddaya know? F Stop's bankroller." To his right Joe recognized Big Casino's basso profundo and glimpsed the brass belt buckle faced downward by his belly.

"Read his titty tattoo," sniggered Little Casino on the left. *"Born to Lose.* No wonder he covers the old man's action."

Before Joe could speak, each sleeved a twentykilo plate on the opposite ends of his bar. He locked his elbows to hold the extra eightyeight pounds aloft, creaking his wrists.

"I . . . aint bankin F Stop no more," he managed to grunt.

Big Casino flashed a gold tooth snarling, "That aint what he tells us . . . *punk.*"

Little Casino pitched in, "He says you'll collect all his markers including the vig . . . Big, I think we should show this pootbutt what weighty matter this is."

Two more iron plates slid onto the bar. Sputtering for breath, Joe fought to keep his quivering arms straight but they crumpled slowly, then collapsed, and nearly four hundred pounds lay crushing his chest.

Big Casino asked, "Is this little interview impressing you?"

All breath was squeezed from Joe and he could only nod. He was afraid his eyeballs were going to pop out of their sockets like corks.

"Good," he chortled. "F Stop's down four yards. I want it in green money at the head of S Wing at chow call *tonight.*"

Joe's world was going black; strange music filled his ears.

"Be there," Little Casino advised, "or we're gonna turn you out for stick pussy."

"Maybe we oughta take this load off him," Big Casino suggested. "After all, he aint heavy, he's our brother."

"You're funny, Big. I'm talkin Vegas funny. You could open for Tom Jones, I bet."

Only the old cons celled there and the others called V Wing the Hole in the Wall. Where Tommy Dorsey took turns with the Texas Playboys scoring sepiatinted dreams of interstate flight in flathead Fords in the days when acquittal could still be won holding court in the streets and a new identity was as simple as one more madeup name. The outlaw then was still the Promethean darling of the republic, hero of pulp rags and Saturday serials, not yet a victim himself of fivecent words that didn't shoot back.

Earl wasn't home. His cell smelled grayly of dirty socks and sour sheets and liniment, old man smells. Joe called to Bony Moroney in the opposite cell. Bony was the institutional Lightbulb Man, a convict remarkable for his height and long white beard. Twenty years Bony had patrolled the Mainline and cellblocks of Coldwater, replacing dead lights with a sixfoot bulbgripper that likened him to an Old Testament prophet.

"He's in the shower," reported Bony. "And the whole wing would take it as a favor if you didnt roust him out. F Stop only takes a notion to wash about once a month . . . if we're lucky."

Joe waited in Earl's cell. The walls were plastered with yellowed maga-zine pictures of oldtime baseball players in baggy uniforms, wearing gloves that looked like raw livers. Mixed in were snapshots with scalloped edges of a younger Earl; standing with his foot propped on the running board of a '39 Plymouth, sitting on a New Orleans fretwork balcony with his arm around a pretty girl, barechested in striped convict pants against a sun-splashed wall topped with broken bottles. Leaning close, Joe made out a gecko lizard sunning itself on the wall and decided it had to be the Louisiana state pen at Angola. Earl had told him once about having to kill that seaman on Decatur Street. The judge sentenced him to ride the lightning and Earl's wife (could it be the girl on the balcony?) had him declared legally dead before his execution even so she could marry a country doctor; then the judge called drunk as they were strapping him in that homely throne of oak and iron, commuted his sentence to Life Without; but he escaped and ran for ten years—or so he said—three of them hiding in the Air Force, where he lost parts of his fingers to frostbite on a highaltitude recon flight over North Korea. Over his cell sink were Scotchtaped several photos from this period. One tickled Joe's memory, perhaps he'd seen someone else in the same pose—tipped back in a chair from a nightclub table dense with bottles and glasses, cap on the back of his head, cigaret dangling from his lip . . .

"Be it ever so humble . . . Where yat, Joe?"

Earl stood in the cell gate with a towel wrapped around his waist. The brow above the blue eye was snaked up in a question mark.

"I just paid off your gambling debts."

Earl opened his mouth and closed it. "You dint have to, no."

"What are you talkin about? You set me up, motherfucker! They almost killed me." Joe related the events on the weight pile. "But what really cooks my cojones is that they did it just for fun. They knew all they had to do was ask, I couldnt refuse. They're McGee's boys. They grease him big time and he protects their action. That's how their runners move so freely after Lights, taking guard action even. That's also why any other convict takin bets gets shook down three times a day until they find an excuse to throw him in the Hole . . . Christ! You were my friend, Earl. You owed me better."

"I'm sorry." Earl pinched the bridge of his nose, squeezing his eyes tight. "I dint mean to get you hurt, no."

"It's Spencer you hurt, you sick old sack of shit. I *told* you I was savin to get him clean blood and real doctors. I *explained* I was finished picking up your markers. And you went and fronted me right off, gambled away Spencer's last hope."

Earl sat on his bunk and stared at the floor. He barely flinched when Joe hurled his portable television to the floor. It exploded with a hollow pop like a giant lightbulb, spraying glass around the cell. Mumbling deep in his throat, Earl busied himself bunching his blanket in his gnarled fist.

Joe shouted, "You go down to W Wing and tell him he'll have to take his chances with the plague because some pitcher's slider aint sinkin . . . or is it a quarterback now who throws more interceptions than touchdowns?"

The opaque gray eye beseeched Joe. "I couldnt help myself, no. It's this jones. I can tell you everything about gamblin cept how not to place that first sucker bet. Just the same as I can tell you everything about jail cept how to stay out and most all there is about livin cept how not to die . . . "

A light shone in the gray eye, igniting its pearly whorls of age, recalling to Joe the worn chip at the bottom of his enamel washbasin at the Monserrat School. Winter mornings when the water left standing overnight froze, the flaw's chaotic Godlike symmetry stared up at him through his own reflection.

"Same as you could tell a person everything about dope cept how to leave it alone," Earl meekly reproached. "You know about them joneses, yeah. Yours made you do things you wouldnt do otherwise. Of all people, yeah, *you* should be able to forgive . . . "

Joe punched Earl the same way he used to break his own reflection in the washbasin; high on the cheekbone, a sound like chopping gristly meat. Earl fell sideways, curling into a fetal position, covering his head with his arms. Rushing to escape the cell and its old man smells, Joe heard him sob, gargling his own blood.

LAWYERS ARE
PEOPLE, TOO

||||

Horace had climbed from parking valet to maitre d' at Rossi's Famous Seafood Restaurant in less than a year. He credited this quick ascent to his drama training. Horace performed every job as a role and transformed each into a minor classic. Horace was a dedicated thespian of the all-life's-a-stage school.

But today, assailed by outrageous fortune, he was having trouble finding his marks. Adolph Menjou, his model for the role of maitre d', would never have taken such an undignified part. Unless it was opposite the Marx Brothers.

The morning started off viciously when the FDA called to announce that their produce had been mistakenly delivered from fields quarantined for the Mediterranean fruit fly, and Rossi's had to use frozen and canned vegetables. It became dreadful when a hot young starlet came in to brunch with her agent and their waiter suffered a vertigo attack and splashed hot coffee down her canyonesque cleavage. The sleazeball agent screamed for twenty minutes how Rossi's would be sued until it bled fish oil for poaching her knockers, defacing public property.

Now—and it wasn't yet noon—Horace saw all the signs of the day shaping into a majorleague disaster. He'd just gotten off the phone from taking luncheon reservations from that horrid valet of Baby Jewels Moses who twisted Horace's arm until he cried the week before. For just winking!

He gulped two more Libriums with his Perrier and slapped his silly hand to keep from biting its nails.

The problem wasn't with the valet, however, but his fat master. Mr. Rossi himself instructed Horace to discourage reservations from Mr. Moses. He was a convicted criminal now, it was in all the papers, the infamia of the movies. Rossi's had enough problems dissociating itself from the public's Italian gangster fantasies without catering to certified hoodlums. And Baby Jewels Moses couldn't exactly be hidden at a back table. But Horace didn't know *how* to discourage that valet when he called. Just his voice turned Horace's insides to zabaglione.

Horace was practicing deep breathing at his maitre d' podium, trying to remember the words to the "Hail Mary," when a purple whiff of lavender slithered up his nostrils and he heard a sibilant doll's voice: "We have reservations, I believe."

Horace's lips were somersaulting over unintelligible responses when suddenly Signor Rossi appeared at his elbow. "But of course, Mr. Moses," he said, bowing from the waist. Spitefully Horace noted his boss's fawning tone when Mr. Moses appeared in person.

Like a mountain seen from a circling airplane, Mr. Moses rotated to face the plump restaurateur. "Well, have us conducted to our table." Behind him the valet smirked at Horace, giving him butterflies. The third member of their party, a haggard man with harrowed eyes, was busy trying to straighten his suit so it didn't look like something he'd worn to sleep on a park bench.

"Of course, of course . . . Horace!" Mr. Rossi snapped his fingers loud as firecrackers.

Mewling Italianate sounds of abasement in keeping with the establishment's ethnicity, Horace led the mismatched trio to the best table in the house. When they were seated, he carefully set a tasseled menu before each on his salad plate. Whether it was the valet's scent of danger or simply that yummy Lagerfeld cologne, Horace almost swooned on top of him. He caught himself in the nick of time and swanned off, leaving them to their conversation. Like every maitre d' in San Francisco, Horace knew of the Fat Man's hatred for intrusive waiters.

"We're going to the wall on this one, Sidney," Baby Jewels simped dangerously. "I had to borrow against my finest gems to make this appeal bond . . . "

"I'm dropping out, Jules," Sidney said.

"What're you talking about, Sidney?—"

They were interrupted by the waiter bringing herring in sour cream for

Baby Jewels, soup for Quick, and decaf for Sidney. The hard little eyes hammered into the Fat Man's huge slick head bored into Sidney's.

"I've considered my position," Sidney continued, "and wish to withdraw from the case. I can recommend competent alternate counsel."

"Alternate, shmalternate . . . I want you on this appeal, Sidney. Now what is it you're talking about, withdrawing? . . . "

Turning his cup of decaf in its saucer and studying the light shivering on its surface, Sidney Dreaks explained in a dry, tense voice his inability to reconcile his conscience with the heinous allegations made in court by state's witness Sunny Deelight.

When he spoke, Baby Jewels's voice had taken on that sinister wheedling tone that squirmed Sidney's skin. "Sidney, how long have we been together? Ten, twelve years? *Tch*, we barmitzvahed your nephew Harry in my very first club, the Blackhawk, down on O'Farrell. And now, what is he? The vicepresident of operations at one of Silicon Valley's biggest microchip producers. We're talking about a long time, Sidney. And in all those years, I never told you a lie. I may not have told you everything, but I never said a lie . . . And now you want to take the word of a shiksa, a prosecution witness and a certified meshuga, against mine . . . I'm hurt, Sidney. That's all I can say, I'm hurt . . . " Baby Jewels got to work doing some hurting himself, punishing the heaping plate of barbecued crab that appeared before him.

Sidney wasn't eating. He ordered another cup of decaf to go with his fresh Salem. Sitting halfway around the round table between them, Quick Cicero was working thoughtfully on a hot sausage hero. Every couple of bites, he'd turn chewing deliberately and regard Sidney with flat eyes the attorney was certain were fondling his soft neck for a garrote.

"Jules, I just cant countenance what that girl . . . "

The Fat Man's fist banged the table, jingling cutlery and crystal. "I'm telling you, Sidney. She's a stone meshuga. Got a psych jacket thicker than your wrist. If your investigators I'm paying for were doing their job, they'd have had her hospital records for you in court."

Sidney sat up. He had guessed Sunny Deelight wasn't exactly superglued, but this was the first he'd heard of any history of mental illness.

"Why didnt you say something?"

Baby Jewels set down his knife and fork and leaned his enormity across the table. "I never thought it was necessary," he said with the cool sarcasm one might use to instruct a master plumber on how to flush a toilet. "I didnt believe we had to further discredit and humiliate an acknowledged addict and convicted prostitute and thief. Not for the purposes of the court. I should have known my own lawyer was a different story! . . . " Baby

Jewels snapped his fingers next to his bulletshaped cranium. "Where was that hospital, Quick? In her home town, wha—"

"Sioux Falls." Quick's eyes measured Sidney for a car trunk.

"So you're telling me you havent produced these socalled snuff movies? . . . " Sidney asked sharply to regain some initiative.

"*Tch!* It's a sad day I have to answer such a question to my best friend. Of course not, Sidney. There's a little roughhousing in some of the loops, but it's acting . . . How many people you see killed on your TV every night? Do you call it snuff TV? Of course not. That's why it's . . . called . . . *acting,* Sidney . . . I cant believe I got to explain this. Can you believe I got to explain it, Quick?"

"I cant believe it, Mr. Moses."

"Sidney, you know the judge signed the warrant just today and they're down at the Menlo Park film lab ransacking my entire film inventory. And you know what they'll find? Of course you do. The same innocent stuff that used to be on my store racks. Fuck and suck and come for the birdie. Will that satisfy you? Because I need you on this one, Sidney. This is all the marbles."

Sidney shifted in his chair and lit another Salem. He spotted two waitresses at the kitchen doors talking behind their hands and pointing surreptitiously in their direction. He had been so long painted with the same notorious brush as his client he almost relished the association.

"All right, Jules . . . "

"No, no . . . " Baby Jewels waved his hand, twinkling a fistful of tawdry lights. "All right isnt quite good enough, Sidney. You got to be a little sorry."

"So I'm sorry already." Sidney actually smiled contritely. "The emotion in court, the heat of the moment . . . you understand."

"*Tch,* Sidney. You're supposed to have freon for blood."

"Lawyers are people, too, Jules." Sidney grinned weakly.

Baby Jules laughed, a flaccid hissing like a leaky air mattress. "I like that. You like that, Quick?"

"I like that, Mr. Moses. I think Sidney here's a real wit." His eyes now sized Sidney for the fiftygallon drum to dump in the bay.

"Sidney, this morning I received by messenger confirmation that our case has been calendared for a certain appellate judge referred to us by someone who owes us a . . . favor. But where are my manners? First a little celebration of our renewed friendship! Quick, tell that dingbat maitre d' to shlep over the the sweet nosh wagon . . . "

Meanwhile, back on the truck ranch, it wasn't like Rings was hanging around because she had to; she got bocoo chances to book. Every day some whiteline Romeo offered the Gypsy Queen of Aces High luxury transport to Memphis to lay a wreath at the King's grave, St. Looie for an earful of the blues, Alaska for a midnight suntan. Working Aces High was like tricking a travel agent—Rings could write her own ticket.

Thing was, she'd changed: her heart had too many stitches, she no longer fell in love at the drop of her drawers. And Rings wasn't one to take up a trucker falsely on his offer. "Commitment" was a word she'd picked up reading *Cosmo* in the truck ranch gift shop. That it was the same word used to put kooks on the funny farm Rings found no coincidence, because that's fur shur where she'd be headed if she fell in love again.

So she'd jellyroll the truckers, treat them to brief bursts of heaven, but whenever one wanted a piece of heart to go along with the piece of ass, she'd squall: "Gag me with yer custom chrome stacks! Gypsy's my name and casual's my game . . . " Then softening, running her nails with a *zzzz* noise up Levi's buttonflies, "Course you could always gag me with Mr. Happy there. For a double sawski, like."

That was before she met Randolph Scott, But Not the Actor.

It happened one rainy afternoon in the cafe. Rings was dancing with herself by the jukebox flaming in the corner when she lamped this prime side of USDA beef at the counter slumped on his forearms, sipping java and looking longsuffering and noble in way that reminded her of Alonzo, the golden retriever Rings rescued from the pound when she was six. Alonzo slept with her and carried her books home from school and everything until Daddy zotzed the pooch for pooping on the new Galaxy plush pile in the rec room. Drilled him in the head with a .22 just for heaving a little Havana! And here, twenty years later, the dog's deadringer shows up at the truck ranch. Total reincarnation, like.

A hurricane blew up in her heart; she started seeping south of the border. Rings had always gone for the strong silent types, though none had gone for her. She picked a stool like casually once removed from his and tried to sit daintily without swinging her leg aboard like mounting a potbellied trucker; ordered herself a coffee, cream and sugar please, and picked up a copy of the *Laramie Roundup* lying on the counter just to show she knew another use for newspapers other than lining cat boxes.

The headline frizzed her hair; she nearly sprayed the paper with major coffee—MOSES AND THE BLUE RUSHES, CALL GIRL FINGERS FAT MAN. Gag me with the Sunday edition, she cried to herself reading on. She knew Sunny Deelight, a real dialtone. But she had the heart to call out the Pimp Blimp and here Rings was hiding beneath skies that weren't cloudy all day—letting down the Sisterhood of the Towel, girl. Shame grumbled in her tummy, building gas. She wouldn't be happy until she went back and did the right thing . . .

"Sumptin troublin you, lil darlin?" The voice down the counter filled her ear with honey.

"Like, radically," sobbed Rings, though truth be told, just the sound of his voice, like oil on rough water, stilled all thought of the trouble in San Francisco. She turned on her stool, wiping woedrops from her cheeks, swinging her fringetop Tony Lamas littlegirlwise.

But Mister Strong and Silent was staring straight ahead again as if they'd never spoken. She tracked the eyes the color of his profusion of turquoise jewelry and saw he was studying the plastic jetblender splashing grape drink. She cleared her throat. "The way it shoots up," Rings sighed, "reminds me totally of the fountain at Caesar's Palace."

The stranger looked at her with interest. "It reminds me," he said, "of an oil strike."

"Rad," she said absently, estimating how perfectly her clit would fit in the cleft of his chin should she sit on his face. "Like, you seen many oil strikes?"

He grinned. "Every time Saint Pete stands up and salutes."

"Huh?" Not another savior trying to haul her to the cross.

"Cmere, lil darlin," he invited with a turquoise wink. Rings scootched to the stool next to his. Gag me with a gear shift, he was pulling out his weenie! He wants me to buff ole Pete's pink helmet right here in the cafe. "No, no," he laughed gently, dashing her hopes. "You've heard of divining sticks for finding water, huh? Well, this here's my Divine Rod for finding fossil fuels. I prospect with him. Every time I walk over an underground reservoir of oil or natural gas . . . " He sprang his forefinger rigid.

Rings poohpoohed, "Next you'll tell me you got a bridge for sale." Though she did closely scrutinize the subject, which seemed to blush, making her drip now like a sponge.

He zipped up. "I advertise Saint Pete in *Christ Today*. See, he gushes for the Lord. Why, he's collectin royalties from a dozen wells already, and I only just discovered his powers last year."

"Powers I'd like to see," Rings said, which she fur shur would, as in a major gusher, only not right here in the Aces High Cafe where she was afraid her tummy gas might trigger it. "What's your name, anyway?"

"Randolph Scott, but not the actor."

"That's . . . distinctive."

"My mama thought so . . . " Randolph Scott, But Not the Actor reached out and covered her hand with his. "I got a load of aluminum siding in the lot. Once I drop it off in Council Bluffs I'm headed south to Louisiana where Pete's already contracted to prospect a field. Ought to yield enough black gold to retire to a life of plenty . . . " He looked away, with long fingers shyly milking his muzzle, and Rings saw in his turquoise eyes tall pumping shadows against southern skies. "And I need a woman to share it," he said with the tiniest little choke.

That like cinched it. Later she would blame it on a combination of his resemblance to Alonzo and the truck ranch's diesel fumes eating the last of her smart cells. But like all she could think in the raingray Wyoming cafe was, What could better grease love's skids than Louisiana sweet crude? It seemed like her first chance at a slice of an American pie that wasn't as stale and tasteless as those racked behind the counter of the Aces High Cafe.

A new sun rose in Rings's belly, and with it a fresh wind dispersing her gas, blowing it out one ear with all memory of love's past labors loused while sucking in the other Blanche DuBois deliriums of nightblooming jasmine and oil depletion allowances.

"Let's beat cheeks to dreamy dreamland," she cried, grabbing his hand, hustling him out to the lot raucous with idling diesels, singing pollywollydoodle all the way.

LIKE A TURKEY
THROUGH THE CORN

||||

Saturday night movies in the Gym were the social climax of the week. Everyone put on the Big Dog. The hucklebuckin hambones Afropicked and jerrycurled their cornrows and donned their baddest bone-roos; the vatos and street bravos wrapped their cleanest bandannas around Dippity-Doed razorcuts and spitshined their Santa Rosa hightops till they glowed like lamps; the whiteboys splashed on fifi water and groomed their mustaches with toothbrushes and wrapped bandannas around their upper thighs, ceremonial tourniquets. The Q Wing punks and B CAT queens greased on party paint and shimmied into tightass state blues, tying the shirts over babyoiled bellies, then draped themselves from the shoulders of their latest Mainline fantasies. Saturday night at the movies was where all the new couples made their debut; it was the time to see and be seen, for posin' to be chosen; a time to qualify to *signify*.

As they did in the Chowhall and other places where they gathered en masse, the convicts segregated themselves in the Gym. Racial mixing was acceptable in the course of informal activities such as job assignments and Yard recreation, but taboo for formal occasions such as the Stroll or Saturday night movies. Whites sat in the southern bleacher block; blacks in the upper half of the northern block, Latinos in the lower half. The handicapped off the Hospital Wing sat along the lower benches on both sides or parked their wheelchairs on the apron of the basketball court between the bleachers and the far wall where the screen hung.

Tonight Joe found a seat beside Carmen Memoranda and another old queen named Fraulein. Fraulein worked in Procurement with Carmen. She learned her arithmetic as an accountant tallying pussy in Nevada whorehouses. Between these two aging queens, thousands of taxpayer dollars were diverted each month to streetside accounts under fictitious names. Lola also tutored convicts studying for their GED's and helped others with tax problems. And there were those who had stranger uses for Lola's aptitude with figures.

"That F Stop has me tabulating production quotas for his freakin armadillo ranch," she complained to Joe. "It's got my mind filled to the horizons with them ugly little things fucking away for America's dogdom. Can you call the old man off?"

As she spoke, Joe spotted Earl taking a seat a dozen rows down. His ambiguous gaze snagged Joe's up the crowded slope of heads, blue flashing remonstrance, gray charged subtly with guilt. Joe shook his head tightly; he was still enraged with the old fool. Earl snapped his head away and sat by Bony Maroney.

"Earl and I arent speaking," he told Fraulein.

"Gracious!" Carmen exclaimed. "You sound like a couple of dueling dragqueens."

"You callin me a fruitcake?" Joe challenged in jest.

"I aint *callin* you anything," huffed Carmen. "But the last time we kissed I opened my eyes and you had yours shut."

Fraulein went on: "I asked F Stop once, 'Have you ever actually fed a dog armadillo meat?' And he says, 'No,' and I say, 'How do you know they even like the stuff?' And you know what the old fool does? Taps his bean and says he had a vision . . . "

"Armadillos, army dildos," Carmen closed the topic.

Joe wasn't alone in liking these old queens. Their hearts were big as churches, their belly laughs could fill circus tents. Their popularity hinged in part on their no longer being in the sexual arena. Younger queens could befriend them without fear of competition; straight cons could play the fool around them without fear of having their bluffs called. Joe enjoyed their bawdy repartee—in small doses.

"Joe," Fraulein tugged his sleeve and husked in a voice ripe with reefer, "Carmen's got a new hustle. The old sow's been overordering Lidocaine and Procaine, local anesthetics used in Dental. She's been selling them on the line for StaHard erection cream."

"Look!" cried Carmen, pointing an arm dripping suety flesh. "Here comes Will Clay with that tramp Agnes of Awful. Doesnt he know while he's out buffin his chest muscles on the Yard, she's on the wing buffin love muscles? . . . Oooh! There's Aunt Jemima this fine evening with her cumdrunk grin. Did you know that coon queen's takin it from Dr. Starkowitz, Chief of Psychiatric Sevices? Now would La Memoranda tell a lie? . . . " The Gym P.A. thumped Marvin Gaye's tribal aria to the perennial lasttoknows, "I Heard It through the Grapevine."

When Fraulein saw Billy Skaggs make his entrance with Angelfood riding his leg, Joe thought she'd faint. "My God, he's marrying Magdalena in the Catholic Chapel in a month. Must he make a spectacle of his infidelity?"

"Why marry Magdalena twice?" asked Joe.

"Oh, this time it's legal. Havent you heard? When she paroled, Magdalena had the sex change operation at Stanford Medical Center, she's tucked and rolled, a genuine woman. Goodness, did the Visiting Room guards hate having to let her use the ladiesroom. The Warden's bound by law to let them get married just like any other man and woman. They're fifth on the Catholic Chaplain's list . . . Although I cant for the life of me imagine why he'd want to tie the knot with that tramp."

Carmen said, "You're just jealous, you old cocksucker."

"Jealous?" Fraulein's hand fluttered to her bosom like a wingshot bird. "You think *I* lust to lie with the beasts of the field? Shame on you, Miss Thing."

"Where's Oblivia?" Joe asked casually. He'd missed her usual grand entrance on the arm of Coldwater's most recent heartthrob.

Carmen turned earnest. "She holds orientation for fish queens Saturday nights, when most of the guards are busy watching the movie and Darth Vader's offduty."

"What's the movie?" Joe asked to keep from thinking of McGee, wondering when he'd make his move for the Moon.

"Something called *Below the Belt,*" Carmen said.

"Here I was hoping to put my mind on hold," Joe said, "and they slip us an intellectual exercise."

"What fun!" Fraulein clapped her hands. "Will there be a quiz afterwards?"

Wearily Carmen honked, "In the showers, Myrtle."

The lights dimmed, the rock faded; the parachute draped flat against the far wall flickered to life . . . An electronic throbbing insistent as a lifesupport system accompanying bloodred credits flowing from beneath the chrome rear bumper of a '58 Impala streaking down an absolutely straight twolane blacktop. The camera halts when the credits are finished; the car speeds off, becoming a speck on the featureless horizon . . . *Cut* . . . A dark and crowded roadhouse, Brenda Lee pining "I'm Sorry" from the juke, laughter, the clink of ice in glasses. A loner with face like a closeup of lunar lava stands at the bar cooling his brow by rolling a cold tallboy of beer across it. A flash of sunlight, a stranger appears with something wrapped in oily rags; approaches the loner and says, "Here, Lucy said it yours. Bury it or pickle it or have it for lunch." He sets it on the bar and unravels the rags to reveal a shriveled blue fetus . . . The Coldwater Gymnasium erupted in riotous cheering, whistling, and bleacherstomping for kindred loser spirits immortalized on celluloid.

SCENE TWO: a raunchy motel room with broken venetian blinds and racketing airconditioning . . . A man lying on the chintz bedspread loosely aiming a large caliber revolver at a bosomy blonde starting to strip at the foot of the bed. She's wriggling up her tube top, one boob bobbles free . . . Wait a minute! It looks like someone just spread vaseline on the lens.

"Picture!" Several convicts cried at once; another screamed: "Projectionist motherfucker. Focus!" But the picture only worsened; now three blurry blondes are shaking six fuzzy leche bags. Everyone joined in the screaming for the projectionist. After all, this was the inmates' cultural issue being fucked with. Then the film froze; the lamp scorched a hole beginning with the tits and burning outward until the screen went white. Pandemonium erupted.

In from the Mainline rushed a gang of guards accompanied by a lieutenant Joe didnt recognize. He bounded down the bleacher steps, struck parade rest at the center of the Gym, facing upward over the writhing frieze of convict ire, and shouted: "Silence! Stop stomping the bleachers!"

The convicts turned their racket down halfway. The lieutenant ordered his men to knock on the projection booth door directly behind Joe. No answer. He ordered them to break it down. The guards took turns kicking until it splintered and crashed inward. They ran up the stairs.

A moment later one of them returned and with a red face motioned the lieutenant to follow him back up. The lieutenant descended the stairs and grimly snatched up the wall phone. A gravelly voice over the P.A. ordered the convicts to return to their units for Emergency Count.

It had to be one of the guards who spilled the beans. The word spread like prairie fire as the convicts filed out of the gym and down the Mainline.

"Goddam projectionist escaped!" "What?" "Busted a hole in the ceiling with a piece of angle iron and went out over the roof." "But the guntowers! . . . " "Take a look out the window. Fog's thicker than soup. All they do is sleep in them towers anyway." "That boy's gone like a turkey through the corn."

After Lights Joe uncapped a Maxwell House coffee jar of pruno, as prison hootch was called. He'd bought it from the Bakery, who had the lock on the prison's yeast supply. Flicking on his radio, he tipped back his head and drank. The first slug torched his throat, the second flamed his gut like a forge. It was the fourth and fifth that set the cell to gently rocking, and Joe fell back on his moonsplashed bunk, yodeling along with a Christian cowpoke over the airwaves about a couple of other dudes in big fixes

> *You delivered Daniel from the lion's den*
> *Sprung Jonah from the belly of the whale*
> *I'm askin Lord, askin once again*
> *When you gonna go my bail?*

SALLY GO
ROUND THE ROSES

||||

The only place Kitty remembered being unafraid as a child was Mama's kitchen in the little whitewashed house off the coastal road on Galveston Island. There the little girl liked sitting on the windowseat beside the big black wood table, amid the warm smells of corn tortillas and roasting carne asada and beans, always beans; watching Mama move with plain and placid surety within the rustling of her bulky black skirts, from cast iron stove to sink to flourdusted counter and back to the stove; wondering at her blunt mestiza fingers blurring like drumsticks beating out tortillas and sculpting tostada crusts and spinning out of modest sugar and flour and the occasional egg elaborate pan dulces commemorating obscure saints; listening to the sizzling oil and the faint metered susurration of the Gulf and Mama softly singing deep in her throat malaguenas, folk laments from her native Nuevo Leon. Next to praying, Mama was best at cooking; she lived somewhere along the nexus joining these two sustaining ceremonies of her existence, the one spiritual and other secular; without either Mama would surely wither and blow away like one of the dry translucent shrimp shells littering the nearby beach. So next to church, the child sensed her mother was closest to contentment in la cocina, what contentment this world offered to her for whom suffering was a birthright, an ancestral and ineluctable and sacred precondition of existence as essential to salvation as the death to deliver her thereto.

"Shitfire!" Kitty more than once exclaimed to her Aunt Juanita, who was a waitress at the Silver Peso where Mama cooked parttime, "When Mama kicks the bucket, ole Saint Pete's gonna shunt her into the express lane cuz she's got credit for time served in Purgatory ten times over right here on the Island."

Now she sat again in the windowseat behind the heavy black table watching Mama; again in the drowsy and fetuslike state within the whitewashed womb of familiar warm smells and sounds. Only now she sprawled, splayed legs supporting her hugely domed belly. And now the child's secret abstract smile was replaced by that of a woman fulfilled; the enigmatic primal halfsmile of the eternal matrix knowing yet once more the species is saved from extinction, granted one more reprieve of three score and ten years through the sole and exclusive agency of her uterus.

"Mama, this brings back memories."

Mama was grinding corn on the flat stone beside the stove. A gritty scrunching sound slowly softening until she stopped and threw another handful of kernels beneath the hardwood spindle.

"Many years, many tears. Eh, baby?" Despite her propriety and abject sanctity, Mama still spoke English like a bordertown B-girl.

"Not so many tears here in la cocina, Mama." Kitty shifted to peer out the window. Across the coast road she could see the shallow Gulf breakers advancing on the dirty beach in staggered ranks. Down the road blue neon tubing in the shape of a Mexican flaked out against a cactus with his sombrero pulled down over his face marked the place of Mama's employment since Papa had the stroke and was sent to the home on the mainland.

"You still think about him, baby?"

"Um-hmm."

"So young to die . . . such a good boy."

"Not *him*, Mama. Jesus! . . . " She was talking about that lunkhead she married to cover up for Papa.

"Not in this house you dont swear, baby. You know my heart cant bear it. The doctor told me I shouldnt even be working. But unless I give up all the social security check, the government wont pay the rest of Papa's ticket at the home. I ask the men in suits, I beg. I say I sick, too. No way, baby, they say. So dont swear in my house or I drop dead. Eh, baby?"

"No. I mean, yes. Oh, whatever floats your boat, Mama."

"What boat you talkin about, baby?"

Kitty sighed. "No swearin, mama. Only just dont act like Joe's someone I dreamed. He's alive. Right inside me now. It's him I think about. It's him I'm goin to."

Mama dropped her spindle, dusted her hands smartly, and stepped to a convenient statuette of the Virgin on a wall pedestal. She crossed herself and hissed fervently for a moment.

Kitty waited until she was finished and had started grinding again, then said softly, "Mama, he's a good man."

Mama ground harder and began moaning a lugubrious cancion.

"Mama!"

"Yes, baby," still singing, grinding her daughter's heart.

"I said he's a good man." God, how she wanted to say better than Papa ever even wanted to be, how she wanted to throw all his violent drinking and philandering and thieving right in her face, even the terrible secret. Or was it a secret? Mama had to know. She only believed herself absolved of the knowing by her furious pagan devotion, as though the shining of her piety could blind God to the abomination of her own house.

"What good man goes to jail? Eh, baby?" she asked finally.

The nerve. Really the fucking nerve. As though there wasn't a bunk in the downtown clink with Papa's name practically inscribed on it.

"He's good to me."

"Sure, he's good to you, baby. But . . . el niño?"

"It's his. He'll know it. I'm certain. Know it and claim it and cherish it and provide for it. All those good things."

Mama finished grinding and rinsed off her spindle. She hung it from a wall bracket and turned, drying her square hands on her apron to face Kitty with those drawn black eyes in which suffering shone like a virtue.

"Baby, you know men like that dont never do the right thing. Out of all the sin of your living I hoped you'd learned at least that. I know what you been doin. You've know many men and I betcha baby I lit a candle for every one. You know how they do, men. Eh, baby?"

"Mama, I believe in Joe. Okay? I believe . . . Didnt you ever believe in someone . . . "

"Sure, baby." Mama turned to find something else to do, another cooking chore to defend herself. "Sure."

Kitty knew then Mama was beyond belief in fallible flesh. There were a couple before Papa, and then maybe she thought she believed in him when he had to marry her or fight her brothers because she was carrying Kitty. She delivered prematurely, after Papa beat her in a drunken rage for having had to marry, the connubial curse by which fate fettered him; beat her so severely the doctors told her to try again was to die and she brought her baby home to a house already bereft of love and now, too, its charade proscribed. Took the baby with her to her own barren bed because Papa had smashed the cursed cradle for kindling to beat her. That night wouldn't be the last he didn't come home, not by a thousand. It was then

Mama swore her life to the Virgin, and Papa, his to a stewardship in the Devil's own wineshop. When Mama abjured earthly love, belief in flesh became apostasy and a renunciation of her jealous faith.

After a moment, Mama said, "Will you take it to the home, baby?"

"To him? Mama, dont ask me that," Kitty warned. His presence invaded the room just as surely as when he would burst in drunk and thrash Mama, way back when Kitty still was small enough to hide beneath the table.

"It would mean something to him." She was seated across the table from her daughter now, cutting crepe paper to weave flowers for the navidad.

"I'm tired, Mama. I'm going upstairs."

"I'm tired, too, baby."

"What you got in the oven?"

"Pan gloria."

"It smells about done. Dont let it burn."

Mama tied a red camelia without answering.

It was the same room, only smaller, the way all rooms are smaller when revisited by the children who once inhabited them. The same cerise cafe curtains on the dormer windows with the same desiccated insect husks between the screen and frame rattling minutely when the wind scudded off the Gulf. The same floralprint wallpaper, a little more curled and yellowed along the seams; the same corny print of a mare and foal, the same crucifix dangling the same gory Christ; the same pine floorboards, whose creaky warps she knew so intimately that she could play "Sally Go Round the Roses" with her bare toes. The same shutup smell of camphor balls and Catholic school missals and old varnish. Everything the same, only shrunken to a degree perhaps commensurate with the unexpectedly trivial significance that this, her former world, now held for Kitty.

Only one thing was unshrunken, unbrittled, unreduced by time: the vow she'd made on a winter evening much like this one, lying just as she was now with a life awake in her belly. Only then it was the monster that kicked and squirmed and soured her milk, the incarnation of the perverse impulse that spawned it; and she knew she was bringing it forth only to destroy it. She vowed to that same cramped dark ceiling that one day her body would bring forth life, not something only living; would create instead of a screaming image of hate and evil, a symbol of adoration and wonder, love itself. That was her vow, and it had lived these years, awaiting her in that room.

"Any day now," she hummed the words to the oldie. That's what the doctor said. Already it was two weeks late but the doctor said not to worry

and she hoped it might wait another ten days. The hospital had a sort of sweepstakes, which would pay the complete delivery expenses of the new year's first baby. That way she could save the last of Dan's ten grand she'd set aside for medical expenses, give her and Joe and the baby a little startup stake. She reached in her blouse and touched a leaking nipple and tranferred the bluewhite juice to her tongue. It tasted sweet and tart both, like new elderberry wine.

Perhaps the charge of sheer joy jumpstarted her womb. The first contraction sprung tears to her eyes; she forgot what the little booklets in doctor's office said and held her breath. The next loosed a cry, but she remembered to breathe deep and count. When it subsided she called out for Mama. No answer. She swung her feet off her childhood bed and that's when the third hit, only now she was ready for it. They were coming so fast she knew it was time.

"Mama!" she called out the door. Still no answer. Must have fallen asleep at the kitchen table. She could smell the pan gloria burning.

Kitty gained her feet and headed to the top of the stairs where she waited until the fourth came and departed; then, holding the steep bannister with both hands, she descended. She decided to call a cab, Mama's driving was too crazy in that old Plymouth.

Kitty stood gripping the frame, swaying in the kitchen door. Mama's head lay peacefully on her arms amid the profusion of bright paper. Kitty didn't have to stagger across to touch the utterly still shoulder, though she did. Neither did she have to look into her face to know her eyes would be upturned like those of the illumined Virgin on her bedside table. She knew it as plainly and implacably as she knew she was bringing forth life. *Shitfire, Mama, you're dead.*

She was dialing the wall phone, staring at Mama across the kitchen, when the next two hit one right after the other. Her strained voice said hold just a second; when the blood cleared her eyes and she had enough breath she said: "One to collect, one to deliver, boys. Toot sweet, as in pronto."

Hanging up, she noticed smoke rolling out of the oven and lunged clumsily for its knobs.

"You havent had any writeups? No fights or sexual misconducts?" were Maas's first questions in the Interview Room between gates.

Joe could answer that one confidently. "Nope."

The attorney was surprisingly young, with a keen glint in his eye. "It's the sexual hankypanky the board frowns on most," he explained. "Violence is winked at, within reason. It's considered a symptom of the system.

But their studies show that inmates who succumb to homosexuality are the worst parole risks. They view sexual deviance as a prime characteristic of the recidivist."

"Studies." Joe's repeated tonelessly.

"Right. Studies," chirped the young attorney. "Dull, unimaginative sorts like parole board members rely on studies. They risk nothing on personal judgment and initiative . . . But writeups arent our problem, are they?"

"I guess not."

Since Maas hadn't had time to review his Central File, Joe spent some minutes briefing him on his institutional and criminal records. As a rule Joe was honest only to doctors he saw for genuine ailments, not narcotics, and lawyers paid for by himself, not appointed by authorities. Offering silent thanks once more to Earl for relieving him of the obligation to explain Pious Wing's killing, he tried to be explicit and forthcoming concerning all the rest. Maas propped a fist beneath his chin and blinked attentively.

Joe felt queer. Reeling off his depredations like this made them seem as petty and insignificant as last year's World Series scores or canceled gambling debts. The longer he was in, Joe realized, the more his trangressions were of lasting importance only to him, not to the state which codified and catalogued them. Long after they were erased from computers and relegated to dead files, they would cast cold shadows in his heart.

When he was finished, Maas made several notes on the legal pad before casually asking, without looking up: "Any silent beefs on your jacket?"

Joe hesitated, nonplussed. "No," he said then testily. "If there were I'd be wasting my money shooting for a coffee break parole."

"Not necessarily," Maas said brightly, busying himself with fitting the legal pad back in his briefcase, adding airily: "There are motions I could file for suppression . . . " Then the attorney's classic closing query, always posed delicately, like a knife to the throat: "Now about my fee . . . "

This had been on Joe's mind since the day he was wiped out by Big and Little Casino. The axiom that it takes money to make money held true in the pen as well, and it was taking Joe a long time to rebuild his nestegg. Every night after Lights Joe wondered how Earl had hurt him more, by sacrificing Spencer's health or postponing his own parole. Yet in a secret way he was glad Earl had betrayed him; it relieved him of having to chose between Spencer's life and his own freedom.

"I'll tighten you up soon," he promised.

"If you cant," smiled the attorney, "I could postpone my fee until after your release . . . "

Joe laughed. "You mean until I got a job?"

"I mean until you could get your hands on the money or . . . something which might be exchanged for money."

"What the fuck are you talkin about?"

"I . . . I was under the impression you had something of value stashed on the streets, something to cash in . . . "

"Where the fuck you get *that* idea?" Joe sized him with a slitted sidelong.

"Never mind." Maas laughed a little forcedly, his mouth and eyes too wide. "I must've got you mixed up with another of my parole clients. I have so many."

JINGLE BELLS

||||

Christmas morning broke clear and cold as the bells of Coldwater heralding it. Joe rolled out of his bunk and brewed a cup of coffee with his contraband heating coil, the hottest selling item in the Maintenance Yard. He tuned his radio to the shitkicker station and, humming along to a chickenfried "White Christmas," pumped hot water into his sink. At least the Boiler Room was manned this holiest of feast days. Joe listened while he shaved to the voices from the other cells:

"Wha*choo* wan for Chrusmuss, buby buoy?" "Jes gimme a date, fate." "All that motherfucker wants is a punk in his bunk." "World! Jes leaves me what I got, three hots and a cot." "Yall shet up! Christmas done got canceled. They picked up Santa's merry ole ass las night on a B&E and booked his elves for Receiving."

Charity baskets were distributed to the convicts on Christmas Eve. Joe's sat on his writing shelf, crinkling the sunlight in his eyes. Nested in its green plastic grass were peppermints, sourballs, a few musty chocolates, a shriveled apple, and a sack of Bull Durham. A sticker on the cellophane read: GIFT OF THE CLOISTERED SISTERS OF THE PRECIOUS BLOOD PURGATORIAL SOCIETY. Sounded like a leather cult to Joe, one allied with that spurious order dispensing rubbers like alms that longago Strip night.

Holiday procedures were in effect for Christmas. Other than the Visiting Room clerks and porters, only inmates assigned to sections essential to plant maintenance were called to work. Of these, the most essential from the convicts' point of view were the Culinary workers. The Chowhall stayed open all day, the steam tables serving up a holiday fare of turkey, yams, mustard greens, and cornbread. The fresh pineapples meant for dessert, unfortunately, had been stolen for pruno. Joe went through the line three times until he had to waddle back to his cell to read and sleep away the afternoon.

With twilight slanting golden through his window bars he awoke and felt the penitentiary buzzing in anticipation of the Christmas Show. It was an annual event put on in the Gym by the Chowchilla Jaycees. Convict bands, guest musicians, variety acts . . . even dancing girls, they said.

All day long Joe had resisted the holiday spirit. He tuned out the relentless *falalas* and *jinglebells* yapping from the Mainline P.A., ignored the convicts trading excited news of their families, ducked the platitudes they flung like slapstick pies. But now he couldn't withstand his own sentimentality; recollections of yuletides past rose in him as irresistibly as bubbles in hard cider.

What the hell, get into it, he exhorted himself reaching into his locker for his boneroos. As he dressed, he looked around his cell, fondly inventory-ing the accumulations of . . . *How long had he been down?* For the first time in ages he calculated . . . almost ten months behind bars.

His writing desk and custom toilet cover, the balsawood airplane hang-ing by a wire from the center of the celestial map on his ceiling; the posters on the walls, one of a ketch on a close reach in tall seas, another Earl had given him of an armadillo; the gewgaws on his window ledge, the legal files beneath his bunk, his personal library recently expanded when the arsonist in the next cell paroled and willed Joe his mystery collection; his zuuzuus and whamwhams, his toiletries, the broom hiding his reefer in its straw. An ordinary prison cell with ordinary cell clutter, T-103 might appear drab and depressing to a freeworlder, but to Joe it was opulently appointed; each item was rich with significance.

He frowned and puffed his cheeks, however, taking in the multitude of pinups on the walls; the cunts and assholes aimed inward as though it were genitalia, not guns, which held him impotent. Quickly he danced around, snatching them all down, and when he was finished wondered how he'd ever surrounded himself with such blatant reminders of what he was bereft.

The bell announcing the show rang. Grinning into the scarified cell mirror, he fitted the cap low over his brow, snapped its bill with his finger, and hooked out of his cell for the Gym.

Moonpie and the Coldwater Cold Cuts were playing a diddybopping

Christmas medley as the convicts flowed through the doors and down the bleachers. The band was set up on the basketball court in front of a stage erected just that day and trimmed with bunting, balloons, and tinsel. There was much activity behind the stage, indicating the outside acts had already arrived. Once or twice a female head poked around a curtain's edge, eliciting a storm of cheers. Along the stage's base, Gooners faced up the bleachers like centurions from Saturn. Joe saw they were armed with tasers tonight, Thomas A. Swift Electric Rifles. Joe had heard McGee had acquired these highpowered stun guns; he supposed he'd issued them to his squad as Christmas gifts.

Joe had never seen so many convict eyes brimming with sheer delight. For one night they were to be catered to by free people. It was an honor few received on the streets. They laughed and shouted and called holiday greetings to men they hadn't spoken to in months. The lights dimmed and instantly came back up, warning of the show's commencement, and the convicts came to order as quickly as any ladies' church group. Joe found a seat halfway down between two men he didn't know; he felt like observing anonymously tonight.

The lights went down and Moonpie grunted *undah one undah two* and the Cold Cuts turned the refrain of "The Twelve Days of Christmas" into a boogiewoogie fanfare and the spotlight followed an Emcee strolling out with Warden Gasse in tow.

The Emcee was a slimy, bald exile from the Borscht Belt. He was draped in a shiny blue tux he could have stolen from a singing Albanian waiter. He opened with a couple of bad lounge jokes about Santa's sex life at which the convicts howled, then he introduced Gasse. So thrilled were the convicts to be getting a show that they applauded the Warden.

"Gentlemen," Gasse held up his hands and cried, "I want you all to enjoy this offering of the Jaycees. It's been a wonderful year and I want to say I am proud to be associated with such a wonderful group of men. Merry Christmas! And Happy New Year!"

The Emcee regained center stage, applauding Gasse as he backstepped behind the curtain. Then he turned back to the bleachers and lowered his voice confidentially. It rasped through the mike like tearing underdrawers. "Just wanted to check one thing with you gents . . . I'm sure you all know what they call a bull who doesnt let his meat loaf, dontcha? Huh? You *dont?* Beef strokin off! Get it? Beef Strogin-*off* . . . " To make sure he pumped a fist into his crotch. There were scattered calls from the restless dark of "Stroke this, punk" but most of the convicts laughed politely. "Gents," he continued, "we got a show so hot tonight the fire department said we had to coat this stage with asbestos, but please . . . no strogonoff!

Ha ha ha . . . " He laughed like a rabid monkey. "Let the show begin!"
The bleachers thundered with feet.

The first act was an old showbiz couple on roller skates who looked with
their glassy eyes and Halloween grins like moonlighting kidnappers.
Around the stage they twirled to the strains of "Greensleeves," doing dips
and pirouettes and for a finale a propeller spin, in which the skeletal male
skater swung his aged kewpie doll over his head, spinning faster and faster
until she was a sequined blur grinning like a sick cat at both ends. The
convicts endured the geriatric rollerskaters silently.

"Awrite! Awrite!" screeched the Emcee. "That's what all the lil girls are
doing these days on the public beach boardwalks. So you best get yourself
a pair or you'll never catch em! . . . And now, some of your female
counterparts from down Frontera way . . . "

His last words of introduction for the Fallen Angels, the California
Institute of Women at Frontera's choir, were drowned in stomping and
cheers as the female prisoners marched out swinging saucy bottoms
and shooting sultry looks into the dark. A matron bowed to the bleachers
and turned to lead them with a little baton. To the spirited if ragged
accompaniment of the Cold Cuts, they ripped right into "Jingle Bells,"
really laying it on for the chorus, "Laughing all the way . . . *Yah! Ha! Ha!"*

Hearing forty bustout whores laughing all at once gave Joe goosebumps;
the Gymnasium went wild. With the matron leading them off, two of the
girls in blue flipped up their skirts and flashed twin moons grinding a slow
tandem orbit and bumping at once. The cons loved it. One of the asses
had eyeballs tattooed on either cheek like a dirty old man in the moon.
Joe thought the roof was going to blow.

From there the show went downhill: a magician whose idea of a good
trick was sawing his rabbit in half and a female vocalist mooing "You Light
Up My Life" while the cons screamed specific anatomical parts worthier
of ignition. Then the Emcee duckwalked out and snatched the mike,
yoyoed it on its cord, did a sudden corny dip and growled: "Awrite,
gentlemen and you not so gentle men, I want you to check see if your seat
belts are fastened because here she comes packin those fortyfour magnums
which she aims to *please* . . . Live and *di*rect from the fabulous Blue Note
Lounge, pound for pound the most effishunt sex machine in the animal
kingdom"—he shot a smarmy aside behind his hand—"Gents, they say
everybody needs milk. But does she have more than her share? . . . You
be the judges!"—the Colds Cuts' drummer started a big rolling beat *Bomp
ba-ba-ba Bomp,* and the opening bars of "Fascination" were Bronx
cheered through a saxophone—"Here she is, the shape that lunched a
thousand faces, the sex-otic sex-sashun, *Brrrrrr-*muda *Schwartze!"*

And damn if ole Bermuda didn't leap through the curtains shaking like a catfish on a pole. She wore a floppy Santa cap on her head, and on her feet velvet fuckme booties with turnedup elfin toes. Every square inch in between was covered with party balloons. She looked like a lifesize model of a Crisco molecule.

Bermuda curled her fingers around the mike, bringing it to her mouth as if she meant to eat it. The Cold Cuts struck up "Santa Claus is Coming to Town," and she purred: "He's knows when you've been naughty, he knows when you've been nice . . . " while the convicts whistled and stomped and screamed. At the song's conclusion, she motioned the band for silence and bubbled: "I get the feelin you fellas dint come to hear me sing. Maybe you wanna see what's under all this hot air . . . " She tweaked and burst a balloon baring some belly and the Gym went wild.

"Well, I've got a little Santa's helper who's gonna help you do just that . . . Oh Dwah-*neee* . . . " And here came Dwan Wand skipping through the curtains in pink dropbottom pajamas. He was smoking a long black cigaret. Now the Cold Cuts segued into "I Saw Mommy Kissing Santa Claus," while Dwan shrieked and cavorted along the edge of the stage and Bermuda started singing squeakily: "I saw Mommy"—BOMP BA-BOMP, Bermuda rolled and swung her hips and shot them north and south, showing what talent Mommy reserved for the merry old elf— "Santa Claus underneath the mistletoe . . . " Dwan skipped around her popping the balloons with the cigaret.

Then she segued into "Santa Baby, Hurry Down My Chimney To-night," and Joe thought the Gym was going to implode with the collective intake of breath as one after another the balloons burst revealing her biomorphic blimpoids. The atmosphere must have been compatible with the silicone; Joe had never seen them more perfectly lifelike. When at last they were totally revealed, she stood stock still for one of those suspended intervals that could have been a millisecond or millennium, who could tell under the spell of those vast and shimmering meringue globes radioing lust into the dark.

Then Dwan, in a paroxysm of jealousy, skipped in and jabbed one siliconic spheroid with the cigaret as though he mistook it for a last very large pink balloon.

"That's my *bwest*, you *bwat!*" Bermuda screeched; and the spell was broken. The convicts howled and hooted, thundering their feet on the bleachers. One Viking whiteboy leaped up and yanked down his pants and wagged his penis at the stage. "This bud's for you, baby!" he cried. Bermuda leaned forward, shading her eyes against the lights. When she spotted the offensive turkey neck shaking just for her, she clutched her throat and gagged.

By now the Gooners were advancing menacingly and the lights went up.

The P.A. announced the show's conclusion and instructed the convicts to return to their housing in an orderly fashion. Joe stood with the rest and started shuffling out.

It was then that Bermuda's squall pierced the tumult: "Joe! It's a boy!"

He spun, but she was being hustled back through the curtains by one of the matrons detailed to escort the Fallen Angels. He shook his head dazedly and turned back into the press of bodies thronging out onto the Mainline.

Earl was standing by Custody. Joe felt the gray eye soldered to him as he passed and heard the softly lilting voice, "Merry Christmas, amigo. And congratulations, yeah."

After Lights, Joe stood at his cell window, thinking. He knew what Bermuda was talking about: a child born to Kitty, a boy she said was his. She must have called the Blue Note from Texas. He couldn't understand why Kitty was being so persistent unless the child truly was his. He thought back: yes, the arithmetic was right, it was some weeks over nine months since they'd been together. He could think of no motive she could have for lying. She didn't know about the diamond, not that it looked like it could do either of them a lick of good anyway. Why continue linking her fate with Joe's unless it actually was, through commingled blood.

Below him, in the pocket yard between the cellblocks, two convicts sat together in the winnowing silver moonlight. One was passing the other candy from his charity basket. The other handed back his sack of Bull Durham. How could they be out there after Lockup? A match was struck. Joe was blinded for an instant by its flare. Then all he could see was a tongue of fire within a gauze aura, a flaming blue tear. Suddenly it was extinguished, and he was blinded a second time. When his night vision returned once more, the pocket yard was empty, and Joe wondered if the convicts hadn't been wraiths and the flame a mirage, like those attributed by the bushmen to the Devilstone.

Joe rolled himself up in dreams of Kitty, her wildsmelling hair like nightmist, her taste like wild fruit and sea spray.

JACKS

||||

With the new year came the rains that lasted into March. By day the slow incessant downpour crowded the Mainline with graywoven shadows; by night it haunted convict dreams with its stonethroated whispering down the walls.

"It's like a broken record," they complained over their grits in the charcoal predawn. "Over and over and over till you're half out of yer head."

Yet Joe found just the way to animate this funerary and featureless rotation of days and nights. For months the rutted pocket yard between W and Z Blocks had preyed on his mind. Its muddy moonscape was useless to men on crutches and suicidal to those in wheelchairs. Then it came to him one day that it might be paved. It seemed the perfect project for the Work Order clerk, who controlled the prison's building trades. Moreover, Joe had become an accomplished convict chamberlain by now, adept at negotiating official channels. He drafted a proposal and within a week had the Warden's signature. He plunged straightaway into organizing the materials and coordinating the work. Not only did the project accelerate his ayems and peeyems—it helped Joe forget what he thought to be true, that the Fat Man was only awaiting his moment to sic McGee on him.

At Work Call every morning, Joe stopped by W Wing to report to the assembly of blind, maimed, crippled, and diseased.

"The work wagons should be rolling soon as the rain lets up," he cried one drizzly dawn, striding into the wing proper and raising his voice to be heard by the AIDS victims crowding the screened upper ranges. "Your yard will be paved by spring," only hoping half of them would still be alive. He received the W Wing version of the standing ovation: croaking cheers, wacky clapping, waving crutches. The plaguers shook the screens, a thunderous gnashing like the beating of great steel wings.

Near the front of the ragtag crowd stood Roy between the handles of Spencer's wheelchair. Spencer looked worse every day. Only patches of lint remained on his scabbed skull; his body was a bog of suppurating sores. With his shriveled skin and shrunken flippers, he resembled something accidentally vomited up from the ocean floor.

He stared at Joe with unnerving intensity. Since Joe had last seen him, Spencer had added a pencil, affixed to his brow with a sweatband, to his prosthetic devices; and he aimed it between Joe's eyes, reminding him of Tarzon's accusatory cheroot.

"Are you going to do it?" he asked. "The jack's our last chance."

Joe flung back his head, staring up to the high shadowed ceiling. He puffed his cheeks and released his breath with a pop.

"We're both walkin off all day," Roy rumbled deep in his chest crypt. "And now that Spencer's comin down with the symptoms . . . "

Joe flung an arm up at the carrier ranges, eyes sprung wide in horror. "You mean . . . Spencer? . . . "

The brow pencil flipped up and down. "Any day they'll lock me in the byebye bird cages. And those boys'll kill me fast . . . "

"What are you talkin about?"

"They have no immune systems to protect them against the other diseases I carry," Spencer said. "I dont blame them."

"Christ!"

A smile froze Spencer's face, the rictus grin of a gambler rolling dice on which his life is bet. With his twisted coathanger he touched Roy's arm. The pair swung away and was swallowed into the cathedraltall gray shadows.

Southward under countrymusic stars sped Rings'n'Things on her harebrained hegira, snugly installed in the overcab sleeper of Randolph Scott, But Not the Actor's tractor trailer, whose bonnet moniker should have read Peterbought, not Peterbilt. They'd dumped the aluminum siding in Council Bluffs and were deadheading down to Dixie where Rings had no old times to be forgotten, lookaway. Never had she known a happiness quite the equal of balling the jack down the highway. She felt everywhere and nowhere at once, free from her future and curtained from her past.

But when in her life hadn't there been a hitch, and how many times this same one? Like, she wasn't getting boinked. Randy explained that he had to save Saint Pete's strength for his prospecting chores. As soon as these were complete, he promised, the Divine Rod would revert to its normal usage, the sacred act of pokeration.

"But it's just a piece of gristle," Rings would beg, "you cant wear it out."

At such profanity Randolph Scott, But Not the Actor cemented his jaw and steeled his eyes. He caught her once trying to trick him by whispering subliminal smut in his sleeping ear. Thereafter he fastened a rubberband around it at night, after the fashion of boxers, to awaken him should it thicken.

It was fur shur beginning to seem to Rings that the only time men wanted her was when they had to pay for it. But she steadfastly refused to accept that because it meant acceding to its corollary, that she would never get to do it for love. Instead she pushed the whole matter from her mind, settling for solos in the sleeper. Cranking up Guns N' Roses on her Walkman, she'd nibble her clit with the earphones, tingling it until she cried out with such selfmockery and abandon that Randy would reach over his shoulder to shake her from her nightmare. To distract him while she caught her breath she'd ask once more how oil came to be, and patiently he'd explain. Listening to his voice like mint juleps laced with Spanish fly, Rings aimed whiteline tracers out the rig's rearwindow and imagined that the dark, humped hills skiproped with telephone wire were the graves of dinosaurs who'd followed this same southern route a zillion years ago to croak mysteriously and get mushed into the subterraneous goo of lamister whore dreams.

Dreams that were about to take shape, taste, and voice because here she was at last swinging on a Louisiana porch shaded by magnolias blossoming on honeysuckle vines. And there, along the lavender horizon flocked with pink, a lonesome figure strolled strumming a Gibson guitar. Rings knew just what Randolph Scott, But Not the Actor was singing, too, "Do Not Forsake Me, O My Darling"—just the tune fur shur to stir the Mesozoic juices.

"You care for a rootbeer, Mizz Scott?" asked the sugar planter's wife.

Rings tilted up eyes brimming with gratitude at the presumption of matrimony. But when she nodded to the woman, her frosted flip wig fell halfway down her brow and Rings had to like grab it, suddenly pretending to swat a fly and push it back up. The wig was part of her new beauty school dropout disguise. It went with the 7-Eleven cherry shades, stems and all, and an armored Maidenform bra exactly like the one Sandra Dee used to speargun Troy Donahue's last faint aspirations to heterosexuality. It made Rings's tits look like the original molds for the '57 Cadillac's bumper bullets.

"A rootbeer sounds pretty good, but a real beer would fur shur be better," chimed Rings, forgetting that she was the guest of evangelic Christians. Hostility flickered between the woman's eyes like the lightning suddenly forking the horizon, and Rings first noticed thunderheads muscling up behind the cypress stand.

"Fetch up a case of the real stuff from the storm cellar," said the man in the shadows at the porch's other end. "Looks like we're gonna need the extra room down there."

As he spoke, thunder rumbled like distant artillery, and low black clouds floated up like cannon smoke, swallowing the strolling silhouette on the horizon; and before Rings had time to worry about it happening, it did, a mighty triton of lightning quivered in the ground where last he stood. Randolph Scott, But Not the Actor's Divine Rod had become a lightning rod before even once poking Rings.

They collected what looked like a crisp strip of bacon from the cane-brake and put it in a box and waked him on the porch where Rings had watched him zapped. The rolleyed preacher hallelujahed Randy a good headstart on the Glory Road, though Rings could see in the mourners' eyes that they believed it was the Devil's work he was about, and the Devil's due he collected.

In closing they all sang "Nearer My God to Thee," and Rings joined meekly in, though she couldn't have felt further from whatever God might be and knew she'd never be any closer until she returned to the Bay City to testify against Baby Jewels. It was the only right thing, the only honest thing, and there was no woman so honest as an honest whore. At the hymn's conclusion, the congregation sang *Amen* and crossed themselves, and Rings did likewise, crossing her broken heart, promising to go back just as soon as she found a way to blot out what happened to Glori girl, what nearly happened to herself. Just a little longer, she prayed—long enough for Humpty Dumpty to fall without her.

Randy died intestate as well as intesticled, and no one knew what to do with the Peterbilt until a man claiming to be his cousin showed up, a spry little guy with wirerimmed spectacles who'd read of the freak accident all the way in Little Rock. Rings was like, Hey, the rig's worth twenty large, this geek better have some proof. "What's your name, buster?"

"Harry Truman," he chirped, "no relation to the president."

"His cousin fur shur," Rings promised the parish justice, who released the Peterbilt. She agreed on the courthouse steps to have a beer with Harry Truman, No Relation to the President. They crossed the road to a crawfish stand and bought two Dixies, which they took out back to a long wooden table littered with bleached crab shells. There as the evening drew on they drank beneath drapes of moss like moldering lace, while fireflies sparked in the cattails and blue herons haiku'd through the swollen purple monotone of frogs and insects.

"I'm a chemical toilet contractor by trade," Harry Truman, No Relation explained. "But by vocation an inventor. Right now I'm designing a zerogravity toilet. *Fascinating* ergonomics. I hope to have its plans perfected in time for the Mid-South Plumbing Convention in a couple of months. They hold it in Houston, home of the Space Center. My ambition is to sell the zerogravity toilet to NASA and be set for life."

Rings looped a lazy brow. "No shit?"

"Why dont you come along? You dont want to be stranded in this swamp. Plus I bet you could show me all the ins and outs of . . ." He paused a beat, poking her with hard eyes, "trucking."

"Quit lookin at me like I'm lunch," she squalled. After all, a girl's gotta put up some resistance.

Joe first missed its mutter on the roof of the Chief of Plant's office and was whiplashed with a chill. He sprang to an eastern window and exclaimed out loud. It had been weeks since the spiny peaks of the Sierras were visible. Trailing tatters of mist, they resembled the overwrought mountains of Chinese watercolors. He heard insects harping, and faintly from the orchards, a dove speaking of sorrow amid the tremolos of meadowlarks.

The rains were over, it was time to roll the dice.

The Maintenance Yard whistle shrieked. Joe snatched the memo typed days ago off his desk and joined the rest of the outside workers thronging into the prison through the Rear Sally Port. With the lifting of the weather, spirits rose; Mainline twostepping resumed and brash dozens rang down the walls. Joe felt alone on the raucous blue flood and judged it was the warrant in his hand to live or die that set him apart.

Custody was bedlam as usual, a hive like a big city squadroom. Loud voices lobbed over the ringing of phones, the crashing of drawers, and everywhere the clacking of typewriters. Joe went straight to Ramsey's desk, dropping the memo in his box. "Baa Baa, expedite this to Tower One. It authorizes the backhoe to enter the Truck Sally Port, circle the access road and enter through the gate in the pocket yard separating W and Z Blocks.

They need it to level the new Hospital yard. Soon as the fuckin ground's hard enough not to swallow the thing, that is . . . "

"Good as done," Baa Baa said. "It's a fine thing you're doin for those dudes . . . "

A dim light flickered in the shadow of the cap. "We'll see."

Baa Baa shrugged. "It'll look good on yer parole jacket."

Joe laughed a single note. Coffee break paroles were bought, not earned. He'd managed to scrape together a couple of hundred to send Maas the week before. The bloodsucker still needed more than a grand. He was going to have to land a windfall hustle fast.

Suddenly he was jostled from behind, knocked half over Ramsey's desk by a gang of guards. Between them they carried a black convict by his chained arms and legs. They tossed him on a bench outside S&I's frosted-glass door, where he lay rocking from side to side, moaning wretchedly.

"Christ! Why not take him straight to X Wing?" Joe asked Ramsey. "Why the pit stop in Custody?"

"He's slated for the front gate, not the Hole. His parole date's today and he wont cooperate."

"He wont . . . leave this place?" Loathing curdled Joe's stomach.

Ramsey shook his head. "There ought to be a way they could just reup, like in the service."

Joe's throat swelled, blood kettledrummed in his ears. Flipping the cap backward, he bounded to the bench and hoisted up the black convict by his shirt front. Shaking the sickeyed face inches from his own, he choked on the closed wing stink.

"What are you?" he shouted. "Some kind of animal that's scared to leave an unlocked cage?" He banged the wooly head on the back of the bench, spraying drool. "There's dudes fuckin dyin to get out of here . . ."

A sudden billyclub beneath Joe's chin snapped back his head and lifted him to his toes. His hands went numb, dropping the black convict. Then he heard that rabid slur he knew from nightmares: "Dont choke him out . . ."

The club whipped away, dropping Joe to his knees. Everything was misted with blood.

"Are you one of those dudes dyin to get out of Coldwater?" the slurp fingerfucked his ear.

Trying to speak, Joe spit up blood. He gained one foot, then the other, and stood shakily, staring into McGee's gloat. Just as the shotgun was slung over his shoulder when he last spoke to Whisper on the fence, now a taser nestled his meaty neck. Joe had seen these weapons used already. He'd watched them sink twin copper electrodes into men, girdling them with lightning, melting them into puddles of feces and semen. He swayed, grabbing a desk corner for support.

"What are you waiting for?" he croaked, thinking, *It's the cap, it must be the cap, fucker knows I've got the rock.*

"What's the hurry, Speaker? None of us is going any place. Except Robinson here . . . " He prodded the black with the taser. "But he'll be back soon. See, he's scared to death of the streets. Someone else's death, that is. He'll kill and kill fast to get home for good . . . "

"Fuck you," it spurted like pus from a wound, and Joe swung, tottering from Custody on unsprung legs.

GASOLINE SHORTS

||||

Belly Blast left the ring trailing hoots and jeers like tin cans tied to a dog's tail. Yeta the Abominable Snowgirl had just whipped her mercilessly in the main event. Hey, this whirleytwat hadn't even been in the national computer ratings until last week and she beat Belly like a rug on a line.

First she used Belly's own championship belt to snake a cobra choke around her neck, then lifted her with her hightop red boots kicking, spun her in a highspeed helicopter and flung her, twirling up into the fourth row of seats. Nothing like *that* in the script. Belly was ready to walk out of the Martin Luther King Auditorium right then and there if the fans hadn't handed her bodily over their heads and boosted her back into the ring.

With a banshee scream, the Snowgirl then seized a handful of Belly's sequined crotch and another of her bangs to loft her high, turning, holding Belly up there for the screaming geeks, before flinging her down on her uplifted knee, snapping her back like trying to break a dead branch. The ole wheel of torture, that *was* in the script, only as Belly's last move, the one to lay the Snowgirl out for the count. Either the Abominable Snowgirl was making up her own moves as she went along or the promoter, Aldo Tortoricci—"The Torturer," in his ring days—had switched scripts to retire Belly on a stretcher. Ugly biz either way, though in a daze Belly chose the latter scenario as truth: the Torturer was promoting his latest bimbo basher. He'd promised Belly a comeback and used her for a fall bitch.

With Belly blocking heavy traffic on Queer Street and the fans screaming bloody murder, the Torturer's new protégée climbed the turnbuckles to balance herself on the topmost, tearing her frosted hair and screeching the Himalayan Hootnanny before executing a flying somersault slam, crushing Belly to the mat, nearly spewing her guts out her mouth.

Some comeback, *chica*.

But the crowning indignity, the stuff of every prowrestler's nightmares and direct evidence Aldo was eightysixing Belly, the Abominable Snowgirl saved for last. Arising after the ref counted Belly out, the Snowgirl brandished a fist with a meaningfully protuberant knuckle. *"Noogie time, noogie time,"* the morons chanted. The Abominable Snowgirl snatched Belly's arm and *triple*noogied it! Now one of the bank tellers or bus drivers out for a night of wholesome fun had an even better idea. "Indian rope burn!" a delirious voice cried out. The crowd, quick to fan the spark of genius, ignited a raging fire. "Rope burn! Rope burn! *Burn* the spic bitch!" Belly was climbing up the ropes, shaking stars out her ears, when the Abominable Snowgirl twisted a hellacious Indian rope burn on her noogiedout upper arm.

Now any wrestler who suffers the insult added to her ring injuries of a single noogie should take a serious look at her career. That kind of humiliating kids stuff just wasn't professional. Then compound that indignity with an Indian rope burn . . . well, you shouldn't need a crystal ball to gaze into or a wrecking ball whuppin' you upside the head to know you were washed up in wrestling circles.

Back down the damp cement walkway trudged Belly Blast, past the faded boxing posters from when the auditorium was still called the Redwood and hosted the sweet science; beneath hissing pipes and swirling steam from many leaks that smelled like wet dirty socks and piss she dragged her cape become her shroud of shame. Chica, now you gotta make fuckie suckie loops for Baby Jewels, was the only thought her mind could link up. Gotta feed the monkey before he eats your bahakas up raw. Then a sudden thought sprang fresh sweat to her brow: *Maybe Gordo paid Aldo to set this up.* The heat was up, his porn players were bolting, he was using every trick to wrangle back his stock.

In the boiler room where her street clothes hung from rustfrozen spigots and gauges, Belly flung aside the cape with a curse. Cold crosses like this, she scolded herself, are the price a dopefiend pays. The Torturer's betrayal was particularly bitter because Belly had spent her best years making him all kinds of money. The mementos of her career plastered on the boiler room wall proved it. The colorful costumes and masks, the profusion of belts and other ring regalia, the posters of her leaping from turnbuckles, spreadeagle in midair, delivering bodyslams to prostrate opponents. There she was flogging the Iron Maiden with her championship belt, here actually chewing *off* Inga, She-Wolf of the SS's ear—and wait, by the door, in case any might snigger she was chicken to take on real men: Belly Blast chasing the Sheik of Pain through the stands with a chainsaw—it's running, you can see the smoke!

Smoke, she chuckled ruefully. That's all Aldo was blowing up your culo with that comeback talk. Gordo couldn't trap you with the kilo, so he used another trick to pin you. She had to go to him now.

She propped her foot on a stool and was unlacing its high red rasslin' boot when her fingers froze in midflight. Her nose twitched, sifting from the mildewed damp the acrid fume that twisted still through her every childhood memory. Her eyes clicked wide. She snapped her head over her shoulder and snarled, "What the fuck *you* doin here, Pop?"

He sat in the corner, on an upturned bucket, smoking his black cheroot. "You dont know how long, how hard I've looked for you."

"But I know how fast and easy you could lose me."

He spoke with his chin ducked, his voice tightly leashed. "All these years you've known the truth but I let the lie stand, I . . . "

She set down her boot and turned on him, arms akimbo, head tilted. "Which lie you talkin about?" she asked in a way that suggested there were many.

"About your mother. How Rosa died."

She laughed, jiggling unraveled sequins in the oily halflight. "I wasnt the only one who knew, Pop. Everyone knew. The cops . . . "

A strangulated laugh escaped him. "The cops?"

"Your *brothers*, Pop. The boys at the Coronado station. They knew."

"How?" Dubiety twanged his voice.

"I told them, Pop. Not that they would do anything. Half of em were gettin greased by border wiseguys, the other half shaking B-girls down for blowjobs, and they were scared you'd pull their covers, so they entered whatever you told them on their reports to protect their own action. But they knew. Next I went to her brother, Uncle Freddy. But he was too scared of you, too . . . "

Now apprehension stretched his words. "What did you . . . tell?"

"I told em Mom was a little light in her huaraches and was seeing a talk doctor, and maybe sex got a little offkey, so you went and got some strange and took her to our Chris Craft at the marina . . . "

"But you were only nine! How did you figure all that?"

"Pop, I was out of school sick that day. I saw her come home, get the gun, and leave again. She kept jabberin bout yer fuckin love boat. So I knew she dint surprise burglars at the marina the way the reports said. She caught you playin hopscotch on someone else's block and was going to maybe shoot you both, cept you got the drop on her."

He said, "It was an accident."

She slumped her shoulders. High overhead the rain prayed on the roof. "Who cares?"

"Maybe just me. Seems I was the only one fooled by my own lie. I thought everyone believed it . . . "

"It doesnt matter anymore, Pop."

It did, he said. He had to hear the truth himself from his own mouth; and he took a breath too long deferred and told how Rosa caught them napping in the fo'c'sle. She must have been drinking because she stumbled down the gangway, awakening him, and he vaulted naked from the bunk and grappled with her; but she was strong, a glandular madness whipped her limbs like sprung tension cable, he still could feel the sugary pain in his wrists. He didn't know who pulled the trigger.

"You did," she intoned, "but it dont matter."

"It does!" He beat a fist on his knee, then drew another breath. "All right. Yes. It was . . . my finger." He almost had the gun wrestled from her when she yanked suddenly into herself, a fierce hug, and it fired, a shuddering explosion rocking the cabin, and she shrieked wildly, a laugh almost, then doubled over like slapping her knees, collapsing.

"Dead," he said, staring at the floor as if seeing again her sideways leer. "You're right. She was going to kill us both. I was defending us. I'm . . . sorry."

"Pop, lissen to me. If I could forgive you, maybe I would. If I could overlook you bopping some bimbo on the boat you named after my mother, I'd try. If I could justify you killin her to defend your infidelity, I'd be willing. But it aint in me."

"Just hate," he guessed.

"Not even that. Hate needs love to burn and I'm just cold. Through and through."

The bucket overturned with a clatter and out he stepped from the shadows. "If there was just something I could say . . . "

"Maybe one thing, Pop. One thing I always wondered. Was it any different?"

"Different?"

"Doin Mom. Did it feel any different from the rest?" His gaze fell before the accusation in her eyes. "Nuhunh. I dint think so. It was just like the legal ones, like flushing a toilet. Just because you had to doctor the facts dint make a difference. You done that before. Written false reports, put throwaway guns in dead hands. You aint protectin the public from homicide, Pop. You are homicide. That's the big lie of yer life . . . "

"I want to take you home . . . "

"This is home." She swept an arm around the dim damp boiler room. "You're gettin old and your guilt's catching up. That's good, Pop. Maybe if you suffer some you can save yer ass. Just dont come round me with that confession shit. I'm your daughter, not a priest. So do me a big favor and fuck right off with that."

"At least you arent workin for the Fat Man."

She stared at him. "You watch the match?"

"No. I wouldnt watch one of those any sooner than I'd watch one of your . . . movies."

"You oughta, Pop. Like part of yer penance. Watch what you done . . . Now get the fuck outta here. I'm tired of lookin at myself all twisted in yer eyes . . . "

She turned her back, planting her boot on the stool again. "Belinda." Never had she heard such longing in her name, and she whirled on him, shaking with a fury at the one thing in her life that was better never than late, his love. "Maybe you want it in writing . . . F-U-C-K O-F-F!"

He winced. "Please think about it . . . Here's my number if you want to talk, make this right."

Helplessly he looked around for a place to lay his police card. She grunted and held out a hand, a hand purple and swollen and pustulant like one he'd seen first in a barrel and last on a morgue shelf. She said, "Dont put on any coffee. Now take yer stinkin pacifier n get out . . . mother-fucker."

Tarzon left the auditorium by a fire exit. Outside a sagging night sky showered silverdollar wishes in puddles swirled with gasoline. He turned up his collar, shrugging deeper into his raincoat, and hooked up the block. He didn't notice the Sting Ray across the rainseething street, nor remark its windshield wipers swipe once, clearing a view for dead eyes briefly lit by the lightning flickering along the rows of dead windows.

After Lights, Joe stood smoking at his window bars. The moon skulked low over the opposite cellblock, scarved in clouds. Convicts called softly back and forth between the cellblocks; the plinking of radios rose and fell on the black wind chanting through the fences.

They'd brought in the backhoe that morning. Joe saw it from the Mainline window, hunkered in the pocket yard mud. They got the jack during afternoon exercise, he guessed. With Spencer directing, Roy had no trouble finding it in the tool compartment beneath the operator's saddle. Easy to bring back inside, say under a blanket on Spencer's lap.

Then what? The jack's only conceivable purpose was to spread window bars. But they'd never fit the wheelchair through. Spencer would have to direct Roy carrying him across the treacherous yard. And what about the double row of fencing? The searchlights pinning them in a crossfire between the towers? The image of their immolation snatched Joe's heart with frozen claws.

But he had to do it, he told himself sitting on his bunk, lighting another cigaret. He owed them this last chance at life. Christ, even if it killed them. Selfsacrifice was every man's right.

Through the long night watch he waited, lighting one cigaret from another's butt, conjuring mystic tricks to steel his soul against his heart's devastation. Yet, despite his best efforts, repeatedly he saw within the moonlit panes shuffling on his cell wall bullets zippering the dirt, plucking poppies from blue shirts; Roy falling to his knees, head lolling, searching in the snap and whine of lead for his music, spilling the bundle from his arms, spectacles smashed, pencil broken in the bluewhite light. *What have I done?* Then the panes dissolved, becoming fog, and the tip of his cigaret pulsed like a police light, and Rooski's face lifted in a doorway framed by barred shadows.

Tower One's siren shattered the slide show. In seconds a hundred clamoring bells and klaxons joined in, followed by the thumping of breaker switches awakening the entire penitentiary and its perimeter in a blaze of light. He heard thundering guard boots on Mainline. An unfamiliar First Watch guard rushed down T Wing, ordering all prisoners to roll out and stand for Emergency Count. Another guard followed him down the cells, thumbing a mechanical counter.

Then, as suddenly as it erupted, the commotion died. First the bells, then the klaxons, finally the lights. The prison was plunged back into seething darkness slanted now with shadows like an old steel engraving as between the cellblocks dawn arose.

No shots, he rejoiced. Christ, no shots!

There was no use going back to sleep now, even if Joe could. He brewed a cup of instant coffee with his heating coil, lit another cigaret and listened to the harsh whisperings up and down the T Wing cells. The convicts concocted increasingly gruesome scenarios to explain the Emergency Count. Fantasies of mass breakouts and the taking of guards for hostages and reprisal raids on X Wing snitches abounded. There was a wishful quality to their imaginings which rattled Joe.

Surprisingly, they were unlocked for breakfast. The Mainline was clogged: it seemed all General Population was making chow that morning. It struck Joe as foolhardy to allow such unrestricted inmate movement while a security breach was still being evaluated.

A cordon of Gooners blocked the W Wing gates. They cut off any questions with gruff orders to keep moving. Slowly passing the gates in the press of blue shirts, Joe glimpsed a confusion of correctional khaki and S&I armor thronging the rotunda. He had almost reached the Chowhall when the call rang out: "MAN WALKIN! Hit the walls and no talkin!"

The convicts scrambled to either wall where they stood three and four deep in absolute silence. An open lane twelve feet wide separated them. The cordon at the head of the Hospital Wing parted and reformed into a guantlet.

Suddenly it was clear to Joe why they waited until now and didn't move them before Unlock. Some genius in Custody—and Joe was willing to bet a month in the Hole it was Rowdy McGee—had decided to make object lessons of Spencer and Roy. They were to be led down the Mainline in full view of General Population.

When Rowdy McGee swung out of W Wing first, Joe knew he would have won his bet. Lustrous armored epaulets had been added to his uniform, and to his armament an electric cattle prod, which he swung like a jeweled marshal's baton. His chin jutted as if he'd been studying photographs of Mussolini. Two Gooners with tasers at high port fell in behind him.

Spencer came out next, his wheelchair pushed by two more Gooners each grasping a handle. Without the necessary extremities to attach the handcuffs and legirons, they were reduced to swaddling the tiny, frail torso in chains. Spencer's countenance was a beacon of triumph.

Next came Ray in full body restraints, staring upward and clanking stiffly like Frankenstein's monster in legirons. The remainder of the Goon Squad followed him. One of them carried the hydraulic jack ceremoniously uplifted like the Ark of the Covenant wrested from the heathens.

Watching this bizarre procession form up, Joe heard a convict behind him lay down the inside skinny: "This bitch, yuh see, she goes into the onliest hardware store in Coldwater and buys threefoot bolt cutters, so natchly the store calls S&I soon as she books with em. Then last night they found the bolt cutters lyin on the access road between the fences . . . Along with enough C2 to blow down the cellblock wall. They was fixin to free *all* the plaguers. *Might* uh, too, if the bitch had the strength to throw the

stuff over both fences. Natchly, since they landed next to the new Hospital
Yard, it was pretty obvious who the stuff was meant for. They shook down
the wing and found the jack . . . Man, that pair woulda stood a better
chance runnin through hell in gasoline shorts."

"How'd dem crips get the jack inside?" asked a second.

"How do I know?" snapped the first. "Aint no clear voyeur."

"However they did it, them boys got *heart,*" said a third.

By then Spencer's wheelchair was passing abreast of Joe. Without looking, the quad hailed him with a jaunty salute of the coat hanger. Up to
this moment the convicts crowding the walls had been subdued. Not by
fear, but awed respect. But the spell was broken by the cavalier flip of the
twisted bit of wire. First several began clapping, then more and more,
louder and louder, cheering and stamping their feet until the Mainline
resounded like a conch shell big as Dallas.

Spinning around, McGee nearly capsized on his gimpy leg. He realized
quickly that there was no quelling this inspired outburst. Terror spurting
from his eyes, he ordered his men to doubletime the escapists to X Wing.

The convicts were too gladdened to bother jeering McGee and his
flunkies. They closed ranks after the retreating procession and redoubled
the cheers for Coldwater's very own heroes who had mocked all odds and
found the way to win for losing.

All they got was thirty days in the Hole for possession of unauthorized state
property—to wit, a jack. Escape charges were referred to the Madera
County Attorney, who declined them. The girl was never identified, so no
one could be charged with either possessing the explosives and bolt cutters
or importing them onto a state reservation.

That memory is brief can be as cruel as it is kind. By the time their
durance in the Hole was up, Spencer and Roy were no longer cynosure of
all Mainline adulation. Population hikes, rumors of brewing gang warfare,
the snitch game, and baseball pools had become the foci of convict attention.

They returned to the Hospital Wing unnoticed. Spencer was gaffled
straight to the carrier ranges. Less than a week later he was found smothered to death on his bunk, killed in selfdefense by the other plaguers as
he had predicted.

Roy went clean Eleven Ninetyeight and punched out three guards and
was sent to Z Block. There he was put on a Prolixin regimen until he
managed to prop his chin beneath the rim of his cell toilet and flush
himself to kingdom come.

IIII

When the green smells of things growing in the earth arose and tiny buds like powdered snow sprinkled the apple orchards; when melting snowcaps festooned the high Sierras with trembly silver ribbons and the uplands swirled their massy wildflower skirts; when the conversations of tanangers and gosbecks on cell ledges roused convicts before the Wakeup bell, which every day followed dawn at a wider interval, the Hospital Yard was paved as Joe had promised. In the corner by the fountain he crouched and wrote their names, their birth and death dates, with his finger in the wet cement.

Standing then, Joe slung his hands on his hips and tipped his head back staring up into clouds like bearded cheeks with seams which seemed to smile. Slowly, deeply through his nose he drew a draught of chilly upland ether and held it till it hurt; then, ballooning his cheeks, held it a bit longer, almost afraid to loose it, until his eyes floated and his face prickled and all the guilt and pain burst from his breast at last with an explosive gasp whose violence bent him double, hands on his knees, dizzy, staring swimeyed at the tracks of his fingers in the cement.

Quickly then, before it set up, he stooped and added the days of Rooski's life.

MATTER OF TIME

||||

"**S**ix in the boneyard," called Joe.

The pickup rattlebanged between the conjugal trailers slouched on cinderblocks and fourbyfour pilings. At each, Sergeant Gene Fortado braked and blared the horn, and a convict waved through a window or door, and Joe ticked off a number on the count sheet.

"Dont know why their women stay with them," Fortado said.

"The ladies love outlaws," Joe pointed out. "Plus they want to make sure these men are availed their inalienable right to pussy."

"You mean the right to alien pussy," Fortado growled, screeching to a halt at the last trailer. From its door, uxurious and connubial, the proud groom Billy Skaggs waved. He wore ribbons in his long greasy curls and a shiteating grin big as Dallas.

Joe had missed the brute's Catholic chapel wedding to the woman surgically paroled from Magdalena's body. Her whole street family had been there, crying their cholo eyes out. Billy wanted all spiritual bases covered and had Swami in attendance. Warden Gasse even showed up to buss the bride—despite the effrontery of the most writtenup cocksucker in Coldwater's history wearing virginal white. Although Joe had to admit, once she got the tuckenroll she really was some kind of born again virgin.

Joe couldn't resist. He stuck his head out the window and mouthed at the cumdrunk villain—"How's it *taste?*"

Billy joined the tips of his forefingers and thumbs to tongue the teardrop of air in between, then swung his hips and smacked his lips loud enough to be heard over the pickup's engine.

Joe laughed, "Six in the meat," and Fortado slapped the pedal to the metal, peeling out of the boneyard. *A travesty of holy matrimony*, he ground his teeth, *a crime against nature*. Joe knew better than to crack wise just then, although he ached to ask whose nature.

The spectacle of Skaggs miming cunnilingus made Joe smile thinking of his bustout babushka, her big ass and chichis, her screwball comehither eye. But his child—a boy, almost four months old by now, figuring from the card Kitty had sent to Oblivia to coincide with Joe's birthday two weeks earlier—his *son?* That notion recalled his own faceless convict father, and he balled his fists until his knuckles popped, shunting aside that fugitive grudge. Christ, just so the child doesn't curse his creation the way I have cursed the incidental hip thrust spawning me.

"Four in the meat," Fortado tallied the heads of convicts setting up running silhouettes of their own kind on the rifle range.

Joe ticked off the Rifle Range and called, "Three on the Staff Service station sheet," and off they sped.

On one side the Sierras swept up to the sky; the penitentiary walls turned slowly on the other. It was hard for Joe to conceive of having spent almost a year of his life inside those colossal stone blocks. The walls seemed unreal, fantastical almost. The stilted guntowers interspersed along the fences could have been designed by the special effects genius who contrived the Martians on flexible steel legs who attacked the San Fernando Valley in Hollywood's version of H.G. Wells's *War of the Worlds.* Joe entertained himself with such thoughts and by occasionally sticking his head out the window and stretching his cheeks to scoop in the rushing air making his skull sing. He felt free outside the fences, from both the prison and himself.

Yet the illusion of freedom wasn't the only reason Joe enjoyed helping the Outside Sergeant make count. He genuinely liked Gene Fortado. A handsome man in his late forties with a high clear brow, a straight thin nose and wavy white hair, he was a careerist who wore the service stripes marking his years on the line proudly. He was intelligent enough to perceive that California's penitentiaries were human waste dumps breeding criminals the way other dumps breed rats, yet not so soured by cynicism that he didn't take his sworn duty to heart and extend convicts his best efforts. He was the apotheosis of the oldline guard with whom Joe was most comfortable, a known quantity in a world of X's, Y's, and Z's.

"Three in the meat," caroled Fortado at the service station.

"Three in the meat," Joe repeated. "Seven in Sewage."

Their last stop was the Sewage Plant situated a mile from the fences to spare the institution its fumes. Gunning through the orchards, Fortado told Joe he was following his brotherinlaw into early retirement. "McGee's forcing me out. He wants someone out here with a chaingang mentality. He has me frozen at my present pay level with no hope of promotion. He's logging derogatory reports on my personnel file, saying I'm too lax, when all I wont do is coerce convicts, play the snitch game . . . " Fortado sighed. "If I dont retire soon, he'll have me cashiered with a demoted pension."

"How do the McGees get the power?" Joe asked in a ruminative vein.

"The same way the violent criminals are getting them on the other side of the bars. By default. When power loses all its positive sources, it reverts to the violent . . . McGee uses his position as Teamster rep here at Coldwater to consolidate and validate his power. He's organizing the guards to agitate for better pay and more manpower. Half the guards are already Teamsters. The other half soon will be or'll be handed their pink slips like me. It's just a matter of time. With population and violence on the rise, the guard force is startin to run scared. And when men run scared, they run to power, not reason."

They turned off the road skirting the fences and galloped along a dirt track, across barren open fields to the Sewage Plant. Joe reclined against the jostling seat, his brogans up on the dash, dreaming out the window where a cloud's purple shadow shimmered up the winedark mountain slopes like a chill breeze over still dark water.

"I'm sure when X Wing tried a mass breakout last night," Fortado remarked sourly, "McGee won some more converts . . . "

"*Last night?*"

"Guess the news didnt hit the line before you broke out the Sally Port this ayem. About five in the morning an inmate on a lower range cried to the First Watch guard that he was suffering an appendix attack. When the guard keyed his cell, the inmate jumped up and overpowered him. Got the keys to two other ranges and the deadbolt box. By the time the Goon Squad arrived, there were fifty convicts runnin loose."

"How'd the Gooners get there?"

Fortado snorted. "The guard called the medics before he went down to the cell. When the medics got to the wing gates and saw what was jumpin off, they called the Squad."

"How'd those guys expect to get off the wing, let alone over the fences?" Joe asked. "What was their plan?"

Fortado swerved to evade a pothole and shrugged. The backward world jiggled in his darkglasses. "They didnt have a plan. Those informants down there in X are just gettin desperate. They sense they're being corralled for slaughter. They'd rather take their chances on the fences or against the Gooners than with you guys."

"Come again?"

The glasses turned to show Joe his own bemused features. "Last night the Gooners killed two of their usedup snitches. The body count's gonna be a mite higher if you guys take over."

"Christ! I guess I never thought of it like that."

"You better start. Mass escape attempts most times signal a major riot in the offing. That loony Hospital attempt was the first signal. Men who've lost their last hope of survival. And those boys in Protective Custody are more desperate than the plaguers. AIDS takes longer to kill than a shank. Call it herd instinct, the guys in P.C. sense what's comin. The convicts can take over this pen any time. We're sittin on a gasoline drum with a fistful of matches . . . Here. Let's count the shit stirrers."

The Sewage Plant was a squat cinderblock building connected by huge pipes to a vast, round, open tank. The sulphurous stink was overpowering. At the blow of the truck horn, the Sewage Workers emerged in their kneehigh rubber galoshes.

The Outside Sergeant's walkietalkie crackled. He stepped from the pickup and walked several yards distance to get better reception. One of the Sewage Workers took the opportunity to approach Joe. Joe had heard this old lifer with a face like a wrinkled oil rag called Dinky.

"I wanter meet witchoo . . . " Dinky winked and smiled slyly. "Inside."

"What for?" Joe leaned back from the stench seeping from his coveralls.

"Got a lil prepsishun to make yew . . . Very profitable," Dinky added with another salacious wink.

Mention of profit recalled Joe's obligations to Maas Dinero. "How about Evening Yard Call? By the horseshoe pits."

The oldtimer nodded and laid a cautionary grimed finger beside a nose twice as crooked as Joe's and slunk back to the Plant Building.

"You're Miguel's first visitor in weeks," the nurse said.

"Mike. His name's Mike Quintana," Kitty corrected her.

"Here he's Miguel," the nurse said primly. "We have to use the same names that appear on the government checks."

Kitty's faint smirk couldn't give a fuck if they called him Cantinflas. Serves him right, she thought. All his badass life he wanted to be Iron Mike. Well, Papa, for the last act you're little Miguel again, the dirty bordertown Chicklet boy.

"My, what a *nice* baby," the nurse said, though her small grimace pitied it. The girl wasn't even married: she signed Kitty Quintana in the Shadowbrook Convalescent Home guest register.

Kitty glanced down at the infant asleep in the canvas papoose harnessed to her breast. "I just hope he stays that way until I get out of here." She clicked a smile on and off.

The nurse stepped from behind the counter, gesturing down a corridor streaky with sunlight. "If you'll follow me, Miss Quintana."

The nurse's nylon stockings and layers of complicated underwear made squinchy noises as she walked, like termites gnawing dead wood. The corridor smelled of unemptied bedpans and unchanged bandages and dead skin. A lunch wagon was left forgotten beside a mop closet. A cluster of flies on a halfeaten plate of macaroni and cheese swarmed as they passed, then clustered back once more. A withered crone in a wheelchair with plastic tubes in her nose clutched Kitty's arm. Kitty looked down into the black toothless hole of a mouth suckling empty air. She shuddered, prying loose the monkey grip, and hurried to catch up with the nurse. Instinctively she touched the sleeping infant's head.

"In here, please." The nurse ushered her into a room divided by curtains on ceiling runners into four cubicles. Papa's was the last, by the window. He also had tubes in his nose. When he saw his daughter, his black eyes flared and turned away. His right arm, the one not paralyzed, pointed furiously downward. His slack jowls trembled making a gurgly noise.

"Oh dear," the nurse said turning an indulgent smile on Kitty. "Miguel's pan is *always* full. Here, I'll empty it. But first, let me get you comfortable, Miguel. Up!" The nurse reached behind his neck with one hand and lifted him. With her other, she punched the pillows. She settled him back down. Shitfire, Kitty gasped inwardly, he's light and dry as an old stick.

"There." She reached the brimming pan from beneath the bed and stood back, beaming. "He's such a dear," she told Kitty. "He only gets grumpy when his roommates die on him . . . " She turned back to Papa and trilled, "But that's to be expected here at Shadowbrook, Miguel!"

Papa's eyes followed the nurse from the room. They remained fixed on the empty doorway a moment before tracking back to his daughter, flooded with fright.

Kitty stared dumbstruck at the frail invalid. For years she had waited for this reckoning, rehearsed it a million times. Now suddenly her passion had deserted her; her gall was evaporated. She felt only pity. An abject and all encompassing pity staining herself even. Because she'd been cheated. She wanted so much to beat him fair and square. Not like this, not now.

She pulled a molded green plastic chair to the bed. She shrugged out of the harness and sat with the papoose in her lap.

"Long time no see, Papa," she said finally. "How's the chow in this dump?"

The bastard's eyes could still smile. Though his face hung in flaccid folds, his black heart still showed. The smiling eyes then posed a question, looking to the baby and back at her.

"I forgot," she said, turning the papoose to face him. The infant awoke and twitched out a tiny fat arm. "This lil buckeroo's your grandson, Joseph. How about them eyes . . . " She pushed the papoose closer. "One's blue, one's gray. Doctor called it heterochromia. Said it runs in families. Says it skips generations . . . " She reversed the papoose, looking curiously in the baby's eyes herself. "Thing is, I don't know anyone on our side . . . must be his daddy's people." She shrugged.

A part of her still didn't believe her own gentle voice. It had been so long her intention to flaunt her womb's second bloom at him who'd blackened its first, prove that another man wanted her despite his defilement of her. Now all that was dead and gone and briefly she felt even more bereft of her hatred for Papa than her love of Mama . . . and then Kitty remembered why she'd come to the home in the first place, that with Mama alive she'd never have seen Papa again.

She set the papoose on the foot of the hospital bed and took his hand and folded hers over it. Again she saw a bright sheet of fear across his eyes, and she said: "Papa, listen to me good. Mama's dead, died natural and peaceful and she spoke last of you . . . "

A shadow fell across the eyes, a veil immediately lifted, and they shone with a soft, sad light while Kitty told how it happened, of the services in the little church of white stones on the grassy bluff over the Gulf, where she herself had been baptized and confirmed; told which cousins came and what they said and what Mama wore and how she looked when they closed her up; then on about the house, which Kitty listed for sale. Already a motel chain had made an offer, Kitty didn't know how much, a lawyer was handling it and if there was enough left over after taxes and fees and all the bills Mama left in the breadbox, well . . . then the lawyer would have Papa moved out of this dump to someplace more comfortable.

She peered critically around the room as she spoke and gripped his hand tighter; and when her eyes returned to his, she felt they were moist, so she weakly joked, "Coupla nurses on the sunnyside of menopause might liven things up, eh Papa?"

She returned the grin in his eyes, then looked quickly down at his hand. She stroked it for a moment, then remembered the letter in her purse from Joe's lawyer saying it wouldn't be long; she looked up.

"I'm taking Joseph here back to California so we can be with his daddy, Papa. So I guess this is sorta hasta la bye bye."

The eyes leaped up in panic, then sank back in his skull, shining softly.

She said nothing more. She sat still holding his hand, watching his eyes in the long Texas twilight falling through the windows.

The Yard was gripped in an enormous rustling silence. Never had Joe seen it so crowded, nor felt it so palpably tense. The vast blue vortex of convicts trudging sluggishly counterclockwise shrank the hundredacre enclosure to the size of a holding pen. An eerie blue nightmist avalanched down the Sierras, sweeping across the plains to billow at the base of the fences. Through it shone a too yellow moon, jaundicing faces. The wind rising up from the valley was sweet, like a corpse, with doom.

Joe spotted Dinky from a distance loitering near the horsehoe pits. Joe suggested meeting there for no better reason than it was where he first remembered seeing Dinky, holding forth to a bunch of youngsters. He was telling them about the old days at San Quentin when the Death House still was smoking. The day they gassed Caryl Chessman, he recounted, all the cons on the lower Yard knew two minutes afterward because the pigeons roosting on the North Block roof keeled over the moment they opened the exhaust vents.

"Let's walk n talk," Joe tersely invited the Sewage Worker.

The way Dinky laid out the drawings, it was so simple Joe was surprised it had been so far overlooked. Huge grills out at the Sewage Plant filtered solid trash from the excremental waste to be chemically degraded. It was amazing, Dinky said with yet another wink, the things people flushed down shitters. Once he'd even recovered a Seiko watch which he used to grease a guard.

"The grill teeth are spaced so . . . " Dinky measured an inch between his fingers. "Anything bigger gets trapped and I haul it out."

"But what do you think you're gonna get from convict shitters?"

Dinky showed sharp blackened teeth in a laugh. "You gotta remember, the Sewage Plant soivices the entire institooshun, not jist the cellblocks. Like all the Admin terlets, frinstints. Like where do the Visiting Room wimmens flush their tampoons? And knowing the size of them things, what do you imagine could be hidden inside em?"

Now Joe got the picture. He rubbed his chin, lit a Camel, adjusted his cap. "What do you need me for?"

"To mule em through the gates . . . See, they shake me down purty thurrah on account I got priors fer sech stuff from other joints. Only reason they give me the custody to work outside is I'm the only man in camp what knows his shit . . . *Hee, hee* . . . Also I'm gettin older n dont know so many line hustlers no more, n you could hep me line up the wives n goilfrens n all."

Joe carried away a sulphurous reek on the hand he used to shake the deal closed.

Back on the wing, Gerald Irons gawked at Joe. "You mean, all my ole lady's gotta do is flush a tampoon loaded with dope down a shitter? You take care of the rest?"

"Yeah . . . But is Dinky regular?" Joe was being careful not to blow his coffee break parole in the process of paying for it.

"Dinky?" Irons laughed. "In Quentin I watched him slide a redhot bunk spring through one of a snitch's ears and out the other."

Joe had to agree, you couldn't get much more regular than that.

The manager of the Rexall's in downtown Coldwater already suspected there was a cathouse booming in the hills east of the prison. What other explanation could there be for the huge prophylactic demand? When a Mrs. Reba Irons came in and placed an order for ten cases of Super Tampax, he was certain he'd met the establishment's madame.

Two weeks later Maas Dinero received by registered mail a personal check from Reba Irons in the amount of five hundred dollars to be credited to the file of SPEAKER, B-83478. The next day he received a check drawn from Joe's Coldwater inmate trust fund for another seven hundred. The Special Circumstances parole was paid up front in full. It only depended now on how fast Maas could get the board members to take that coffee break. A matter of time. That same stuffless matter separating Joe from oblivion at the whim of Rowdy McGee or the rage of riot.

Z BLOCK

||||

Dawn spread like fire on the Pacific fifty miles outside the Golden Gate, where twin islands like stalagmites pointed rocky fingers to a heaven black with birds. The ocean breathed in long, slow swells, rocking the trawler like a cradle.

In the trawler's stern stood a fisherman, legs spread for balance, one hand resting on the net winch. He had fished in the lee of the desolate Farallones since boyhood and knew the tides and currents as well as he knew his mother's face. With narrowed eyes he watched the sea flow in iridescent wrinkles between the island rookeries. Not long now, he thought. He listened carefully to the cries of the frigate birds and cormorants, sweeping his gaze across the waters beneath which his net drifted. He flexed the fingers of his winch hand.

There! Broad flashes beneath the waves, a school of fish turning as one, this way, then that. Netted! He leaned full sinew into the winch, chattering its ratchets. The wheeling birds lifted their cries.

The fisherman smiled feeling the heft of the net. Then he saw the silver bodies, waferthin and bright, tumbling upward. Nearing the surface, the light caught them, gilding them, changing them into golden coins. He locked the winch, pitched the derrick hook over the side, and hauled the bulging, wriggling net from the water. The birds made runs for the net, spearing it with razor beaks. He swung the net over the open deck and yanked the draw rope. The fish cascaded to the deck, moiling, flashbulbing in the rising light, funneling down the open hatch.

But not all the fish. Something was snagging the net, something that didn't slip and slither. The net swung with its weight. A crab, thought the fisherman. He was used to them. Or a piece of garbage. Plenty of sportfishers spent their weekends at the Farallones tossing trash in the water.

Peering between the overlapping squares, he jabbed at the net with a gaff. Whatever it was was round, festooned with seaweed, he thought at first, a rock perhaps. He jabbed harder, hooking the gaff's spur in the net, and yanked. The object broke free and fell tumbling to the deck with a soggy crack, and the fisherman cried out. It was a human head, a girl's head from its profusion of matted black hair cut in bangs; though it was impossible to read the age of the bloated and garishly madeup face.

The fisherman staggered backward, the trawler's pitch rolled the head after him. It rocked to a rest at his boots, ogling him with bulged eyes ringed with grease. Her cheek had been eaten by fish, baring her teeth in a howl that echoed the cries of the helixing birds and the fisherman's imprecations.

Washing his hair, Joe leaned up into the showerhead as if it were the boom mike at the Grand Ole Opry, twangtonsilin *I'm breakin rocks in Georgia, she's breakin hearts in Tennessee.* Rinsing off, he segued into "Make the World Go Away," his curtain number when he'd really wrench it up from the gut, echoing blue roadhouse purgatory around the tiled showerroom.

Shutting off the water, he heard solitary clapping and wondered who it could be. He snatched aside the curtain and was staring at Rowdy McGee, who slurped, "I'm here to do just that, make your world go away." Behind him several underlings traded arm punches and bellylaughs. "You're going to Z Block, bowelbaby."

Joe eyes flicked to the hooks where his clothing hung. The cap was gone. Terror spilled into his skull.

Joe Sing scoped the Goon Squad swing out of Custody and followed them down to T Wing, though he didn't enter. He leaned on the Mainline wall gazing out a tall window where the sharp Sierras raked cotton from the sky. Then the wing gates crashed again and out swarmed the Squad frogmarching Joe Speaker in their midst. The Barker was naked. The obsidian stare in the black bandanna's shadow followed them until Joe Sing was certain where they were headed. Z Block, the terminal Psych Unit. It was time to make that call.

C.O. Ng looked up from his desk in Y-1 Pharmacy and smiled at the familiar lanky figure before his desk. Ng was the avatar of the sublimely venal refugee from overseas war games, weaned on Yankee waste and corruption, who fit so seamlessly into state agencies.

"I need to call a lawyer," Joe Sing said.

"Put in a request slip," returned Ng's toothy grin.

"No time." Sing nodded at the outside line beside the institutional phone on Ng's desk. It was Joe Sing and his boys who protected Ng's drug traffic from the Wah Ching. At a snap of Joe Sing's fingers, Ng's Jaguar would be repossessed.

"Long distance I have to place through the switchboard . . . " Sing shrugged. "What's the number?" Joe Sing passed him the card. Ng picked up the receiver with one hand and took the card with the other, reading aloud, "Marvin Maas . . . "

Out of the steel elevator the Goon Squad hustled Joe onto the highest security wing in the state of California. Z-3, the third level of Z Block, had no bars. The cells were solid iron boxes running the length of an iron corridor. The convicts were fed through locking food slots like gun slits. Above the slots were riveted narrow ports of twoinch glass. Through these the guards monitored convict movement by the light of yellow dimwatters behind grates in the iron ceilings.

McGee howled to the guards for the keys to the interview room at the head of the wing. He was answered by screams and moans and manic laughter reverberant from the boxes. The iron echoes merged in a single sustained ululation of madness and horror that had yet to abate by the time they entered the room.

Joe was chained to a metal folding chair. McGee ordered his thugs from the room. Blood trickled down Joe's cheek from a wound opened on his brow when they hurled him in the elevator; he twitched his mouth, tasting its salt. McGee turned another chair backward and sat facing Joe over its back. He extracted a toothpick from his breast pocket and began picking his teeth.

"Life expectancy up here's less than six months, penis blossom. There's only one way you'll get off this wing alive." Loudly McGee sucked a shred of something barbecued stuck between his teeth, smudging his lips with orange. "Tell me where the Moon is at."

Joe strained forward in his chains, grimacing with disbelief. "Moon? What is this, an astronomy quiz?"

"You're a smartass, Speaker. But brains dont matter in Z-3 any more than love in a whorehouse . . . You robbed Baby Jewels Moses. You ripped a blue diamond. He's asked me to help him get it back."

"You took your time . . ."

McGee chuckled. "Oh, I wasnt going to let you make your little coffee break parole, if that's what you mean. I knew you caught my little act in county jail. Those bowelbabies who threw me off the tier at San Quentin might have hit my head but they didnt hurt my memory none . . ." McGee clunked the heavy Teamster ring against the steel plate. "I also know it was you who helped smuggle the jack to those crips, making me a fool . . . So you see, I was goin to air you out anyway, Speaker." McGee swung his nerveless leg off the chair and lurched across to stand over Joe. "But now I'm willing to cut a deal. You tell me about the diamond and I'll let your ass off . . . What's wrong? Dont believe me?"

"Ha! Why shouldnt I believe you?" Joe hadn't meant to betray surprise.

"I get a headache when folks dont believe me," slurped McGee. "Now where the fuck is it, pootbutt?"

"I dont know what you're—"

The studded gauntlet nailed Joe on the chin, humming his teeth, gonging his head. He twirled, crashing to the floor with the chair chained to his back. Through blood he saw McGee's lustrous laceup boots a foot from his head. Bending his knee, Joe braced his foot against the wall. Gathering all his hatred in his lungs, he screamed, springing off the wall, snapping his back to spin the chair so that one of its sharp legs struck McGee's boot, cutting clear through the leather at the heel, where it was softest, drawing a spurt of blood.

McGee loosed an oath and booted Joe behind his ear. He felt himself slipping down the dark, damp walls of a cold well. From far away, as though McGee leaned over the well, calling down after him, he heard: "I'm not wasting any more time today, Speaker. You like dope, dont you? You'll be getting plenty up here. I'll be back soon to see if you've remembered where the ice is . . . Pleasant dreams."

Sheer force of will lifted Joe back up the slimy dank walls to peer over the well's lip at the bloodied boot limping from the room.

He struggled to right himself and succeeded only in turning onto his side with the chair chained behind him. Through a corner of wiremeshed glass in the door, he watched the clock in the Z-3 corridor. For an hour while his blood crusted on the linoleum, he lay waiting. He felt relief hearing the door at last. But then his eyes flew wide with fear.

There were five of them. Four guards and an MTA in white ducks and shirt. The guards carried batons and wore helmets with the smoked Plexiglas shields down. They carried halved prison mattress shields. With their polished plastic head shells and shiny black bubble eyes, they resembled giant malevolent insects.

But the guards at least were familiar. All they could do was beat him, and he was so numb now he scarcely feared that. What iced his heart was the implement upheld by the smiling MTA. A very large hypodermic syringe filled with red viscous liquid like cough syrup.

"No! Dont medicate me down," he gasped. It was like begging not to be buried alive.

They closed on him suddenly. Half a cell mattress covered his head, muffling his cries as his kidneys were clubbed. He felt his chains removed from the chair and resecured; heard the chair skitter across the linoleum and bang against the wall. A sharp knee savagely pinioned the small of his back to the floor. Hands ripped at his clothes. They were stripping him; he was naked. He felt the sudden prick of cold steel, felt the heavy lowgauge needle slide into his tensed buttocks, the liquid gush into his muscles. He screamed into the stinking batting.

They left him melting into a big muddy puddle on the floor. He spread across the room filling the seams between the linoleum, seeping through the cracks beneath the baseboards. His head lay sidelong on the cool floor watching himself being soaked up.

Now he was flowing down the corridor beneath the bright lights. He was a molten ectoplasmic stream coursing in a smooth, straight bed. He felt nothing but motion. The motion bent suddenly, turned and flowed through rock that opened and closed for it. The sky turned to iron that made rolling thunder. A weak sun shone behind its prison bars.

He was thirsty. It was so dark. But he was thirstier than it was dark. There, an iron sink in the corner. To reach it, he had first to recall all his molecules and command them to resolidify. To do that he had to think. It was harder to think than it was dark. The sun never moved, but he thought it took him days to reintegrate and crawl to the sink and haul himself up and he was just pursing his lips to drink when the iron world thundered again and the iron sky broke with light and he felt the cold deep in his flesh.

Once they were late dosing him. He decided to kill himself. Such a good idea, he smiled. But he was naked, nothing to hang himself with. No zippers to hack open his veins. No matches either to set himself on fire. Crawling along the wall of the cell, he came to the steel shitter and remembered how Roy toilet paroled. But feeling around, he found no flush button. *Of course, they're flushed remotely,* his mind groped through its psychotropic mists. And at irregular intervals.

He heard singing and his dopey smile widened. Jumpshout gospel reboant from a nearby box. His senses coalesced sufficiently for Joe to grip his food slot and crawl up to peer through the observation port. There, directly across the corridor, a black's face filled his observation port singing *hallelujah, hallelujah*. The Z-3 guards had the corridor door to his cell open but couldn't open the inside door to his box. Joe murkily understood them to say he had shredded his blanket, stuffing it between the door and its jamb so there wasn't enough play to turn the lock's tumblers. They used sledgehammers to break the lock. He sang "Peace in the Valley," metering the hymn to the strike and rumble of iron. Louder and louder, big eyes rolled up to home until the box was breached and wildly milling clubs felled him from the port, spraying it with his blood. No easy ways out the back door even of Z-3.

Then they cracked Joe's own iron box and sank another needle deep in his buttocks.

The hallucinations overlapped and sometimes played out simultaneously. Men in white gowns entered his world through the sky and measured him with calipers. The needlesharp tips measured his head, his limbs, his hips, buttocks, and penis. When they left, he was visited by a formless shadow which spoke, not in the voice of one but many which, differing in their rhythms and pitches and accents, echoed in his iron box with the familiar cadences of his dead, and he screamed and fell through the floor down a corkscrewing tunnel like large intestines which dropped him light as a feather onto the streets of a city he didnt know. And there before his eyes floated a teardrop of blue light. He reached for it; it danced away, just beyond his fingertips. He chased the teardrop up and down the topsyturvy funhouse streets that seemed level, only he kept falling. He lost it and ran to a newsstand to ask where it was and Hymie the Hat spit it in the air, where it gyred wildly before floating through the doors of a strip club. "Enter, enter," beckoned Pious Wing, tipping his bishop's miter. "Get you harder than Chinese rithmetic." Joe chased the tearshaped flame inside. A fat old stripper with a clown's face and greasy sacklike breasts lay on the stage rasping "Short time, sugar?" and spread her meaty thighs and the teardrop glistened in her cunt like the Devil's blue cum. Her belly changed to Rooski's face, and her cunt to a shotgun barrel that popped out the teardrop slow motion. It drifted over Joe's head. He leaped and caught it finally, only it turned to water trickling through his clenched fingers. The stripclub wall became Whisper's face, and now the teardrop froze at the corner of his eye becoming a burning point of blue light lancing his skull, then bursting, vaporizing into aquamarine mist . . .

It was within a misty streetlamp cone of that same color that Joe sat one summer evening when his mother had company and he wasn't allowed inside the little house. Instead he played with a cockroach in the gutter with a stick. The cockroach was trying to reach a storm grate; Joe blocked its passage, flicked it backward over and over just before it reached its goal. It kept trying, would keep trying forever, when Joe heard his friend Melvin call. Melvin was on his bike; Joe heard the playing card snickering in its spokes. Could Joe come to his house for dinner? He stood and squashed the cockroach and followed the sound of the flickering card down the dark street.

On the wall at Melvin's house, a mounted fish who had lost a longago battle rolled its dusty eye down at Joe while he munched the salami sandwich. Melvin was talking to his mother in the other room. Joe heard her say never invite Joe to their house, his father was a convict. He leaped up screaming and threw the sandwich at the big stupid fish. He ran from the back of Melvin's house across the dark yards littered with upended refrigerators and old tires and rusted barbecues. Pounding along the boards of their back porch, he heard his mother's cries. He burst through the kitchen into the living room. She was bent naked over the back of the couch, crying, and the naked man stood grunting behind her, thumping her, hurting her. On the mantle behind them the boy saw the photograph of his strange young father slouched smoking at a nightclub table, a funny cap like a cop's tipped back on his tall head. He screamed. His mother's head flew up. The man jumped back and laughed. His angry purple thing shrank back into its bush. His mother jumped naked around the couch all flapping tits screaming and slapped him . . .

Only it wasn't his mother, it was McGee, who had come into his box through the crack in the sky and stood over him. Joe couldn't hear what he was telling McGee. Something about the moon in Davey Jones's locker.

Once they took him for a Psychological Review hearing in the Interview Room. He didn't know how he got there. He felt drool dripping from his mouth but he couldn't wipe it away because he was chained. A shrink asked him a question he couldn't understand, though he tried to answer, if only he could tell they'd let him go, but too much dope, his lips were like a flat tire and all that came out was a flubbery moan. An alarm klaxon went off on one of the lower wings. Joe threw back his head and imitated its howl, laughing and crying at once.

WHAT FEAR REALLY IS

||||

"**R**ick. Dental was enough for ID. Unnecessary for you to view the head." The Medical Examiner spoke habitually in shorthand as if dictating autopsy minutes.

"I had to," he said huskily. "Belinda wasnt only my daughter, she's the newest subject of an ongoing murder investigation." With fingers cramped from trembling he peeled the cellophane from a fresh Hav-A-Tampa Jewel.

"*Ah-* aaah." The M.E. pointed to the NO SMOKING sign affixed to the tiled wall behind his desk, the sympathetic blinking over his halfmoon spectacles begging Tarzon to understand that rules, after all, are rules, regardless of circumstances.

Tarzon settled for chewing the unlit stogie's plastic mouthpiece. "Where'd they find the torso?"

The M.E. questioned his own memory, "Dumpster?" Delicately, like drawing a sheet over a cadaver, he folded over the file's top page. "Yes. Outside Cow Palace. Dumpster already on truck forks, being emptied. Sanitation worker saw torso tumble into rotary jaws. Extracted before much damage."

"And the cause of death?"

The M.E. looked up in surprise. "Why . . . decapitation."

"That much I gathered, Ralph. Maybe I should have asked what means.

I've seen my share of severed heads, but never one so cleanly cut. Almost like a meat slicer . . . "

The M.E. leaned back and aimed Tarzon a scholarly squint down the bridge of his nose. "Saw a portfolio once. In medical school. Postmortem cadaver sketches. Victims of the Reign of Terror following the French Revolution. Guillotine." The M.E. stretched the word into three exaggerated syllables, jumping at the crack of the mouthpiece between Tarzon's teeth on the last. In a flurry he produced from his desk's file drawer a quart of whiskey and two Dixie cups. He uncapped the bottle. At the inquiring lift of his brows, Tarzon nodded tightly. The M.E. filled a cup and Tarzon tossed it back, loosing a moan of such desolation that the M.E. asked if he shouldn't be at home under a doctor's care.

"No. I have two more questions. First, was there evidence of sexual battery?"

The M.E. nodded, busying himself refilling Tarzon's Dixie cup.

"What, for Christ's sake? I'm not a father anymore, but I'm still a cop. What evidence?"

The M.E. smiled painfully. He joined his hands in a soft clap. Rubber wheels squeaked down the hall outside; distantly, the muffled whump of a morgue drawer rolling shut.

"Semen. Anus and throat. Different strains. Throat strain diluted by sea water. Anal strain can be matched by DNA fingerprinting."

The force of Tarzon's exhalation bugged his eyes. He lifted his fists, beating them once against his temples. He drilled another shot and said, "She was wearing some kind of heavy makeup. Like a clown or something."

"Encore brand base makeup. Footlight brand eyeshadow, lipstick, et cetera. Cosmetics mixed with chemicals to absorb strong lighting. Used by TV and film actors."

There was no mistake, Tarzon's worst nightmare was confirmed. He cursed himself, thinking: *They must have followed me. They couldnt have made the connection unless I led them to her. Trying to save her, I won her a snuff film contract. But why? Not just for spite because she was my daughter. Why not kill me then? How much I would have preferred they had killed me than . . .* His blueshadowed cheeks rippled as he envisioned pale hands slipping from numbered postal boxes the record of the horror wrapped in plain brown paper. He was gripping the M.E.'s desk to stand when the phone rang.

"For you, Rick."

Tarzon took the phone in his cold sweaty hand. At first he couldn't make out what the Homicide sergeant was saying. He wiped his hand over his clammy brow. "Lieutenant Tarzon, did you hear me?"

"Just run that by me again, Pete."

The young cop took a breath. "OK. Santo Crespi, aka the Troll, called our office. He saw your daughter's picture in the obit. He swears it's the same girl who left the shooting gallery with Speaker and Chakov."

Tarzon's jaw dropped, he unstuck the unlit stogie from his nerveless lip. *Of course!* It was no coincidence that McGee made his move on Speaker the same day her head was fished from the sea. Belinda knew Speaker stole the diamond, had known all along. Moses wasn't taking revenge against Tarzon. He tortured his daughter for Speaker's name and made a film of it. All along Rick Tarzon had been haunted by a feeling that his search for Belinda and his quest for the diamond were linked. He'd just never imagined so directly. He hung up and turned for the door.

The M.E. cleared his throat. "Her . . . remains."

He looked at the M.E. in desperate confusion. For one whose profession was death, Tarzon was woefully unschooled in its last rites.

"Made arrangements, Rick?"

"Yeah. First I'm gonna get drunk, then I'm gettin even."

The M.E. ducked his head, batting his brows. "The body."

"For Chrissakes, Ralph. Whatever they do with bodies, do. Send the bill to my office."

It goes to show you never can tell, because today felt to Rowdy McGee like a day when nothing could go wrong. From his home the night before he had called Baby Jewels Moses telling him where to find the diamond. When he got off shift that afternoon, he was driving to San Francisco to pick up his two G's reward. Who knows, maybe a little Chinese dinner, a cable car ride—hell, he might even get laid. Rowdy appreciated life's simple pleasures. Of course there was the unfinished business of Speaker, but that he could postpone . . . *savor.*

On the way to work he stopped at Dunkin' Donuts for a box of their class stuff, with the pink speckles and all. None of that dayold junk on this red banner day. Setting the box on the table in the Goon Squad Muster Room, he shelved his armored belly beside it and with his hand stamped down his nerveless leg Sumostyle. Using his cattle prod to gavel his gang to order, he smeared a smile around the room. "Aint we got some convict ass to kick this morning, studs?"

Such familiarities were the stuff that endeared McGee to the squad. C.O. Shepherd, the youngest and handsomest Gooner, and McGee's favorite, reported first. "During the first watch we raided Bakery and found three gallons of pruno brewing over the venting ducts. We conducted a thorough search of the job area, including opening the working ovens and . . . their cornbread fell . . . "

"Awww!" the squad chorused.

Laughing, Shep dusted a raspberry cruller's sugar from his hands and continued: "We also ascertained that an acetylene torch requisitioned to repair ovens is missing. Short of shaking down the whole institution, no means of recovering it are available."

"Not to worry," slurped McGee. "They'll probably use it to torch themselves extra assholes . . . Next . . . "

Muldoon, who of all the squad looked most like a Goon, looped a Neanderthal brow at his commander. "Some inmate broke into our evidence room, sir." Silence fell. "But nothing was taken," Muldoon hastened to add, "except that baseball cap you confiscated from the Work Order clerk."

"Find it!" McGee rolled a wild eye around the room. "Turn this joint upside down, cavity search every inmate, but *find* it . . . I dont ever want to see another penis blossom wearing it . . . Ever."

"Why not set Fraulein on it," Henderson suggested to break the tension. "Hell, she's our most productive snitch. Last night she gave up the Rubber Queen . . . "

"What?" Delight lit McGee's face and fizzed spittle at the corners of his mouth. "We got the Rubber Queen?"

"Not exactly, sir. But we know who she is now. We were only waiting in case you wanted to gaffle her personally."

McGee smiled; how quickly he had taught his studs the basic courtesies.

"Yes sir!" sang out Henderson, proud to deliver his commander his fondest wish. "Fraulein says the Rubber Queen is inmate Arthur Gottlieb, Reilly's old clerk. She's stashing the rubber supply on third tier W Wing Quarantine. Fraulein says she has enough stockpiled there to keep this pen fucking for a year. The reason the topmost range of Quarantine is being used, sir, is because it's an opentiered block and it's widely believed you're as scared of heights as you are of the plague."

"They say . . . *what*?!" Now apoplectic congestion purpled McGee's face. Henderson repeated himself, crestfallen for not omitting these last insulting details. "We go now!" McGee spurted. "They think I'm scared? I'll show those fuckin bowelbabies what fear really is. Muster dismissed. Fall out to raid W Wing."

Convicts on the Mainline dispersed wildly seeing the whole squad in battledress pour out of Custody with McGee lurching doubletime in their lead. At the W Wing gates, McGee pummeled an MTA with his prod for being slow keying them in.

"Now I want you studs to dress ranks right here in the Rotunda. I'm going up alone. I have to put these fuckin rumors to rest." He torqued his squad a pink eye livid with import. "It's not every day we get to neutralize Coldwater's biggest contraband operator . . . What cell did Fraulein say that cunt Gottlieb is using for a stash house?"

McGee heaved himself up the winding iron stairs. Twice he stopped to catch his breath, but didn't dare look down. By the time he reached the third tier, his heavy synthetic armor sloshed with sweat.

With bright shining eyes, the plaguers silently watched McGee's progress. When he reached the topmost rail they hooked their hands through the cyclone fencing and began shaking their screens. It began as a low rumble and built into a mighty thunder, swaying the catwalks and humming the rails.

McGee wrenched off his helmet in alarm. Something was very wrong. He shouted at them to stop shaking their screens and was answered with jeers and more violent shaking, shuddering the air. He ordered the plaguers on the third tier to clear his way, but instead of scurrying, they slouched; and in their eyes he saw not fear but only a sullen hatred. He screamed over the rail for his squad to follow him up; he hadn't noticed behind him the plaguers blocking the ladderways with burning mattresses and bedclothes. The plaguers in their cells shot him looks of open scorn and defiance. A black queen named Caledonia unzipped and slapped her penis on a crossmember. "Bite it, you big ole fonky bitch you." McGee began to tremble, and to babble beneath his breath.

And that's when he smelled the scorched steel and saw wisps of blue smoke clinging to the grating underfoot and knew in a blaze of terror why they were shaking the screens. He was nearly down to the end of the tier now, breathing in great wet gasps, holding cell bars with one gauntlet and the rail with the other.

Suddenly a convict stepped sideways out of a cell into his path. He wore the cap with the letter "B." He tipped it with gnarled fingers truncated at the second knuckle.

McGee froze with a cry. He looked down at his squad eighty feet below and screamed again. The shaking of the screens redoubled. The catwalk on which he stood began swinging like a rope bridge. The convict wearing the baseball cap said something, soft and deadly. McGee looked at him and bellowed in rage. He unslung his taser, staggering to take aim. His stamping boots broke the catwalk free where it had been cut by the welding torch. It fell in one piece, McGee bicycling shadows. His howl was drowned in the rumble and gnash of steel.

DASYPUS
NOVEMCINCTUS

||||

Tarzon spent the night alone in his office. It took nearly three quarts of Hiram Walker to burst the dam of shock, allowing him at last to weep, a flood of grief raging through the lonely hours. Toward dawn he drained the last tears with the last drops of whiskey. Sweet sad tears for a onceupon little girl, while freighters moaned out on the tide, bitter ones for her failed father and long dead mother as the sky feathered rosy and yellow behind the downtown towers; and, finally, with the light rising like candycolored steam in the purple canyons where streetlamps trembled, about to go out—beads of fire for Belinda's killer, Baby Jewels Moses, who seemed further from his grasp than ever.

Then he locked his office door and snapped shut its blinds and unfolded the cot he kept in the closet and slept like the dead.

He awoke in the midafternoon. His brain ticked as brightly as a brass clock whose works have been dismantled, soaked in caustic solution, scrubbed with wire brushes, and reassembled with new springs. He ordered up coffee and turned his attention to the most pressing matter at hand, the status of Joe Speaker. Four days had passed since Maas first got word from Sing that Speaker was in McGee's clutches on the psych unit. The lawyer had promised Tarzon he was doing everything in his power to get Speaker released. Four days. Tarzon shook his head dialing Maas's Sacramento number again. No way could Speaker still be holding out. He had to have surrendered the ice. He just prayed Speaker hadn't surrendered his ghost as well.

Maas's secretary said he was in court but would be back within the half hour. Awaiting the parole attorney's return call, he peeled the cellophane from a fresh Hav-A-Tampa Jewel and collated his mental index cards on the Moses case.

A grand jury had heard the Cowley girl's testimony, but alone it was insufficient to bill the Fat Man. Not only hadn't she personally witnessed a single murder, she was also an admitted addict and convicted thief and prostitute, the least desirable of state's witnesses.

On to the killing of Rosemary Hooten, aka Rings'n'Things. The only eyewitness to the suspect in orderly whites fleeing the Hall of Justice was a seventyyearold newspaper vendor who, when brought to the squadroom to identify the personnel mug from McGee's CDC file, developed selective amnesia. Tarzon suspected one of the cops on the Fat Man's pad had gotten to him. He also suspected that the police were involved that same day in the shooting of Undersheriff Collins. An official inquest was held which failed to determine what the Undersheriff was doing on the kitchen loading dock just minutes after the Sick Bay slaughter. It found Collins's slaying to be unrelated and coincidental, most likely the work of a mugger. Tarzon distrusted coincidences as much as he doubted there was a mugger so brazen as to attack the Undersheriff inside the courthouse.

Then there was Alice O'Shea, aka Fay DuWeye. The slim chance she held out of identifying Gloria Monday's black trick, possibly the man who beat her prior to her slaying, was scorched with her brain circuits in the brewery.

Tarzon slammed his fist on his desk. His last hope had been Joe Speaker. But by now Baby Jewels had probably recovered the diamond and had Speaker zipped. Tarzon cursed himself for not arranging a pardon for Speaker the day he met McGee at the Coldwater Gate House and made him for the Sick Bay killer. He could have had Speaker released from custody within a week. Instead he had opted to continue playing cat and mouse, hoping to trick Speaker into leading him to the diamond. And for what? To mete out justice to the Fat Man? No, the immediate threat to Speaker's life occasioned by Tarzon's own carelessness should have overridden any hypothetical prospect of gaining evidence against Moses. He had left Speaker in harm's way for purely selfish reasons. He hoped to get Moses before Moses got his daughter. And as he'd failed Belinda all her life, he'd failed her there too, and now she was dead. How would his conscience bear up, Tarzon bitterly wondered, with Speaker's life added to that weight?

Fool, he upbraided himself. Whatever crimes Baby Jewels is guilty of you have compounded with your own complicity. Belinda was right: you've crossed the line; you've become the same evil that you fight, like a fire, with fire. It's time to lay down your sword before you fall on it. But not before you bring down the Fat Man. Belinda must be avenged and your own soul exorcised.

He snatched up the phone before its first ring ended. Maas's voice reminded him of a glitzy game show host's, at once snide and smarmy. "I got your boy off Z-3 on a writ of habeas corpus last night."

"Thank God . . ." Tarzon crossed himself.

"Not that I needed to," Maas went on. "The only threat to him fell off a top tier yesterday. Broke his neck."

"Wait a minute . . . Are you talking about Rowdy McGee?"

"That's the name . . . The departmental release says the tier was old and poorly maintained and collapsed accidentally under McGee. The inside skinny is that the cons helped it along with a blowtorch."

Another coincidence, thought Tarzon. "How's Speaker?"

"He's in pretty rough shape. But I think I can get him sprung in a matter of days."

"How much will he owe you when he gets out?" Tarzon asked. His original plan had hinged in part on the price of the coffee break parole forcing Joe to recover the diamond as soon as he hit the bricks, leading Tarzon to it quickly.

"Nothing," Maas said. "He's paid up in full. Musta had some hustles inside."

Tarzon sighed. "I should have known when you told me my help wouldnt be needed wiping out that silent beef. Speaker's jointwise. He's got friends in there. McGee's death proves it. Lemme know as soon as you got him a date."

Maas chuckled. "Speaker's instructed me to alert some broad in Texas, too."

"Katherine Quintana," Tarzon said, flipping her card to the front of his mental stack.

"There's apprehension here that Coldwater might blow," Maas continued. "Population's at twice the recommended level, violence is way up . . . Hell, a lower court has already ruled that confinement there in and of itself constitutes cruel and unusual punishment."

"A riot? What happens if the shit flies the same time Speaker's slated to raise?"

"Not to worry, Loot. A parole carries the weight of a court order. If they can get to him, they'll cut him loose."

Hanging up, Tarzon wondered fiercely if McGee was killed before or after getting the secret of the diamond from Speaker and relaying it to Baby Jewels. The fact that Speaker was still alive seemed to hold out hope. It made no sense for McGee to leave him breathing once he knew where the diamond was.

The next Joe knew was water, warm and lushly green. His body rolled in the long undulant sea growth along the bottom; he felt mossy tendrils stroking his face. The shadowed gloom was so peaceful, like the aquarium. Then he felt a buoyancy; he was rising, turning slowly and rising. Above he saw light wavering on the surface, and he rose faster. The riddling light widened and widened, rushing up to meet him . . .

"Welcome back." Duck Butter sat on the edge of the bunk, sponging Joe's face. The sun through the cell window blinded him. He tried to sit up and shield his eyes. Duck Butter pushed him back down by the shoulders and covered his eyes with a towel.

"Rest easy, Joe. You been through hell and back . . . No, dont say nothin. The doctor says it'll be a few more days before the Prolixin's outta your system. He say they give you enough up there on Z-3 to kill a hoss. See your hand quiverin? . . . You been beat pretty good too."

"What . . . happened?" he managed to blubber.

"Yer lawyer writ yer ass off Z-3 . . . "

"How long was I there?"

"Four days . . . "

Joe swiped the towel from his eyes and squinted at Duck Butter in the brightness. "That's all?"

"I'm lyin, I'm dyin. It mighta seemed four years, but it was jest fo days. N you've been here jest overnight. It's the end of June still, Joe . . . N the doctor say you better keep your eyes covered, get used to the light slow."

Joe lay back down and let Duck Butter drape a fresh towel over his eyes. Slipping down shiny walls to sleep, he heard Duck Butter say from far away: "Know where you are? In Spencer's old cell on the Hospital Wing."

When he awoke, his eyes were uncovered. The cell was steeped in long blue shadows. Outside the window he heard wheelchairs and crutches on the Hospital Yard. A frisbee fluttered into the window bars. He smiled.

"Here's yer cap, amigo." It was Earl, holding out the Dodgers cap. "One of McGee's snitches stole it from you in the shower. I got it back yesterday."

Joe propped himself on his elbows, taking the cap. "Where's McGee?" Just saying the name frosted his heart.

"Dead, yeah. Fact he died ten feet from where you layin. Fell off the top tier here yesterday."

"Accident?"

Earl shrugged.

Joe slapped the cap against his thigh. "If only Whisper could *be* here. Someone finished the job." Triumphantly he fitted the cap back on his head. "Thanks."

"Dont mention it, no."

Joe suddenly remembered they hadn't spoken since the gambling confrontation. "Christ! Why are you here? After what I did to you? . . ."

"I promised Jack Moran, yeah, to look after you. I failed back then. I was all the way wrong."

"Not as wrong as me. Christ, of all people I know what a habit can make you do. And all these months I've waited to set it right and now you've gone and beat me to it . . ."

"Dont matter who set a thing right, just so it's done."

"Got another square?" Joe's head swam when he sat up. His bare feet on the floor were still numb. Earl passed him a lit cigaret.

They smoked in silence. The lights in the opposite cell block came up with a blaze. Joe caught a glint of reflected blue from Earl's eye.

Earl said, "I got some more vital stats on the armadillo for you, yeah . . ."

"No, no . . . anything but that." Joe laughed weakly.

"No, this you'll appreciate. You realize the armadillo lived a million years without a natchl enemy? The world was his oyster, yeah. Till the *next* armored thing come along—the automobile. It become the armadillo's only predator. See, what happens is them little suckers hypnotize theyselves nufflin around after roots and grubs and they dont notice the automobile till it's right on top on them, no. Then up they jump in the air, legs spraddled, and get creamed . . ."

"They should stay off the highway when they're drinking that Lone Star beer. Besides, there aint no grubs and roots growin in concrete."

"Yeah you right," he heard Earl respond thoughtfully.

The next time Joe awoke, it was pitch black. The penitentiary was quiet as a tomb. It had to be three or four in the morning. Earl still sat on the toilet cover, his right eye a blue pilot light in the dark. Joe sat up and asked him for another cigaret and wondered at the silence.

"The quiet before the storm," Earl said portentously.

Feeling black air rush into the hole opened suddenly in his stomach, Joe slumped back. "They've been sayin that for months."

"It's truth this time. Riot comin, yeah. The kites are everywhere. It's how the pen talks to itself, kites. They say hostages are gonna be taken and all the snitches killed. There's a stack of em in Custody right now, ones they confiscated. Shit, cons are startin to send them to their favorite free personnel warnin em to take early vacations, yeah."

"Why dont they do something?"

Earl laughed. *"Errp errp* . . . Why, Joe, aint you got it figgered yet? A riot's just what the Department wants. The legislature'll vote all kinda new money for them to steal. See, society aint gonna blame *them* for the riot. They'll blame theyselves for not givin the Department what's needed to contain and correct the conditions the convicts created. Heck, a riot's the answer to their wildest prayers. Afterwards, no one'll dare not give em all they want, no."

Thinking reactivated the Prolixin the way stepping in swamp mud releases its gases. Joe started slipping down those shiny walls again.

"Tell me more about those army dildos, Earl. The more I hear about em, the more I think we should hitch up out there, you and me and Kitty and the kid, buy us some land and raise them lil drunk fuckers for dogfood, like you say."

Earl slapped a bony knee. "I *knew* you'd see the light, boy. Well, lemme see . . . Your basic dasypus novemcinctus, he come to the Mississippi River n he want to get across, yeah. How he gonna do that lil thing? . . . I'll give you a hint, yeah. He got two choices."

"Some hint. You just made it twice as hard."

"Cmon, boy! . . . "

"Okay. He can wait for the ferry or hitch a ride on a gator."

"Errp errp." Earl leaned forward, hugging his hands between his knees. "Truth is he can hold his breath and walk cross the bottom," softly, in a voice still with mystery, "or he can swim cross the top like a damn amphibious tank. *That* how he do it, yeah."

"Crazy ole fool," Joe heard himself calling from across a rolling meadow trembling with wildflowers beneath a butteryellow sun. "Crazy ole fool."

THE FAT MAN
HAS NO CLOTHES

||||

Kitty woke up with a hangover out of West Hell. Her head hammered, her heart fluttered, she felt spooky as a tree full of hootowls. Yesterday she signed the final estate papers and last night went out with Aunt Juanita to the dogtrack where they got higher than witchdoctors, sucking lemons and Jose Cuervo.

"I'm buzzin like a cheap TV," she relayed her latest symptom to Aunt Juanita over coffee. "It wouldnt be so bad cept I gotta watch Joey n I got so much to do today if we're gonna hit the road tomorrow. For starters, I got to buy a tragic used car."

Say no more, said Aunt Juanita. She'd watch Joey, Kitty should just go on and do her thing. Only don't forget to buy Pampers, they were almost out, and call if she'd be later than five when Juanita had to be at work. Kitty poured herself another cup of java to chase the four Tylenols she found in the bottom of her purse, jumped in and out of the shower, and caught the bus to Houston.

A kid sitting in front of her cradled a boombox on his arm playing rebop rhapsodies she remembered from her Blue Note nights. She leaned her cheek against the window where it was cool from the AC vents blowing up through the sill, surrendering herself to the very fears she drank off her mind the night before. Now that it was time to go, she was scared. She kept remembering what the cop told her about Joe stealing something from someone who would kill to get it back. A diamond, the cop had blurted in the garage. Until the baby came, she never questioned Joe not giving it up. He'd lucked into something big, something dangerous to parlay, yet danger was the real drug of the capering Life.

But now that baby was here, she felt differently. Nothing was worth gambling its newborn life. But she couldn't be sure Joe felt the same. Shitfire, she couldn't even be sure Joe wanted the baby. Maybe potty training wasn't what he had planned for his freedom. But Kitty wasn't long for this sort of thinking. She bucked herself up remembering Joe's last words to her—"Till the wheels fall off." And what was it she was bringing him? A brand new wheel, that's what.

She stepped off the bus into the airtight heat of a dusty boulevard lined with scorched palmettos, where usedcar lots did battle for a threadbare dollar with secondhand appliance outlets and cutrate drilling riggers. She spotted the car she wanted from the sidewalk, a primercoated Chevrolet Caprice wagon on the back row of Smilin' Jack's World on Wheels.

Smilin' Jack wore a stringtie and aftershave that would have kept the flies off a dead carp. He sold all his cars with a ninetyday warranty, which was more than Kitty was willing to give his life if the Caprice broke down.

"Lissen hard," she said, "I'm pickin up Leroy at the Texas State Penitentiary at Huntsville tomorrow. He just done a flat twenty for murder. The first place we're goin is his mama's for dinner, and if this lil wagon give us a problem n Leroy's plate got cold . . . Well, let's just put it this way, you wont be smilin past sundown, Jack."

Smilin' Jack agreed eight hundred was a little high and had his mechanic change the oil and rotate the tires before giving it to her for five.

Kitty drove to a mall where she counted her money. She still had twelve hundred left from Dan's dough and decided to kick herself down a few dead presidents for an outfit to wear meeting Joe. She spent the afternoon fretting and foraging through boutiques, settling at last on a Mexican peon blouse that bared her shoulders, a new pair of stonewashed 501's, and cowboyboots with silver toe and heel brackets. She struck a pose in the fulllength mirror, tossing her hair and heaving her chichis . . . and started crying. It was all so innocent, she felt like a tragic teenager, and what if it wasn't enough that Joe gave the diamond back, what if . . .

She tossed her purchases in the back of the wagon and booked back Galveston way. Shitfire, girl, she ragged herself, speeding down the highway. You haven't come this far to get spongy. The sun was setting by now, oozing orange and black along the rim of the Gulf, where offshore drilling rigs pumped like fornicating sea monsters. What you need is a drink, girl.

Need? Whaddaya doin', trading the cooker for a shotglass? Just one. Two tops.

She passed up the roughneck jukejoints stringing the night with neon and the roadhouses licking it with steel guitar riffs. She wanted someplace quiet enough to hear her own blues. Whoa! Hit that turn signal, girl. A Ramada Inn, airconditioned lounge, WELCOME MID-SOUTH PLUMBING CONVENTION. It seemed just the anonymous purview for her troubled heart.

Off the highway she steered into the crowded parking lot, aiming for the neon martini glass marking the lounge. She swung wide around a Peterbilt tractor trailer and nearly creamed a Lincoln Towncar backing out of a space.

Inside was cool, sprinkled with spuriously sophisticated piano notes, flickered with the artificial intimacy of candles in red tulip glasses. Kitty took a stool where the bar doglegged to meet the wall and ordered a Wild Turkey and beer back.

She'd hardly taken a swallow before some geek in a seersucker suit sidled up and offered to stand the next round. A little squirt with wirerimmed spectacles, he wore a Mid-South Plumber lapel pin. He shot his cuff before propping his elbow on the bar, making sure his Rolex gloated openly. As if Kitty could have cared less if it was a Kotex strapped to his wrist. Still, she enjoyed the squirt's attention; it had been awhile since she'd felt attractive, and it was hard feeling blue at the same time. And a convention-eer! It was just like back at the Blue Note. She drilled her shot and arched her brow.

"Encore," calls this smooth operator to the bartender; back to her— "Harry Truman's my name, no relation to the president . . . Whom do I have the pleasure of drinking with?"

The squirt.

"Vanna White, only no free spins."

"Ha ha!" His lip pulled back like a donkey's, laughing *hahahahaha* until he figured out the joke was on him and huffed up. "Dont flatter yourself thinkin I'm tryin to pick you up," he straightened Kitty out. "I already have a lady friend, thank you. A girl just as pretty as she wants to be. She's jumpin out of a cake ten minutes from now in the banquet room, if you care to see for yourself."

"Girls actually do that?"

Now it was the squirt's turn to look askance, clearly signifying that he knew plenty of things girls actually did and was only being tactful sparing Kitty the details.

Kitty tossed back the Wild Turkey. "This I gotta lamp."

The banquet room was jammed to the rafters with drunk plumbers. The smoke was thick as movie fog, but Kitty and the squirt found two chairs against the back wall. A threepiece cowboy combo was hoking it up on a makeshift stage, across which a banner was strung that boasted MID-SOUTH PLUMBERS LAY LONGER PIPE. The plumbers sat at long folding tables, sopping up the last of their chili dinner. From the shiny strained look around their eyes, Kitty guessed some weaponsgrade gas was brewing. The combo wrapped up "Mama, Don't Let Your Babies Grow Up to Be Cowboys," the guitar player picked a country fanfare, and a voice over the P.A. congratulated the Mid-South Plumbers Association on having fewer Chapter Elevens than any other national trade association, and hoped they'd all stay so *flush*. Guffaws. Then the lights dimmed and the voice rasped, "Run yer cattle up the hill n hide yer women cuz it's des*sert* time!" The combo started in with "Happiest Girl in the Whole U.S.A.," and two slobs rolled out a giant cake in the shape of a toilet.

"Get ready," warned Harry Truman, No Relation to the President.

Kitty couldnt have guessed how ready she ought to be. Hardly had the squirt spoken than the toilet cake sort of exploded. What happened was, the girl inside tried to flip up the meringue lid, but somehow it was stuck. In a claustrophobic fit she started flailing around and first one arm broke through, now the other in a burst of icing; then the whole commodious confection disintegrated into angelfood rubble from which crawled to her feet a floyfloy floozie, platinum beehive gunked with pink frosting. She brandished a big cookie in the shape of a monkey wrench, wailing, "Gag me with a plunger!"

The potted plumbers, being by profession accustomed to helping women in distress, rushed the stage, dabbing at her with napkins, dunking pitchers of beer over her head, ripping off their shirts to wipe her down. Two began licking the stuff off her legs. "What kinda mamas you got anyway?" she cried, breaking the monkey wrench over their heads. The squirt jumped on the stage and began pulling the others off, screaming, "That's my Gypsy! You can look but you cant touch." A big plumber laid his ass out.

Kitty only stared. As the cake and frosting fell away, she saw that the naked girl had more tattoos than the Seventh Fleet. It was the one on her tummy, the half man, half motorcycle, that Kitty remembered. Shitfire, it was the same girl who'd worked at the Casbah Club with Kitty two years ago. A plainclothes Vice came in one night and asked if he could get oral sex and this tattooed tragedy told him all night long and they busted her. She told the judge she thought he meant *talk* about it, but he fined her a hundred clams anyway, and she quit the Casbah, telling Kitty she was going to go back to slinging pussy since she was paid up for the privilege anyway.

Kitty jumped to her feet and cupped her hands to her mouth.

"Rings'n'Things!"

On his penthouse terrace, a nude Baby Jewels lay prone on a massage table custommade for his bulk. A masseur in white ducks and T-shirt stood on a footstool to reach the rounded pink heights of the flesh mountain. His hands blurred *slappity slap*, shivering talced blubber. The Fat Man hissed like a happy bicycle pump.

"Boss!" Quick Cicero stepped through the sliding doors onto the terrace.

The rhythmic hiss stretched into a wheeze of worldclass fatigue. "When will the weary be at rest and the wicked cease from troubling?"

"This wont wait."

"Tch. That's all for today, Eddie." The Fat Man held out his arms for both men to hoist his enormity upright.

When the masseur had left, Quick said: "Truck Infante called. He said his torpedo got zotzed."

"You mean McGee?" The eyes nailed into the fatty pod gimleted. "How?"

Quick related the incident as it was reported by the Department of Corrections. "But Connie said the convicts used a torch to make cuts in the tier supports. He says Speaker's tight with this prison outfit called the Aryan Brotherhood, a buncha Nazi morons who never liked McGee anyway. They did the same thing to him at San Quentin years ago and probably wanted to see if he still bounced. Connie says it sounded like their style."

Baby Jewels made abstract kissy sounds assessing this theory. "It sounds more like *your* style."

"Thanks!"

"Saves us a coupla large," wheezed the Fat Man. "And he lived long enough to tell us where the diamond is at least. With Speaker dead, we can take our time fishing it out."

"Speaker aint dead, boss."

The wheeze opened into a whoosh. "What the fuck you talkin about? McGee said . . . "

"He said as *good* as dead."

"Tch. That means we gotta get the diamond right away." The Fat Man balled his twinkling fists. "As for this Speaker character, he knows we're

on to him, he has to be scared, and he might run to the cops. So we also gotta clip him . . . fast."

"Might be tough findin another guard fast . . . "

"Then use a convict!" sprayed the Fat Man. "Killing's how they got there. Call Connie Truck, Quick. The punk's got it coming anyway. Clip Speaker."

"Yo, boss . . . Say, look!" Quick produced a golden lozenge tin from his pocket, tearing off the cellophane. "They just got a new flavor in from gay ole Paree . . . Mandarin orange."

Gurgling naughtily, Baby Jewels jerked a dimpled arm for the tin. But in so doing his eyes chanced down across his pink subcontinent of flesh. He started, knocking aside the tin, spattering the terrace with lozenges like candy hailstones.

"What am I doing sitting here naked?"

Quick was too engaged staring hurtfully into the empty tin to respond.

"You see me naked, you're supposed to tell me, you putz!"

Rings was like, *Eeek, who's screamin my real name?* It took her several seconds to make out the tall girl with black hair waving her arms in the back, another two or three tics to remember Kitty Litter from San Francisco, and about two shakes of a toilet brush to sock one plumber in the jaw and kick another in the nuts and run out of the banquet room.

Theyre after me! was all she could think in the utility room, climbing into her Sandra Dee duds. She didn't even take the time to rinse off the cake and frosting that hadn't been sluiced or licked away. *They comin to finish what they started in jail.* She ran out a service entrance, leapfrogging across the hoods of cars, beelining for the highway, her thumb already unlimbered.

"Girlfriend!" she heard behind her. "Rings baby! Wait. It's Kitty Litter."

"Dont know you!" Hooking her arm around a lightpole, Rings swung a right angle and kept running.

"Then why . . . *huff huff* . . . you beatin cheeks?"

Cold logic always gave Rings pause. She turned, skipping lightly backward, holding up a finger. "Kasj. So I know you. Only I dont know what you want . . . "

"I gotta put down them cigarets," Kitty gasped, lurching to a halt.

"How'd you find me?"

"Pure chance. I didnt . . . Oh, lemme get my fuckin breath!" Kitty fanned her face with her hands.

Rings giggled. "You know what they call me when I do that, flap my hands by my ears?"

"Whadda they call you, girlfriend?"

"An airhead refuelin!"

Kitty groaned.

"So what do you want from me?" Rings asked, all business again.

Kitty stared at her, then stared around at the Ramada Inn parking lot, the headlights streaking down the highway, a single plane blinking across the night sky. "I dont know," she said. "Maybe just a familiar face from home. See, I been stuck here in Texas for months. Only I'm goin back to California tomorrow."

Mention of the Golden State awoke Rings's ruling sorrow. "I totally wish *I* could go home," she sobbed.

"Say what?" Kitty approached, sliding her arm around Rings's shoulder. "Cmon, girlfriend. You gonna make *me* cry. Lets sit down and you read me yer beads. Why cant you go home?"

They sat on the lip of a culvert pipe running beneath the Galveston highway, Kitty hugging Rings to her while the Illustrated Hooker spilled her refritos to the song of the tires above. As she talked, Rings felt Kitty tense with excitement. When she finished, the big TexMex gal made her go back and repeat the stuff about what happened in Glori girl's apartment, about the blue diamond and all.

"It's gotta be the same rock," Kitty whispered. She seized Rings by both shoulders, turning her to stare wildly in her eyes. "You mean if you turn state against Baby Jewels, they'll put his fat ass on ice?"

"Fur shur. But I'm like scared."

"I'm scared too," Kitty admitted. "That's why I ran after you, I needed someone to talk to." And she told Rings about Joe and the baby then and how her testimony would take the heat off the three of them.

Rings gazed at her as she spoke, thinking if Kitty had a feather up her ass, and Rings had her looks, they'd both be tickled. "That totally settles it," she announced once Kitty had laid bare her soul. "We'll go back together. Neither of us got nothin to fear with the other watchin her back."

"You'll be a star witness," bubbled Kitty. "Shitfire! Get asked on talk shows, maybe pose for Penthouse."

"I just wanna do what's right," Rings insisted modestly.

Kitty hugged her. "I got a car right over there. We'll leave tomorrow. Book right back where we started from." She felt Rings's hand cup a chichi.

"I can make kasj chicken salad for the road, girlfriend," Rings husked. "And deviled eggs to die for."

Kitty slapped away the fingers rolling her jalobie like tuning a radio dial.

THE KITE

||||

Joe sat alone behind the wheel of the Outside Sergeant's pickup parked deep in the folded shade of a eucalyptus stand in the foothills. Drinking coffee from a thermos, he watched the penitentiary broiling on the sunblasted plain. The cellblocks shimmered in the record July heat; the bonewhite walls seemed to gently swell and shrink like the flanks of a great somnolent beast breathing back the light. There were the kites, Earl said. The beast was talking in its sleep. Joe watched and dreaded its awaking.

It had been two weeks since his release from Z-3 back onto the Mainline, yet his focus on reality remained blurred. Time after time he was overcome with a feeling of helpless panic, like a hydroplaning automobile, that sickening feeling when the wheels lift off the pavement. Joe wasn't sure if it was the slow halflife of the Prolixin or the increasing surrealism at Coldwater.

His eye strayed across the Movement Sheet on the clipboard hanging from the dash. He snorted amusedly seeing Jesus Molina, aka Magdalena, alongside an X Wing number. The week before it was discovered the Stanford Medical Center records attesting to her womanhood were forgeries. The Goon Squad busted her in the Visiting Room. Ripping off her dress in the Strip Room, they found one still swinging down there. True to the legacy of their fallen leader, they hung a snitch jacket on her to coerce the names of her accomplices in Records who had helped perpetrate the fraud. Now she was locked up with the rest of the damned.

Thinking of McGee, Joe frowned. In a perverse way he missed the sick monster. His absence from the Mainline removed the last restraint, however malignant, against chaos. Even Hell had its Satan, its arbiter of order.

Static sizzled the stillness. Joe picked up the radio lying on the passenger seat and mumbled a set of call numbers to Tower One. Sergeant Fortado had yet to be replaced, and Joe made the outside Second Watch counts alone. It was the final joke, the animals guarding their own cages. But Joe wasn't laughing; the jest was homing in finally, turning deadly.

A hot wind down the arroyo lisped through the eucalyptus and Joe's eye was drawn once more to that vast canker on the plain. It was a thing to be strongly smelled and tasted and felt, reminding him of the great pyramids, the nearly palpable power of their mystery. But the penitentiary was more, it was a numinous malignancy he had dreamed within so long that he and it were conjoined as much as if he were turning to stone and it, to flesh and blood.

At last the light was falling over the dusty plain. Sirius, the dog star, rose over the fences between towers Five and Six. The bright tip of the new moon's scimitar pricked the Gym roof. Beyond the penitentiary the lights of Coldwater were coming up. Early Saturdaynight cruisers were pulling into the Kwik Fixx for sixpacks. The last crepuscular flush of day rinsed the prison walls a sleepy warm vermilion, reminding Joe of his cell, calling him home. He released the emergency brake, rolling down the hill in silence.

Earl waylaid him outside Custody. Wordlessly he gripped Joe's arm and led him down the Mainline toward the Hole in the Wall Wing. Blue eye sparking, he answered Joe's protests in a tense whisper, "You cant go to your cell. Please, just this once listen to a man with more experience . . ."

At the head of the Hole in the Wall Wing, Earl told Joe to wait while he hurriedly conferred with old Art Sweeny, the Third Watch wing guard just coming on duty. Art looped Joe a mournful look and nodded. Earl motioned Joe onto the wing and led him briskly down to his cell. Inside, he turned and snapped a folded piece of paper from his pocket.

"Custody found it shakin down the Gray Goose. Read it."

Joe unfolded the scrap and read,

CARNAL FLACO DE LA OILSLICK . . . HECTOR DE UNION CITY FLIES THIS KITE. HIS BONES ARE TRUE. THERE ARE MANY SPARKS IN THE HILLS. WHEN THE FIRE COMES TO THE PLAIN THE BUTCHER BOYS WILL DANCE. THE SPACE COWBOYS STAND WITH THE

FAMILIANOS. ONE COWBOY IS PICKED TO DANCE
WITH A BLUE WHO HAS NO HEART. COACH SAYS HE
MUST TIPTOE THROUGH THE TULIPS. HIS NAME IS
JOSE NARRADOR. VENCEREMOS. CARNAL CHICO DE
FOLSOM

Joe handed it back, laughing. "I like choke poetry."

"All right, you dont want to get it, so I'll read it to you in plain English,
yeah. 'Homeboy Flaco, Hector from Union City carries this message. He
is a member of the Nuestra Familia. There are many signs of riot, and
when it breaks out, our killers will make reprisals against our enemies. The
Aryan Brotherhood are our allies. One of them is contracted to kill
an inmate with no gang affiliations. This is a Teamster hit. His name is
Joe . . . ' " Earl's blue eye flicked back and forth between Joe's surprised
brown ones. "You know what *narrador* means?"

"Yeah. Talker. In this case, snitch."

"You wish, yeah. It's your name, Speaker. This little note," shivering
it in his hand, making a tiny crackling like distant flames, "is a formality.
Notification to Flaco that someone's operating on his turf. There's a space
cadet on the line with your number on his blade . . . as we speak, boy!"

"But I'm aces with the A.B. here at Coldwater," Joe objected. "Malec
and Irons are my homeys."

Earl shook his head. "Dont make no nevermind, no. This comes down
over their heads. This comes from the folks who pulled McGee's strings,
the Teamsters. That's who 'Coach' is. Them gumbas bankroll the A.B.
street action up and down the state. The A.B. has to carry out any hit they
order . . . Do you hear me?" Earl gripped Joe by the shoulder. "You a dead
man walkin!"

Joe shook his head to clear the Prolixin fogging it. "All right, Earl.
Suppose you're right. What the fuck can I do? Lock up? X Wing's the
fastest place to get hit. There's no place to hide in this joint."

Earl sucked his eyeteeth, the last not bought by the state. "I'll figure
something . . . " As if to assist thought, he started humming "Saint James
Infirmary."

"Will you give me a fivecent break with the funeral noise?" Joe snapped.

"Sorry, amigo. I was jist lookin at yer cap n rememberin Jack Moran,
yeah. Wonder what he'd think of the pass things have come to in these
pens. In the old days a convict could walk the line with a little pride, a
little dignity. I often think Whisper knew his day had gone n left him
behind. Hittin the fence was the only way left to catch up . . . "

"You're a romantic ole fool," Joe said. He removed the cap and examined it himself, turning it in his fingers. He picked a piece of lint from its crown. "Although I've often thought myself that there was more than a little magic in this ole cap."

A bell rang from the Mainline signaling fifteen minutes until the movie.

"Let's make the flick," Joe said. "It'll take our minds off this shit. Lemme take a piss n we'll head down to the Gym . . . " He laid the cap on Earl's bunk and stepped to the toilet, moaning softly as he drained his bladder of all the coffee he drank watching the prison like a mad dog sleeping. "Earl," he said, "we gonna have to hook up if ever we raise up. Christ, the more I think about it, the more I wanna give this armadillo business a shot . . . Just dont ask *me* to jerk the lil motherfuckers off for hair cream . . . "

The cell gate crashed behind him; its deadbolt fell with a clang. Joe whirled buttoning his fly. Earl stood on the other side of the bars wearing the cap and a faraway smile. The blue eye burned like a planet on a clear night, the grey shone like a pearl.

"This is the only way," Earl said. "Dont bother hollerin for Sweeny, he aint gonna break you out . . . "

Joe rushed the bars, lunging his arms through. Earl skipped nimbly back.

"Where do you think you're going in my cap?" Joe shouted.

"The picture show, amigo." He tugged the bill. "So long, Joe Speaker. It's been a reward knowin you. Adios."

With that, the old coonass yanked the cap lower, snapped a big knuckle to its bill, and was gone.

Joe shook the bars and screamed for Sweeny, but as Earl had warned, to no avail. He pled with passing convicts, who ignored him. He heard the movie bell ring again, the ragged tramp of feet down the Mainline to the Gym. Earl's gone clean Eleven Ninetyeight, Joe told himself.

He gave up and sat on Earl's bunk, lighting a cigaret. He laid back with his hands laced behind his head. The pen was eerily quiet. Then he heard a sound, a rasping from above. He pleated his brows staring at the ceiling. It sounded like gnawing rats, if at last a mutant had evolved that relished concrete. The cadence picked up, something scraping . . . Suddenly Joe knew what it was, someone above with butchery on his mind was fashioning the implement to articulate it, sharpening a strip of metal on his cell floor.

Joe jumped up and punched the PLAY button on Earl's cassette machine. The scraping from above was washed away on Hank Williams's adenoidal lament:

> *No matter how I struggle and strive*
> *I'll never get out of this world alive*

Joe distracted himself looking again at the gallery of cracked and yellowed photos stuck right with toothpaste to the old con's cell walls. Distantly he heard a roar from the Gym. A breeze through the window bars fluttered the old photos, chattering their curled edges.

There Earl was in New Orleans again, drinking coffee on a wroughtiron balcony, a girl nuzzling his shoulder. They had that quiet smug look of having just made love in the room through the French windows behind them. It was hard imagining Earl as young as the man in the photograph. And here, in Angola, the smiling kid killer. But he looked so bashful, innocent. Or maybe it was just the way the sun had to be behind old cameras, making their subjects duck their heads and squint. Maybe Earl really had been some kind of badass desperado.

Next, the baseball idols of the kid from the town they called the Big Easy. Their vintage proved Earl to be older than Joe had estimated. Roger Hornsby, Ty Cobb, Eddie Stankey, one of the Babe himself, when he still pitched for the Boston Browns. All with those crazy raw liver gloves, baggy uniforms, teeny beanies, and granny spikes. The last portrait in the corner smiled out of a sunny centerfield beneath bleachers strewn with straw skimmers. Joe bent closer to read the signature. He frowned first, then his eyes popped wide. He snatched the photo from the wall and sprang to the cell window. By tilting it to the light of the sodium searchlamps atop the opposite cellblock, he could make out the signature clearly now—*Tris Speaker.*

The tumblers fell crashing in his head with a force that quivered his legs like freshly killed meat. That day in Vacaville R&R, Earl's head lifting behind the camera like a bad moon rising, asking his name, mentioning the mythic ballplayer. *Christ! All my life I've carried this false surname of a John Doe father stolen from his childhood idol.* Joe loosed a plaintive groan. He whirled to the opposite wall, where he knew the Air Force snapshots were grouped. There it was, the one in the nightclub with the cap on the back of his narrow head, cigaret dangling from a crooked smile. It was the same face beside the big airplane beaming down from the mantle, the face belonging to the man his mother once loved.

You're just in time to be too late, ole Hank read Joe's beads.

He rushed to the bars, pressing his face between their cold. His howl was swept up on the sudden storm of klaxons and alarms ringing the penitentiary like Hell's own jackpotting slotmachine.

THE CURSE

||||

Tarzon sat huffing a Hav-A-Tampa Jewel at his desk. He still didn't know whether McGee had forced Speaker to reveal the diamond's hiding place before diving off the tier. And if he had, whether McGee had time to get the information to the Fat Man. Tarzon hadn't been able save his daughter's life, his only hope now was to avenge her death. And for that he needed the diamond.

Reaching across the desk for his Screaming Eagles Zippo, his eye fell once more on the newspaper folded to the announcement of the recovery of Belinda's head. Juxtaposed to the article was an advertisement heralding the opening of a new exhibit at Steinhart Aquarium. Idly he examined it for the first time. He was bitterly noting the blurb ENTERTAINMENT FOR THE WHOLE FAMILY when the aquarium logo, a leaping blue dolphin, triggered something deep in his memory. Where had he seen it? He thumped his head with the heel of his hand. Of course! The ticket stub in the Porsche's inventory! The one he'd presumed belonged to its owner.

Suddenly the jigsaw pieces clattering in his skull these past months were fitting themselves together like an animated cartoon. The shells in the Porsche's tire treads, the petals pasted to its fenders; the reference the Cowley girl made to the earlyblooming cherry blossoms at the Japanese Tea Gardens . . . right across the bandshell park from the aquarium!

The cheroot sprang erect in a wild and wiley grimace. The stub was Speaker's! From a ticket bought that fateful evening.

Tarzon jumped up and snatched his jacket from the wooden tree beside the door. In less than five minutes his unmarked had rocketed up the underground police ramp and was using its pulsing blue light to nudge through rushhour traffic.

He wheeled into Golden Gate Park at Oak Street. The winding road was empty. Already the night fog off the Pacific was stealing on the city through the darkling trees, blurring the roadside lamps. This must be about the same time Speaker came this way, he thought, reaching down for his lights to bore two fuzzy shafts into the misty blueblack.

He came out of the trees by the DeYoung Museum, pale and somber as a mausoleum. Across the bandshell's formal garden loomed the aquarium's long low monolith. He shut off the engine in the oblong lot of the Japanese Tea Gardens. It was paved with white shell chips. He softly closed his door and took a deep breath of moonlit fog scented ghostily with cherry blossoms.

In the silence he heard another door slam—right in front of the aquarium. But it was closed, had been for over an hour. Who else had business there, unless . . . Tarzon reached into his car for his handradio and stole across the deserted bandshell park.

Approaching, he saw the armorplated Mercedes. He crouched behind a hedge and whispered its plate numbers into his handset. Awaiting a response, he peered anxiously around. The car's occupants were nowhere to be seen; had to have already entered the aquarium.

The radio blatted softly; he cocked his head, smiling in the dark. As he suspected, registered to Climax Produxions. Not only had Speaker given up the secret, but McGee had passed it on. Yet fate had placed Tarzon on the scene at the hour the Fat Man chose to recover the diamond.

He set out stealthily circling the building. In the rear he found the jimmied fire door, its bolt taped, its alarm circuit bypassed with magnesium wire and alligator clips. Tarzon slipped inside, grateful for his rubber soles. Down the shadowy corridors he stole, left and right through the maze of silent shimmering marine light. Past the tidal pool tank, circling the crocodile pit, and around a corner where he spotted another taped door, this one marked EMPLOYEES ONLY.

"To the left, the left, you nebbish!" Tarzon's scalp tingled hearing the odious baby voice. Baby Jewels stood not ten feet away in front of the shark tank. Tarzon had missed his huge shape in the shadows. He ducked back around the corner.

"Next to the wooden steering wheel, you klutz!" the Fat Man squealed. Tarzon peeked back around the corner. Moses was throwing a tantrum, beating fat flashing fists against the glass, enraging the sharks, which began gliding in swift circuits.

"*Tch!* Your brain needs trainer wheels," he screamed. Tarzon heard Quick Cicero's muffled protests. Baby Jewels answered, "What good am I doing kibitzing from here? You want a job right, you do it yourself. My father Izzy taught me that . . . I'm coming up there." He waddled to the service door, flung it open, and disappeared.

Tarzon eased around the corner and took up station in the shadows across from the tank. He admired Speaker's ingenuity. Somewhere in plain sight, among all the phony gems, the deadly diamond blinked as it had blinked for countless other eyes since his search began. He had only to wait for the Fat Man and Quick Cicero to show him where before arresting them for the murder of Gloria Monday.

He heard Baby Jewels's heavy footfalls on the scaffold above the tank. A glinting hook like an inverted question mark was shuffling the planes of coral and aquamarine. Tarzon saw it jerk as Baby Jewels snatched the gaff from Quick Cicero. The hook quested deeper into the tank, followed by the gaff's wooden shaft. Tarzon watched the hook tremble with light as it groped the junk jewelry heaped on the sand. He smiled faintly within the wavering shadows recalling how distorted underwater objects appear from above. A jeweled hand broke the surface as the Fat Man reached deeper still. There, the hook snared a necklace, an elegant length of gold beaten into the shape of tongs. Where the tongs were joined, a diamond burned. Funny, Tarzon thought. He didn't even know diamonds came in blue.

Slowly the Fat Man withdrew the hook. Like an enchanted bird the necklace lifted off the bottom, streaming an opaline train of sand. The Fat Man grew impatient and pulled faster; with an oddly sentient grace the necklace floated off the hook. Angrily the jeweled hand jabbed the gaff after it. The hook grazed a Mako's flank. Sweeping its tail like a giant sickle, it whirled and seized the gaff in its grinning jaws and snapped it like a matchstick.

Tarzon heard Moses scream in fright and watched the shadows whirling in the tank as he windmilled his arms above, fighting for balance. Then a slimmer shadow grappled with the huge one, Quick Cicero trying to steady his boss, and that's when the scaffold began to crack under their combined weight. First it splintered, then, with a report like a gunshot, snapped in two, tumbling both men into the tank.

Quick Cicero cracked his head on a scaffold brace. Unconscious, he floated limp and spreadeagle, ribboning the water with blood. Baby Jewels somersaulted slowly underwater, getting his bearings, then began flailing, fighting for the surface. But it was too late. First one shark, then another and a third thudded into them, scissoring off flesh in pulpy chunks.

Baby Jewels tried breaking through the glass with his fists, pummeling a soft slowmo tattoo. Tarzon stepped close and grinned into the mad infant eyes. He pressed a fist with its middle finger straight up against the bloated face. It was the Fat Man's last earthly sight. A Tiger shark seized the huge cranium in its jaws and, bullwhipping its monstrous sleekness, ripped it entirely off. The slowly falling torso was quickly swallowed within its own billowing blood.

Smiling, Tarzon patted himself down. The smile inverted, becoming a frown. He patted himself down faster. He cursed.

Of all the times to be out of cheroots.

JAILHOUSE ROCK

||||

For hours Joe clung to Earl's cellgate, listening to the storm of riot rage through the penitentiary; the incessant din of alarms, the screams of terror mixed with bellows of wrath, the furious rumble of convict feet up and down the Mainline. Through the window bars he watched headlights surround the institution, shining inward through the fences.

At midnight the main power was shut off. The prison plunged into a gloom helldancing with red and orange shadows cast by fires set by rioters along the Mainline. Rank smoke coiled down V Wing, through which stumbled a wildeyed youth in ripped and bloody blues, the first convict Joe had seen since the riot ignited. Darting frightened looks over his shoulder, the youth shook the gate of each cell he passed, seeking one unlocked. He's looking for a place to hide, Joe realized, calling out to him, "Homeboy, find someone with keys to unrack me!" The youth swung a pretzeled mask of horror on Joe. He pointed a shaking finger, babbled a mad procession of obscenities, and rushed off the wing.

Joe scarcely had time to wonder at his terror. Within seconds he ran back down the wing, chased by four other convicts wielding bunkframe sections and baseball bats. Three were masked with pillowcases; the fourth wore a Gooner helmet, faceshield down, and carried a taser. Cornering his quarry at the rear of the wing, he fired the stun rifle, sinking the electrodes in the youth's belly. The fifty thousand volts jumped him three feet in the air, flinging him against the wall. There, pinioned by the charge, the youth convulsed grotesquely, squirting piss down his pantleg. Finally the helmeted hunter released the taser's trigger, breaking the circuit, and the youth dropped to the floor. There he lay, convulsing still, legs and arms loudly slapping the concrete, until one of the other masked rioters crushed his skull with a fire extinguisher wrenched from a wall bracket, spurting brains like pulp from a burst fruit. The hunters celebrated the kill by cinching their arms with bandanna tourniquets and injecting themselves with drugs looted from the Y-1 Clinic. Blissfully stupefied, they slumped to the floor beside their victim, nodding to the fevered rockenroll echoing through the cellblocks from a thousand convict boomboxes.

Next a boy unknown to Joe marched down the wing. Around his waist were tied tin cans, which he beat with broken chair spindles; eyes turned up showing white like the eyes of the truly holy, mad, or dead, tapping a metallic *rattatat* like a drummer boy in antique battle.

"They're using stump blasting charges to blow the X Wing gates!" screamed the next convict to rush down V Wing, a black armed with a shovel. He paused to straddle the dead whiteboy and hack off his head. A terrific boom cannonballed down the Mainline. "They done it!" he exclaimed, severing the neck with one last chop. "Now they gonna torch into the cells so's we can kill up all them snitches."

Dawn drenched the walls with red. For those convicts for whom violence awakened its companion urge, several enterprising queens were running a combat whorehouse in the cell opposite Earl's. Their pimp stood at the cell gate collecting drugs, ducats, cigarets. The convicts in line were mired in offal. Some fingered the prophylactics it was their prudent habit to employ. They called to their mothers while sodomizing the yelping punks. Finished, they swept out of the cell, buttoning their trousers to rejoin the massacre.

In numb amazement Joe watched a number of Hole in the Wall convicts return to their cells to collect their dirty laundry because it was the wing's assigned day at Clothing Exchange. Others he heard organizing betting pools for baseball games to be played in distant cities. In the course of these mundane prison pursuits, they joked of the wholesale carnage. Childish delight shone in their bloodspattered faces. A surreal circus feeling was abroad, a lunatic holiday spirit infiltrating the rockenrolling gloom. Death left behind his cowl and scythe when he came to Coldwater, donning instead his motley with its squirting lapel flower, gladhanding his delegates with a shake disguising a trick buzzer.

Up front in the wing's TV Room, the set was turned up loud, flickering the shifting murk with bulletins of the riot. Calmly munching zuuzuus and whamwhams looted from the Commissary, the convicts gathered there stared raptly as the electron beams bore belated witness to their grisly festival. For these children of the global village the images on the screen were real and those populating the Mainline phantoms. Their reality required the certification of the video eye: helicopter aerials, ranting newscasters, blustery officialdom, anguished families . . . body counts.

They brought the three correctional officers being held hostage onto V Wing before noon, corralling them in the rear of the wing near Earl's cell. Two of the hostages were gravely injured. Joe overheard their convict guards say they couldn't be defended in the Gym from marauding bands of blooddrunk rioters. One of the convict guards Joe knew, a plumber from the Maintenance Yard named Owen Jenks.

"You're better off in there," Jenks said when Joe asked if there wasn't a convict with a torch who could cut him out of Earl's cell. "Look what happened to your friend, the Rubber Queen. The plaguers rushed the Hospital Yard fence and the National Guard started bustin caps. She ran to the fences and started pullin em down. One of the weekend warriors drilled her through the neck . . . Stay locked, Joe."

The two wounded hostages died while Joe watched. One, a black officer whom Joe saw once hug a convict whose wife had died, bled to death from the repeated anal rapes by riot baton administered him in the Gym. The second, a burly white officer whose face was obliterated by a teargas canister fired pointblank into it, from massive brain hemorrhaging.

The third hostage was the idiot who blew the hole in the guntower roof. Though terror verging on madness glazed Ray Savage's eyes, he was drinking the coffee and eating the donuts brought to him by sympathetic convicts. His wounds appeared limited to a broken leg, which Jenks was setting, using a broken mop handle for a splint.

Dr. Raggedy Mouth suddenly rushed down the wing, towing Nefertiti by the hand. "I wants to see Savage suck some of this geechee poontang," he shouted, pointing where the black queen's diseased dick dangled through her fly. She began milking it erect; it oozed from a dozen sores. She spread a smile at the quaking hostage.

"It was Savage," Raggedy added for justification, "who run his mouf how the plaguers oughta be taken out to the range n shot. I wanna see how he feel once he got it."

The convict guards shrugged at one another and raised eyebrows sympathetic to the Doctor's logic.

"No," Joe shouted through the bars. "Savage is the last hostage. If we harm him we lose our last bargaining chip. They'll slaughter every last swinging dick in the joint when they retake it."

"Yo, Joe!" Raggedy exclaimed, seeing him for the first time. "What you doin in there."

Joe explained how Earl had locked him.

Raggedy's eyes widened. "Earl's dead, Joe. He was the first, they killed him in the Gym. It kicked off the riot."

Joe laughed. "No he isnt dead. Dont put me on."

"Yes he is, Joe." It was Bony Maroney. In his hand he held the Dodger cap. "I found this beside his body. He was wearin it in the Gym n a gunsel mistook him for you in the dark n stabbed him eleven times . . ."

"Shut up!" Joe cried. "Dont fuckin do this to me!"

"Here," murmured Bony, passing the cap through the bars. "I reckon you want it."

Joe snatched the cap with a howl of unutterable anguish. He shook the bars until the concrete seating them showed cracks. He cried aloud, demanding the gunsel's name, swearing to kill him.

That aint why he died, Joe," said Bony.

Joe sagged at the bars, swaying helplessly. "*Noooo,*" he moaned. Earl hadn't died so that his blood could be avenged; he died so his spirit might be vindicated. But what gave him the right? Joe balled the cap in his fist and slammed his head against the bars. *Christ! To die in my place! You've gone and hogged the high road to Heaven and left your son with the work of angels cut out for him . . .*

Fitting the cap to his head, he told Bony in a fierce mutter, "Get me outta here. I got things to do."

Bony nodded knowingly. He disappeared to return momentarily with a scrofulous whiteboy who lugged two fistfuls of keys conveniently tagged for identification. In no time Joe was unracked.

"Dont you jist hate it when they start the party without you," this keykeeper's carious grin asked.

One of the convict guards had Savage's head in a choke hold; Nefertiti was spreading her legs, straddling his face, guiding her ulcerated penis into his slack mouth.

Joe jumped between them, pushing the black transister back. "No!"

"Aint your beef, homeboy!" Raggedy cried.

"You're wrong, Doc," Joe said implacably. "Only I aint gonna explain. Just this. You gotta kill me first."

"You dead, then, punk," said Raggedy. He ripped off his shirt and shot Joe a crab, a ritual fighting pose like hugging an invisible tree trunk that flared his massive deltoids and trapeziuses. Calmly Joe reversed the cap on his head in preparation for battle.

"Stop!" cried Bony, thumping his bulbgripper on the concrete. "Fighting over Savage would be paying him the biggest compliment of his life."

Raggedy snorted. Together he and Joe unlocked their stares. "Dont give a fuck what you do with him," Raggedy said, taking Nefertiti by the arm and leading her off the wing. Over her shoulder she snarled at Joe, scorching him with coalbright eyes.

"Thanks," Joe told Bony. The ancient murderer stroked his beard and nodded.

Joe turned and looked down at Savage. Christ, if any guard deserved annihilation, it was this vicious little idiot, which was precisely why he must be saved. Joe was wondering how when he noticed the radio on Savage's service belt and was seized by an inspiration.

"Quick, Jenks. Help me make a stretcher. He cant walk . . . "

"Where you takin him, Joe?"

"I'm surrenderin him at the Yard gates . . . "

"You cant!"

"I have to. We cant protect him in here. If they kill him, that's all the hostages dead. It'll be a real bloodbath then when they retake the joint."

"He's right, my homeys," Jenks told the other convict guards.

"Just dont ask us to help drag him down the Mainline," one said. "The others spot us, they'll kill us."

"I'll do it," Joe said.

Jenks and Joe fashioned a trace stretcher by knotting the corners of a blanket and rolled Savage onto it. Then Joe dragged him sliding off the wing onto the Mainline.

By now plumbing had been ripped everywhere from the walls and the Mainline was kneedeep in water that swirled with every conceivable scrap of prison garbage, including human parts. Joe reversed the stretcher, hauling it with one hand by the knotted corners supporting Savage's head so he wouldn't drown in the muck. Surprisingly, the roving bands of masked killers paid Joe no mind. Perhaps they guessed he was dragging Savage to a secret place to perform a private horror.

He passed X Wing, its gates blown wide. Through the ringing shrieks of the snitches and the oaths of their killers Joe heard the lisp of acetylene torches breaching cells and the hollow thud of teargas launchers pulping skulls.

Sloshing down the Mainline, he flexed the fingers of his free hand and marveled that he could live so long without once considering what intricate miracles hands were. He lifted it before his eyes; its skin was translucent, he could see right through it; the tendons, bones, the flowing veins. Everything was brightening, brightening, lost in a gauzy white world; the gloom banished by a sourceless aortal light, the rockenroll muted by the silent music of those same spheres that once sang for Roy.

Then he was out the Yard gates. He dragged Savage to the nearest fence, propping him against it. Savage started to sob and Joe slapped him, saying, "Just be grateful you're alive." He unhooked the radio from his belt and dashed back through the gates before he drew any fire from the guntowers.

Inside he crouched beneath a Mainline window, from which obelisks of slategrey sunlight pierced the roiling smoke. He snapped out the radio antenna and punched CALL.

"Voice One to Outside Command . . . Voice One to Outside Command. Surrendering hostage Savage at the yard gates. Repeat, surrendering hostage Savage at the Yard Gate fences. Have ambulance standing by southern perimeter, his leg is broken . . . Do you read me?"

He held the radio to his cocked ear. The airwaves were a flatulent sea of static. He gritted his teeth listening to the hysterical, garbled call numbers. He recognized National Guard and State Police and CDC units. He repeated his call. So intently did he listen for an answer out of the crackling morass, so singleminded was he in what he must do, that Joe didn't notice the convicts running up the Mainline, nor hear their shouts: "That's him, the one with the cap we just seen on TV givin up the hostage. He's no better than snitch his own damn self. Kill him!"

Suddenly, as if in answer to the first prayer in Joe Speaker's life not for himself, the radio fried: "We read you, Voice One . . . Identify yourself by name and number . . . Identify . . . "

Before he could respond Joe was hit on the head from behind, sent chuting down sparkly corkscrewing walls that echoed Bony Maroney's voice: "No! Dont kill him. Joe Speaker's a homeboy. He only did what he had to. Just lock him in his cell."

Two hundred miles away, Lieutenant Tarzon in his office was listening to the riot bulletins over his police scanner. When Maas said the joint might blow, he imagined a bunch of convicts barricading themselves in the Chowhall, demanding chickenfried steak once a month. He didn't expect Coldwater to become a war zone. Tarzon half expected to hear an air strike ordered next.

He was worried about Speaker, and he wondered why. He had no further professional interest in him; the diamond had been recovered and traced by a police gemologist to Justice Bell. Neither did he feel a personal responsibility for his life any longer. Were Speaker to die in the course of the riot, it wouldn't be Tarzon's fault. Any harm in whose way he had placed Speaker was removed with Moses and McGee both dead.

Nonetheless, Tarzon felt a keen personal stake in Speaker, and he judged it was because the wily dope addict's life had intersected in a fatal way with Belinda's, and that finding a meaning in that convergence might unlock the significance of her tragedy. Rick Tarzon's was not an accidental universe. All things happened for reasons, revealing truths.

The scanner blurted with sudden excitement. An inmate was radioing from inside the charnel house of Coldwater. "Voice One, Voice One surrendering hostage . . . " Tarzon laughed aloud. He didn't need graphs this time to identify Speaker's voice. *You sweet motherfucker, it isn't just a hostage you rescued.* Rick Tarzon's spirit, so accustomed to famine, was glutted, making him giddy. He clapped his hands and lit a fresh cheroot.

There were just two ends left loose, and in a flash he conceived just how to tie them together. The cheroot leveled like a saber at the charge. He reached for the phone.

LIKE, A NEW CAREER

||||

On the frayed edge of the Tenderloin, at the triangular corner where O'Farrell slanted into Market Street, the Golden Spike Bar and Grill still offered a shot and a beer for six bits and all you could eat for a deuce. There, in the cool breeze through the doors on both streets, horse degenerates traded ponies and hookers updated their date books in dark booths beneath daguerrotypes of steam locomotives.

Rings'n'Things came striding in from the blaring end of day through the O'Farrell Street entrance. Spotting Rick Tarzon at a rear booth beside a window, she did a Cuban grind between the tables and plumped down beside him. They ordered drinks and the waiter gave them each a mimeographed menu and Tarzon began, "Rosemary . . ."

"Gag me with Rosemary! Call me Rings."

"Okay," he smiled. "Rings. I know how disappointed you must be to get back here to Frisco . . ."

"San Francisco," she corrected him a second time. "Folks who live here think it's hokey to call it Frisco."

"Yeah. Folks who were born in New York. As I was saying, you must be let down that your testimony isnt needed . . ."

"Like radically," Rings made sure he understood. Though in truth she was relieved to know that the Pimp Blimp had already crashed. The big Disappointed Act in Tarzon's office had been for Kitty's benefit. Not that it impressed the big TexMex gal much. She kissed Rings's cheek and said they'd meet again in that overly cheery way that meant they never would, then booked with the baby in the stationwagon they'd driven all the way from Texas together. Rings thought fur shur she'd be happy to be home until she found herself all alone there.

"But maybe I can make up for it," Tarzon was saying, firing up a cheroot and ordering a fresh rum and coke.

Aint no maybe about it, Rings wanted to say. *Like, abuse me in ways no other men have discovered.* The very thought tripped her love trigger, juicing her drawers. But instead she suggested, "You could start by gettin me something to eat."

"Sure. Whatever you want."

BREAKFAST 24 HRS was one of the Gold Spike's claims to fame, and Rings decided a couple of eggs over easy would fur shur knock the wrinkles out of her belly. But lamping the shortorder cook behind the counter, she changed her mind. A pasty dude with a wilted pomp, he shook with major D.T.'s.

"I may as well get em scrambled," she told Tarzon, "cuz that's how they'll end up anyway. Look at him whip n jingle."

Tarzon laughed. "That's Fabulous Frank, the Wizard of Odds. Just another life transformed by the touch of Baby Jewels Moses." He sounded a little drunk. "Well, look here. Our guest of honor."

A tall black man wearing an elegant dark suit stood uncertainly a few feet from their booth. His sunglasses reflected the Golden Spike like security mirrors. *Gag me,* went Rings. *Is this why Tarzon invited me to dinner? To pawn me off on some fly ponce?*

"Look, buster," she had Tarzon know. "I dont flatback for nobody. Aint no way, aint no how."

"Dont worry," Tarzon chuckled, suddenly sober again. The voice he raised was dipped in acid. "Glad you could join us, Bell. Have a seat."

Cautiously the black man approached the booth, tucking his forearm to his middle, folding himself into the seat opposite theirs. Rings frowned at the scent of his expensive cologne.

"Who's this?" Bell asked distastefully, tipping his head her way.

Tarzon snarled through the teeth clenching the cheroot. "A young woman who had the guts to come forward with the truth while you were hiding behind cheap sunglasses . . ."

Bell snatched off the glasses, uncovering eyes like knife thrusts. "I thought this meeting was confidential."

"Those confidences," flipped the cheroot, "have cost lives, my daughter's included."

"You know I regret that. I didnt know . . . "

Rings busied herself flipping through the jukebox station on their table, regretting that she'd spent her last quarter on the Vibro King unit attached to her hotel bed. Before she could interrupt to ask for another one, her eggs arrived, and she busied herself dumping a half bottle of ketchup on them.

"You didnt want to know," Tarzon said.

Bell gaveled the table, jingling the glasses.

"Hey!" squawked Rings. "Like, my eggs is scrambled enough awready."

"Let's get one thing straight," Bell told Tarzon. "I wont be intimidated again, I wont sit still for abuse. If you intend to expose me, go ahead. I've lived so long with the threat I'd almost welcome it. I thought we had an understanding, but if not, go ahead and do your worst—it might be best for me."

Tarzon sighed and said, "No, I'm not going to expose you. You're a good judge and have to go on being one. The same as I'm a good cop and have to go on being that."

Chewing her toast, Rings stared out the window down which twilight sifted a lavender dust past the asterisks of streetlamps. The Golden Spike's lights came on, and she saw the reflection of Tarzon's cheroot uncoiling its smoke.

"Did you talk to your wife?" Tarzon asked.

"Yes," Bell said. "I told her everything. She agrees to your terms. She'll auction the Blue Jager Moon and donate the proceeds to whatever drug rehabilitation fund you designate . . . "

Rings started. What moon? Wait a sec. *That's* where she last smelled the cologne. Fur shur! In an elevator on Nob Hill.

She dogeyed Bell. "You were Glori girl's sugardaddy."

"That's right," Bell said, smiling sadly.

"I did some digging last week," Tarzon said, "and discovered Miss Cywinski was on your payroll."

"You are thorough," Bell admitted.

Rings made a face. It was like they were feeding each other lines all of a sudden.

"Apparently the same federally funded job training program is still in place. I think I know a particularly worthy candidate, one who would actually show up at the office to learn a profession . . . "

Complicity lit Bell's eyes and wreathed his face. "Oh, yes . . . " He turned to Rings. "Yes, indeed. If you wouldnt mind starting in the mail-room, Miss . . . "

"Hooten," Tarzon supplied.

Rings gave up trying to understand what was going on. On they talked of other things with the eager intimacy of strangers who had discovered a mutual friend. The Golden Spike filled with the early evening crowd, sneering pimps and bellylaughing whores and bookies with backcombed hair. Outside, the great purple and green bubbles of twilight swelled up from the pavement and bulged against the buildings and burst in the indigo zenith, melting into night; and she noticed suddenly that Bell's reflection was missing.

"You got a job," Tarzon said. He was slumped in the booth with a fresh drink in his hand and a bittersweet smile on his face. He explained that she would be paid a salary to work parttime in the judge's offices while she got her GED and enrolled in college.

"Like, a new career," Rings said, a little scared.

"You're all set," he mumbled with just a twinge of resentment, and ordered another drink.

"Aint you had like enough, sailor?"

He puffed fresh life into his cheroot and, jetting a long stream of blue smoke across the table, flicked a shy look at her.

"Say, do you ever do it for . . . fun?"

And here Rings thought she'd never be asked.

DON'T LOOK BACK

||||

Joe came to the following night on the floor of his own cell. He felt behind his head. The gash already was scabbed. He stood shakily and found cigarets and lit one, stepping to his window bars. A fire on a floor above glowed the opposite cell block. Behind it, smoke from the burning Admin Building squidded oily black ink into the midnight blue.

He heard the ugly stutter of helicopter rotors. The noise swelled, then smashed the night with clattering as the great iron locust crested the cellblock, washing the barred window sockets with bluewhite light, driving Joe backward to his cell gate.

When the stars swam from his eyes, he saw that the the other cells on his wing were standing open and empty. From the Mainline, the measured tramp of boots: not guards, not convicts—soldiers. The pen had been stormed and retaken. The tramp dimmed; the cellblock refilled with a dreadful thunderous peace.

On the morning of the third day, the National Guard officer found Joe sitting in his cell like Jonah beneath his trick gourd. Joe smiled hearing civilization's first utterance following the long night of the Butcher Knives.

"Hey, asshole! Roll it up. Some damn thing called a 'Special Circumstances' parole just came over the wire for you."

Joe sloshed behind the soldier's clanking battledress down the flooded Mainline. Guardsmen stood every fifteen feet, M16's at port arms. Joe was chained hand and foot: the final irony, being bound over to freedom. The windows all were smashed, the walls blackened. Torn centerfolds, half-burned trial transcripts, discarded masks, love letters, looted disciplinary chronos stirred sluggishly as Joe slogged through the alluvial ooze of convict wrath. Amidst ribbons of their fathers' blood floated children's smiling photos.

He was escorted through the burned and gutted Admin Building to R&R, where he signed his parole papers and was issued a hundred dollars in gate money. Miraculously his street clothes had escaped the fires. He stripped off his blues and put on his old jeans and T-shirt, his boots and dragon jacket. They let him keep the cap despite regulations prohibiting an inmate from leaving the institution with any apparel he didn't possess when he arrived. But he couldn't wear it for his Dress Out mugshot. This would have been Earl's job, and sitting in the plywood booth Joe had to blink fast and swallow hard not to give away his grief.

Out in the bright morning Joe bellowed his lungs, flushing them of death. It was a moment he'd so long dreamed of, it had acquired the surreality of a dream. Unchained, he walked through milling soldiers to the Gate House. Police cars, media vans, army jeeps, and ambulances jammed the entrance drive. The dusty cars of the convicts' people stretched a mile either way along the fences. Joe heard the iron gonging of their hearts.

Moving through the freeworlders he felt he'd known them all before, known them intimately: the civilians with their leeching eyes, the clamoring reporters, brows pleated with predatory concern, the soldiers, fear barricaded behind parade eyes—known them intimately some time before, yet now they were subtly but utterly altered. He felt like a bit movie player moving across the set of some disaster epic, mistaken for its star and pelted with questions neatly typed on a script beneath the arm of someone just out of sight.

"What's it like in there?" shouted the first reporter.

"You all should see," he said, shouldering politely past.

The reporter skipped nimbly around, blocking his path.

"Who's this guy 'Voice One'?"

"It doesnt matter, could have been any of em."

Joe stood on his toes scouting the crowd's nearest edge and knifed toward it, ignoring the multiplying questions as they realized he was one of them. They closed like hounds to a wounded stag; the bristling microphones, the cyclopean cameras, the clamoring bloated faces lit in the false dawn of their kliegs until he halted and growled with unmistakable menace and the hounds shied back.

Walking alone, he passed one last spectator, a pudgy and disheveled old gent whose wilted seersucker suit was straining a fresh dark sweat in the rising heat. A halfpint of cheap whiskey was upended in his dissolute mouth. Seeing Joe from the corner of his eye, he sucked it dry and tossed it twirling into the high grass along the fences.

"Looks like it's fixin to get hot as a twodollar pistol . . . " he began with the hasty jocularity of one caught at something shameful. Then, pouched eyes squinting with mean surmise over Joe's shoulder, demanded, "Why those boys killing each other up in there?"

Joe stopped and stared blankly at him. "It's all that was left to do."

"Fuckin animals," smacked the greasy lips.

"Wrong, amigo. Men built those cages for themselves."

Then he was swinging down the road, humming a rebop "Saint James Infirmary," when he heard her voice to the side:

"Fella, you better have a kiss in both pockets cuz there's two of us now."

He was laughing as he turned beholding those goofy eyes like the five ball off the eight, the hard way. She took his kiss swiftly, on a cool cheek that smelled of soap, then eagerly held up to him the bundle she carried. His cautious finger parted the tiny blanket. He stared with astonishment at one gray eye, one blue staring back with that profound consternation of infants that verges on anger.

He bent to kiss the downy globe, and a tiny fist jerked up and popped him in the nose. He jerked back with a bemused and crooked grin. "Christ!" he breathed. "Everything comes around . . . "

"Whoa!" Now it was her turn to jerk back. She tucked a fold of lip between her teeth to bite suspiciously, gunned him that savvy sly ole slantendicular, and said, "Dont tell me you went and caught religion in there . . . "

Joe ballooned his cheeks and popped his lips. He tipped his chin toward a distressed Chevy wagon with Texas plates facing away from the penitentiary along the fencing.

"That heap belong to you?"

"Shitfire, no! That tragedy belongs to us. So dont say if it was a horse, I'd have to shoot it."

"All I got to say is, let's blow this popstand," already striding toward the stationwagon.

"To which I'd say you got a bright ideer . . . " She followed him, swinging the infant onto her hip to open the passenger door.

"Fella, you got some drawings for your new family?"

Joe cocked his head and torqued an eye to slant her a speculative sidelong across the car. Dropping his voice and stretching it confidentially, he asked: "Do you have *any* idea how an armadillo crosses the Mississippi?"

"No, and that very question's been pesterin me all my life."

"I'll pull your coat when we get down the road a piece," he promised, slipping behind the wheel.

She sighed settling in beside him with the infant. "I dont judge another few minutes of suspense will kill me."

"I'll give you a hint, though. Something to think on." He cranked up the aged short block; it fired up with a bang and burst of black exhaust. "They got two choices."

"I knew it couldnt be as simple as waddlin across a bridge."

Laughing, Joe swiped off the cap, hung it over the rearview mirror, and dumped the Chevy into Drive.

ABOUT THE AUTHOR

||||

SETH MORGAN was born in New York City, where he attended private school. Later he studied at Hotchkiss, the American School in Switzerland, and Butler Institute in Mexico. He then attended the University of California at Berkeley. He was a strip joint barker, an ironworker, and a chef. In 1978, he won first prize in the PEN American Prisoners' Writing Contest.